Other ImaJinn titles by D.B. Reynolds

The Vampires in America Series

Raphael (Book One)

Jabril (Book Two)

Rajmund (Book Three)

Sophia (Book Four)

Duncan (Book Five)

Lucas (Book Six)

Aden (Book Seven)

The Cyn & Raphael Novellas

Betrayed

Hunted

Lucas

Book 6 of the
Vampires in America Series

by

D. B. Reynolds

ImaJinn Books

This is a work of fiction. Names, characters, places and incidents are either the products of the author's imagination or are used fictitiously. Any resemblance to actual persons (living or dead), events or locations is entirely coincidental.

IMAJINN

ImaJinn Books
PO BOX 300921
Memphis, TN 38130
Print ISBN: 978-1-61026-100-5

ImaJinn Books is an Imprint of BelleBooks, Inc.

ImaJinn Books was founded by Linda Kichline.

We at ImaJinn Books enjoy hearing from readers. Visit our websites
ImaJinnBooks.com
BelleBooks.com
BellBridgeBooks.com.

10 9 8 7 6 5 4 3 2

Cover design: Debra Dixon
Interior design: Hank Smith
Photo/Art credits:
Cover Art-Pat Lazarus
Man (manipulated) © Francesco Cura| bigstock.com
Background (manipulated) © genefleeman| renderosity.com

:Llko:01:

Dedication

In loving memory of my brother Daniel.

I miss you every day.

Prologue

Quantico, Virginia

SPECIAL AGENT Kathryn Hunter lay on her stomach in the dirt, the butt of her Sig Sauer 3000 rifle snugged into the curve of her shoulder. She leaned into the Leupold scope and settled the crosshairs on her target. Data ran through her brain, was processed and let go. Like all snipers, she tended to step out of the moment when she was shooting, focusing only on the target, the shot. She concentrated on taking shallow, even breaths, her entire world reduced to what she could see beyond the crosshairs.

It was a relatively easy shot. Eighty yards, less than the length of a football field. A slight breeze was blowing, but at this distance, that wasn't enough to matter. The target was stationary, but armed. Not a problem. Law enforcement snipers were trained to go for the head shot, to immediately incapacitate a subject holding a weapon, if necessary. It was a shot she'd made a hundred times on the range. No hesitation, no nerves. Just line up the shot and take it.

Kathryn heard the go-ahead come over her radio. She exhaled slowly and squeezed the trigger.

"And bye-bye terrorist! Kathryn, baby, you are the best!" Eduardo Saver, her friend and the day's range supervisor, said over the radio, confirming what she already knew. She'd hit the target dead on. His enthusiastic reaction wasn't exactly protocol, but there were only the two of them on the range this afternoon, so he'd gone for friendship instead of professionalism. Kathryn grinned as her heart started pumping again, and she felt the rush of adrenaline begin to fade. Her body didn't care that this was just another practice shoot in a long line of practices. Once she got behind the scope, everything narrowed down to the crosshairs and the annihilation of her target.

"Thanks, Eduardo," she said as he came up behind her.

"You going out with the rest of us later?" Eduardo asked. "Time to let some hair down, *chica*. All work and no play . . ."

Kathryn turned as she sat up from her prone position, her hand going self-consciously to her hair in its tight French braid. She forced a laugh. "Maybe. The usual place?"

"Naturally," Eduardo said. He looked down at her with a leering grin. "I'll be waiting."

"Uh huh." She rolled her eyes at him. Eduardo wasn't interested in her that way. She was too tall and too pale for his tastes. "I've got to stow this," she said, indicating her weapon. "But maybe I'll see you there."

She stood, reaching automatically for the cell phone on her belt and switching it back on. It was always off during range exercises. The phone vibrated almost at once, and she pulled it off her belt one-handed, frowning at the message she saw there.

"Problem?"

She looked up. "I don't think so. It's Penelope Bateman, my brother's agent. He's on one of his solitary photo adventures, and she's probably just calling with a message from him. He does that sometimes if he can't get a hold of me."

Eduardo touched her arm to get her attention. "See you at the bar."

"Yeah," she agreed absently, giving him a brief glance before returning to the call log on her phone. Penny had called several times in the last hour.

She placed her weapon on the wood plank table and popped the magazine, checking automatically to be certain the weapon was empty. She then wiped it down and used a soft brush on the scope lenses before placing it in the custom-made hard shell case. After closing the case, she made a few notes in her field book, mostly range and target information, since shooting conditions had been as close to ideal as they ever got. As she wrote, she bemoaned, as always, that so far she'd never had a chance to fire her weapon anywhere *except* on the range. She was a skilled shooter, but since 9/11, the FBI's emphasis was all about terrorism. She spent far more of her time sitting at a desk than she did out in the field, and had begun to regret the Quantico posting she'd been so excited about a few years ago.

She sighed and tucked the field book away, then pulled out her cell phone and hit the call back on Penny's last message.

"Kathryn!" Penny answered almost before the phone had stopped ringing the first time.

"What's up, Penny, did you—"

"Something terrible's happened! Danny's missing!"

Chapter One

Two Weeks Later
Near the Minnesota/Wisconsin Border

THE HUGE SUVS were three black blurs of speed as they roared through the night. Lucas Donlon sat in the middle seat of the second SUV, listening to the chatter of his vampires, both around him and through his headset for those in the other trucks. They were hyped and ready for action, almost *too* hyped after the hours of travel to get this far. Even with a private jet, it took time.

But they were here now, and Lucas was with his warriors in feeling the rush of impending battle, the pump of adrenaline as he prepared to fight to the death. It was a rare thing in this civilized world, with its laws and cameras everywhere. But tonight's confrontation would mark the beginning of a war between vampires—something this continent hadn't seen in nearly a century. And how better to start a war than with the death of a traitor? Alfonso Heintz didn't know they were coming for him, but he would soon, and his fear would taste just as sweet as his blood. Maybe better.

The trucks rolled down the unlit rural roads, running dark. The vampire drivers didn't need the lights to see by, and Lucas didn't want to advertise his presence to anyone yet, human or vampire. Not until he had his prey cornered. Alfonso Heintz was sworn to Lucas, but had recently moved his entire household just over the border into Wisconsin, near the small college town of River Falls. It was no more than thirty miles from Minneapolis, but crossing the border between Minnesota and Wisconsin took him out of Lucas's Plains Territory and into the territory of Lucas's enemy, the Lord of the Midwest, Klemens.

Had Lucas needed it, Heintz's move over the border would have confirmed the vampire's guilt. But Lucas already knew he was guilty and needed no more evidence. In truth, if the traitor had known his betrayal had been discovered, he'd have moved much farther than a few miles over the border. As if a few miles, or a few *thousand* miles, would ever stop Lucas from exacting the justice he was due. This was war. Boundaries no longer mattered.

But whether or not Heintz realized he'd been discovered, he would surely have a guard or two on lookout. Unfortunately for Heintz, most of the vampires hiding away with him were also sworn to Lucas, a fact that he clearly didn't fully appreciate, in terms of its ramifications for security. Lucas could drop any vampire sworn to him with nothing more than a thought. It was likely, of course, that one or two of Klemens's people would be in the house tonight, and they'd require close up killing. But then, Lucas had no intention of winning this battle from a distance. He intended to punish the traitors in a very up close and personal fashion. In fact, he hoped Heintz and his fellow miscreants put up one hell of a fight, because Lucas and his people were ready to rock and roll.

The target house was big and wide, a two-story clapboard with a long, covered front porch. The building was completely dark when the SUVs skidded on the light snow covering the dirt patch of a front yard. It appeared empty, but the large number of cars and trucks parked around back told a different story. Lucas sent a small tendril of power creeping into the house and found thirteen vampires, all wide awake and jittery with nerves. By now, Heintz and his people knew Lucas had arrived, and they were probably wishing they'd hidden themselves a lot better than they had.

Lucas reached forward and clapped his lieutenant on the shoulder, where he sat in the front passenger seat. "Let's be polite, Nick. I'm sure Heintz and his minions will be excited as hell to receive a visit from their rightful lord and master."

Nicholas laughed and issued a few terse commands into his throat mike. The doors popped open on all three SUVs, and black-clad vampires poured out, deploying quickly to surround the house. Every one of them was a highly trained and powerful fighter. By virtue of their vampire blood, they were weapons unto themselves, but they also carried whatever human weapons they preferred, from 9mm handguns to compact submachine guns. And no doubt a knife or three thrown into the mix.

Lucas himself carried no weapon other than the power which made him one of the most feared vampires in North America—a vampire lord, ruler of the Plains Territory. Thousands of vampires literally lived and died at his command. Including Alfonso Heintz. Traitor or not, Heintz was still beholden to Lucas for every breath he drew, every beat of his heart. Klemens might have used Heintz, but he hadn't offered his protection, hadn't taken his oath of fealty. Which meant if Lucas wanted, he could have shriveled the unfaithful bastard's heart in his chest without ever leaving South Dakota.

But where was the fun in that?

Nicholas caught Lucas's eye and nodded once, then took up position to the left and slightly ahead of his Sire. They climbed three short steps up to the covered porch, and Nicholas knocked on the door. Or perhaps pounded would be more accurate. It was the adrenaline. Lucas stifled the urge to laugh. He loved this shit. After weeks of playing nice, of waiting while various vampire politics played out, he was ready for first blood.

The door creaked open, and a slender vampire stood there, his eyes wide with fear. "My lord," he managed to stammer out. "We didn't expect you."

Well, that was a lie, Lucas thought to himself. No one, neither human nor vampire, could lie successfully to a vampire lord. This was not a very auspicious beginning. Who was this child anyway? Not one of his.

Nicholas didn't bother with further niceties. He simply shoved the vampire out of the way and pushed the door open, slamming it against the wall. No invitation was necessary since this was a vamp house.

Lucas followed him inside. "Where's Heintz?" he asked the trembling vampire.

"Forgive me, my lord, but he's not here. He had to—" The sentence ended on a squeak as Lucas picked the vampire up by his throat and dangled him several inches off the ground. "Fool. Do you think you can lie to me?"

"Please," the vampire rasped. "I only—" Lucas had no interest in what this one had to say. Heintz had sent him forward as a sacrifice, and he had fulfilled his purpose. Lucas granted him the mercy of snapping his neck before he incinerated his heart with a short burst of power.

"Nicholas?" he said sharply.

"Ready at your command, my lord."

Lucas sent his power raging through the big house. It spread outward like a massive concussion of air, rushing up the stairs, sending furniture crashing into walls, slamming open doors and breaking windows. Screams sounded from deep inside the structure, some of them muffled, as if in a vault or safe room. Lucas laughed out loud and turned to his lieutenant.

"The command is given," he said and strode forward, his eyes flashing gold fire with the furnace of his power, his fangs in full view and gleaming. "Alfonso!" His voice boomed out like the wrath of God, or the wrath of a vampire lord, which was eminently worse. God was rumored to have a sense of mercy, whereas Lucas had none, especially not for traitors.

His vampires moved in from all sides, and the battle began, the air filled with the enraged roars of the combatants and the terrified screams of the dying. There were no humans in the house. Heintz had been that smart, at least.

Lucas passed several fights in progress, but he ignored everything in his search for Heintz. The coward was hiding. Lucas laughed gleefully and picked up his speed, racing through the house until he stood in front of a daytime sleeping vault. Heintz was behind that door, along with . . . Lucas tilted his head as his mind reached out . . . two other vampires. And they both belonged to Lucas. What an ass. These vaults had been designed to withstand human assault, not that of a powerful vampire. If the traitor was going to try to hide here, he should at least have been clever enough to hide behind someone Lucas couldn't easily control.

Almost bored with the simplicity of it, Lucas sent his mind out and touched each of the two vampires cowering inside the vault with Heintz, ordering them to open the door and present themselves to their master. He could have ordered Heintz to deliver himself, too, but it was much more pleasurable to drink in the sweet taste of the bastard's terror when he realized what was happening.

The heavy vault door swung open to reveal the two vampires already dropping back to their knees, heads bowed. Even Heintz had assumed the penitent posture. As if that would save any of them from their treachery.

Lucas entered the vault, moving with the preternatural speed of his vampire nature, and ripped the heads off the two vampires flanking Heintz. Blood sprayed from their severed arteries, coating Heintz in the thick red stuff. He swayed, moaning with fear, hands clasped in front of him as if in prayer.

Lucas regarded him dispassionately. "The sniper talked, Alfonso. He didn't even bother to put up a fight. Saved himself the agony of torture. Unlike you, he was smart enough to see the writing on the wall."

"Please, Master," Heintz whispered. "I had no choice—"

"Silence, worm. You had a choice. You simply made the wrong one. Bad enough that you betrayed *me*—" Sudden rage rose hot and heavy in Lucas's heart, nearly choking him with fury. He shoved his closed fist into Heintz's open mouth, shattering his fangs as he rammed the fist down the vampire's throat and used it as a lever to lift him into the air.

"You conspired with my enemy and hired a human to assassinate my *Sire*," he snarled, and saw Heintz's already terrified eyes fill with horror. Very few vampires still alive knew that Raphael was Lucas's Sire. Both of them wanted it that way. It was a weapon they wielded in secret, and Lucas only voiced it now, because he wanted Heintz to understand the full magnitude of his sin before he died. Painfully.

The vampire was trying to shake his head, making guttural sounds deep in his throat, no doubt of denial. But it was far too late for that.

Lucas shook Heintz off his fist, dropping him to the floor.

"I beg you—" The worm began whining almost immediately, and

Lucas flicked his fingers, silencing him.

He gazed down at the sniveling vampire dispassionately, then stepped back and started breaking bones, beginning with the little ones, fingers and toes, the delicate bones in the hand. Heintz groaned softly at first, but by the time Lucas had started on the big bones—the tibia and fibula in the calf, the thick femur in the thigh—the vampire was grunting like a rutting pig, the only sounds of pain he was able to make. Bloody tears streamed down his face as he groveled on the ground, unable to even wipe the snot from his chin.

Lucas worked systematically, splitting the skin open when he ran out of bones, slicing the abdomen and watching the vampire's gray entrails spill onto the blood-slicked floor, making certain to keep the spinal cord intact and the heart beating. He wanted Heintz to feel every last ounce of pain before he died.

He was crouched over the bloody form of ruptured flesh and shattered bone when Nicholas found him. Heintz was whimpering weakly, his heart still beating, his vampire blood keeping him alive despite the destruction of every other major organ.

"Well?" Lucas asked Nicholas, never taking his eyes off Heintz.

"The other twelve are dead and dusted, my lord," Nicholas said, crouching next to him and eyeing the wreckage of Heintz curiously, like a bug splayed for study. "What about this one?"

A small smile tipped the side of Lucas's mouth. "His heart is still beating," he said. "I could take him with us, see how long it takes him to regenerate enough to crawl."

Nicholas winced. "He'll get blood all over the new Gulfstream."

Lucas laughed. "Good point. Very well." He dug through the gore until he found Heintz's beating heart and ripped it from its moorings. The vampire gave a final squeal of pain, and then died as his heart burst into flame on Lucas's palm. The bloody mess turned to ash in moments, leaving nothing but a dark stain as testament that Alfonso Heintz had ever lived.

Lucas stood, slapping his hands together and eyeing his clothes in dismay. The black fabric went a long way toward concealing the blood, but he knew it was there. It was wet and sticky and damned uncomfortable. And it would soon begin to stink. Plus there was the new jet's interior to consider.

"It's late," he said, automatically sending his thoughts out, verifying the well-being of each of the vampire warriors he'd brought with him. "We'll take the trucks back and overnight at the Minneapolis house."

"What about our FBI visitor? Even if we leave first thing at sunset tomorrow, it'll be hours before we get there."

Lucas shrugged. "She's dealing with vampires. If she's stupid enough to show up too early, she'll just have to wait. God knows she's made me wait long enough." He spared the stain of Alfonso Heintz a final glance, then started for the front of the house. "Come on. I want this place burned to the ground before we leave."

Chapter Two

Quantico, Virginia

"HUNTER, COME IN."

Kathryn stepped into SAC William Fielding's office. It was as neat as the man, obsessively neat, in her view. And that was saying something, since Kathryn wasn't exactly known for her messy work habits.

"Close the door," Fielding directed.

Kathryn complied, her jaw tightening automatically as she considered what it meant that he wanted the door closed. Fielding was better known for leaving the door wide open, especially where female agents were concerned. He was convinced women were naturally predisposed to sleep their way to the top and had a morbid fear of sexual harassment lawsuits.

Fielding wasn't a bad looking man, and she was sure he'd had his share of admirers over the years, but culturally, he was trapped in the fifties. And he made no secret of the fact that he believed the FBI had made a mistake in opening its ranks to the weaker sex.

Of course, since most FBI agents were male, if you eliminated the *weaker* sex from the Bureau, there would be hardly any agents left. Kathryn bit her cheek against the urge to laugh at the inside joke, which reflected the opinion of pretty much every female agent she knew.

"Have a seat, Special Agent."

Kathryn sat. If this bastard tried to cancel her vacation leave, he'd have far worse than a sexual harassment suit on his hands. Mayhem seemed likely. The man wouldn't have any hands *left* when she was done with him! Which was no more than exaggerated wishful thinking on her part. The truth was, if he cancelled her leave, she'd grit her teeth and take it, because the only alternative was going AWOL, which would probably cost her her job. And she didn't want that. She'd worked hard to get where she was. It was the only career she'd ever truly desired, and she was the perfect cog in the giant Bureau machine. Always on time, always willing to work the extra hours, the weekends.

Maybe Eduardo was right. Maybe it was time she loosened up a little, broke free of her own rigid rules.

And that reminded her of why she'd requested vacation leave. Her brother was the free soul of the family, and look where it had gotten him. Disappeared, missing . . . and . . . *"Oh God,"* she pleaded silently, *"please don't let anything terrible have happened to Dan."*

Fielding cleared his throat, drawing Kathryn's attention back to the here and now. "I hear things, Hunter," he said.

There didn't seem to be any response to that, so Kathryn waited.

"I know your brother is missing. How long's it been now?"

"Nearly two weeks, sir," she confirmed, keeping her expression carefully blank, while wondering where he'd heard about Dan's disappearance. Kathryn had been careful not to talk about her brother's situation, though she *had* made a few phone calls. From home, of course, so no one could accuse her of slacking off on the job. She'd called the sheriff in the small town where Dan had been staying while shooting in Badlands National Park, and might even have used her position as an FBI agent to set up an interview or two. That was assuming she could finally get her boss to approve some vacation time. Which was why she was sitting in Fielding's office right now.

Fielding leaned forward, his brows coming together in a scowl. "I sympathize with your situation, Hunter. But you cannot use your position, your authority as an FBI agent, to put pressure on or interfere with the local authorities."

"No, sir!" Kathryn hoped she sounded sufficiently shocked at the very thought of such a thing. "My brother is an artist, and something of a free spirit. He's done this before, dropping off the grid for weeks at a time."

What she didn't say was that while Dan might drop off the grid, he'd never dropped off her *personal* grid for this long. She'd dismissed Penny's initial hysterics over Dan's missed check-in. The woman was a frustrated actress and tended toward the dramatic in almost every situation. But when a week passed, and there was still no word, she'd begun to worry. She and her brother had a system, and even when he missed his calls to Penny, he'd never once failed to get a message out to Kathryn, somehow, some way. Until now.

"Good to hear."

Kathryn nodded and hoped Fielding didn't get chatty and start asking about her vacation plans. She'd hate to lie, but she would if he pushed her.

"Well, then," Fielding said, sitting back abruptly, as if suddenly aware that in leaning across the desk that way, he'd gotten far too close to her for safety . . . *his* safety, that was, given his potent male charisma. "Enjoy your vacation, Hunter."

Kathryn stood immediately, as anxious to get out of his office as he was to have her gone.

"Thank you, sir," she said and managed to leave the office without once entertaining an improper sexual thought about SAC Fielding.

DANIEL HUNTER struggled to sit up, his head pounding, eyes blurry, though it was hard to see anything in his prison. There was a ceiling light, but the switch was in the hallway just outside the locked door. His jailer turned it on when he brought food and water, or when he visited. The fucking freak.

Dan had no memory of how he'd gotten here, didn't even know where *here* was. His last memory was of having a drink at the local bar. He'd tried to piece it together and figured the freak must have drugged his drink. But why?

He leaned against the rough wall and tipped his head back to stare at the lone window, high above his head. It was tightly covered. He only knew whether it was day or night by the small spot of sunlight that squeezed through a hole in the corner sometimes. He'd taken to ticking the days off by scratching a line on the plaster wall with a shard he'd salvaged from the ceramic cup he'd smashed on the first day. His jailer had picked up all the pieces, or so he'd thought. But once he was gone, Dan had scrambled around on the floor feeling for any sharp bits left behind. It had felt like a victory when he'd found the sharp wedge beneath the bed. And now, it was all he had, those lines on the wall, his small rebellion against captivity. That and the reminder that days were passing, that with every day that went by, his sister Kathryn was a little closer to finding him. And she'd never give up until she did.

He sighed and tried to make himself more comfortable on the thin mattress. If the bastard was going to trap him here, the least he could do was provide a decent bed. Not for the first time, he wondered why he'd been taken. Money was the obvious answer, but he was beginning to get a bad feeling about this setup. With every visit from his jailer, it felt a little more personal, a little more like an obsession. And that thought put him in mind of the great Stephen King book, *Misery*, and not in a good way. Although it brought back good memories, too. Dan and his sister had snuck away one Saturday to see the movie, and Kathy Bates had scared the shit out of them. He smiled, remembering, but the memory sobered him once again. Kathryn would be worried sick by now.

South Dakota

Kathryn glanced at the GPS and made a right turn, quickly spotting the sheriff's office down the block. She'd gone directly from Quantico to the airport, her bag all packed and waiting for her in the trunk of her car. A late night flight had gotten her as far as Minneapolis, where she'd spent the night in an airport hotel, catching a 6:00 a.m. puddle jumper into Spearfish, South Dakota, which was the nearest town of any size.

She had her brother's itinerary. He always e-mailed it to her before he went on one of his trips, even though he insisted she didn't need to worry about him. But whom else did she have to worry about? Easy for SAC Fielding to tell her to leave the search for her brother to someone else. Fielding had a wife and three kids, not to mention a whole plethora of relatives, including two brothers, a sister and a backyard full of nieces, nephews and cousins. He'd invited Kathryn to a barbeque one summer, along with a bunch of others from the office, and she'd been amazed at the sheer number of blood relations.

She and Daniel only had each other. Although that wasn't completely accurate. Their father was still alive, but he had remarried and was engrossed in his new family. It wasn't that he'd turned against Kathryn and her brother. She knew he still loved them, but she supposed he preferred to forget the tragedy of losing his first wife, their mother, to cancer when Dan was still a baby, and the hard work of raising the two of them mostly on his own. She couldn't blame him, really. It had been rough on all three of them. Fortunately, she and Dan remained close. They had each other, and that was all they'd ever needed. Even as kids.

But because Dan was all she had, because she'd all but raised him, the idea of standing by and waiting while someone else made desultory efforts to locate him wasn't even an option. She *had* to do this.

Kathryn parked in the small side parking lot of the sheriff's office, noticing the number of SUVs and trucks alongside. She was glad she'd upgraded to the midsize SUV instead of taking the standard 4-door sedan. It had been a dry winter in this part of the country, but dry was a relative term. They'd had snow, just not as much of it, and spring had come early. Still, she was glad for the 4-wheel drive on the SUV. She drove a Jeep back home in Virginia, but the best the car rental could do was a Toyota Forerunner. It did the job, and at first glance, let her blend into the local scenery. She wanted a chance to look around before everyone started pointing at her and saying FBI, or at least cop. She'd even made a point of wearing jeans and a black turtleneck for the flight into Spearfish this morning, trying to avoid standing out any more than necessary. But even so, she knew she had that FBI look about her—a little too stiff, a little too conservative. A little too conservative in other ways, too, as the few men she'd dated had been happy to point out. Too many of them had been excited by the idea of dating a gun-toting woman, and then been disappointed when she also turned out to have a brain and a will. She'd only dated one guy, a homicide detective, who'd actually accepted her for what she was, at least at first. But he'd eventually moved on to some air-headed bimbo. Okay, that wasn't true. The bimbo was a pediatrician, and so probably *wasn't* an airhead. But she wasn't a cop either, and that had been the problem for her homicide detective. There'd been too much shop talk and not enough of anything else between them.

She'd pretty much given up on dating after that. Her vibrator had become her favorite companion, and Ben and Jerry her best friends. And she'd buried herself in work. Until Daniel went missing.

Despite the patches of snow on the ground, it was warmer than she'd expected when she climbed out the SUV. She left her heavy jacket in the truck and went with her standard FBI blue blazer over her sweater. She wore plain, black, flat-soled ankle boots for two reasons—one, they were comfortable enough to run in, if necessary. (Forget Agent Scully's three-inch, blocky pumps. Never happened.) And the second reason was that at nearly six foot, Kathryn tended to be taller than a lot of men even without heels. The FBI was still largely a man's world, and too many of those men copped an immediate attitude if they had to look up at her. So she wore flat soles on the job. Of course, technically, she wasn't *on* the job today, but since she was about to defy SAC Fielding and use her FBI credentials to push the investigation, she figured she'd better make a pass at looking the part.

The station door opened as she climbed the stairs. Two men in jeans, long-sleeved shirts and well-worn cowboy boots emerged. Kathryn sized them up automatically, noting height, weight, coloring. They looked alike, probably a father and son from their ages, with the older one well into his sixties. The younger one tipped his hat and held the door for her.

Kathryn smiled and hurried up the last step. "Thanks," she said and ducked past him and into the station.

There were three plastic waiting chairs against the wall and a battered wooden counter with a skinny deputy at a desk on the other side. With his neatly trimmed brown hair and guileless brown eyes, the deputy looked all of eighteen, but Kathryn figured he had to be older. Although not by much. He glanced up as she approached.

"My name's Kathryn Hunter. I'm looking for Sheriff Sutcliffe," Kathryn told him. "I think he's expecting me."

The deputy didn't seem impressed. He eyed her carefully, then slowly picked up the desk phone and hit a number.

"FBI's here to see you, Sheriff," he said unhurriedly.

Well, so much for blending in, Kathryn thought.

The deputy eyed her unblinkingly while he waited. "Yes, sir. Will do, sir."

He hung up the phone with deliberate movements, then, with all the speed of a sloth, stood, walked around the desk and over to the swinging door of the counter's pass through. Reaching beneath the counter, he hit a release of some sort. A buzzer sounded, followed by the click of a latch as the door nudged open. He stood there holding the button, listening to it buzz for a good ten seconds before he finally said to Kathryn, "The sheriff will see you."

Kathryn wanted to slap his hand away from the damn buzzer, but forced herself to bare her teeth in a semblance of a smile and push through the low, swinging gate. Sloth boy finally released the button and preceded her past several empty desks and down a short hallway where he stopped in front of a closed door. The top half of the door was frosted glass, and the name "Sheriff Max Sutcliffe" had been stenciled in gold lettering.

The deputy knocked three times on the wooden frame, pausing between each one. Kathryn blinked, hoping she wouldn't fall asleep while waiting.

"Get in here, Henry," a voice barked impatiently from behind the door. Clearly the sheriff shared Kathryn's sentiments regarding his deputy.

Henry opened the door, and Kathryn scooted past him politely, but determinedly.

"Sheriff Sutcliffe," she said, crossing to the desk and holding out her hand. "I'm Kathryn Hunter. We spoke on the phone."

Sutcliffe was already standing by the time she reached the desk. His gaze did a quick up and down appraisal, and she saw the slight flare of appreciation in his eyes. Kathryn was used to the reaction and didn't comment. Some men, too many men, automatically assumed any woman in law enforcement would be either ugly or a lesbian. Or both. The opposite couldn't be more true. Not to mention the fact that most of the lesbians she knew were pretty damn good looking. But she wasn't here to correct the sheriff's perceptions about FBI agents, lesbians, or anyone else. She had one purpose, and that was to find her brother. For which she needed the cooperation of this man.

"Ms. Hunter," Sutcliffe said, holding her hand just a little too long. She noted the absence of her proper title and let it pass. "A pleasure," he continued. "Please sit. Close the door, Henry," he ordered, looking over the top of a pair of reading glasses, which he quickly slipped off and tucked into his shirt pocket. He waited until the door closed before sitting down again.

"Now," he said pleasantly. "What can I do for you, Ms. Hunter? Would you like some coffee? Water? I've got it here, so you don't need to worry about waiting on old Henry out there."

Kathryn chuckled dutifully at the comment, but shook her head. "No, thank you, Sheriff."

"Call me Max."

"Max," she corrected, then added, "and I'm Kathryn."

"Kathryn. Beautiful name. My mother's name."

"My great-grandmother's too," she commented with a smile, then sat on the edge of the wooden chair in front of his desk and pulled a small notepad from the inside pocket of her jacket. She still took written notes when interviewing people, no matter the case. The FBI's policy on recording interviews and confessions was inconsistent and more complicated than it needed to be. It was easier to assume that recording wouldn't be permitted. Later on, she'd transfer it all to her laptop anyway, and if a recording was made available, it was a nice bonus. But this way she always had her written notes to fall back on. Kathryn flipped open her notepad. She'd already marked the page containing her notes on Daniel's disappearance, so she didn't have to search for it.

"As you know, Max," she started, "I've been trying to track down a photographer who went missing around here a couple of weeks back."

Max nodded. "Daniel Hunter," he confirmed. "Your brother, if I'm not mistaken," he added with a smug look.

Kathryn wasn't surprised he'd made the connection, even though she hadn't mentioned it to him. Hunter was a common enough last name, after all. But what she knew of Max Sutcliffe already told her not to underestimate him, so she didn't bother denying it, either.

"My younger brother, and only sibling, as it happens."

"He didn't tell you where he was going?"

"Dan sent me his itinerary, including flights and hotel, which is his usual routine when traveling. I'm based out of Quantico, and Dan lives in California, so we don't see each other as often as we'd like, but we're close and stay in touch by phone and computer whenever possible. What I know, Max, is that my brother has *never*, and I mean *never* in the ten years we've lived apart, disappeared like this."

"Well, hell, Kathryn. I don't care how close you are, there's all sorts of things a man wouldn't want to share with his sister," he said, suddenly seeming uncomfortable with the direction of the conversation.

"I'm sure you're right. But not this. A couple days, even a week, I could buy. But Dan wouldn't go this long without getting in touch. He knows I'd worry, and he knows what I do for a living. He wouldn't want me calling out the troops if he was just off on a romantic fling," she finished with a smile that she hoped didn't look as forced as it felt.

"I believe you, or at least I believe *you* believe it. And I've checked around some since we spoke last. Last time anyone saw him was at a private club over in Spearfish."

Kathryn looked up in surprise. This was new. "A private club? What kind of a private club?"

Max squirmed uncomfortably, and Kathryn felt a depressing sense of inevitability. Her brother was openly gay, and she had a feeling Max was one of those people who weren't comfortable discussing—

"It's one of those vampire things," Max finally said in disgust.

Kathryn's dismay was replaced by shame that she'd assumed the other. Max's unease was apparently focused on vampires, not sexuality. And the vampire connection wasn't a complete surprise to her. The last time she'd spoken to Daniel, he'd mentioned meeting a vampire or two and said something about a party, which might be the same as the private club Max was talking about. In fact, it was her brother's comment about the local vampires that had motivated her to set up an interview with the local vampire honcho. Max's information only made that interview more important.

"In the last conversation I had with Dan, he mentioned meeting some vampires," she told the sheriff. "I actually have an appointment to meet with"—she checked her notes—"Lucas Donlon later tonight. I understand he's leader of the local vampires?"

"Lord," Max said sourly. "He's not a bad sort, but he does title himself a vampire lord. His people even call him Lord Donlon, like this was the Middle Ages or something."

"I've heard that title also. Not about Donlon, but a couple of others. Vamps tend to lie pretty low usually, but the FBI does have *some* information on them. Mostly from the one or two who live more in the public eye."

"Yeah," Max said glumly, "when I first became sheriff, I ran a check on Donlon and any of his people I could get names for. They don't have so much as a traffic ticket in South Dakota. Leastways, not that I could find."

"Arrests aren't common," Kathryn agreed, "but when they do happen, the lawyers come out, and it goes away. These vampire lords seem to have plenty of money, and they're not afraid to spend it on the right lawyers and politicians."

"Why should they be different than any other rich asshole, right?"

"I'm afraid so. Should be interesting, though, to see how Mr. Donlon responds to an FBI investigation, which is quite a bit more serious than a traffic ticket."

"I wish you well with that," Max said, but with so little enthusiasm that she didn't find it very encouraging. "You got a navigation system in that SUV you rented?" Kathryn nodded, and he continued, "You'll want to use it going out there after dark. You'll never find it otherwise."

"Thanks, I will. Back to Daniel's last known whereabouts. I know he planned to do some backcountry camping in the Badlands, but he frequently goes off on his own when he's working, and he's an experienced camper."

Max opened a drawer, pulled out a full-color brochure of the Badlands, and handed it across the desk. "Ordinarily, something like this, I'd assume he was just another lost camper. There aren't too many trails in the park, and it's easy to get turned around or injured. But I spoke to the rangers at the visitor center. They confirmed that Daniel Hunter stopped to check in with them on his way into the backcountry, and then again when he was leaving the park. And they haven't seen him since. It makes sense that if he bothered to check in the first time he set out, he'd do it again if he was going back for more. So I'm assuming whatever happened to him, it didn't happen in the park. Leastways, not in the backcountry."

"Would you mind if I talked to the rangers myself?" It was a courtesy question. She didn't need his permission, but his cooperation would be helpful.

"Not at all," Max said readily. "It's the Ben Reifel Visitor Center in the Park Headquarters out on highway two-forty. There's a small map in that brochure, and road signs will show you the way, too."

"Thanks. And what about the witness who saw him leaving the club?"

"Well, now, that one's more complicated. He just left on his third tour of Afghanistan two days ago. But I record everything on video these days, more for our protection than theirs, so I can give you a copy of that."

Kathryn wanted to scream in frustration. Two days! She'd missed interviewing possibly the last person to see her brother by two measly *days!* She felt something digging into her fingers and looked down to see her hand gripping the pen so tightly that her fingers were bloodless. She forced her hand to relax and dug up a smile for Max.

"I'd appreciate that, Sheriff," she managed to say. "A flash drive would be great if you have it. Or a DVD, if you don't."

"Uh, yeah. Computers and I don't exactly get along. Henry handles all that. I did ask him to make you a copy this morning, so we'll see what he came up with. He ought to about have it ready by now," he added dryly.

Kathryn took the hint and stood. "Thank you for all your help, Sheriff. If I come across anything else, I'll let you know."

"And I'll do the same on this end. If you need anything at all, you just give me a call. I'm either here or reachable by cell phone pretty much seven days a week."

Kathryn stopped on her way out and picked up a flash drive from Henry. Once back in the SUV, she stowed it in her briefcase to play later. Right now, she wanted to get out to the visitor center at the park. She had little doubt they'd have nothing more to tell her than what they'd already told Max, but she needed to do this her way, and that meant checking off each item personally.

She did a quick search on her laptop, piggybacking onto the Wi-Fi from the small cyber-café and sandwich shop across the way. Locating the Ben Reifel Visitor Center, she studied the map, then shut it down without bothering with the nav system.

As Max had told her, getting to the park headquarters and visitor center was pretty much a no-brainer. There were signs everywhere and not much in between. Less than an hour later, she was pulling into the parking lot. There were no other cars, just a couple of official pickup trucks. Despite the cool weather, it seemed this wasn't the park's busy season. Most people tended to take their vacations in summer, when the kids were out of school. Even the people who didn't have any kids *in* school. It made more sense to her to travel when places were less crowded, but maybe that was because she'd never taken a summer vacation as a child, and so had no preconceived notion of what a vacation was supposed to be. The closest she and her brother had come to a vacation were the summers spent on their maternal grandparents' farm. But then their grandparents had died within a year of each other when she was only twelve, and that ended that. Nonetheless, her time with them made up some of her fondest childhood memories.

Kathryn shook herself back to the present. She had no time for memory lane. The visitor center was a typical national park building, a plain single story structure with a concrete walk out front. The interior had the usual displays and dioramas of the park's history, with racks of brochures for free, and a few glossy books and touristy souvenirs for sale. Kathryn looked them over, thinking about what Daniel had told her in explaining why he'd chosen the Badlands for his next project. He'd said he'd seen a brochure at a friend's party and had known he could do better. She picked up the free visitor's brochure which was identical to the one Max Sutcliffe had given her. She wondered if it was also the one that had brought her brother all this way from San Francisco.

"Can I help you?"

Kathryn turned to find a young woman with long, brown hair pulled back into a neat ponytail and brown eyes with just a touch of mascara. Her face was makeup free, clean and pink-cheeked, as if she spent a lot of time outdoors. The name *Belinda* was stitched over the pocket of a neatly pressed U.S. Park Service uniform.

"Special Agent Kathryn Hunter, FBI," she said, flashing her credentials and hoping none of this ever came back to bite her in the ass.

"Oh!" the young woman said, frowning a little. "Sheriff Sutcliffe said you'd be coming. You're Daniel's sister."

Kathryn blinked. "I am, yes. You remember my brother?"

"He went backcountry twice, and I spoke with him before and after the second trip," Belinda said, but her already pink cheeks had gone even redder.

Kathryn smiled at the woman's reaction. Her brother was charming and charismatic, and had a way of making people believe he really cared. And sometimes he did, even if it was only for the ten minutes he was talking to you.

"So, how does that work exactly?" Kathryn asked.

"Everyone's supposed to check in with us before they head into the backcountry, although, of course, not everyone does. We try to make sure people know what they're doing. It's very rough out there in any weather, and hikers are completely on their own. I was a little concerned when I saw Dan was going solo, but after talking with him . . . well, it was obvious that he was an experienced hiker, and he was well-supplied."

"But he'd already been out and back once by the time you talked to him, right?"

Belinda nodded. "He went out twice for ten days each time. That's a long while to be out there alone, but the time I saw him come back through, he seemed fine. Better than fine, actually. Exhilarated. A little tired maybe, and ready for a shower, but when he left, he said he just wanted a few days of hot running water and good food, and he'd be coming back again."

"He was healthy? I mean, no obvious injuries, limping, bandages, that sort of thing."

"No," Belinda said, frowning and shaking her head. "Like I said, a little tired, but other than that, he actually seemed happier than when he went out."

"You only saw him come back the once?"

She nodded again. "The last time he was here. That's why Sheriff Sutcliffe said you'd want to interview me, because I was the last person he talked to here."

"Did Dan check in with you guys the first time he went out, too?"

"Yes, but I wasn't here. That'd be Cody Pilarski. We rotate shifts so there's always someone here."

"But you're sure it was Dan's last trip when you talked to him."

"Definitely. And I sure hope nothing's happened to him. He was a really nice guy."

"He *is* a really nice guy," she corrected, emphasizing the verb. Her brother might be missing, but he was still alive. She knew it in her gut. Something terrible had happened, but not the worst. Not yet. And not ever if she had anything to say about it.

"Thanks," she said to Belinda. She turned over one of her official business cards and wrote her personal cell number on it. "If you hear anything, or if anyone mentions seeing Daniel, please give me a call."

Belinda took the card, glanced down at it briefly, then tucked it into her breast pocket right under her name. "I'll do that, Agent Hunter. I sure hope nothing's happened to him," she repeated, half to herself.

Kathryn nodded absently as she turned away, her mind already on her next task, the next item she had to check off her list. Everything Belinda had told her coincided with what she knew. Dan had actually called her when he emerged from the backcountry. He'd left a message on her voicemail, telling her he was all right, that he was going to enjoy a few days of civilization and head back.

When Penny had first called her, saying Dan had missed his regular check-in, the first thing she'd done was access his phone records. Since he traveled to a lot of places where cell service was spotty, he always carried a satellite phone with him, which enabled him to make calls without being within range of the town's cell tower. She found only one other call after the one Dan had made to her, and that was to Penelope in San Francisco. Unfortunately, Dan also had a tendency to pick up a disposable phone whenever he was in range of a cell signal, using that and then throwing it away, instead of carrying around the more expensive, and heavier, satellite phone. So while Kathryn knew when he'd called her and Penny, she had no way of knowing whom else he might have called locally.

On the one hand, it was good to know that her brother had been well and happy when he'd left the park two weeks ago. But on the other hand, so far she hadn't learned anything she didn't already know.

She beeped the locks on her rental SUV, opened the door, and then just stood there for a moment, leaning her forehead on the warm metal of the door frame. Her chest ached, and tears threatened as she fought off a wave of despair. If she could find even one clue, a single hint that would tell her what had happened . . . she needed a direction, and she didn't have it.

The slam of a truck door behind her had her straightening, blinking away the tears. She turned quickly, afraid someone might have seen her. But there was only a flash of khaki as one of the rangers disappeared through the side door of the visitor center.

Kathryn drew a deep breath and slid into the driver's seat, surreptitiously wiping away the few tears. She pulled over her laptop and checked the list she'd already memorized. Next stop was the motel where Dan had stayed. His room was still there, still racking up nightly charges. She'd assured the motel manager on the phone that she would pay for it, although she suspected the motel was pretty empty this time of year anyway. But she didn't care about the money. She'd just wanted to be sure Dan's things were left untouched. Maybe that was where she'd find that one clue she was looking for.

The motel was the only one in town—flat-roofed, one story, and without a single identifying characteristic. Even its color was a boring beige that blended so well into the desert one could probably miss the building entirely on a hot day, with the heat rippling the air. It was a long step down from the type of hotel her brother usually stayed in, although, as with the backcountry camping, Daniel was more than willing to rough it to get the shot he wanted.

Kathryn parked in front of the office and went inside. The day manager's name was Jason Kenton.

"Mr. Kenton," she said, "I'm Kathryn Hunter. We spoke on the phone." She didn't use her FBI ID for this one. She was already feeling guilty about that, and it wasn't necessary in this case since she was paying the bill.

"Daniel's sister," Kenton said, looking up from a cluttered desk behind the check-in counter. He looked groggy, as if she'd woken him from a nap. He stood slowly, stretching out his muscles and yawning without any attempt to conceal it. Kathryn waited impatiently until he finally strolled across the six feet separating them and reached for a key hanging on a numbered board.

"His things are all in there, just like you asked. I haven't even let the maid clean. Didn't see much point, and I didn't want to mess anything up, just in case."

"Thanks," Kathryn said, smiling as she took the key. "I'll be staying a few days, so I might as well use the room, if that's all right with you."

Kenton shrugged. "You're paying the bill. Don't matter to me who sleeps there, as long as there's nothing funny goin' on."

Kathryn blinked, trying to imagine what sort of *funny* he had in mind. But her brain was too tired. "Nothing funny," she assured him. "You ran my card?"

"Yes, ma'am. No problem."

"Okay. Thanks again." She backed out of the door, feeling suddenly awkward, as if he expected her to stay and talk a while. Or maybe he'd expected her to question him like they did in all the television shows. Whatever it was, she didn't have the energy.

She climbed into the SUV and backed down the empty parking lot to room 18. It was an end unit, but other than that it was exactly the same as every other one. She thought Daniel might have requested the end, hoping for a little more privacy and quiet, but like everything else in this case, she was just guessing.

Her only suitcase was a small, rolling overnighter, so she grabbed it, then locked up the truck and let herself in. She was immediately swamped by a sense of loss. The room was a mess, with dirty clothes tossed haphazardly into an open suitcase on one of the double beds, and still lying on the floor where Daniel had left them. She knew they were dirty, because his clean clothes were all neatly hung in the closet. This was so typical of her brother that it brought tears to her eyes.

She glanced around, noting that among the dirty clothes were some obvious pieces of hiking gear. The single chair held Dan's backpack, which appeared deflated and forlorn. His well-worn hiking boots, some *really* dirty pants and T-shirts, and several pairs of thick socks lay in a pile on the floor next to it. One thing Daniel had always told her was that he never stinted on clean socks when he was hiking. Everything else could be stiff with dirt, but he always took several pairs of socks.

She frowned, then stepped farther into the room and saw his camera equipment neatly stacked between the second bed and the wall, where it wouldn't be obvious to someone standing in the doorway. Dan's cameras were worth a small fortune, but even more than that, he'd told her they were irreplaceable. Not because he couldn't buy another one, but because over time a photographer's camera became a part of him, as if the physical characteristics of the equipment mutated with use to become unique to the photographer.

She dropped her things on the bed and crouched down next to the pile of equipment. She couldn't tell if anything was missing. Maybe his agent Penny would have been able to, but she wasn't here.

Kathryn went to stand and had to grab the wall when the room spun around her. She was beyond tired. She'd slept very little in the last two weeks, too worried about Dan. And then there'd been the flight yesterday—she could never sleep on planes—and the sleepless night in Minneapolis waiting for the morning so she could get here and start looking for him.

She sighed and began stripping off her clothes. The jacket came first, then her badge and her gun, which was the FBI standard issue .40 caliber Glock 23. She set both badge and gun on the table, placed her spare magazine next to the gun, then snapped her holster from her belt and threw it on the other bed on top of her jacket. Stepping out of her shoes, she left them where they were and skimmed off her jeans. She was about to toss them on the bed, then thought better of it and folded them instead. She hadn't brought that many clothes with her. Knowing she'd be more comfortable wearing her usual work attire later tonight for the interview with Donlon, she pulled her slacks and blouse out of her case and hung them up in the closet, hoping to get rid of any wrinkles. She hated ironing, but didn't want to present herself to Lucas Donlon looking like she'd slept on a plane, either.

Picking up her jacket and shoes, she shuffled over to the closet, dropped her shoes on the floor and hung up the jacket next to the pants and blouse. She eyed the bed warily, then yanked the bedspread down, piling it on the floor. She never slept on those things. They were crawling with bacteria. She was tired, but her mind was racing, and she knew she'd have to check out the witness interview from Sheriff Sutcliffe before she'd be able to sleep. Her knees sank into the too soft mattress as she dragged her laptop over and inserted the flash drive. She watched it all the way through, intending to go back and make notes on a second viewing. But when she reached across for her notepad and pen, her head spun dizzily. She put her head on the pillow, intending to close her eyes for only a moment. She registered that the sheets were surprisingly fresh and clean when she pulled them up to her chin. And that was it.

Chapter Three

Minneapolis, Minnesota

LUCAS OPENED HIS eyes and stifled the immediate desire to groan. He was in Minneapolis. Not that this was a bad thing in itself. The Twin Cities were exciting and vibrant, and he maintained a residence here, which he visited several times a year. So, it wasn't that he minded being in Minneapolis that made him swear with his first waking breath. It was the knowledge that he had to rush back to the ranch in South Dakota, because some damn FBI woman was coming to visit him tonight.

Visit. Huh. Interrogate was probably more like it. Lucas had never met a cop he trusted, and he'd met a lot of cops. He also admitted that this prejudice might have something to do with his misspent youth on the streets of Dublin and London, but that didn't change the fact of the matter. Especially not when it came to cops and vampires. The people in charge never liked it when someone else was more powerful than they were. There was a level of distrust between vampires and the human authorities that would never go away, and he didn't see that changing between now and later tonight when the FBI invaded his ranch.

A hot shower dispelled much of his bad mood, as did the memory of their successful hunt last night. He was standing in front of his closet, trying to decide whether to go with a business look for the FBI, or stick with jeans and leather, when his cell phone rang. He reached out and picked it up without looking.

"Yo, Nicholas," he said.

"My lord," his lieutenant responded. "I just spoke to Magda. Klemens called your private line."

"She didn't pick up," Lucas confirmed. None of his people were allowed to pick up that line as long as he was alive to do it.

"No, my lord. But when you didn't answer, he called the business number, and Magda told him you were unavailable. Nothing more."

"Ah. I'm sure he'll be—" He was interrupted by the incoming call signal. He pulled the cell phone away from his ear long enough to check the caller ID and then said to Nicholas, "Speak of the devil, and he will surely appear. Klemens is on call waiting. I'll get back to you." Lucas switched over to the incoming call with the flick of a finger. Modern technology was a marvelous thing!

"Klemens, old chap, what can I do for you? Or more to the point . . . *to* you?"

"Cut the crap, you fucking Irish gutter rat. Who the hell do you think you are taking out a house on *my* fucking territory!"

"*Your* territory? I have no idea what you're talking about. I disciplined one of *my* vampires last night, along with his fellow traitors."

"Two of those vampires you killed were mine, and you know it."

"Two of yours? How sad. Well, as my dear old Gran used to say, if you lie down with dogs, boyo, you'll surely get fleas."

"Your fucking Gran was a pox-riddled whore on the streets of Dublin."

Lucas laughed. "Quite right, Klemens. I had no idea you'd met her."

"I've never been to that useless country of yours and never will. It's full of thieves and drunks."

"And the thieves are drunk, too!" Lucas agreed cheerfully. "Ah, good times. But I don't think you called to stroll down memory lane with me. So the house was yours? Things get a little muddled that close to the border. And speaking of borders"—he added, as if it had just occurred to him—"Raphael is quite vexed with you, I'm afraid. Apparently you took a shot at him, and in Colorado, no less. Terribly bold, Klemens. Hitting Raphael on his own territory."

"Stop babbling, you fool. I had nothing to do with that."

"Ah, but you have heard about it. From whom, I wonder? I'm sure Raphael would dearly love to know."

"I don't give a shit what that bastard wants. If someone took a shot at him, more power to them."

"I'm afraid not," Lucas commiserated. "The sniper missed rather handily, and, from what I hear, he's no longer among the living."

"You want me to believe Raphael shares that kind of information with the likes of you? You can't be trusted to keep your own secrets, much less anyone else's."

"True, but since Raphael is convinced you were behind the hit, we've become quite close. The enemy of my enemy, you know."

Lucas could hear Klemens breathing hard, either trying to control his famous temper, or trolling through his thick brain for something clever to say.

"In any event"—Lucas said, continuing the conversation, such as it was—"if the house was yours, I did you a service by burning it to the ground. It was quite bloody when we finished. And there was dust everywhere."

"This isn't the end, Donlon," Klemens snarled.

Lucas dropped his guise of humor, his voice hard when he said, "No, it's not. This is just beginning." He disconnected, not waiting to hear what would no doubt have been some obscenity-laced threat from Klemens. He punched up Nicholas.

"Ten minutes, Nicholas, and we're out of here." He threw the phone down and pulled on a pair of worn and comfortable denims. He was in no mood to play nice for the fucking FBI.

Chapter Four

South Dakota

KATHRYN SWORE AS she missed her exit on I-90. She took the next off-ramp, doubled back and took the correct exit as her GPS began recalculating for her mistake. Sheriff Sutcliffe had been right. Lucas Donlon had an address, but not much of one. She frowned as the nice GPS lady told her to take the next right turn. She slowed, eyeing the unpaved road that presented itself. There were no lights out here, just her headlights and the full moon, which was barely peeking over the mountains. And there was a lot more snow on the ground, big clumps of it piled against boulders and beneath the trees. The so-called road was two strips of dirt, visible only because they were paler than the rough fields of grass and ice-pocked rock that surrounded them. But it had to be reasonably well traveled, or the two strips wouldn't be worn away at all. Sutcliffe had also warned her that Donlon didn't welcome visitors. Maybe leaving this unpaved was his way of discouraging people.

Unfortunately for him, Kathryn wasn't going to be put off by a little rough road. She switched on her high beams and made the turn. A quarter of a mile later, she was having second thoughts. The other reason she'd chosen to rent a 4-wheel drive SUV was because she'd assumed that, in this part of the country, there would be the occasional dirt road to travel. But even then, she hadn't counted on driving down dirt trails carved through unlit, half-frozen fields of knee-high grass and unfriendly looking trees. What sane person intentionally left the main road to his residence in such a dangerous condition? Especially since most of the traffic out here was probably after dark. Even a vampire had to leave his ranch eventually, and he'd have to take this road, too. The myth that vampires could fly was just that—a myth.

And what about his employees? There must be *somebody* who worked for him. They'd have to navigate this impossible thing every day! Her car hit two potholes in a row, one right after the other, nearly jerking the steering wheel out of her hands. She growled beneath her breath, keeping up a steady stream of muttered curses. She should report the bastard to OSHA. Serve him right. Maybe he didn't worry about the FBI, but he'd sure as hell worry about the Occupational Safety and Health Administration. The sheer volume of paperwork they'd demand would make Donlon's life a living hell. She grinned at the thought, then hit a new pothole and swore, "Stupid damn . . . oh."

With no warning, the road evened out, becoming smooth as silk, her tires virtually humming over the hard surface. She loosened her grip on the wheel, shaking out her hands to restore circulation, feeling the nerves in her fingers and arms still vibrating after—she checked her GPS—only five miles of that tortuous road? It had seemed much farther than that.

But it was behind her now, and she was making good time on what the nav system told her was the last leg before her destination. She saw a flash of white in the distance as the road rose briefly before dipping into a deep ravine. When she came up the other side, a white rail fence was paralleling the road, and about a mile farther on, there was a white arching gate with a name stenciled overhead.

Kathryn slowed and made a right turn that took her through the open gate. Looking up, she saw that it wasn't a name on the wooden arch above her, but a stylized D. The kind one associated with livestock brands, although she was fairly certain they didn't brand animals anymore. She seemed to remember seeing a report on TV, or maybe it was the Internet, about how ranchers had gone to something more technological, like implanted data chips or something. If the vampire had herd stock, maybe she'd ask him about it. Although she found it unlikely that a vampire would actually raise cattle. A sudden thought struck her, and she frowned. Could a vampire exist on animal blood?

She shook off the unpleasant image that question conjured, and focused on the road in front of her, which wasn't at all a straight line. It looped around stands of trees and grassy humps, many of which had piles of jagged boulders buried on their hillsides. In the far distance, silhouetted by the pale moon, was the sharp peak of Lookout Mountain, which she recognized from the research she'd done online.

After a mile or so, another open arch appeared over the road, but this one was sturdier, made of beautiful river rock with wood accents. That same stylized D was worked into the wood. Jeez, maybe the guy was afraid he'd forget his name unless someone reminded him at every turn.

A stone wall angled out to either side of the entrance, tapering down to a low decorative border before it disappeared altogether in the deep grass. Two figures appeared beneath the arch as soon as her headlights splashed over its surface. They stood in the roadway, blocking her access. From their formidable size, she assumed they were male. One was a bit taller than the other—six-foot-two to his buddy's five-nine—but they were both heavily muscled and moved with an economy of effort that told her they had some training. Obviously, this was Donlon's security, although that was some serious heft for gate guards. And they weren't relying on muscle alone, either. Both men were carrying what, from a distance, looked like H-K MP5 submachine guns on combat slings over their chests, and she wondered if they were licensed to carry that kind of weapon. South Dakota had some very liberal gun laws, but she didn't know if they included the personal use of submachine guns.

Not that this was her problem. She wasn't even here on official FBI business, much less anything else. She'd come here to interview a vampire. She snickered as she thought the words and only *hoped* her subject looked like Brad Pitt.

Focus, Kathryn!

She wished someone *had* interviewed Lucas Donlon, or any of the vampire lords. There had been scattered pieces here and there on the Internet, mostly blogs devoted to the paranormal genre. But even those gave away very little about the vampires themselves. She supposed living hundreds of years made one an expert at deflecting questions from nosy interviewers, especially given man's violent history toward things he didn't understand. But the sum total of what she'd been able to uncover about vampires—and she'd had a lot of places to look, given her job access—was very little.

Vampires were almost a nation within a nation. They policed their own people, and from what she'd been able to find out, tolerated no dissent. And as long as they didn't cause any problems, like littering the streets with bloody bodies, the human authorities didn't seem to mind. At least no one complained. The vampires even had a new ambassador of sorts in Washington, D.C., Duncan Milford. He was more of a lobbyist than an ambassador, representing vampire interests in the halls of Congress. It was the public information on Duncan more than any other that had given her most of what she knew.

As far as the local vampire bar, the one where her brother had been seen last, the witness, who was now out of touch in Afghanistan, claimed to have seen her brother speaking to a known vampire. He also thought they'd left together, although he hadn't personally witnessed that part of the evening. He *had* seen them walk out the front door, but since he'd been inside the club, he couldn't verify what had happened outside. He was, however, certain that the person with Daniel was a vampire, because he'd been to the club before, and apparently it was pretty obvious who was and wasn't. Unfortunately, he only knew the vamp's name. Sheriff Sutcliffe's report had gone on to say that there was one more witness who claimed he'd seen Daniel leave the bar with the vamp, but his report was questionable. He'd admitted to being drunk at the time, so drunk that he had no memory of his own actions later that night.

It wasn't much to go on, but it was all Kathryn had. So, vampire honcho or not, Donlon was going to give her some answers.

LUCAS STRODE INTO his office, still pissed that he'd been forced to rush back here for the convenience of the FBI. He slumped down into the chair behind his desk and watched sullenly as Nicholas called Magda for a situation report.

"Talk to me, gorgeous," Nicholas said, then listened as Magda talked. He laughed abruptly. "Not happy, I can tell you that. Okay, see you in a few." He disconnected and regarded Lucas warily.

"The FBI has landed, my lord," he said. "She's on her way up to the house as we speak."

"Shit." Lucas looked away, thinking. "Did Magda see her?"

"No, but she got a report from Kofi at the checkpoint. He says she's right proper."

"I swear that limey bastard just says stuff like that to piss me off."

Nick chuckled. "I believe he means she's buttoned up tight, stick up her butt, by the rules . . . Shall I go on, my lord?"

"No. Fuck. I know what it means. I suppose I have to meet with her."

Nicholas gave him a disbelieving look. "I thought that's why we rushed back here."

"I know, I know. All right." Lucas tapped one finger on the arm of his chair. "Have Magda meet her and bring her in. Tell her to take it slow, sit and chat a bit. And tell Maggie to play it human. Maybe our FBI visitor will give something away if she thinks she's speaking to a sympathetic ear."

Nick dipped his head briefly. "My lord."

"And, Nick." Nicholas stopped in the doorway, looking back. "Make sure you come back. I want you with me."

"Aw, come on, Lucas."

"Fuck that. I'm not suffering alone."

KATHRYN BRAKED to a stop with the front end of her SUV just beneath the arch of the stone gate. It was either that or run over the big guy standing in the middle of the road glowering at her. And his finger looked a mite too twitchy on the trigger for her peace of mind. She caught movement in her side mirror. The second guard had circled around her vehicle and was coming up on the driver's side from the back. Probably hoping to surprise her, maybe watch her jump when he tapped on her window unexpectedly. Not gonna happen.

She hit the button and had her window already sliding down before he could go for it. He gave her a sour look, as if maybe she'd spoiled his fun. Like she cared. She flashed her FBI credentials. "Special Agent Kathryn Hunter," she said. "I believe Mr. Donlon is expecting me."

The guard studied her silently for a moment, and she studied him back. Black male, shaved head, brown eyes, and she'd been right about the height and weight. About the muscles, too. Not an ounce of fat. He was still staring.

If he thought to unnerve her with his sphinx act, he was going to be disappointed. She could stare at him all night. She wondered if he was a vampire. She'd never seen one before. They were notoriously camera shy. Even Duncan. He was making the rounds of Capital makers and shakers, partying with the best of them, but while his name was frequently mentioned, she'd never seen a photograph of him. And it wasn't because of that old superstition about vampires not appearing in mirrors and, by extension, cameras, either. That was just stupid. Simple physics said if a body occupied mass, it interacted with the universe in predictable ways, including mirrors. No, he was simply one step ahead of the photographers, that's all.

Vampires lived and breathed just like everyone else. Although, maybe not *quite* like everyone else, since they certainly lived a hell of a lot longer.

The sphinx was still staring. She was about to say something when the big guy in front of the car beat her to it.

"Boss is waiting, Kofi," he called.

A flash of irritation crossed her guard's face before he smiled . . . and displayed two very long, wicked-looking fangs. Kathryn almost groaned out loud. Please. Did he think *that* was going to put her off? Was she supposed to shriek and race away in her little SUV, never to darken his archway again?

Kathryn bared her teeth back at him in a perfect smile that was the product of four miserable years of braces as a teenager.

The sphinx finally grunted and stepped back, nodding at his buddy to do the same.

"Thank you," Kathryn said politely. She buzzed her window up, more against the dust from the road than the cold, and continued toward the house. A glance in her rearview mirror showed the sphinx on a cell phone. Probably warning his boss that she was on her way. Good. If they were ready for her, she wouldn't have to waste time waiting.

The road very quickly entered a patch of trees that combined pine trees and a bunch of others. Kathryn didn't know trees. Anything that resembled a Christmas tree was pine, and everything else was just a tree. Good enough.

It was even darker once she passed under the thick branches. She was tempted to flip on her brights, but figured she'd only be turning them off soon enough. And she didn't want to show any kind of weakness or fear, especially not of something as straightforward as a little bit of heavy shadow.

The trees thinned out, and the road straightened. A white rail fence appeared on her right, and she recognized the enclosure as a paddock. It was dark at this end, but there was a well-lit structure in the near distance with more white-fenced enclosures. And in the one closest to the barn, she could see . . . horses. She blinked, not quite believing her eyes.

"Oh, please," she muttered. "A cowboy vampire? Like I believe that."

As she drew closer, it was obvious the horses were well cared for and well-bred. These weren't family pets but expensive animals. Was someone training them? Or maybe breeding? Was horse breeding profitable? She wouldn't have thought so, but she'd have to look it up. She hadn't found anything in her research to indicate Lucas Donlon was breeding livestock, but that didn't mean anything. As far as she knew, she was the first federal agent of any kind who'd made it this far. She slowed slightly as she drew even with the paddock. The brightly-lit structure was a horse barn, with a long aisle down the middle and stalls on either side. It all looked very tidy . . . and very expensive.

Kathryn felt the weight of someone staring at her. She turned her head sharply toward the far end of the paddock and saw that it wasn't one pair of eyes watching her, but several. Even the horses seemed to be studying her. She knew that was nothing more than a fanciful thought, but there was no mistaking the suspicion of the men. She frowned. Maybe they were all vampires like the gate guard. Did vampires ride horses? Wasn't there some superstition about animals being more sensitive to vampires than humans were? She supposed it was unscientific of her to give any credence to that kind of superstition, not to mention it was probably politically incorrect. Vampires had fought and won several civil rights lawsuits which took into account their unique natures.

Not wanting to draw any more attention to herself, she sped up once again, following the road as it circled around the barn, slowing as it dipped alongside a small creek bed for what felt like a hundred yards, then circled around a grassy hill to finally reveal . . .

Oh. Now that was lovely. And not at all what she'd expected from a vampire's residence. She hadn't been foolish enough to imagine he lived in a creaky castle with bats circling around the turrets, but she hadn't anticipated this, either. This was a beautiful house, built into the hillside and glowing a warm gold in the wash of landscape lights. It was a Craftsman style with a peaked roof and skylights, somewhere around 8000 square feet would be her guess. But there was probably a basement level she couldn't see, and who knew how big that was? That was one thing the myths got right about vampires. They didn't like sunlight, which made the skylights an unusual feature, but if the house had windows, why not skylights?

She drove up the short hill to the foot of the front steps, where a woman appeared to be waiting for her. She wore a severe black pants suit and a blindingly white, tailored blouse, with a short red tie. If not for the spiked heels, Kathryn would have thought she was *trying* to look like a man. But those heels gave it away. She was either a dominatrix or a lawyer. Kathryn was betting on the latter.

The woman walked over to the truck as Kathryn was climbing out. She slammed the door and turned.

"Agent Hunter," the woman said, holding out her hand. "I'm Magda Turkova, Lord Donlon's attorney."

Bull's eye! Kathryn thought to herself and shook the other woman's hand. "Special Agent Kathryn Hunter," she said unnecessarily.

"Lord Donlon is expecting you," Magda said, her attitude all business, but there was a slight edge of hostility beneath it all.

Kathryn followed the attorney up the stairs and into a slate-floored foyer that completely lived up to the promise of the golden exterior. The house was single story, but the ceilings were high, the walls raw stucco and painted a blend of warm hues. The décor was decidedly western, but elegant and reeking of wealth. Apparently, it paid to be a vampire, especially one with a title.

Magda continued through the entry, leading Kathryn around a handsome, double-sided fireplace and into a living room which had clearly been decorated with a male sensibility. Big couches and chairs were gathered around a huge slab of glass that was perched on a piece of rock and served as a coffee table. The room was nicely done, but there were no dainty designer accents, no carefully posed vases or works of art. Instead, there was a pile of magazines comprised of mostly sports and business, with a big screen monitor gracing the main wall. A bookshelf next to the monitor boasted a collection of videos and games and at least four separate gaming consoles. Next to that, a wall of windows looked out on the front of the house and down across the property, with its dark clusters of trees. Kathryn noted the slight distortion that told her the glass in the window was bulletproof. Apparently, all was not happy in the land of vampires.

The lawyer indicated the seating area. "Lord Donlon will be with you in a moment." She walked over to a wet bar.

Of course, there was a wet bar. What else would there be in a man cave like this? Kathryn thought cynically.

"May I offer you a drink?" Turkova asked. "Or no, you probably can't drink on duty, can you? We have water, or soft drinks?"

"Water would be nice. Thank you," Kathryn said. Normally, she wouldn't accept anything to eat or drink from a person she was about to question in relation to a crime. But first of all, she wasn't certain a crime had been committed. Secondly, she had no evidence that Lucas Donlon was directly involved in her brother's disappearance, and, in fact, doubted that he was. And finally, she was thirsty.

Magda retrieved a bottle of water from the under the counter refrigerator and grabbed a glass from the overhead rack. "Would you like ice?"

"No, thank you. And I don't need a glass. Just the bottle will be fine."

Magda gave a brief smile. "My own preference, as well. I can rarely drink one of these things—" She held up the bottle. "—in a single sitting. I like to take it with me rather than throw it away."

Kathryn took the proffered water. It was icy cold, the bottle slightly wet with condensation. "So, Ms. Turkova," she began, but the woman interrupted her.

"Magda, please. We don't stand on ceremony."

"But you do have guards."

Turkova gave a dismissive shrug. "A necessary precaution for my lord's security."

Kathryn tipped her head to one side in curiosity. "You refer to him as lord. Is that a hereditary title of some sort?"

Magda laughed lightly, sounding genuinely amused. "No, not at all. Vampire society has a feudal structure, Agent Hunter. And Lord Donlon rules a substantial territory."

"Feudal .·. ." Kathryn repeated, thinking that if nothing else, she'd gain substantial knowledge about vampires from this visit. "Do his subjects—"

"Not subjects. His people. We *have* made *some* concessions to the modern age."

"Of course. His people. But if the system is feudal, do they tithe to him?"

"Naturally. He protects them, defends them from both humans and other vampires. He also runs a considerable corporate empire, which I'm sure you know. Many of his people work for him directly, others he underwrites. Lord Donlon is a businessman, a very successful businessman."

"I see."

"And you, Agent Hunter, what brings you to South Dakota? I know for a fact that you are not based out of our jurisdictional field office, which is in Minneapolis."

Kathryn chuckled, shivering intentionally. "Minnesota's a little too cold for my bones. No, I work out of Quantico."

"I see. And what does Quantico want with Lord Donlon?" Magda's tone was just as casual as it had been, but her gaze was abruptly intent. The lawyer emerging at last.

"I've made no secret of the reason for my visit, Ms. Turkova. I'm investigating the disappearance of someone. A photographer from California who was here to shoot the Badlands. He's an artist of some repute and has friends in high places. Hence, the FBI's interest in what normally would be a matter for state or local authorities."

"I see. And what is this photographer's name?"

Kathryn smiled, knowing that Turkova almost certainly knew Daniel's name already. "I'm here to interview your client," she said mildly, but firmly, "not you, and not to be interviewed by you, either. Is Lucas Donlon available?"

Magda bared her teeth in an unfriendly smile. She wasn't as blatant about it as the sphinx-like guard had been, but Kathryn clearly caught sight of two delicate white fangs. "It never hurts to try," she said.

"Understood," Kathryn agreed.

Magda pulled a cell phone from her pocket and hit a number. "Agent Hunter is here," she told someone, then disconnected and slipped the phone back into her pocket. "Lord Donlon will see you now."

KATHRYN FOLLOWED Magda Turkova out of the comfortable living room and down a long, tile-floored hallway. Turkova's high heels tapped loudly on the hard surface, and all Kathryn could think of was how cold these floors must be in winter. This was South Dakota, after all. She'd never lived in any of the truly cold states, but she saw the weather reports like everyone else, and South Dakota was usually buried in snow for months at a time. The heating bill for this house must be cosmic. But she supposed if you could afford a place like this on a ranch this big, then you didn't worry much about heating bills.

Turkova's cell phone rang. She glanced at the ID and scowled, but she answered before it rang a second time.

"Magda." She listened, then said, "Yes."

And that was it. Kathryn figured it was Donlon calling, maybe asking if they were on their way or something. Maybe he was anxious to get the interview over with and return to his vampire business, whatever that was. Actually, her data run on Donlon had listed considerable financial holdings, but everything was owned under his corporate identity of Donlon Inc. It was a private corporation, which meant he wasn't required to make the details of his holdings and/or earnings public unless he wanted to. And he clearly didn't want to. Usually, even private corporations made *some* things public—charitable stuff that was good for their public image, or information they intentionally let slip to influence a particular business transaction. And sometimes political donations were revealed, when it served their corporate interests. But Donlon didn't seem to care about any of that. She hadn't been able to find a single article on him or his corporation, not in the major journals, not even in the local newspaper.

Kathryn and Turkova were met halfway down the corridor by what she took to be another gatekeeper. Male, presumably a vampire, six-foot-three, blond and brown, big shoulders and arms, so probably two twenty-five or more in weight. He was good-looking in an all-American football captain sort of way and gave her an openly friendly smile before stopping them in front of a pair of big wooden doors with iron belting.

"I'll take it from here, Magda," he said, as if he was the one in charge. "Agent Hunter," he said, turning his attention Kathryn. "My name is Nicholas. Lord Donlon is waiting, if you're ready?"

Kathryn scowled inwardly at the use of the honorific for Donlon, but outwardly she only nodded briskly and said, "Yes, thank you." Unfailingly polite and professional, that's what the FBI expected of their agents.

Nicholas opened the door. Kathryn started to step forward, but stopped in surprise when he strode in ahead of her. It threw her off enough that she paused on the threshold until Magda made an impatient noise behind her.

Kathryn continued into the room, her gaze sweeping the space, cataloging everything she saw. It wasn't quite what she'd expected, but then so far, nothing about this vampire's lair *had* been. The room was big and airy, very masculine, but tasteful, with a grouping of dark leather furniture to one side, in front of an even darker row of wooden bookshelves that lined the entire length of one wall. There was a fireplace on the opposite wall, with a carved wooden mantle, and above that a beautiful oil painting depicting moonrise over what she assumed was the nearby Badlands, although it could just as easily have been Monument Valley in Arizona or another similar desert setting. She wasn't that familiar with any of them. But the artist had caught the surreal look of those landscapes, and the rising moon gave it such an alien cast that if someone had told her it was another planet, she would have believed them.

On the side of the fireplace nearest the hallway door, the wall was unadorned except for a series of black and white photographic prints. Kathryn's eye ranged over the photographs as closely as she could without being obvious about it, and there was no doubt. She had none of Daniel's talent, but she had a terrific eye for detail, and she knew his work. They were from a series he'd done on Ireland some years ago.

Her gaze shifted to the vampire she'd come to see, Lucas Donlon, but the broad-shouldered Nicholas was still in the way. Impatient now, she started to walk around him just as he addressed Donlon, saying, "My lord," and stepped aside, like a magician revealing his trick.

LUCAS SPRAWLED behind his desk, consciously projecting an image of negligent ease, which was at complete odds with what he was feeling. The timing on this FBI investigation sucked overall, although he was glad to get it over with at last. With his incursion last night into Klemens's territory, war had been declared. Up until now, the Midwestern vampire lord had limited himself to an occasional, if irritating, foray along the border in an attempt to seize assets he knew belonged to Lucas. His success had been limited, but with the assassination attempt on Raphael, and now Lucas's response, the gloves would be off. And Klemens was a dirty fighter.

Vampire wars in general were fought differently than human wars. For one thing, there were no grand battles. There weren't enough vampires on either side for that, and most of *those* were civilians, who everyone agreed should be left out of the bloodshed as long as they didn't insert themselves into the confrontation. Or hang around with traitors like Heintz.

Instead, the war would consist of a series of skirmishes, short-lived and bloody. Every vampire lord had his warriors, some more than others, but no one had more than a few hundred. Because wars were fought with a limited number of combatants, there were lulls in the fighting. Like now. With Lucas's successful strike last night, and especially since Klemens had suffered the loss of both property and vampires, it would be at least a few days before Klemens could pick a target and rally his forces for a counterattack. That didn't mean Lucas could relax. His people were on alert all up and down the eastern border, and his warriors were staged in such a way that at least a few of them could reach any attack point fairly quickly. Their job was to hold the line until backup arrived.

So, if Lucas *had* to deal with the FBI, this was as good a time as he would get for the foreseeable future. But this whole thing was a waste of time. He didn't know anything about a missing person, and neither did any of his vampires. He'd questioned them specifically about this matter so that none of them could weasel out and lie to him. A vampire couldn't lie to his Sire or his sworn master, and Lucas didn't permit anyone to reside within his territory unless they were at least sworn to him. Most of the vampires living on the ranch itself were his own children, and that included everyone who worked closely with him in the main house.

But then, this was South Dakota. There weren't that many vampires in the entire state. There weren't even that many *humans*. Fewer than a million people lived in South Dakota, which was one of the lowest population densities in the country. The majority of South Dakota's vampires lived or worked right here on Lucas's ranch. There was a small cluster in Sioux Falls, but they weren't suspected in the FBI's missing person case because this Agent Hunter seemed certain her man had gone missing while hanging around in the Badlands, which, by the way, was a good eighty miles from Lucas's ranch.

Lucas had his main headquarters here because he loved the area. When most people thought of South Dakota, they thought of the crags of Mount Rushmore with its famous presidents, and they figured the whole state looked like that. But his ranch was beautiful and green—during most of the year, anyway. His estate was over a hundred and fifty acres of rolling grasslands and mature trees, with two separate creeks running through it. It wasn't as green as his native Ireland, of course, but in the centuries he'd been alive, he'd never been anyplace that was. He loved his ranch, though. He loved raising horses, loved riding them through his land and knowing it *was* his land. He had other houses throughout his territory, some in much bigger cities. But he always came back here. This was home.

And now the FBI was invading his home. He didn't trust the police; he never had. He'd grown up on the mean streets of Dublin when they were truly mean, and the Garda had never been his friend. That was another thing about South Dakota. They left a man alone. As long as he didn't do anything to draw their attention his way, the authorities didn't bother him. He wished he could simply tell this FBI woman to go away, but he couldn't do that. Regardless of his personal preferences, he was responsible for thousands of vampires throughout his territory, which spanned several states. Anything he did could redound on them in unpleasant ways. So, he would see Agent Hunter, and he'd tell her what he'd already said on the phone. He didn't know where her brother was. Speaking of which, he found it very suspect that Agent Hunter had never bothered to mention that the man she was looking for was her brother. Did she really think he didn't have the wherewithal to find out details like that? She had surely done a data search on *him*. Did she think that he wouldn't do the same on *her*?

Granted, his contacts within the FBI weren't what they'd once been. For years, the vampire community's best and most secret asset within the Bureau had been Phoebe Micheletti, a former FBI tech and later forensic consultant. Phoebe's loyalty had been unquestioned because she was a vampire herself. But recent events in Washington, D.C. had shown that perhaps someone *should* have questioned her more closely. The situation had ended with Phoebe and her longtime mate both dead and the loss of an inside track at the FBI.

But there *were* still some vampires employed by the Bureau, especially in the technical areas where they could work at night. They might not have the contacts that Phoebe had once enjoyed, but they were still good enough to know that Kathryn Hunter wasn't here under official FBI auspices. As for discovering that the missing man was her brother, that took his computer guy all of seven minutes to find on the Internet. Thirty minutes more, and Lucas knew all sorts of things about Hunter.

He picked up his cell phone and rang Magda.

"Magda," she answered immediately. Normally, she used his title to answer when he called, but since she was currently escorting the FBI agent to his office door, she wisely didn't want to give away that he was the one calling.

"Reach out again to our people in the FBI," he told her. "See if they've got anything more on Kathryn Hunter. Personal stuff. But make sure they're discreet, Maggie. I don't want to set anything into motion until I know more."

"Yes," she said, the one word clipped and short.

Lucas disconnected, smiling. Magda absolutely hated it when he called her Maggie. Which was why he did it, of course. He heard footsteps a few seconds later, Maggie's heels and a nearly silent tread that he assumed belonged to Agent Hunter. Nick had been waiting in the hallway for them, and he spoke as soon as the two women were close enough.

"Agent Hunter?" Nicholas said.

"Yes." The woman's voice was deeper than expected, sexy. Her voice over the phone had been much more businesslike. It was too much of a difference to be explained away by the idiosyncrasies of phone transmission alone. She probably worked at sounding professional, but as far as he was concerned, she'd only sounded robotic. Maybe he should tell her. Maybe he would.

Out in the hallway, Nicholas could be heard introducing himself, and then the door opened. His lieutenant entered first, which was probably unusual in a human corporate setting. In his experience, the guest would normally be permitted to enter first, followed by their escort. But in Lucas's world, especially while they were at war with their neighbor, Nicholas would never permit a stranger to approach Lucas directly. And then there was the fact that Kathryn Hunter was FBI. Nicholas had been infected by Lucas's distrust of police authorities, and so he entered first, with the FBI agent sandwiched between him and Magda, who stood at the door.

Lucas didn't stand. Why should he? Agent Hunter wasn't a guest. She was an interloper, an interrogator. And she certainly wasn't due any respect of position from him. He was far more powerful than she was.

"My lord," Nicholas said formally, and stepped aside, giving Lucas his first real view of Kathryn Hunter.

Well, well, he thought to himself. Agent Hunter was definitely not what he'd pictured. He'd expected someone who lived up to that robotic phone voice—some sort of Brunhilde with sturdy hips and shoulders to match. What he got was the sexy-voiced version instead. Kathryn Hunter was quite lovely. Or, she would be if she permitted herself. She was tall, nearly six-foot despite those sensible boots. Put her in a pair of lipstick-red, fuck-me heels and she'd definitely top six-foot. Lucas liked tall women. He liked to fuck tall women. Well, okay, he liked to fuck women of pretty much any height. But his *favorite* fuckable women were tall because he was well over six-foot himself, and he liked to kiss the women he bedded. He especially liked to kiss them while he was inside them, and that was always easier when the parts matched up so nicely.

And speaking of kissing, his personal FBI agent had a mouth to match the voice. Soft, puffy lips that were made for wrapping around a man's cock, and she was wearing just a hint of pink gloss that she probably considered practical. But it gave her mouth a vulnerable, little-girl-lost look. Not that she was a little girl. Oh, no. Miss FBI was very much all grown up. She was, however, very prim and proper, just like Kofi had said, with her long, blond hair pulled into a high and tight pony tail, and every hair in place. Her figure was slender for the most part, although he suspected her breasts were much fuller than they appeared. She probably wore some sort of sports bra to flatten her natural assets. He supposed it made sense, given her profession, but it only made him more curious to see the real things.

The rest of her body was camouflaged by a boring, dark blue pants suit and a white button-up blouse that was *definitely* buttoned up . . . all the way to her neck. His fingers itched to twitch open that top button and reveal her delicate neck. Actually, they twitched to do a lot more than that, but he'd settle for that top button. No woman should ever be *that* buttoned up.

Slender hips, long legs . . . his perusal traveled back to her face and a pair of dark blue eyes that were regarding him with something short of a friendly look.

He grinned unapologetically. "Agent Hunter," he said, without rising.

Her jaw tightened, but she stepped forward and reached across his desk to offer her hand. "*Special* Agent Kathryn Hunter," she said, aiming for crisp, but that bedroom voice of hers wasn't made for it.

Lucas stood slowly and took her hand in his. It put her at a disadvantage, because she'd stretched across the desk to reach him. She was now left leaning forward while he stood straight, holding her in place by virtue of their joined hands. Lucas made no attempt to alleviate the uncomfortable position. He kept his gaze steady as he wrapped his fingers around hers, catching the slight flair of concern in her eyes as she quickly rebalanced.

"Lucas Donlon," he said smoothly, still grasping her hand. "And you've met my lieutenant, Nicholas. How can I help you, *Special* Agent?"

Hunter immediately tried to take her hand back, but Lucas wasn't ready to let her go, and she clearly wasn't willing to force the issue by jerking her hand away from him. She was aware of him, though. A slight flush lit her cheeks, and it was more than just embarrassment or even anger. Her pupils were dilated, and her heartbeat had just kicked up a notch.

He released her hand with a wink. She took a step back from the desk at once, putting distance between them. She didn't wipe her hand on her pants leg, but he could tell she wanted to. Kathryn Hunter was clearly used to denying her more feminine urges. She probably had to, working where she did. But Lucas was a vampire lord. When he touched a woman, she knew she'd been touched, and, in this case, desired.

And Kathryn Hunter didn't like being reminded of that.

KATHRYN FOUND herself staring. If everything she'd seen so far in the vampire's headquarters had surprised her, Lucas Donlon himself was the final stunner. And that was the right word, too. Because he was one of the best looking men she'd ever seen. He had straight black hair that wasn't long so much as it looked in need of a trim. It touched his collar in back and threatened to drop over his forehead in front. He didn't bother to stand up, the ass, but lounged back in his chair like some sort of bad boy making a point. Still, she could see he'd be tall and well built. Not as thickly muscled as his bodyguard, or whatever Nicholas was, but his shoulders were wide and appeared well-muscled beneath the leather jacket he wore over a black T-shirt. She met his eyes briefly. They were hazel, she supposed, but the brown had so much gold in it, they almost defied classification. And they were scanning her from head to toe, lingering in all the inappropriate places. She waited until his perusal finally made it back to her face, then gave him her most frigid stare.

He grinned in response, and some deeply buried feminine part of her shivered at the sight. Kathryn steeled herself against it.

"Agent Hunter," he said lazily, still not bothering to stand.

Kathryn suppressed the urge to tighten her jaw in irritation. She leaned across the desk and offered her hand. "*Special* Agent Kathryn Hunter," she said, meeting his arrogant gaze.

He remained seated, but his big hand closed over hers, his fingers hard and a little rough, as if he did more than sit behind this desk all night long. He stood then, uncoiling a tall, well-muscled body with a grace that only emphasized his looks and strength. Kathryn almost groaned. The black T-shirt was tucked into a pair of faded denims that showcased his flat belly and clung to his narrow hips like a lover's caress.

His standing unbalanced her, and she gripped his hand tightly before looking up and meeting his eyes for an awkward moment. She steadied quickly enough and tried to give his hand only a perfunctory shake, but he didn't release her. Her heart slammed against her ribs, and she cursed her body's instinctive reaction to his overwhelming masculinity.

This shouldn't be happening. Kathryn worked in a man's world where women were still barely tolerated by too many. SAC Fielding was only one example of the misconceptions and resentment she faced all the time. She'd long ago come to grips with the fact that in order to succeed, she'd have to set aside her femininity and be simply one more agent, since she would never be one of the guys. She wore no makeup other than a touch of nearly clear lip gloss to keep her lips from drying out completely, and while she couldn't bring herself to cut her long hair, she always wore it pulled away from her face, either in a French braid or a ponytail so severe she didn't think she'd ever need a facelift.

But somehow Lucas Donlon had broken through all of those precautions with nothing more than a look and a handshake. He'd managed to awaken feelings and desires buried so deeply that she'd all but forgotten she ever had them. And she wanted them left buried. This was her job, her career. This was what she did with her life, and she wasn't going to let some handsome vampire or anyone else shatter her carefully won reserve.

"Lucas Donlon," he was saying, "And you've met my lieutenant, Nicholas. How can I help you, *Special* Agent?"

Kathryn thought of all sorts of things she'd like to say to him, most of which involved sharp, pointed objects drilling into his heart. But she reined in her temper and forced herself to back a couple of steps away from the desk, telling her heart to stop acting like such a fool.

"As I explained on the phone, Mr. Donlon—"

"Lucas," he said easily. "And do sit down . . . *Kathryn.*" He slouched back into his own chair like a big, graceful cat, and regarded her over steepled fingers.

Kathryn sat, using the motion to conceal her irritation at his familiar use of her first name. She considered correcting him, reminding him of her title and that she represented the FBI. Except she didn't in this case, not really. That thought shocked her back to the matter at hand. She had ten days to find her brother, ten days before her bosses would expect her back on the job. She didn't have time to waste bandying words with Lucas Donlon. Besides, she had a feeling it would only encourage him if she insisted on her proper title.

"As I explained on the phone, Mr."—Donlon raised one eyebrow, and she switched words mid-syllable—"Lucas. I'm looking for a photographer who went missing after completing a shoot in Badlands National Park."

"There are several towns closer to the park than we are."

"I'm aware of that. But he was staying very near here, and this area is where he was last seen."

"And how does this relate to me . . . *Kathryn?*"

Kathryn blinked. He was actively flirting with her, although flirting was too tame a word for anything Lucas Donlon did. And damn it, her body wanted to respond to the seduction in that deep voice, to the crooning way he kept repeating her name. Kathryn bit her tongue, letting the sharp pain redirect her senses. She didn't have time for his games. She needed to find Daniel.

"Daniel Hunter is the man who's missing. An eyewitness places him at a local nightclub."

"We've quite a few of those in the surrounding area, as well."

"Yes, but this particular club, according to my sources, is owned and run by vampires."

Donlon lifted his eyes, looking over her shoulder at his lieutenant, Nicholas. The exchange was silent, but it told her he hadn't expected that particular piece of evidence.

"A blood house," he said, returning his gaze to her.

Kathryn blinked at him. "I'm sorry?"

He smiled briefly and repeated, "A blood house. The club you're referring to is called a blood house. That's not its name, but that's what it is. It's where humans go to . . . mingle with vampires."

"Mingle," Kathryn said softly. "You mean—"

"Many humans are fascinated by the vampire . . . culture, shall we say. They go to blood houses to flirt with what they see as the darker side of humanity. And they give blood, of course."

Kathryn frowned. "Give blood. You mean from their own veins?"

Donlon laughed. "Don't look so shocked, Kathryn. It's a *very* pleasurable experience for all involved."

"Are you telling me people go to these places and let vampires *bite* them?"

"Yes, indeed."

"But that's . . ." She was about to say revolting, but thought better of it given current company.

Donlon grinned as if he knew anyway. "Don't knock it 'til you've tried it. And you will," he added with a slow, smoldering look.

Kathryn felt her lips pinch with irritation and forced her face to resume a bland expression. He had a way of goading her completely out of her comfort zone.

"In any event," she said briskly, "while I can't imagine Daniel enjoying something like that, he always *has* been an adventurer, so it's possible he—"

"Daniel?" Donlon said, catching her slip. "So, the last name isn't merely a coincidence. A husband? Brother? It's unlikely that he's old enough to be your father."

"How do you know how old he is?" she demanded at once.

Donlon shrugged, unconcerned. "I don't. But I can certainly guess at how old *you* are and extrapolate how old your father would have to be. My manager at that club is very careful about whom he lets in. And a man old enough to be your father would never pass muster. Too dangerous."

"Dangerous for whom?"

"The older man, love. As I said, having a vampire drink from you is *very* enjoyable. Not everyone's heart can handle it."

"Lovely," she muttered.

"Indeed," he agreed, not at all put off. "But as to your missing . . ."

"Brother," she supplied. There was little point in trying to conceal it. Sutcliffe knew, and she suspected Donlon knew, too. Despite his little games, she found it unlikely the efficient Magda would have let her get this far without checking out every aspect of her purpose in being here.

"Your missing brother, yes. I don't often visit the blood houses, but the vampires on my staff do frequent that particular one, among others. If you have a photograph of your brother, I'd be happy to show it around and ask if anyone saw anything."

"I'd rather check it out myself," Kathryn countered. "If I could have your club manager's name and those of any vampires who visit the club regularly . . ." She took out her notepad and pen, prepared to write names.

Donlon didn't move except to give her a lazy blink of his eyes. "I'm afraid that's not possible, Kathryn. My people rely on me to protect them, and I take that responsibility very seriously. It was not so long ago that your people were hunting mine down and slaughtering them for no reason. As I said, I'm more than happy to show your brother's photograph around, but that's all you'll get."

"What I'll get," she said sharply, "is a judge's order requiring your people to submit to questioning."

"Will you?" Lucas came to his feet so fast, she didn't see him move, and she shot up defensively.

Donlon's expression was no longer lazy, his voice no longer teasing. "Go ahead, *Special Agent* Hunter. Get your warrant. Oh, but wait, you can't, can you? Because you're not here in an official capacity. In fact, I suspect your supervisors told you to leave this alone, but here you are anyway."

Kathryn gave a mental shrug. So he knew she was off the reservation on this one. Powerful men always had ways of finding out things, and she didn't make the mistake of thinking Donlon was any less powerful just because he was a vampire. If anything, it was likely to make him more powerful. He could bring to bear not just economic and business pressure, but that visceral fear of the unknown as well. She *had* hoped to milk her FBI connection a bit longer, but . . . she sighed inwardly. It looked as if she'd have to play nice with this incredibly handsome bastard, after all.

She met Donlon's cool gaze evenly and gave an easy shrug. "It was worth a shot," she said, sitting down again. "Yes, I'm on my own for this one, and, yes, my superiors would rather I leave it alone. But I suspect their reluctance stems in large part from a desire not to piss you off. I don't really care about pissing you off. I just want my brother back, and I think you or your people know something about what happened to him."

"Just because he went to a vampire bar?" Donlon slouched back comfortably into his big chair. Did the man *ever* sit up straight? "There are many bars in South Dakota," he continued. "And very few of them are owned by vampires."

"Yes, but I have a witness who saw him leaving *your* bar with someone they say is a vampire. And that's the last time anyone saw my brother."

"Who's the witness, and what's the vampire's name?"

"I won't tell you that," Kathryn said instantly. The last thing she wanted was to have Donlon discover that her only witness was in Afghanistan. "But he's been to the club before, and he's certain the man leaving with my brother is a vampire."

"How can he be sure?"

"Because—" Kathryn looked away from the vampire's too perceptive gaze, feeling her cheeks heat with embarrassment. "—he claims to have been with the vampire in question. I assumed he meant sex, but now that you've explained . . . what you've explained . . ."

She chanced a glance at Donlon and found him watching her with blatant amusement.

"It's usually the same thing, Kathryn," Donlon said, clearly enjoying the moment. "Taking blood from the vein is a very sensuous experience. Sex usually follows. Or precedes. Or sometimes even both," he added with a teasing grin.

Kathryn bit her already sore tongue, using the pain to center herself. She was not here for Lucas Asshole Donlon's amusement.

"You don't know me, *Lord* Donlon," she said tightly. "Oh, I'm sure you know the basics, maybe even more than that. But you don't know *me*. I love my brother, and I will move heaven and earth to find him. I will be the thorn in your side, the stone under your foot. I will make fucking with your existence my damn mission in life until I find out what happened to him."

"And if he's dead?"

The air left Kathryn's lungs. She hadn't dared to ask herself that question. Hadn't dared to even consider the possibility. She forced herself to meet Donlon's curious stare.

"If he's dead," she said in a thin voice she didn't recognize. "Then I want to take him home."

Donlon's gaze softened with something close to pity. But she didn't want his pity. She drew a deep breath and stiffened her spine.

"The vampire you're looking for," he said. "He's not one of mine."

"How do you know?" she demanded.

He leaned forward, golden eyes glittering. "Because I've asked my people," he said in a hard voice, "and I trust them. What's the vampire's name?"

Kathryn thought about not telling him, but decided he couldn't help her if he didn't know whom to look for. And if he wasn't willing to help her, it wouldn't matter anyway.

"Alex," she said. "The witness didn't know a last name."

Donlon frowned. "There is no Alex among my vampires, not locally." He glanced briefly at Nicholas, and Kathryn would have sworn there was some communication going on there. She also noticed that he'd said not *locally*. Did that mean there was an Alex somewhere else, and they suspected he'd moved into the area? Or that this Alex visited on occasion? She drew a breath to ask him, but he turned his attention back to her, and she waited to see what his next move would be.

His scowl was still in place, but then, suddenly, as if a curtain had been drawn, everything about him changed. The sardonic gleam was back in his eyes and his mouth quirked into a cynical half-grin as he winked at her. "Tell you what, Kathryn. Come back Friday evening, and we'll take a tour of the club. You can ask around yourself."

Kathryn studied him distrustfully. "But today's only Wednesday, Why do we have to wait so long?"

"Because the club isn't open," he explained slowly, as if she should have known that. "Friday through Sunday only."

Shit! Kathryn thought to herself. Possibly her best lead, and she had to sit on her hands for two more days?

"What if they won't talk to me? I mean the vampires and whoever else is at the club."

"Trust me, they'll talk to you," he said silkily. "But I'll do even better, since I'm certain you'd rather not postpone your investigation while you wait. I'll make some inquiries here and elsewhere. Come back tomorrow night, and perhaps I'll have something for you."

Kathryn wondered about Lucas's almost Jekyll and Hyde transformation, but even more, about his sudden willingness to cooperate. Did he know more than he was admitting?

"You could just call me if you find something," she said ungraciously.

He only smiled and murmured, "But where would be the fun in that?"

Kathryn stood. "I'm not really here for fun, Mr. Donlon."

"Och, and don't I know it?" he responded, with a very genuine-sounding Irish lilt flavoring his words for the first time. Was he Irish? For that matter, how old *was* he? Vampires lived a long time, if what she'd heard could be believed. She tended to think at least some of it was vampire disinformation. But if even part of it were true, Donlon could easily have been born in some long ago Ireland. The there-and-gone lilt was just one more piece of the mystery that was Lucas Donlon. And she'd always loved a good mystery.

She stood, as if to leave, then shifted her gaze deliberately to the photographs on the wall next to the fireplace. The ones she knew for a fact that her brother had taken, although that didn't necessarily mean anything, since Dan's work was sold in galleries worldwide.

"These are beautiful," she said, crossing to the wall and moving from one photo to the next. "Ireland, isn't it?"

"*Éire* we call her," Lucas murmured directly into her ear.

Kathryn's heart slammed against her ribs. He'd somehow come out from behind his desk and walked over to stand right behind her without her being aware of it. He stood looking over her shoulder, so close she could smell the spicy scent of his skin, could feel the warmth of his breath on her cheek. She had to fight the urge to reach for her gun as she turned her head and found herself looking directly into his strange golden eyes.

He smiled, a bare upward tilt of his lips. He knew he'd startled her, and he took pleasure in it. Kathryn wanted to step away, wanted to ball up her fist and slug his beautiful, smug face. But she couldn't do it. She could only stare and try to breathe.

"Have you been to my country?" he asked in a voice so soft she wouldn't have heard him if they hadn't been standing so close.

It took her a moment to find the words to answer. "Your country?" she repeated.

"*Mo Éireann álainn. Mo Chroí mo go deo.*"

The Irish words flowed like beautiful music. "What does that mean?" she whispered, unwilling to dispel the echo of the lovely sounds.

He leaned even closer, and for one wild moment, Kathryn thought he meant to kiss her. And the worst part was, she was pretty sure she'd let him. Fortunately, he spared her from making that terrible mistake by saying softly, "Someday maybe I'll tell you."

He straightened a little, putting just enough distance between them that she could think rationally again, and indicated the photo nearest to her left. Daniel had caught three horses in full movement, running over a grassy paddock, with trees closing in all around. The youngest was still a foal, his back legs kicked up in play.

"That's Kildare," Lucas murmured to her. "Heart of the Irish thoroughbred country. My grandfather had a place there. Nothing this grand, of course. Just a patch of dirt and an old plow horse. I only visited there once, but it was a memorable event in my too short childhood."

Kathryn was surprised he'd told her that much. She glanced over her shoulder. "My grandparents had horses, too," she offered, and was rewarded with the most glorious smile.

"Well, then . . . it seems we've something in common, *a cuisle*. You'll have to come riding with me sometime."

Kathryn's cheeks heated with embarrassment. She didn't know what he'd just called her, but she knew it crossed that invisible line between agent and witness. What was she doing? She wasn't here to be romanced by Lucas Donlon, no matter how handsome and charming he was.

Lucas must have sensed that their moment of connection was over. He gave her an "*oh well*" kind of shrug, then stepped back a pace and studied the entire series of photographs. "I don't know who took these. Magda found them for me. But the photographer has captured my homeland like no other I've ever seen." He gestured at the images. "I'll probably never live there again, so I'm grateful."

Kathryn looked from her brother's photographs to Lucas, trying to decide if he was genuine, or if he was playing her. But there was that comment about his grandfather between them, and his expression held such yearning as his gaze traveled from one photograph to the next, that she believed him.

"Then you should probably help me find him," she said.

Lucas gave her a puzzled look. "Find whom?"

Kathryn tilted her head toward the photographs. "The photographer. Daniel Hunter."

He regarded her blankly for a moment, then his eyes widened in surprise. "Your brother took these?" He grabbed one of the framed images from the wall and turned it over. Kathryn knew what he'd find. There was a label on the back with her brother's name and contact information, as well as a statement of copyright.

Lucas read the label quickly, then turned the photograph over again and searched for a signature on the image.

"Lower left corner," Kathryn said. "Very small, but it's there. Just his initials, D H."

She watched his eyes as they traveled over the print and saw the moment he found what he was looking for. "Son of a bitch," he swore softly. "Nicholas," he said without turning. "Get Magda in here now."

Kathryn heard Nicholas on the phone, but her attention was all for

Lucas, who was staring at the photos with new interest.

"What is it?" she asked. "What do you see?"

"It's not the prints," he said, shaking his head slightly. "It's where she bought them."

"What do you mean? Daniel's work is carried in a number of very fine galleries—"

"Yes, but what about *this* gallery?" he asked, rubbing a square tipped finger over the gallery's name on the back label of the frame he still held.

"Which one—" Her question was interrupted by the opening of the door. Lucas held up his hand, asking Kathryn to wait as he turned to address Magda.

"Maggie," he began, and she saw the woman's expression tighten with irritation at the nickname. She would have found that intriguing if she hadn't been far more interested in Lucas's reaction to her brother's photographs. "These photographs," he continued, gesturing with one hand. "The gallery owner is Carmichael, right?"

"Yes, my lord," Magda said, clearly puzzled by the question. "He has a small gallery in Minneapolis, but I believe he brought these from his main gallery in Chicago, because he thought you'd enjoy them."

She saw a knowing look pass between Lucas and Magda and knew there was something they weren't telling her. Something about Carmichael?

"Why is Carmichael important?" Kathryn demanded. "What does it matter where you bought them?"

Donlon shrugged and hung the photograph back on the wall. "It occurs to me that he might be an admirer of your brother's work. Admiration can sometimes turn to obsession."

"You think Carmichael kidnapped Daniel?" she asked, doubtfully. "My brother's a big guy, taller than I am, and very athletic. He wouldn't be easy to grab."

"Don't be naïve, Kathryn. Even the strongest man can be taken down by the addition of any number of available drugs to his drink. And your witness did say Daniel left the bar with someone. Perhaps it only had the appearance of willingness."

"But the witness also said the man was a vampire."

"Perhaps he was wrong about that, or perhaps your brother didn't actually leave with the person he saw."

Kathryn studied his too handsome face, trying to determine whether he was telling her the whole truth. But she might as well have tried to read a statue. Lucas stared back at her with nothing more than a vaguely puzzled expression, as if he couldn't figure out what *her* problem was.

"All right," she said at last. "What time Friday night can we visit this vampire bar?"

"If you want to get a feel for the place, it will have to be late. What do you think, Nicholas?" he asked, turning to his lieutenant. "Eleven o'clock?"

Nicholas nodded. "On a Friday, yes, my lord."

Lucas swung back to her with a pleased grin. "It's a date then. Eleven o'clock on Friday. Shall I pick you up?"

"No," she said immediately. This was *not* a date, no matter what he said. "I'll meet you there."

"Very well." He sighed, as if disappointed. "But do wear something appropriate."

She frowned and glanced down at her white blouse and dark blue pants.

"If you want to get information, *a cuisle*, you can't walk in there looking like you're about to raid the place."

"Of course," she said dismissively, as if she'd already considered that. And she was sure she would have. Eventually. Damn it. Damn *him*. She'd have to go clothes shopping, because the raciest thing she'd brought with her was a cotton tank top.

Lucas winked conspiratorially, as if he knew what she was thinking.

Kathryn scowled. She'd clearly gotten off on the wrong foot with Lucas Donlon. "But we're meeting again tomorrow night, right? Same time as tonight? And you'll speak to your people?"

"I shall count the hours, Agent Hunter."

The urge to punch him was growing stronger. Anything to wipe that satisfied smirk from his face. But she had a feeling he was hoping for just that, so she turned and strode out of the office instead.

"Kathryn," Donlon called just before she reached the door.

She gritted her teeth, but managed to turn around and inquire politely, "Mr. Donlon?"

"Do you ride?"

Kathryn frowned in confusion. "Ride? You mean horses?"

Donlon gave her a knowing wink, but had enough grace to say only, "Well, yes."

"It's been a while," she said, her face hot with embarrassment as she belatedly realized the obvious innuendo in her words. "The grandparents I told you about died when I was very young, and their place was sold." And why the hell was she telling him that?

"Excellent. Wear some jeans tomorrow night, then. You do own a pair of jeans, don't you?"

Kathryn narrowed her eyes in irritation. "Of course. But why—"

"You'll see."

She stared at him, tempted to tell him where he could shove his cryptic comments, but then she remembered her brother and swallowed whatever she'd been about to say. She couldn't come up with anything nice to replace it, however, so she simply turned on her heel and strode out into the hallway where Magda was waiting to escort her.

LUCAS LEANED back in his chair and watched the lovely FBI agent storm gently from his office. She was good at concealing her emotions, good at keeping them from showing on her face, anyway. But he was Vampire. He didn't need her face to tell him what she was feeling. And she was pissed as hell. Not at having her bluff called about the missing man being her brother. She'd clearly expected that, if perhaps not so soon. Mostly, she was pissed because she couldn't figure out what to make of Lucas himself. She was attracted to him, though. She didn't want to be, but she was. No denying that. Her arousal had been subtle, and she'd fought against it, but it was there. Especially to a vampire's senses. He frowned briefly.

"You ever bed a cop, Nick?" he asked idly, listening to Kathryn's and Magda's footfalls fade down the tiled hallway.

With the FBI agent safely away and no longer even a potential threat to his Sire, Nicholas flopped down on the same visitor chair Kathryn had occupied moments before.

"Just one."

Lucas focused on his lieutenant, one eyebrow raised in question.

"You remember Sandi Hager, down in Kansas City?"

"Sandi? I thought you were seeing her sister?"

"I was." Nick shrugged. "Turns out the ladies didn't mind sharing, if you know what I mean."

"Shit." Lucas laughed. "Those were some big women, Nick. You're lucky they didn't drain you dry."

"Who says they didn't? Worth every minute of it, though." He grinned, then asked carefully, "You thinking about the FBI agent, my lord?"

Lucas tapped a finger idly on the chair of his arm. "Pretty lady. Great legs, world class ass, too. Must be a runner."

"Yeah," Nick said thoughtfully, then stiffened when Lucas shot him a hard look. "Not my type, though. Nope."

Lucas stared at him a moment longer, then sat up. "Is Judy still working with Nightshade down below?" Judy was his head horse trainer, a human who'd been with him since he'd first bought this ranch more than fifty years ago. Judicious doses of Lucas's blood kept her from aging, so Lucas didn't have to look for a new trainer every generation. Most of the people working in Lucas's stables were vampires, but horses were prey animals, and while there were plenty of prey animals who'd evolved to use the darkness for safety, horses weren't among them. They needed sunlight, and that meant someone had to be there to supervise and work with them during the day, especially the foals.

"Far as I know," Nick said, answering Lucas's question about the young stallion.

"Good. Let's get down there. I need to talk to Kurt about Daniel Hunter and see what he knows."

KATHRYN FOLLOWED Magda's swaying hips down the hallway, wondering how the woman managed to walk on those heels without breaking an ankle. She had nothing against high heels. In fact, she appreciated the way they made her already long legs look even longer. But if she wore stilettos like those, she doubted she could stay upright. Not to mention, she'd tower over most everybody she met. And fuck Lucas Donlon for making her feel like a drab worker drone.

Jesus! Where the hell had that thought come from? She didn't give a rat's ass what Donlon thought about anything, much less how she dressed. Granted, he was a sexy guy. Okay, probably the sexiest guy she'd ever met. But he was a vampire! He wasn't a guy at all. It was just her hormones reacting to his good looks. Maybe if she got out more, she wouldn't go all vaporous at the sight of a good-looking man, er, *vampire*. She had to remember that. Vampire.

Magda led her directly to the front door and opened it. "Was there anything else you needed, Special Agent Hunter?"

Kathryn studied the female vamp. The question had been polite enough, but the tone had been something else altogether, and the subtext was clear: good-bye, and don't let the door hit you in the ass on your way out. And wasn't that interesting? She thought about Lucas and his comment that admiration was only a short step from obsession. Her brother Daniel was very good-looking and charming as hell. Women loved him and, even more, wanted to *take care of* him. If Magda had been the one who chose the photographs . . . Kathryn knew it was a long shot, but went for it anyway.

"Mr. Donlon said you did the decorating in here," she said, gesturing at the beautiful house around them. "Is this a new residence?"

Magda tilted her head in a peculiar way, as if trying to decide whether to answer the question or stab her with a knife. Kathryn actually draped her hand casually next to her weapon, just in case, and saw the vampire female's eyes follow the movement.

Magda showed her teeth in what Kathryn assumed was supposed to be a smile. "The original residence is a quarter mile from here. The property is old, but this particular house is fairly new. *Lord* Donlon oversaw the design part of the process. He had a very clear sense of what he wanted here and in the stables. But after that . . ." She shrugged. "He asked me to handle the interior. I know his taste, so I found a decorator I thought could handle it. She took me to some galleries, private showings, and I made choices. Carmichael was one of those, and when he found out whom the photographs were for, he brought the Ireland series to my attention.

"Do you honestly think *I* had something to do with your brother disappearing?" she abruptly asked, mockingly.

Kathryn shrugged. "It was only a question. I'm grasping at straws at this point, but maybe if I keep grabbing, I'll eventually get the right one."

"I see."

"Do you? Do you have any family, Magda?"

"I am Vampire, Agent Hunter," she replied coldly. "Whatever family I had, I have no more. My family is here now, with my lord . . . and the others."

"Well, I have Daniel, and I won't stop looking until I find him."

Kathryn walked out the front door and down the stairs, beeping the locks on her SUV as she went. The truck was right in front of the house, and she was inside with the key in the ignition before Magda had even closed the house door.

Kathryn turned the key without thinking, but then sat for a moment, breathing deeply, trying to still her thumping heart. The very fact that it was pounding troubled her. She wasn't a raw, rookie agent. Granted, at twenty-eight, she wasn't exactly a grizzled veteran either, but Donlon was far from the first suspect she'd ever questioned. And he wasn't even a suspect. She hadn't thought going in that Donlon had a direct role in her brother's disappearance, and, having met him, she was even more convinced of it. But she *did* think he could help her find whoever was involved. And given his admittedly protective attitude towards his people, she was worried he'd be more concerned with protecting his vampires than finding her brother.

Kathryn's hands tightened on the steering wheel. She believed with all her heart that Daniel was alive, and she wanted him back. That was her goal. Her only goal. She closed her eyes, forcing herself to calm. If she wanted Daniel back, she needed to be smart about Donlon. He could help her, and he was attracted to her. He'd made that obvious. She didn't mistake that attraction for anything other than lust, the desire of a charismatic male to carve another notch on his bedpost. But if that's what it took to get his help, Kathryn would play along, although she wouldn't play all the way into his bed. Not that sex with Lucas Donlon would be a chore. The man, or rather the *vampire,* was gorgeous. Unfortunately, he was also arrogant, snide and probably a killer, to boot.

The lights from the big front windows, which had been spotlighting her car, were suddenly doused, casting her into darkness. It reminded her that she'd been sitting there too long, and she put the SUV in gear, flipped on her lights and pulled away.

As she retraced her path down the winding drive, she wondered if sex with a vampire always involved blood. She supposed it did. In his videotaped interview, the now-deployed Marine who'd seen Daniel leave the bar had admitted that the reason he knew Alex was a vampire was because Alex had taken blood from him during sex. He'd offered the information readily and seemed almost proud of the fact, as if he'd scored a coup of some sort. He thankfully hadn't offered any details, but there'd been a dreamy longing to his words, as if it had been a wonderful experience.

Kathryn couldn't imagine it. How could having someone bite your neck hard enough to draw blood be anything but painful?

She came around the hill, drawing even with the barn and paddocks once again. There were more men out there now. She slowed down to watch and recognized Lucas among them. He'd taken off the leather jacket and wore only his black T-shirt and jeans. The jacket had emphasized the breadth of his shoulders, but without it she could see the definition of his chest and flat belly. No doubt about it, Lucas Donlon was sex in cowboy boots. He pushed a black cowboy hat onto his head, and Kathryn rolled her eyes. A black cowboy hat? And at night? Wasn't that pushing the stereotype just a little? Lucas strode out into the middle of the ring. A huge, black horse immediately loped across the paddock, stopping right in front of him and butting its head against his chest. A human would have been knocked back a few steps by the force of that greeting, but Lucas didn't budge. He only laughed and returned the greeting with a nose rub for the horse.

Kathryn couldn't help smiling as she watched, but the longer she watched, she noticed something else. There was a pattern to the men surrounding Lucas. They moved and shifted, but he was never isolated, never alone. These weren't just random cowpokes watching the big man ride himself a horse, these were his bodyguards and, from what she saw, well-trained bodyguards. They were probably all vampires, too.

She saw Nicholas, the vampire who'd been introduced as Lucas's lieutenant, lean over and say something to Lucas. The vampire lord looked up then, his gaze crossing the intervening paddock and field to where Kathryn sat in her SUV silently observing. His white teeth flashed in a grin, and he tipped his hat in her direction.

Kathryn felt foolish at having been caught, especially since she really hadn't meant to linger so long. She quickly put the SUV in gear and hit the gas, breathing a sigh of relief when the road was quickly swallowed up by the first dense cluster of trees. She'd have to be careful with Donlon. She wasn't stupid enough to deny her attraction to him, but she was *smart* enough not to do anything about it. Lucas Donlon was not the kind of person an ambitious FBI agent could afford to get involved with. He was part of a secretive society that ruled itself and ignored U.S. law whenever it suited them. No one had ever been able to pin a crime on any of the vamps, though they'd certainly tried. There'd been a case out in L.A. not too long ago. It had been quickly hushed up, but the word underground was that the LAPD had tried to arrest someone very high up in the vampire hierarchy on suspicion of multiple murders.

The operative word there was *tried* to arrest him, because the warrant had been voided less than forty-eight hours after it was issued. And the big vamp had been released with so many apologies from the higher-ups, it was embarrassing. Adding insult to injury, it had been the vamps who found the real killer, the very *human* real killer, and turned him over to the authorities.

But even in cases where a vampire actually *had* committed a crime, the perpetrator disappeared before human authorities could get to him. No one knew for sure if the vampire offenders were imprisoned or executed, or if they were just moved somewhere else, but they were never heard from again. She supposed that was justice of a sort. Not very satisfying for the human authorities, but it saved the taxpayers the cost of a trial, and the outcome was about the same. Maybe even better.

Kathryn slowed as she approached the stone arch with its low, decorative wall. The same gun-toting guards were there. One of them waved her on. She nodded her thanks and kept going, until she saw the gleam of the whitewashed picket fence. A left turn took her back onto the paved section of road, and then the rough two-track again, until, finally, she hit the highway. She checked the dash clock. There was plenty of time left tonight. She would go back to the motel and check out the witness statements again, make some notes, then get a good night's sleep. If she was going to be sparring words with Lucas Donlon again, she'd need all of her brain synapses firing on full. And if only she could stop the rest of her body from firing on full for an entirely different reason, she'd be in great shape.

KATHRYN DIDN'T know what to expect when she arrived at Donlon's ranch the next day during daylight hours. She'd considered and rejected the possibility that the gate would be unguarded. Even if the vampires were tucked away safely in their beds somewhere, there was the house and barns to consider. And the animals, which to her untrained eye looked valuable. But more than anything, she just couldn't see Donlon being that lax about security. He pretended to be an easygoing, ain't-life-wonderful kind of guy, but there was another side to him that she imagined could be quite deadly when it came to the fore. When she'd insisted on questioning his vampires directly, any sense of the playboy had fled, and, in that moment, he'd been all business. And when he'd ultimately told her that his people would talk to her simply because he ordered them to do so . . . she could tell he believed it absolutely. Hell, maybe it was yet another vampire thing.

In any event, there were guards in all the same places and then some compared to the previous night, but they were human instead of vampire. Whereas the white wooden arch off the highway had been unguarded last night, today there were two human guards blocking her way. She showed them her credentials, and they checked her name against a list. Since Donlon was expecting her, albeit later this evening, Kathryn wasn't surprised when they permitted her to proceed past this first checkpoint. The second stop, the one with the stone arch, had four human guards in place of the two vampires from last night, although all four of them looked remarkably like their vampire counterparts. If the sun hadn't been shining, Kathryn wouldn't have been able to tell them apart. She gave a mental shrug and turned over her FBI credentials one more time. The list was checked again, and she was permitted to continue with one cautionary piece of advice.

"The main house will be locked, ma'am," one of the four humans informed her politely. "And there's no one there to answer the door. I suggest you wait down by the barns. The trainer's there, along with her staff. She'll be able to give you a cold drink and a place to sit, if you'd like."

"Thank you," Kathryn said. "I'll do that."

And that's why she found herself parking in front of the main house and walking up the flagstone paved driveway until she reached a set of wooden stairs that dropped down the twenty or so feet to where the barn and paddocks were located. It was a beautiful, sunny day, the sky a baby blue with not a cloud in sight, despite the cool temperature. Lucas's snide remarks about her clothes the previous evening had stung, so she'd dressed casually this afternoon. Her hair was pulled into its usual tight ponytail that hung below her shoulders. Her jeans were soft and comfortable, well-worn in all the right places, and she had a white tank top tucked in at the waist. The air was chilly, despite the sunshine, so she'd pulled on a light blue dress shirt, wearing it open like a jacket. At least her footwear was good. At the last minute back home, she'd shoved her boots into her suitcase, after flashing on a sudden mental picture of herself in her FBI blue suit sticking out like a sore thumb on the streets of a dusty, wild west town, complete with raised wooden walkways and hitching rails. The only thing missing had been the *Lonesome Dove* soundtrack. She'd felt silly at the time, but now she was glad to have them with her. The town was a bit more modern than her vision, but she'd seen plenty of people wearing boots, so she'd been right to bring them. And it had nothing to do with Lucas Donlon and his snarky comments.

At the bottom of the stairs, she followed a well-worn path through the grass that took her to the main paddocks. There were no horses in the barn paddock this afternoon, but in the fields beyond that, she could see several animals grazing in the sunshine. They appeared well cared for and content, and not at all concerned that their owner was a vampire. Kathryn smiled to herself as she made her way past the paddock and around to an open side door.

This was a horse barn. Kathryn stopped just inside the door, struck by the unique scent of warm horse, clean hay and packed earth. It brought back memories of her grandparents' ranch. Their place hadn't been anywhere near as grand as this one, but horses pretty much smelled the same everywhere. Other animals probably had their scents, too. Cows certainly did, and pigs. But there was something uniquely clean about the scent of a horse barn.

She looked around and found herself on the main walkway between a double line of box stalls, every one of which appeared to be filled. Several of the horses poked their heads out to check out the new arrival, watching her with big, brown eyes. One or two nickered softly, while a big black—even bigger than the animal she'd seen Donlon with last night—snorted his displeasure, his head bobbing up and down as he kicked the wooden side of his stall.

Kathryn gave him a wide berth, heading toward the closed end of the barn where she could see a tack room through an open door. Before she got there, a woman emerged, looking not at all surprised to find a stranger in her barn. She was on the short side, no more than five-foot-two, probably less without her boots on. Kathryn would have pegged her weight at 115 to 120, but well-muscled, no doubt from working with horses. Most people didn't understand how big horses really were, and how much strength it took to ride one properly so it would do what you wanted it to. The woman wore no makeup or jewelry. She had blue eyes and strawberry blond hair that was even longer than Kathryn's, her braid hanging all the way down her back to her butt.

"I'm Judy Peterson," the woman said with a friendly smile. "And you must be Special Agent Hunter. Lord Donlon said you might come by." She took the leather glove off her right hand and held it out.

Kathryn took it, feeling the rough skin and callouses of hard work. "Kathryn Hunter," she said. So Lucas had expected her to come early? It wasn't enough that he was unsettlingly handsome and charming, he had to be a mind reader, too?

"I wanted to see the place in daylight," Kathryn admitted.

"Looks different, doesn't it?" Peterson said agreeably. "Especially my babies." She gazed down the long line of box stalls with a proprietary air.

"You're the trainer?"

"Head trainer. I have a couple of assistants and some grooms. Lord Donlon spares no expense when it comes to his animals."

"He breeds them?"

"Some. Mostly he rides for pleasure. But he loves horses, and he's proud of what we've done here, so he doesn't mind letting one of his stallions cover the occasional mare or two. For a price, of course."

"Of course. Does he ever go outside his own stock for stud?"

"No." Peterson shook her head. "If he's interested in a particular line, he'll buy the stallion outright. It's a thing with him."

"Men and their dicks, I suppose," Kathryn muttered.

Peterson laughed. "You'd be right about that."

The big black suddenly kicked the side of his box stall hard enough that it rattled the whole structure, causing several other horses to protest.

"*Tromluí* doesn't like being ignored. He's a big baby that way." She walked past Kathryn to the stallion's stall and held out her hand. The horse immediately stuck his nose into her fingers and tongued up whatever had been there. "Carrot," Peterson said, rubbing the animal's nose with a fond smile. "He's got a sweet tooth, this one."

"*Tromluí*," Kathryn repeated. "That's his name?"

"It's Irish," Peterson told her, without looking away from the big horse. "Means Nightmare."

"How appropriate."

"Isn't it? Yeah, this one's Lord Donlon's special sweetheart."

"Does Donlon do any of his own training?"

"Quite a bit, though he leaves some of it to me, too. He's mostly interested in the stallions, but he takes on the occasional mare. Likes to sweet talk 'em first, 'til they don't even notice he's climbing into the saddle."

Peterson gave such a lusty chuckle that Kathryn knew she'd intended the double entendre.

"He breaks them himself?"

Peterson smiled, as if remembering something pleasant. "Breaks isn't the right word for what he does. I swear these animals understand every word he says. He can take a horse like *Tromluí* here and have him literally following him around like a baby goat. It's a sight to see. Not to mention the pretty picture the two of them make together. Two beautiful beasts moving as one. And that man *does* know how to sit a horse, let me tell you. MmmMmm."

Kathryn grinned, then hid it quickly. She might agree that Lucas was yum-worthy, but it wouldn't do to let him or anyone else know it.

"Does it bother you," she asked Peterson curiously, "to call him *Lord?* I mean this is America, after all."

Peterson shrugged. "The Queen of England comes over to visit, and everyone has to learn how to curtsey, right? They don't call her Liz, or even Missus Whatever-the-fuck-her-last-name-is. It's kind of like that for Lucas. He's a ruler, I guess you'd say, in his own society. It's only polite to grant him his title. Besides, he's a good employer. He respects my opinion and lets me do what I love for a living. I don't mind granting him a little respect in return."

Kathryn nodded. Put that way, it made sense to her, too. Besides, deep down she knew she was only trying to poke holes in Lucas Donlon to avoid dealing with her attraction to him. She couldn't afford to be attracted to anyone right now. She needed to be focused on one thing, and that was finding her brother Daniel.

"You ever notice any strangers around here, Judy? Maybe vampires you don't see regularly?"

Peterson didn't answer right away, but seemed to be giving it some thought. "Lord Donlon doesn't get too many visitors out here. This is his escape. You know, from all the decisions he has to make everywhere else, all the people coming to him for favors and stuff. He goes away for a few weeks every now and then, and when he comes back, I can see how stressed he is. Then he comes out to play with my babies, and he gets happy and becomes himself again."

Kathryn eyed the trainer in some surprise. That was a very thoughtful assessment of Donlon. Apparently, Peterson's talents for understanding animals extended to vampires, as well. Or maybe it was just to stallions, no matter the species.

"Lord Donlon said you'd be riding later?" Peterson said, with a sideways glance. "You ever ride before, Agent Hunter?"

"Call me Kathryn," she said, "and, yes, I've ridden, though lately not as much as I'd like to. I learned as a child and picked it up again in college. I had a friend whose parents owned a small farm not far from Charlottesville, where the UVA campus is. I used to go there sometimes, especially later when—" Kathryn stopped herself from running off at the mouth. She hadn't talked about that part of her life for such a long time, it felt odd to do so now. And with a perfect stranger, too.

The truth she'd almost blurted out was that until her brother started college on his own, she'd spent every weekend home with him, and almost every weeknight, too, making certain he stayed on the straight and narrow path to college himself. Even back then, he'd had a rare talent for photography, and they'd both known it would be his career. But he'd also been a daredevil, challenging the world at every opportunity. He still was, which was why he'd walked off into the backcountry of the Badlands by himself for two weeks. It was rather ironic that when trouble finally caught up with him, it had been at something as ordinary as a private club. Of course, there was the vampire angle to give it a little edge. From their conversations, she knew that touch of danger had appealed to him.

"I'm sorry, I was rambling," she dissembled, cutting herself off. "The short answer is, yes, I ride. Not well enough for that monster," she gestured at *Tromluí.* "But well enough."

"No one rides *Tromluí* but Lord Donlon, anyway," Peterson told her. "Isn't that right, my beauty?" she added, scratching the big horse's cheeks as if he were a fluffy kitten instead of nearly a ton of muscle and attitude.

Kathryn glanced at the digital readout on her watch. 5:47. "What time's sunset around here?"

"This time of year, six or thereabouts. It's getting later every day with spring coming on."

"I should probably get up to the main house, then, huh?"

Peterson shrugged. "Lord Donlon said to expect you, so he's likely to come looking down here. Takes 'em a while to wake up and get going anyway, just like you or me in the morning."

"Okay. Is there something I can do in the meantime?"

"I got some stalls need cleaning out," Peterson said. She laughed at Kathryn's grimace of reaction. "Don't worry, I'll start you out easy. You know how to work a curry comb?"

"Now that I can handle."

"Then I've got just the horse for you."

LUCAS OPENED his eyes seconds after the sun dropped below the horizon. His daytime sleep had been anything but restful. He'd lain there through the hours of sunlight, plotting strategies for dealing with Klemens, identifying places where the vampire lord's hold was weak, his people dissatisfied. The latter wasn't hard to find. Klemens was a benevolent despot at best, and a heartless bastard at worst. He'd toppled the previous ruler of the Midwest through the time-honored tradition of challenge and a fight to the death. It was the way things were done in the world of Vampire, but it didn't always make for a favorable outcome.

In Klemens's case, the Midwestern territory had gone from a lord who held his power gently to Klemens, who ruled with an iron fist. Every vampire lord, Lucas included, had the right to tithe the vampires they ruled and protected. But, like Lucas, most exercised that right sparingly.

Klemens, on the other hand, tithed every single vampire in his territory, regardless of their individual situation, and enforced it like some sort of medieval king. Lucas had taken in more than one vampire who had crossed the border just to get away from Klemens and his thuggish collection agents.

For decades now, Lucas had lived side by side with Klemens in a state of mutual distrust but no outright hostility. It was kind of like North and South Korea. There was the border, and they had both watched it closely, but until now neither had wanted to pay the price of outright war.

Something had changed with Klemens in the last year. Lucas wasn't certain what precipitated that change, although he suspected it had something to do with Raphael and the way he was gathering the other vampire lords to his side. He'd already allied with Rajmund in the Northeast and even Sophia up in Canada. In the South, Jabril had died unexpectedly, and Raphael had stepped up to support the new lord, who was too weak to hold the territory on his own. Raphael claimed it was only for the sake of stability. Lucas doubted that, but didn't care either way. He had no problem with Raphael's long term goals. He was, in fact, a party to them. But even he didn't know what had really happened with Jabril. There were rumors that Raphael's mate Cynthia had been involved somehow, but he'd never managed to get beyond the rumors. Not even Raphael would discuss it with him. Since Lucas and Raphael were far closer than was usual among vampire lords, his Sire's reluctance to even broach the subject gave credibility to the rumors of Cynthia's involvement. Raphael had always been very protective of those he loved, especially the women.

So, it was possible that Klemens had seen Raphael gathering the reins of power into his own hands and decided to make a move before it was too late. And since he'd always coveted Lucas's territory, it was the most natural target of his new expansionistic impulse.

Lucas leapt out of bed and went directly to the shower, thanking the gods of invention for modern plumbing as he did every evening. With the hot water pounding him into submission, he considered Kathryn Hunter. She was like a dog with a bone when it came to the search for her brother. And he supposed he couldn't blame her. If he'd had a brother, he might have done the same. Hell, for all he knew, he had a whole tribe of brothers that he wasn't aware of since his father had split when Lucas was still a baby. His parents had never married, and his mother had always refused to talk about it. Lucas suspected his father had been married to someone else, his mother no more than a summer night's fling. When she'd ended up pregnant, the fling had become a burden, and his father had fled back to the safety of his wife and family. Lucas didn't have any proof of his theory, though by now he had the resources to pay someone to dig it up if he'd wanted. For that matter, he could have hired Raphael's mate Cynthia to track his ancestry as so many of the others were doing.

But the truth was he didn't care all that much. That life, his human life, was long behind him and didn't have a place in what he was now.

His phone rang as he was climbing from the shower. Drying his hair with one of the fluffy towels, he walked into the living area of his underground vault and snatched up his cell.

"Nicholas," he said. "What's up?"

"My lord, I wanted you to know that Agent Hunter is on the premises."

"Is she, now?"

"Yes, my lord. She's down in the barn . . . currying."

"Currying?"

"Yes, my lord. It appears Judy has put her to work."

Lucas laughed. "She has a habit of doing that with people. Okay, Nick. I'm going to finish up here and go down to the barns myself. I'm fancying a ride in the moonlight with my personal FBI agent."

"My lord . . ."

"Go ahead, Nick," Lucas sighed. "Say it."

"She's not just a cop, Lucas. She's a Fed. The forbidden fruit of cops."

"Aye, she is. Which will just make it sweeter when she drops into my hand."

HE FOUND KATHRYN exactly where Nicholas said she'd be, with the sweet smell of fresh hay and horses all around her, using a curry comb on Sassy, who despite her name, was one of his more mild-tempered mares. Kathryn had donned a pair of faded denims, and they showed her ass to perfection, just as he'd known they would. Much better than the boxy slacks she'd worn the previous night. The barn was warm, despite the cool night air, and she was working hard. A tailored blouse hung outside the box stall, leaving Kathryn in a stretchy white tank top that accented her smoothly muscled arms with every stroke of the comb.

Lucas tilted his head and listened. Kathryn was talking to the horse as she worked, speaking so softly that even his vampire hearing couldn't pick up the words.

He started to say her name, then changed his mind. She was so entranced with the animal and the repetitive motion of the curry comb that she hadn't even noticed he was there. The mare noticed him, of course. But after a soft whicker of greeting, she ignored him. Which left only Kathryn. Walking as quietly as only a vampire can, he stepped up right behind her and dipped his face into the crook of her neck, inhaling deeply as he deposited a soft kiss just below her right ear.

Kathryn gasped and spun around, her hand going to her hip for the weapon she'd left sitting on the tack box beneath her shirt. That didn't hamper her any, however. She swung the damn curry comb instead, and if he hadn't been a vampire, he'd have been wearing more than a few stripes on his face.

Lucas caught her wrist gently, laughing in both surprise and appreciation. He did love a woman with spirit. And he should have expected it from Kathryn Hunter, he thought ruefully. After all, a woman didn't make it in the man's world of the FBI without being able to take care of herself. Nor did such a woman traipse halfway across the country looking for her missing brother. He was lucky he wasn't sporting a bloody face about now.

Kathryn wrenched her arm away from him and shoved him back a step. Neither of which she could have done if he hadn't let her, but she didn't know that yet.

"You're lucky that pretty face of yours is still intact," she snarled angrily.

Lucas widened his eyes. "Was that a compliment, Agent Hunter?"

"No, you ass, that was a warning. Don't ever sneak up on me again. What if I'd been armed?"

"Then I trust you'd have held me gently as I bled onto all this nice, clean straw."

She bit her cheek, trying not to smile, but it was a lost battle. "Are you ever serious?" she asked, trying to recover lost ground.

"Only when I have to be."

Tromluí bellowed angrily from his box stall at the other end of the barn, demanding Lucas's attention.

"Excuse me a moment. *Tromluí* is very possessive. You and he will have to work something out if we're going to continue this relationship."

"What relationship?" she muttered behind him. He smiled as he made his way down the uncluttered aisle to his beautiful black. The stallion poked his head out before he got there, blowing and snorting as if to say, "What took you so long?"

"Och, boyo, I missed you, too," he murmured, rubbing the big horse's broad nose.

"Is this the horse I saw you working with last night?" Kathryn asked from several steps away.

Lucas glanced over his shoulder and received a solid head bump from *Tromluí* for his trouble. The stallion rolled his eyes in Kathryn's direction and shifted behind the gate of his box stall, as if trying to interpose his considerable bulk between his beloved master and the interloper.

Lucas laughed at the horse's antics. "You've nothing to worry about, *mo Tromluí*," he crooned, then spoke to Kathryn in the same smooth tone, without looking back at her. "The horse last night was Nightshade, *Tromluí's* oldest son. He's barely a yearling, while *Tromluí* is a strapping man of four."

"He's gorgeous. I mean, they both are, but *Tromluí* is larger than life."

"Did you hear that, boyo? The lady thinks you're handsome." He glanced at Kathryn.

"Judy thinks the two of you make a pretty picture."

Lucas laughed easily. "The truth is he'll take no other rider. It's a bad habit, but one I indulge since we both enjoy the relationship. Speaking of which, it's a beautiful night, would you like to ride?"

"Now? I mean, in the dark?"

"It's not dark. The moon is only a day past full. Besides, the horses know the trails, and we'll stick to the easy ones for now."

"But I'm not dressed—"

"You're dressed just fine, Kathryn. Even wore your boots. Are you looking for an excuse? Afraid to be alone with me?" He glanced at her again, long enough to wag his eyebrows suggestively.

"Of course, not. But I left my jacket in the car, and—"

"Jackets, we have."

They'd been having most of this conversation with Lucas directing his words at the jealous *Tromluí*, but now he turned and called down the aisle, "Judy!"

"Yeah, boss?" Judy Peterson's head popped out from the tack room. He'd known she was back there, because he'd heard the television. She liked to hang around in the evening just in case he managed to get down to the stables. Usually, if he didn't make it in the first couple of hours, he wouldn't be coming at all, or if he did it would only be to visit *Tromluí*, not to ride.

"Saddle Sassy for Kathryn, would you?" He turned to Kathryn. "You do ride western, don't you? You're not one of those horse snobs?"

"That's hardly snobbery, Lucas, but, yes, I ride Western, as well as English."

"If it's English, *a cuisle*, it's not worth doing."

Kathryn rolled her eyes at him, but he only grinned and turned his attention back to the stallion. "What do you say, *Tromluí*? Nothing like a fine moonlight ride with a beautiful woman, is there?" He stepped back enough to open the stall. The stud surged out as soon as the gate was wide enough, but Lucas was ready for him. It was a little trick his horse liked to play. The animal had a bit of the devil in him—more than a bit to be truthful—and he did love to see the silly humans run.

Lucas didn't run from anyone. He grabbed the stallion's head and brought their faces together. "You be good now. You're embarrassing me in front of the lady."

He knew the horse didn't actually understand what he said, but his tone got through well enough. *Tromluí* rubbed his big head against Lucas's chest.

"Aye, I love you, too, boyo." He grabbed the stallion's bridle from the hook next to the gate and was about to slip it on when his cell phone rang. He frowned. Most of his calls were routed through the main number at the house, so this could only be Magda or Nicholas, both of whom rarely disturbed him when he went riding. Lucas pulled the phone from his pocket.

"Nicholas?" he answered.

"I'm scrambling the troops, my lord," Nicholas said urgently. His voice was jumping, as if he were running as he spoke. "We just got a call—"

And that quickly every plan Lucas had made for the evening was changed. He stopped listening to his lieutenant, his mind already searching the thousands of vampires in his territory for whatever it was that had Nicholas gearing up for battle.

"Fuck," he swore softly. The compound in Minnetonka, Minnesota was under attack. It was filled with civilians, which should have put it off limits, but Klemens was breaking all the rules in his hunger for power. Civilians wouldn't stand a chance against Klemens's fighters, but at least the compound's leader, Thad, had some combat experience. And the compound itself should have had security in place. "Who called us?"

"Some kid, my lord. Says his mom's mated to one of ours—"

"Dex. His mom's been with Thad since the kid was a baby. Not mated, though. What'd he say?" Lucas began walking *Tromluí* toward the open barn doors at the other end. He walked the stallion out and released him into the big paddock which was always empty and reserved for him. The horse would throw a major tantrum if Lucas tried to put him back into his box stall now, and Lucas didn't have time for it.

"They hit a half hour ago. Thad rallied a defense, but the kid doesn't know how long they can hold it. He was pretty upset. A lot of screaming in the background."

"Where is he?"

"He was on his way home from a friend's. Saw Klemens's troops arrive and was smart enough not to go running into a situation he couldn't change."

Lucas walked back into the barn and caught Judy's attention. "Judy," he said in an aside as he listened to Nicholas. "I have to leave. Let him run awhile, then bring him inside. I won't be back until late, if at all."

"Yes, my lord," she said briskly and immediately began putting away the saddle she'd just gotten out for Kathryn.

"What's our ETA?" Lucas asked, going back to Nicholas.

"Sikorsky's on its way—" The big helicopter rumbled by overhead, preparatory to swinging around for a landing in the flat field behind the main house.

"Just landed," Lucas said unnecessarily. "Flight time?"

"Two, two and half hours. Good news is we can land directly on-site. Thad's got that field he uses for baseball in the summer."

"Baseball," Lucas muttered. "Might just save his life tonight. All right. Give me five, and once we're in the air, I'll do what I can from there."

Lucas hung up and caught sight of Kathryn eyeing him like a woman ready to go into battle.

"What's going on?" she asked, matching his running pace out of the barn.

"Nothing you can help with," Lucas said, forcing himself to maintain a human's slow speed.

"A transport helo just came in," she pointed out, "and I'm guessing this isn't a search and rescue. I'm trained law enforcement, Lucas. Let me help."

He stopped and turned to face her. "I'm sorry, Kathryn, but this is vampire business. I'll call when I can. And now I have to run." Before she could stop him, he fisted his hand in her long ponytail and pulled her in for a hard, fast kiss, and then he was gone, no longer pretending that he was anything but Vampire. His people were dying. He had no time left for pretense.

Nicholas was waiting for him at the helicopter. The last of his fighters jumped aboard as Lucas raced onto the field. The big helicopter was designed for sound reduction, but the noise of the main rotor was still considerable. Nicholas handed him a pair of headphones as soon as he got close enough, and as Lucas climbed on board he saw that each of his vampires wore the same.

The pilots, both vampires, took off almost as soon as Lucas was aboard. Nicholas pulled a duffle bag from underneath the seat and kicked it over to Lucas, who nodded his thanks. He immediately went to work, changing the clothes he was wearing. What was suitable for a pleasant evening's ride was not at all what he needed to go into battle against his own kind.

Black leather pants replaced his worn denims, the white T-shirt he'd put on so that Kathryn could see him more easily in the dark was stripped off in favor of solid black, and laced-up combat boots finished the look. A black leather jacket was pulled on over it all, making it easier for him to maneuver in the shadows against his enemies. Because one thing was certain. The vampires Klemens had sent to attack the civilians at the

Minnetonka compound were vicious and out for blood. They'd demonstrated that by attacking a peaceful enclave against all the precedents of war. But as cruel as they might be, none of them was a vampire lord, and none of them would be able to stand against Lucas himself.

KATHRYN WATCHED, frustrated, as the helicopter took off into the night sky. Within minutes, it was airborne and gone, even the sound of its departure no more than a memory. She squinted into the distance, but the helo had been painted a dull black so that it disappeared despite the full moon.

She sighed. A few moments ago, she'd been looking forward to a moonlight ride with a handsome man—okay, not a man, a vampire. But vampire or not, it was the most pleasure she'd gotten from a man's company in a long time. Lucas was charming and clever. And he loved his horses. Who would have thought? When she'd first heard he lived in South Dakota, she'd imagined some sort of cowboy wannabe, sitting up in his big house with cowhide everywhere, and never stepping foot into a barn, much less riding a horse.

But she'd been wrong. She also would never have believed she could be attracted to a creature who sucked blood to stay alive. But she'd been wrong about that, too. More's the pity.

And now, she was standing in an empty field, having lost both her vampire expert and her riding date all in the space of a few minutes.

She stared moodily in the direction the helicopter had taken. She'd only been able to hear Lucas's side of the conversation, but she'd gotten a glimpse into the helicopter just before it took off, and judging by the very speed with which this whole thing had been put together . . . well, if they'd been in a war zone, she'd have guessed the enemy had just attacked. That helicopter had all the marks of a rapid response team. But what were they responding to?

Whatever it was, she doubted it would be in the morning papers.

She started back toward the house where her SUV was parked, frustration and worry gnawing dual holes in her gut. She wasn't a single step closer to finding Daniel, and so far her investigation had turned up a whole lot of nothing. Lucas supposedly had people looking into it, but now he'd rushed off before telling her if they'd found anything. She couldn't even check out the club herself, because the damn thing wasn't open until tomorrow night. She frowned, wondering if Lucas would be back in time to make their club appointment tomorrow, and decided it didn't matter. If he showed, great. If not, she'd go by herself. Too much time had already been wasted while the local authorities had ignored her insistence that something was wrong, and while she'd waited for her bosses in Virginia to give her a few lousy days off. Kathryn knew too much about this sort of crime to think it didn't matter. With every day that passed, the trail grew colder, and it became less likely she'd locate Daniel before it was too late.

Too late for what, she couldn't say, or maybe wasn't prepared to admit.

She reached the parking area in front of the big house and beeped the SUV's locks open. A light came on somewhere deep in the house, visible through the dark windows of the man-cave front room. Magda was probably in there somewhere, probably hadn't gone off to whatever battlefield had pulled Lucas away. The female vamp didn't strike Kathryn as the fighter type, except maybe in the courtroom. She was probably a real killer in that setting.

Kathryn briefly considered knocking on the door and asking Magda if Lucas's inquiries had turned up anything, but discarded the idea right away. She wasn't really up to dealing with the prickly lawyer, and besides, even if Magda knew anything, she'd withhold it just to prove she could. Kathryn knew the type, women who disliked other women as a matter of principle. Magda functioned best in an environment where she was the only female, and as far as Kathryn had seen, that made Lucas's ranch pretty much ideal. Other than Judy Peterson, she hadn't seen any other women around the place.

Kathryn reached for the truck door, then paused, wondering if Lucas and Magda ever . . . The stab of jealousy she felt at the idea of the two of them together surprised her with its intensity. All right, so she found Lucas Donlon attractive, sexually attractive. But who wouldn't? She'd have to be dead not to. The vamp oozed sexuality, and he knew it, too. He used it ruthlessly to get what he wanted.

She opened the door and reached across the seat for the light jacket she'd left there earlier. Pulling it on, she slid behind the wheel and closed the door, then spun the temperature control knob to its highest setting in hopes of getting the heat to work faster, even though she knew it didn't work that way.

While she waited for the SUV to warm up, she tried to decide what to do next. She'd pretty much tapped out the local witnesses, with the exception of the club, which was out. So who else was there? Her gaze rested on the house in front of her, with the golden glow of its interior gleaming through windows and skylights. Magda might be a shrew, but she'd done an excellent job of decorating.

Kathryn's thoughts skidded to a halt. The photographs. Magda had said that Daniel's photographs on Lucas's study wall were from a gallery with branches in Minneapolis and Chicago. She glanced at her watch, gauging time zones and distance. Chicago was unrealistic, but she could probably still catch a flight to Minneapolis tonight. She could have all day there tomorrow and be back in time to meet Lucas for their club date. Not that it was a *date* date or anything.

She cursed silently, remembering Lucas saying that the owner of the galleries, Carmichael, was a vampire. So, maybe she wouldn't be able to catch him personally, but his gallery was sure to be open at least partly during the day. Most of them were, and he'd have to compete, after all. Which meant someone would be working. Someone with access to sales records, specifically records of who else had bought Daniel's work, and who might have seemed a little too interested in the photographer himself. And if they were reluctant to talk, Kathryn wasn't above flashing her badge to persuade them. She waited for the inevitable twinge of guilt at the thought of using her position that way, but it never came.

Chapter Five

LUCAS SAT WITH his eyes closed, head leaning against the hard back of his seat. The helicopter was configured for maximum troop transport, not comfort, which meant the seats were sturdy and utilitarian. Nicholas was on the phone next to him, but Lucas tuned him out. He trusted his lieutenant to make the right decisions when it came to deployments of this kind. Lucas had more important things to do. His mind was with his vampires in Minnetonka, seeing the battle through their eyes, feeling their fear and pain.

Every vampire lord had talents that were unique to him alone. Raphael was powerful beyond measure. Duncan was the strongest empath Lucas had ever met, and possibly the strongest vampire empath ever. Lucas's talent was different than even Raphael's. He had a unique connection to his vampires, especially those who were his own children. He could see through their eyes, which wasn't unusual for a vampire lord, but more importantly, he could lend them his strength—both physical and psychological—giving them the ability and confidence to fight against seemingly overwhelming odds. If the vampire wasn't too critically injured, he could also channel enough energy to keep him alive until help arrived. But with the battle now raging, even Lucas's considerable power was being taxed. There were too many of the enemy, and too few of his own on the scene.

Of the Minnetonka vampires, only Thad had any battle experience. They were civilians—merchants and skilled laborers. That Klemens had attacked them was so far beyond the pale that Lucas didn't think any of the other vampire lords would find it acceptable. There were good reasons for vampire rules of combat. Their people were not numerous, but their vampire natures had them fighting with each other all the time. If they started wiping out entire civilian enclaves, their numbers would dwindle even further. Not to mention that bloody battles of that sort would draw the unwanted attention of human authorities. It was one thing to lose even a houseful of warriors at a remote outpost like the one Alfonso Heintz had set up. It was another to wipe out a compound like the one in Minnetonka with human women and children inside. There were at least four human females living in the Minnetonka house, and Dex was only one of several children. Lucas knew Dex was safe, but he was too caught up in the battle itself to know about the others.

He became aware that Nicholas had grown quiet. Lucas opened his eyes.

"My lord," Nicholas began. "Four warriors are on their way out of Minneapolis. I couldn't risk more for fear that this was a feint by Klemens, and the real target was the HQ in the city."

"How long before they arrive?"

"Minutes. It's only twenty miles or so. It probably took them as long to get geared up and into the truck as it will to drive there. They'll ping me when they arrive."

Lucas nodded silently, no longer seeing his surroundings, though his eyes remained open. He was already back in Minnetonka with his vampires. "Tell them to hurry, Nick. Klemens's troops have broken the first perimeter." His eyes closed as pain knifed his heart. "They're sparing no one," he added in a whisper. Lucas wept bloody tears as he witnessed the carnage, as he felt the agony of his vampires. Klemens would pay for this. If it was the last thing Lucas did on this earth, he would make that bastard pay with his life for this *and* for Raphael.

The journey became an endless blur of rage and agony. Some part of him heard Nicholas tell him the four Minneapolis vamps had arrived and were engaging. He heard murmured casualty reports, but he didn't need those. He knew what the situation was on the ground, knew just how desperate it had become. The four helped, but they weren't enough.

Finally, he felt the helicopter tilt as it began its descent. At the same moment, he heard Nick tell someone they were minutes out. Lucas opened his eyes and scanned the vampires he'd brought with him, wanting to be certain they were ready. He'd lost enough tonight. He didn't want to lose anyone else.

Clicking the appropriate switch on his headgear, he said, "Gentlemen." Every head turned his way. "Scorched earth. None of theirs walks away from this."

His warriors nodded grimly. They hadn't been privy to his firsthand observations, but every one of them would have heard Nick's conversations. First with the vampires in Minnetonka, and then with the Minneapolis contingent once the four arrived at the enclave. They knew how brutal Klemens's attack had been, not only to the Minnetonka vampires, but to the humans, as well.

They were still a hundred yards off the ground when Lucas stood and yanked off his headset. He barely registered the deafening noise as he stood in the helicopter's open doorway and took in the scene on the ground. The stench of the battle hit him first, familiar in so many ways. Blood, flesh and fire—no matter how far man progressed, the smell of a battlefield was still the same. But there was more than the physical smell to this battlefield. He was a vampire lord, and these were his people. Their terror was an acrid taste on the back of his tongue, their deaths a deafening scream in his mind, an ache in his heart.

He scanned the Minnetonka enclave as the helicopter descended. It wasn't a single structure but a walled compound, with several buildings gathered around the central hall. Some of the smaller structures were individual homes, while other, larger buildings were shared by several vampires. The wall had been breached, but he knew that. The attackers had blown through the sturdy gate, which had never been intended to withstand an attack of this nature. It was designed to keep the vampires safe from human intrusion and curiosity. And until today, it had never been called on to do anything more.

"My lord," Nicholas shouted as they hovered well off the ground, preparatory to landing. "Let me go ahead—"

That was all Lucas heard as he leapt to the ground and raced toward the battle, his vampire speed taking him out from under the whirring rotor of the descending craft. In a split second, he identified his own vampires, separating them in his mind's eye from those sent by Klemens. He ripped into the first enemy with a roar, tearing him bodily off the male vampire he was fighting and ripping his head from his body with a vicious twist. He tossed the two pieces aside and kept going.

"Inside, my lord," someone shouted, and Lucas's head turned, following the voice as he kept moving. "The main house, Sire!" Lucas recognized Thad, bleeding and broken, in a fight for his life. He started toward him to help, but Nicholas appeared out of nowhere, stepping between Thad and the brute he'd been holding off despite being outclassed by fifty pounds or more.

Lucas raced into the main building, taking the outside stairs at a single leap and bursting through the door. Time seemed to slow as he took in the huge room with a sweeping scan. Blood and bodies were everywhere. A battle raged at the foot of the big staircase, and he recognized twelve-year-old Dex holding a thick-bladed ax, tears rolling down his cheeks as he swung the heavy weapon in a wide arc, trying to hold off the two hulking vampires who were toying with him. What the hell was Dex—

A very human scream sounded from upstairs, and Lucas understood. Dex's head swung toward the sound, and one of the enemy vamps grabbed the ax, yanking it from Dex's hand, nearly pulling the boy with it. The brute reached for the human child, but his fingers never made it that far. Lucas rammed his fist into the vampire's back and tore his spine in two. Before the injured vampire had even begun to collapse, Lucas had taken out his sadistic buddy, as well, lifting him bodily and tossing him in the direction of the door where Lucas's fresh and bloodthirsty warriors were following in their master's wake.

"Watch the boy," Lucas growled and tore up the stairs faster than the human eye could follow.

He didn't have to look for the attackers; he followed the scent of blood. Human blood. The women had been gathered upstairs. For safety, no doubt. Thad and his troops had made their last stand in this building, and God knew they'd lasted longer than anyone had the right to expect. But it hadn't been enough.

Lucas rounded a corner and howled furiously at the sight that greeted him. He'd feared a bloodbath awaited him, and there was blood enough. But it was savagery of a different sort that caused it. Klemens's vampires had attacked the compound's women and raped at will, while their allies held off the defending males down below. And the rapists were still at it. Lucas's rage sent waves of power coursing through the entire house, rattling the walls and shattering windows. The two vampires he'd caught in the act jumped up, ready to fight until they saw whom they were facing. They stumbled back then, edging toward the windows in their desperation to escape. But there was no escape. Not for the murderers of innocent civilians. And not for rapists.

Lucas advanced slowly, holding the two attackers in place with a thought. He felt more than heard some of his own vampires enter the room and spoke without turning. "Get the women out of here. Gently."

The women whimpered in fear when Lucas's vampires approached them, and he spared a wisp of power to send them all into sleep. He would speak to Thad when this was over and recommend the leader permit him to wipe the women's memories of the events in this room. Not the attack. People had died here today. There could be no forgetting that. But these women didn't need to remember the rest of it. Not if they didn't want to.

He focused again on the two enemy vampires now cringing before him, trying to shrink into the floor itself. They were covered in the blood of their victims, fangs fully distended, and they were both huge. Taller even than Lucas, and far more heavily muscled. The vampires in the yard had been the same. Klemens had apparently been gathering thugs for some time, preparing an army for the day he would make his move. Lucas sneered privately. It would take more than a few slabs of beef to win this war.

He crouched in front of the nearest attacker. He hadn't touched the vamp yet, but then he didn't need to.

"What were your orders?" he asked.

The vampire had the good sense to shake his head. He might be terrified of Lucas, but Klemens was no one to cross lightly either.

"How about you?" Lucas asked, addressing the second prisoner.

Clearly emboldened by his fellow thug's success, he too shook his head and uttered a grunting sort of noise that Lucas took for a negative.

Lucas bared his teeth. "Oh, I *so* hoped you'd feel that way. Nicholas," he called over his shoulder, having felt his lieutenant enter the room. "Ask Thad if he has a soundproofed room where I can converse with these two. If not . . ." Lucas turned back and eyed the captives lazily. "I'll just have to rip out their vocal cords and take the truth from their tiny brains . . . after we play a bit, of course. I bet Thad and his people would love to spend some quality time with them first."

One of the vampires whined in fear. Lucas studied the bastard as he would a piece of shit on his heel. "You'd rather I kill you quick?"

The vampire nodded, his eyes begging for mercy. But Lucas only laughed. "Where would be the fun in that?"

Chapter Six

KATHRYN TURNED off the alarm on her cell phone before it could ring. Despite what she'd thought the night before, there hadn't been any flights into Minneapolis until this morning. So she'd booked the first one at six o'clock this morning, and then gone looking for a gym to work off some of her nervous energy. That had been a bust, too. She'd driven up and down every street before admitting a 24-hour Fitness Center wasn't going to materialize on the next corner. She could have driven to Spearfish, or even Rapid City, but that was a good hour's drive each way, and she hadn't been *that* eager to work out. She'd finally stopped at the local Starbuck's—apparently there was no town too small for Starbuck's—and forced herself to stick to decaf coffee while using their Wi-Fi connection to dig up what she could on Carmichael and his gallery. That hadn't taken much time, and without caffeine there didn't seem to be much point to the coffee, so she'd gone back to the motel and tried to grab a few hours of sleep. She didn't know why she'd bothered. Every time she closed her eyes, the facts of Daniel's case would appear—her personal checklist imprinted on the inside of her eyelids, with every item checked off and the inescapable conclusion that she still knew absolutely nothing.

And if that wasn't bad enough, when she managed to erase the checklist, it was only to be replaced by an endless loop of speculation as to where Lucas had been off to in such a rush last night.

She rolled out of bed, booted up her laptop and immediately began searching law enforcement databases for reports of recent and unusual violence. That made for a pretty broad search, but she didn't know what she was looking for. She narrowed the time window to the last twelve hours, which helped a little, and limited the search further to cities within a helicopter ride of her current location. That was more problematic, since it depended on the equipment, and there was always the possibility they'd refueled somewhere. But even eliminating that possibility, the target area was so big that it was impossible to weed out any one violent event from another. America was a violent country. On any given night in a major city, there were too many crimes to count. Add in the problem of smaller jurisdictions that weren't represented in the search parameters, and it was the proverbial needle in a haystack. Worse, she didn't even know if it was a needle or not.

Giving that up as a lost cause, she took a quick shower and got dressed. She didn't bother to pack, taking only her briefcase, with her laptop inside. And her weapon, of course, which she wore in her belt holster. Everything else she left in the motel. Since she hadn't been able to fly out last night, she'd have to make it a day trip, coming back in time tonight to meet Lucas for their visit to . . . what did Lucas call it? A blood house. Great.

Her flight this morning would get her into Minneapolis just after noon. She could go directly to the gallery, talk to the owner if he was available, or his staff if he wasn't around. Three hours later, she'd be on her return flight, arriving in plenty of time to do some bloody clubbing with vampires.

KATHRYN STARED at the sign in the art gallery window in disbelief. Closed for lunch? Who the hell closed for lunch? And for two hours? She looked around the busy Minneapolis street to verify that she was indeed in a big American city and not somewhere in Europe where the two-hour, everything-shuts-down-for-lunch break was the norm.

She checked her watch. There was one hour left before the gallery would reopen. A gust of wind blew down the wide street, and she shivered, pulling her jacket closer as she searched the surrounding area for a way to kill an hour. Her gaze fell on the huge Mall of America in the distance, and she groaned inwardly. She hated shopping. But according to Lucas, she needed something *appropriate* to wear tonight, and a warmer jacket would be useful, too. She sighed and headed for her car with dragging steps.

An hour later on the dot, she was back, sliding her rental sedan into a parking space on the street which opened up just as she cruised past. Taking that as a good sign, she was feeling optimistic when she pulled open the heavy glass door on the gallery. It was fairly typical inside, with pale walls and track lighting which could be maneuvered to accommodate the varying shows over time. Floating walls hung blankly in midair, and Kathryn wondered if they were in the process of transitioning to a new showing.

The sharp click of high heels sounded on the hardwood floor, and Kathryn turned to find an intensely fashionable woman bearing down on her. She was older than Kathryn by at least ten years, with straight black hair parted in the middle and brushing her shoulders. Her makeup was perfect, her skin so pale Kathryn would have thought her one of Lucas's gang, if not for the bright sunlight beaming outside the UV protected windows. Contact lenses changed what Kathryn thought were probably brown eyes into a brilliant turquoise that nature had never produced in the human eye.

A tight pencil skirt forced the woman to walk with mincingly short steps as she approached Kathryn. "Good afternoon," she said in a pleasant but sophisticatedly cool voice. "And welcome to the

Carmichael. How can I help you?"

Kathryn smiled back and produced her FBI identification. "Special Agent Kathryn Hunter. Is Mr. Carmichael around?"

The woman studied the badge carefully before switching her gaze to Kathryn and saying, "I'm sorry, Mr. Carmichael isn't here."

"When do you expect him?"

"I'm afraid I don't. Mr. Carmichael isn't in town this evening."

"I understand he has a gallery besides this one?"

"Yes, his main base of operations is the gallery in Chicago."

"He's in Chicago then?"

"I can't say for certain. Mr. Carmichael doesn't clear his schedule with *me*."

"But if you wanted to get in touch with him, that's where you'd start?"

"If I wanted to reach Mr. Carmichael, Agent, I'd call his cell phone," the woman drawled, as if explaining the marvels of modern technology to an idiot.

Kathryn studied the other woman silently. Long enough that she finally reached up with nervous fingers to straighten her already perfect hair. "Was there something else?" the woman asked.

"I'm sorry," Kathryn said. "I didn't get your name."

"Francoise."

"Francoise? That's it? Like Cher?"

Francoise pursed her lips unhappily, which wasn't kind to her perfect makeup, revealing a starburst of unattractive creases around her lips that made Kathryn up her estimate of the woman's age by another ten years.

"Francoise Reyos," she said grudgingly.

"I notice you've recently taken down a collection, Francoise."

"Yes, a series of photographs by Daniel Hunter," she said, her expression suddenly animated. "A talented photographer and very popular with our clients. Not to mention a handsome and charming man."

"You know him well, then?"

"Oh, yes. Not as well as Alex knows him, of course, but we're very friendly."

"Alex?" Kathryn repeated, trying to keep her voice from giving away the fact that the name meant anything special to her, that this was the name of the vampire with whom Daniel had been seen leaving.

"I meant Mr. Carmichael, of course. Alex Carmichael."

Kathryn froze. Her research had listed the owner as George A. Carmichael, but both Magda and Lucas had been careful to call him only by his last name. Lucas had known she was looking for an Alex, and he wasn't stupid. He had to know Alex Carmichael would immediately jump to the top of her list. So, why hadn't he mentioned it?

And here she'd begun to think of him as a friend, maybe more. That lying bastard.

Francoise was staring at her worriedly, and Kathryn immediately banished all thoughts of Lucas. She'd deal with him later. She forced herself back to the present.

"Will Alex be around tomorrow morning, by any chance?" she asked Francoise, wondering if the woman knew her boss was a vampire.

Francoise dropped her eyes and looked away before answering. "I don't expect him back before tomorrow evening at the earliest. Evening is our busiest time. That's when Alex likes to be here."

"Of course. Do you happen to have a photograph of Alex?"

"The brochure," Francoise said brightly, and hurried over to a narrow table of blond wood against one of the floating walls. Kathryn followed, taking one step for every two of Francoise's in her tight skirt. The gallery assistant picked up what looked more like a booklet than a brochure and flipped it open to an inside page.

"That's Alex," she said with some pride and pointed at a color photograph of a handsome middle-aged man with silvery blond hair. The title under the photo identified him as G. Alexander Carmichael.

"What's the G stand for?" Kathryn asked.

"Oh," Francoise murmured, leaning in conspiratorially. "It's George, but he hates that name. It's on all the legal sorts of documents, but he never uses it. It's always Alex."

Kathryn's heart skipped a beat. The witness had described "Alex" as blond and older, but to a twenty-year-old Marine corporal, middle-aged probably *was* older. And Alex Carmichael was definitely blond. There were too many coincidences here to ignore.

"Do you have Alex's cell number handy?" she asked.

Francoise looked as if she wanted to say *no*, but that would have been foolish. She'd just admitted having the number not five minutes earlier. So she nodded sharply and minced away on her skinny heels, walking over to a minimalist glass desk and retrieving a business card from an elegant mother-of-pearl box.

She held the card out to Kathryn, who'd followed her to the desk. Kathryn studied the card before tucking it into her pocket.

"Thank you, Francoise. If Mr. Carmichael calls, don't tell him, or anyone else, that I was looking for him."

Francoise appeared surprised by the request. She nodded, but Kathryn saw the rebellion in her eyes and knew she was lying. The minute Kathryn walked out the door, Francoise would be on the phone leaving a message for her vampire boss.

And speaking of vampires, Lucas had a few lies to answer for. Maybe he knew far more than he was saying about other things, too. Like what had happened to her brother and where Daniel was right now.

KATHRYN THREW her bags down on the bed when she returned to the motel, still debating whether or not to go to the club without Lucas. Her flight had been delayed on the ground in Minneapolis longer than it took to fly back to Rapid City. She'd raged privately, but there was no sense in yelling at the gate attendant as she'd seen a couple of businessmen doing. After all, the poor woman had nothing to do with the delay, nor could she magically conjure up a new plane just to be sure those two assholes got home in time for dinner.

The plane had finally taken off, but it was nearly ten p.m. by the time she walked back into the small town motel room she shared with Daniel's clothes and equipment. She'd left several messages for Lucas, both before leaving Minneapolis and once she was back on the ground, but he hadn't returned any of her calls. She checked her phone one more time, half-expecting to find a message from him canceling their appointment. She had no doubt that the ever helpful Francoise, or her boss Alex, had made sure Lucas knew Kathryn had visited the gallery and now knew about Alex Carmichael.

She'd hoped he wouldn't cancel, though. Hoped that he was arrogant enough to bluff his way through. Because while she intended to have it out with him about Carmichael, she still needed him to make sure that she not only got into the club tonight, but that his people answered her questions. Once that was done, she could confront him about what he knew. Two could play at lies and half-truths.

But since Lucas hadn't bothered to call, she now had to decide whether to try the club without him. She had no guarantee he would still hold to their agreement, even if he showed up. And now that she knew about Carmichael, he might decide to send her off on a wild goose chase while he covered his vampire buddy's ass.

That decided it for her. She wasn't waiting for Lucas or anyone else. This was America, and she was, by God, a sworn federal officer. She was going to that club tonight, and she was going to get the answers she needed, or she'd arrest everyone and shut the whole damn thing down.

"Damn right!" she shouted, pumping her arm once in an act of defiance. She caught sight of herself in the mirror and started laughing. Okay, so maybe she couldn't shut the club down, but she could and would go there and ask some questions. And she definitely wouldn't be waiting for that snake Lucas to do it.

LUCAS STORMED into his office, still wearing the bloody leathers from last night's battle. He'd been forced to sleep through the day at the Minneapolis house, along with the survivors from Minnetonka. The enclave had been too badly damaged for the vampires' safety, and the humans had been too shattered by the violence to stay there anyway. The enclave would be rebuilt, maybe even in that location. But it would take time, and Thad and his people would need that time to heal themselves. Lives had been lost last night. Granted the enemy had lost far more, but that was little comfort to the dead or those who'd loved them.

The attack had taught Lucas a hard lesson. No one was safe in this war, not when Klemens was willing to reduce himself to the brutality of human warfare, not when innocent civilians were targets, and rape was an acceptable weapon.

Lucas hadn't wanted to remain in Minneapolis after the battle, but it had taken several hours to clean up the scene in Minnetonka sufficiently to avoid scrutiny by the human authorities. The compound hadn't had any close neighbors, but it had been necessary to repair the worst of the damage to the wall and, especially, to remove the human bodies. The vampire bodies had taken care of themselves, but there was no concealing the destruction of the buildings. Klemens's people had done Lucas a favor by torching everything. It made the damage easier to explain and provided an excuse for the sudden absence of people living there. But the fire had also drawn a crowd. Fortunately, the relatively remote location meant it was a small crowd, but Lucas had been forced to manipulate their memories to support his preferred version of the events.

Between that and getting everyone to safety in Minneapolis, then meeting with Thad and several of Lucas's people, there'd been no time to return to the ranch before dawn. His only other choice would have been flying home with a human pilot at the controls, traveling through the daylight hours and sleeping at the airport until sunset. He hated that idea on two fronts. One was his personal paranoia, inherited from his Sire, Raphael, about putting a human solely in charge of his safety. And the other was his aversion to sleeping on the plane at all.

He had a penthouse in St. Paul where he usually stayed when visiting the Twin Cities, but time had been so short this morning that he hadn't bothered with that, either. He'd ended up spending the daylight hours in one of the bedrooms of the Minneapolis HQ vault, and flown back to the ranch this evening. It hadn't been that simple, of course. He'd had to meet with Thad again before leaving, and he'd made a series of phone calls to the leaders of his other regional nests, advising them of Klemens's new and dangerous tactic. He'd ordered them to get the word out to the civilians in their areas.

On any other night, Lucas would have lingered in Minneapolis even longer, but he had a nagging feeling that his favorite FBI agent wouldn't hang around waiting for him to escort her to the club. After his abrupt departure the previous night, she'd probably spent all day today chomping at the bit, cursing vampires in general and him specifically. But despite all of that, he still had one more call to make before he called Kathryn.

He circled his desk and lifted the receiver of an ordinary-looking phone sitting on the elegant credenza behind his desk. It was a landline, and in lighter moments, Lucas jokingly referred to it as the bat phone. It had only seven numbers stored in its memory, the numbers of his seven fellow vampire lords, and it was rarely used. Vampire lords tended to be hostile toward one another, which meant there were no chatty catch-up phone calls on this line. On the occasions when Lucas wanted to catch up with Raphael or Duncan, he used their personal cell phones. The landline was for emergencies and warnings. Like the one he was about to give Klemens.

Lucas waited until he heard Klemens's hated voice, then snarled, "Rape, you son of a bitch? That's what you've come to?"

Klemens laughed. "War is war, my dear Lucas, no matter the venue. But then you micks always worry too much about protecting the ladies."

Lucas ground his teeth. "Those women were mated to vampires," he snarled. "*My* vampires."

"Really? I thought they were simply whores brought in to amuse," Klemens drawled, not even pretending he hadn't ordered the atrocity.

"Well, know this, asshole. There is no mercy for rapists. You're officially thirteen vampires shorter tonight. Your army is shrinking, Klemens, and that means I'm one step closer to you. It's time to start saying your farewells to anyone foolish enough to care for you."

Lucas slammed the phone down so hard it cracked the base. "Fuck!" he spat and swept the damn thing to the floor in frustrated rage, spinning with a snarl when his office door opened.

Nicholas took one look and froze in place.

"I want a fucking target," Lucas ordered. "Klemens is staging his people somewhere along the border. I want it found, damn it. No civilians, but it has to hurt. I'm tired of reacting and letting that bastard set the pace."

"Yes, my lord."

Nick was still in the doorway, eyeing Lucas as if waiting for the other foot to come crashing down on *him*. Lucas rubbed a weary hand over his face and waved him inside. Nick looked even worse than Lucas felt. Like Lucas, he'd changed his shirt, but still wore the torn and bloody leathers from the previous night. Unlike Lucas, he'd also been severely wounded. One of Klemens's vamps had gotten lucky and ripped Nick's jaw open to his teeth. The deep, raw-looking laceration traveled from the outside corner of his eye down to the curve of his jaw bone. The fact that it wasn't healed more than twelve hours after the injury spoke to how serious it had been. Still, one more day, and it would be a healing pink scar. A day or so after that, and Nick's cheek would once again be without blemish. The healing would have gone even faster, if Lucas had been able to give Nick some of his blood to drink. But in times like this, when an attack could come from anywhere at any time, it wasn't wise to weaken himself even the slightest bit unless the need was critical.

"Fucking Klemens doesn't even pretend to apologize for his rapists," Lucas said quietly.

"At least it proves what we already suspected, my lord. That he gave the specific orders."

"Oh, he gave them all right. Bastard *bragged* about it." Lucas collapsed onto his desk chair, falling hard enough that it skidded back a few inches. "Sit, Nick. And stop with the *my lord* bullshit. I'm not gonna hurt anyone, especially not you."

"Well, that's a relief," Magda drawled as she strolled into his office. She crossed to the desk and propped a hip on the edge, her narrow skirt sliding up to reveal an expanse of toned thigh as she turned to look at him. "Agent Hunter called this evening. Several times."

Lucas swore softly. He probably should have called her from the plane, but he didn't want the FBI to know his business and figured it was at least possible she'd have known he was in the air. Grabbing his cell phone, he pulled up her number, checking the time as he did so. Just past eleven. Damn it, he was late. Kathryn's phone was ringing for the third time. Surely, she wouldn't have—

"Kathryn Hunter," she answered in a cool voice. Lucas rolled his eyes. She had to know it was him calling, since his number would have come up on her Caller ID.

"Yeah, Kathryn, it's Lucas," he said, identifying himself needlessly and playing along with her little game. "Look, something fairly serious came up. We'll have to do the club tomorrow night, instead."

"Oh, that's all right. I'm already here."

Lucas pulled the phone away and stared at it, wondering if he'd heard correctly. He brought it back to his ear. "Excuse me?"

"I'm at the club," she said loudly, enunciating each word, as if she honestly believed he hadn't been able to hear her. "In fact, I'm just about to go inside."

"Bad idea, Kathryn," he said, striving for calm, although his brain was screaming at her to get the fuck out of there. His warriors were about to descend on that club. They were fresh from the battlefield, high on the defeat of their enemies, looking for the blood and sex release they *hadn't* had time to get last night . . . and there she'd be—one righteous, blond FBI agent directly in their path.

"Excuse me?" she mimicked archly.

"Bad. Idea," he repeated, trying not to snarl, knowing intuitively that if he got angry or demanding, it would have the opposite effect he wanted.

But she only laughed. "I'm sure I'll manage, Lucas. This isn't exactly my first rodeo."

Lucas said a quick prayer for patience. "Kathryn," he began, then stopped in disbelief. She'd hung up on him! Lucas shouted wordlessly and threw the phone across the room, raging. No one fucking hung up on him. Ever!

Even worse, now he'd have to drag his ass to that stupid club, or Kathryn was going to end up as someone's dinner. He had a sudden image of her pressed up against a wall, legs spread, her arms around some hulking vampire's back while that vampire bent his head to her neck and—Oh, hell, no!

"Nick, we're leaving in five."

"Why?" Magda demanded impatiently, her vampire hearing having given her both sides of the conversation. "She's a big girl, and no one forced her to go there alone. Let her deal with it."

"What a great idea, Magda," he snapped, an Irish lilt flavoring his words as it always did when he got angry enough. "Let's send the fucking FBI agent into one of our blood houses to be blooded and possibly assaulted by a battle-raged vampire or two. Fucking fantastic." He leaned across the desk until he was only inches away from the female vamp who was his lawyer. "I don't know what your problem is with Kathryn, but you need to *deal* with it and do your job."

Magda flushed red with anger and embarrassment. "I'll tell you my problem," she shouted. "I've seen you with a lot of women, hundreds of fucking women. And not one of them has ever mattered to you. But this one does, and I don't like it. She's dangerous. Not just to you, but to the rest of us, and you don't seem to give a shit about it!"

Lucas straightened to his full height and stared at her coldly. Magda paled, suddenly realizing she'd gone too far. She slid to her knees and glanced up at him once before lowering her gaze to the floor. In that brief flash of her dark eyes, he'd seen his own reflection, his eyes burning gold with power.

"Are you suggesting I don't protect what is mine?" he asked in a dangerously calm voice.

"No," Magda whispered instantly. "No, my lord, please. I didn't mean—"

"Silence."

Magda's words were choked off on a sob.

"For the sake of our history together, I've indulged your petty jealousies, Magda. I now see that was a mistake."

She raised her gaze to his, unable to speak, her dark eyes beseeching.

"It may be time for you to try your skills elsewhere. Unfortunately, I don't have time for this now. You're excused for the evening. I'll send word tomorrow as to your new assignment." He waved his hand, lifting the compulsion and permitting her to speak, then turning his back and walking away.

"Sire"—she sobbed behind him—"please."

Lucas stopped and turned enough to give her a silent look. Magda immediately cast her eyes back to the carpet, biting her lips to stifle her sobs. Lucas strode out of his office, taking the side door that led to his private quarters. Once out of sight, he picked up his pace. He had to get to the club before Kathryn, or someone else, did something he couldn't undo.

Chapter Seven

KATHRYN ACKNOWLEDGED that she hadn't been quite honest with Lucas. When he'd called her, she'd just been turning into the club's parking lot and could easily have waited for him. But his high-handed attitude that she would rearrange everything to suit his schedule had pissed her off even more than being stood up, so she'd bent the truth just a bit. Besides, as she'd told him, this wasn't the first time she'd gone to a potentially hostile location to interview witnesses. It might have gone smoother with Lucas at hand, but it was doable with or without him.

She grabbed her FBI ID and headed for the front of the club, only to be confronted by a long line of people waiting to get in. Both men and women were there, although significantly more women than men. And despite various styles of dress, they all had one thing in common—there wasn't a covered neck among them, with most baring a hell of a lot more than just their necks. She eyed some of the women, with their swooping necklines and tiny skirts, and recalled what Lucas had said about clubs like this. The vamps took blood from human partners and gave them a mind-blowing sexual experience in return. She looked again at one or two of those butt-cheek-baring skirts and decided she didn't want to know what else those women were or were *not* wearing.

Not wanting anyone to mistake her own purpose in being there, she made one small change in her own attire. Walking back to her SUV, she pulled open her cargo hatch and debated her options. The only clothes she had with her were the ones in her gym bag, which were left over from her futile search for a place to work out yesterday. She unzipped the bag and pulled out a pair of plain, black leggings, slipping them under the black knit cocktail dress she'd bought in Minneapolis. The dress was wool, with simple, straight lines, long sleeves and a modest boat neck. It was a little more form fitting than she'd normally wear, but at least the hemline fell closer to her knees than her ass. And the belted waist gave her a place to anchor the clip-on holster for her Glock. She hadn't been sure when she bought the dress whether she'd be carrying a sidearm into the club, but now she was glad for her foresight. Not wanting to advertise the gun's presence, however, she pulled her black jacket back on over everything, concealing both the weapon *and* the clingy fit of the dress. Unfortunately, there was nothing she could do about her shoes, since her only alternative was the gym shoes from her bag. And since she had to get in the club's front door, she didn't think that would work. Most places like this—by which she meant trendy clubs, not specifically vampire clubs since she'd never been to one—had informal dress codes with the bouncer at the door having complete discretion about who got in. She could only imagine that the door guy at a vamp club would be even more selective, and somehow she didn't think clunky athletic shoes and a black dress would cut it.

Even the leggings were pushing it, but if worse came to worst, she could badge her way in. She hoped it wouldn't come to that, though. Contrary to what Lucas seemed to think, Kathryn didn't plan on thumping tables and demanding answers. She could be subtle when she needed to be.

Her worries about passing the bouncer's inspection proved unfounded once she got to the door. The bouncer at Lucas's club was big. Not just tall, but thickly muscled with arms that bulged around a black T-shirt which seemed too insubstantial for the cold weather. And apparently he was perceptive, too, because he spotted her as a cop the minute she bypassed the long line of customers and stepped up to him.

"Welcome to the club, officer." He laughed and dropped the velvet rope, which should have made Kathryn happy. But his laugh sounded more like a warning, something cynical and knowing that had made her instantly suspicious.

She considered turning around and walking away right then and there, but she was too stubborn to give up that easily, thereby effectively admitting that Lucas had been right. So, instead, she flashed her FBI badge and said, "I'm not a cop."

He grinned. "Close enough, sweetheart. Don't suppose you'd consider turning over your weapon?"

It was Kathryn's turn to laugh.

"That's what I figured." He sighed. "What can I do for you?"

Kathryn pulled out her brother's picture and showed it to him.

"You ever seen him before?"

He looked down at the photo almost dismissively and then frowned in surprise. "Yeah," he said. "Don't know his name, but he's been here a couple of times."

"Twice," Kathryn clarified. "All of these people coming and going, but you remember this one?"

The bouncer shrugged, massive shoulders moving up and down. "Because he had a camera with him. We don't usually allow customers to bring cameras into the club, not even cell phones." He gestured to a table where new arrivals were turning over purses and turning out pockets. They were also signing some sort of form, but she couldn't read what it was from where she stood.

"This guy," the bouncer indicated Daniel's picture, "had a camera around his neck, and not the touristy kind with point and shoot, either. I told him he'd have to check it, and he balked. Said it was too expensive. Anyway, it was early, and we weren't crowded yet. The boss happened to see what was going on and told me it was okay, that your guy was some sort of famous photographer." He shrugged again. "So I let him in. Same thing the next night."

"When was this?"

"Two weeks ago? Maybe a little more?"

"Did you ever see him leave with anyone?"

"Lady, I keep people from sneaking in, not going home."

Kathryn sighed. She'd known it wouldn't be that easy. "Okay. So, who's your boss, and where can I find him?"

"Name's Kurt, and he's in the same place he is every night we're open. Behind the bar."

"Thanks."

Kathryn bypassed the check-in tables and strolled into the dimly lit bar, trying to conceal the fact that she wanted to gawk like a tourist. Lucas had described what they did at these clubs, but that hadn't prepared her for the reality of it. The place was crowded enough that she wondered about the fire code, and everywhere she looked people were going at it with each other. On the dance floor, in the booths hugging the walls, and in dark corners sporadically lit by twisting lights in the ceiling. Some were engaged in sexual acts that would have gotten them arrested anywhere else, while others . . . She stared despite herself as a vampire lifted his mouth from a woman's neck, eyes rolling up to meet Kathryn's shocked gaze as he licked the twin puncture wounds and then his own lips, as if savoring the flavor of a rich wine.

Kathryn averted her gaze quickly, but not before she saw the vampire's fangs flash in a mocking grin. Determined to do what she'd come for and leave, she made her way through the crowded club, surrounded by sweaty, horny humans and way too many hungry vampires. The music was incredibly loud, the pulsing bass so persistent that she had to fight the urge to put her hands over her ears and wince like some cranky old lady. In order to get to the bar, she had to skirt the edge of the dance floor, which meant being jostled from all sides until she was ready to pull her gun and scream at the top of her lungs for everyone to *get the hell out of the way!* Including—no, *especially*—a particularly clueless testosterone jockey who absolutely refused to take a fucking hint and move along.

In her mind, she'd conjured up an image of a club filled with Emo-styled, twenty-something vampires. She knew the sort of places her brother preferred when he went clubbing—at least she thought she did—and this wasn't it. These guys looked more like Dwayne Johnson clones who'd overdosed on Viagra. And the way they were humping the mostly female patrons, she didn't think too many of them would be attracted to her brother, either.

The place was creepy, and maybe a little frightening, although she wasn't going to admit that, even to herself. And she sure as hell wasn't going to leave before talking to the bossman behind the bar who'd known her brother well enough to recognize him from across the room.

Kathryn finally squirmed her way out of the mass of dancers, feeling like she'd been squeezed out of . . . okay, not a pleasant thought. Not gonna go there.

She made her way around to the service bar and caught the nearest bartender's eye. There were three of them back there. Two were working the bar itself, while the third appeared to concentrate on filling orders from the beleaguered wait staff.

Kathryn leaned across the bar to him and shouted, "Is Kurt around?"

The bartender winced, as if she'd hurt his ears by yelling. But even a vampire had to be deaf with all the noise in here, so she figured the bartender knew who and what she was and was just being a prick about it.

He moved down to the opposite end of the bar and said something to one of the other bartenders. That guy turned, and Kathryn caught a brief flash of fang before he gave her a long look. After a moment, he said something to the prick and switched places with him.

As she watched the new guy making his way toward her, she noticed the original prick talking into a cell phone. It could have been coincidence, but somehow she didn't think so.

"I'm Kurt."

Her attention was drawn back to the club manager. He was big and physically fit, like they all were, with blond hair and light-colored eyes that she assumed were blue, though it was hard to tell for sure in the dark club. He appeared to be in his early twenties, but appearances were irrelevant with vampires. He could be a couple of hundred years old, and he'd look the same.

"Special Agent—" she began and reached for her credentials, but he stopped her with a light touch on her arm.

"I know who you are. What do you want?"

"If you know who I am, then you know what I want. I'm looking for Daniel Hunter. He was in this club, and you knew him well enough to tell your doorman to let him in with his camera."

"Yeah? So?"

"How well did you know him?"

Kurt shrugged one shoulder. "He was only here a couple of times."

Interesting, Kathryn thought to herself. He'd deflected her question while pretending to answer it.

"Did you meet him here at the club?" she persisted.

"No."

She gave him an impatient look. "Look. I'm trying to find my brother. If you don't have anything to do with his disappearance, you've got nothing to worry about from me. Where did you meet Daniel?"

Kurt stared at her for a moment, then said, "In the Badlands. I like to hike, which means I hike at night, preferably when there's a little bit of moonlight to see by. I was out hiking last month, and I came across Dan shooting pictures of the park at night. We talked. I liked him."

Kathryn studied Kurt's closed down expression and realized something. Kurt didn't just like her brother, he *liked* him. And he was worried about him.

"Do you have any idea where he might be?"

Kurt shook his head. "I wish I did, Agent Hunter. He came in here two nights in a row. When he didn't show up the next night, I thought he'd gone backcountry again. He'd already told me that he'd only come into town for a hot shower and a few nights in a real bed, and then he was going out again after that. I figured I'd find him on my next hike. But he wasn't there, and, believe me, I looked. I know that whole park better than just about anyone. And then the sheriff started asking around, and the next thing I knew Lucas told me you were coming to town."

Kurt looked across the crowded club for a moment, then back at Kathryn. "If there's anything I can do to help you find him . . ."

Kathryn smiled. Here, finally, was someone who was as worried about Daniel as she was.

On a whim, she pulled out the brochure from Alex Carmichael's gallery and showed him the owner's picture. "How about this guy?" she asked.

"Alex? Yeah, sure. He's in here a couple of times a month."

"I thought he lived in Chicago."

"He's got a place in Minneapolis, too. But he doesn't like to circulate in the cities where he works. Says he doesn't want everyone knowing his business, but I think he's just one of those guys who likes to go for a bit of strange sometimes."

"Strange?"

Kurt gave her a puzzled look, then laughed a little. "Strange, as in not his usual partner, if you get my drift. I get the impression Alex has a steady squeeze back home, but he likes to play. So he comes here once in a while. We get humans from all over the state, especially in summer, and year-round there are two good-sized cities in easy driving distance."

"Lovely," Kathryn commented. She started to fold the brochure back into her pocket, but Kurt interrupted her.

"If you're thinking Alex had something to do with Daniel being gone . . . I think you're wrong."

Kathryn tilted her head curiously. "Why's that?"

"He and Daniel talked, but it was business. And like I said, Alex comes here to circulate. If he wanted Daniel, he didn't need to come here to get him."

She thought about it for a moment, then nodded and held out her hand. "Thanks for your help, Kurt."

"Yes, ma'am. You should know . . . I haven't stopped looking for Dan. I think he's in this town somewhere, or if not that, then he's lost out in the Badlands. But if I'm wrong, if you find him first, tell him to give me a ring and let me know he's okay. Now, I need to get you out of here, because this crowd is about to get pretty excited, and, believe me, you don't want to be here when that happens. Let me tell Gary, and I'll be right back."

While Kurt walked over to let the other bartender know he'd be gone a few minutes, Kathryn eyed the gyrating couples already packed in like wiggling sardines and wondered how things could get any more *excited* than they already were. But she'd gotten what she came for and had found an unexpected ally, too. So if that ally was telling her she should make like the birds, then she was ready to take his advice and get the flock out of there.

She turned back to see what was keeping Kurt and barely managed to dodge aside as a pair of howling vampires with a screaming woman between them shoved out of the crowd and into the bar, knocking aside several patrons who promptly yelled happily and joined in the mayhem. Kurt roared and started tossing bodies back into the crowd, but it was too late. One of the vamps slammed over the bar and crashed into the stock of liquor, breaking bottles and shattering glassware, and the scent of alcohol rose over the whole disastrous scene in a sickly sweet cloud.

Kathryn had backed away to the safety of a corner wall when the first trio had slammed into the bar, not wanting to get caught up in the violence. But now she stepped away from its relative protection and scanned the scene. It was obvious Kurt wasn't going to break free anytime soon, and compared to the brawl at this end of the bar, the rest of the crowded club seemed almost tame. She drew a deep breath and had just girded herself for a return trip through the mob, when there was a roar of male voices followed by the excited squeals of vampire groupies in heat, and everything went completely to hell.

Chapter Eight

LUCAS WAS ON his way to the club when Nicholas's cell phone rang. Mason was driving, and Nick was sitting up front in the passenger seat, but Lucas could clearly hear both sides of the conversation.

"Nick, where the hell is Lucas? We need him here *now*, man!" It was Greg Monterossa, the doorman cum bouncer at the blood house. The very same blood house where Kathryn had defiantly gone without him.

"Give me the phone, Nick," Lucas growled. Nick handed it back to him. "What is it, Greg?" he asked, even though he had a pretty damn good idea. Talk about the perfect storm. Combine one stubborn FBI agent and a bunch of adrenaline-driven vampire fighters, and he had a disaster in the making.

"A bunch of the guys just showed up, juiced up from the fight and still reeking of blood. The crowd's going nuts with happiness, but that FBI chick is still in there somewhere, my lord," Greg said, clearly exasperated and striving not to show it. "Kurt tried to hustle her out first, but now he and the rest have their hands full, and I can't close the door, we'll have a full-on riot. You want me to—"

Nick's phone beeped with an incoming call. Lucas checked the ID and went back to Greg.

"Kurt's on the other line. Stay where you are; I'm only a few minutes away from you."

He disconnected the doorman and brought up Kurt. "I just spoke to Greg. I'm on my way."

"I tried to get her out of here, Sire, but it all happened too fast."

"Yeah, she has that effect. I've got Nick and Mason with me. We'll be there in—"

"Two minutes," Mason provided from the front seat.

"I heard that," Kurt said. "I'll do what I can from here."

Lucas disconnected and handed the phone over to Nick, considering his options. If there weren't so many humans involved, he could simply drop his vamps where they stood and put everyone to sleep. But if the club was as crowded as Greg indicated, there were probably as many humans as vamps, if not more. And he had no way of knowing what they'd do if the vampires started passing out around them. Most of the humans were bound to be at least friendly, if not straight up groupies. But if only one or two were in the club for other reasons, if they maybe hoped to take down a vamp or two, instead of having a good time . . . well, a lot could happen in two minutes. And he wasn't about to leave his vampires helpless in an unknown situation.

Nick dropped the cell phone Lucas had been using into the SUV's center console, then looked over his shoulder and said, "What's your plan for when we get there, my lord?"

"There's only one plan, and that's to extricate Kathryn Hunter as quickly and bloodlessly as possible. As far as I'm concerned, everyone else knew what they were signing up for when they walked into the club. But I don't think our special agent had a clue, and I'd rather she not find out the hard way. I'd hate for any of my warriors to end up paying the price for her stubbornness."

KATHRYN ONLY wanted to get to the front door and get the hell out of this club. Like right now. But they wouldn't let her. Two large, sweaty, and she was pretty sure bloody, vampires had taken a liking to her and were now stopping her from leaving while they eyeballed each other in some sort of vampire pissing contest. She wasn't sure what they hoped to achieve since she certainly had no intention of spending any time with either of them, but every time she managed to inch in the direction of the door, one of them would shift to block her path. That wasn't difficult in the crowded room, especially not since all hell had broken loose once these two and their buddies joined the party. All of the other women in the room were literally throwing themselves at the new arrivals, but for some reason these two had declared war over *her*. She'd tried showing them her badge and demanding they get the fuck out of her way, but they'd barely glanced at it before going back to their growling contest. Apparently, the prize, i.e. Kathryn, didn't have any say in the matter.

Kathryn was irritated and somewhat puzzled by this turn of events, but not all that worried. Either they didn't believe she was actually FBI, or they thought it was all a game, an interesting new bit of foreplay before the big finale. *She*, at least, knew that wasn't the case, but she was still trying to decide the best way to extricate herself from the situation. She was reluctant to pull her weapon in such a crowded room, especially with the testosterone level as high as it was. And that was her last choice anyway. She had no doubt she could escape any attempt to control her physically. Vampires were amazingly strong, but she didn't need to defeat them on points, she only needed to get away. And she had no intention of being anyone's dinner and/or bedmate tonight.

When one of her suitors made a grab for her left arm, Kathryn decided she'd had enough. She slipped her right hand inside her jacket and had managed to unsnap the safety strap on her sidearm, when the two vampires suddenly began bumping into each other aggressively, like two wooly mammoths battling for supremacy. Kathryn squeaked—and thank God no one could hear *that* over the general noise—and ducked down, lest she be crushed between the two behemoths. They began snarling, muscles bunching across their huge chests and arms, fangs blatantly displayed and gleaming in the low light. Under other circumstances, she might have been intrigued by that development. Where had the fangs come from? And how did they *deploy* them? Was it any intense emotion that did it? Or did it have to be intentional?

But then the two huge vampires went after each other, and she was roughly shoved out of the way. Kathryn glanced around, but no one else seemed to care. There were a few screams and some grunts of displeasure, but they were lost in the general mayhem. And everyone adapted fairly quickly, shuffling aside and giving the combatants room to figure out whose dick was bigger, or whatever the hell they were fighting about.

Kathryn, on the other hand, saw this as her chance to escape. She spun around and was heading straight for the door with long purposeful strides when a wall of solid muscle stepped into her path. She looked up into a pair of glowing red eyes.

"They're battling over you," the new vampire said, lisping slightly around his very visible fangs. This close up, she could see the tight pink flesh of his gums stretching around the tops of the unique teeth. The vamp was smaller than the other two, his height almost identical to hers with the heels, but his shoulders were thick and broad, and he had a deep barrel chest. He grinned at her, and Kathryn fought the urge to grin back. She had to fight it too hard, actually. She'd heard stories of vampires' ability to project emotion and thought and wondered if that was happening here, or if this guy was just naturally charismatic. But whichever it was, Kathryn wanted no part of it.

"Excuse me," she said pleasantly and started to go around the newcomer.

He laughed. "Playing hard to get, Blondie? Not nice. No one likes a fang teaser."

Her eyes narrowed in anger. "Get out of my way. Now," she demanded and put her hand on the Glock where it rested on her right hip.

"You gonna shoot me with your little gun?" he mocked.

Kathryn pulled and shoved the gun into his crotch. "No, I'm gonna shoot your balls off with my little gun," she said sweetly.

He snarled and raised a hand as if to reach for her. Kathryn feared she really was going to have to shoot this idiot's nuts off, when a big hand grabbed the back of his neck and pulled him aside. The red-eyed vampire's first reaction was to yowl like a jungle cat, but then he froze, nearly choking himself on his own outrage as he stared up at the vampire who'd grabbed him.

"Go," Lucas said.

Red Eyes disappeared into the crowd as Lucas turned his impatient stare on her instead. "*Special* Agent Hunter," he said.

"What do you want?" she snapped at him, jamming her gun back into its holster. She started to shove past him, but he looped an arm around her waist and bent his mouth to her ear.

"Is that any way to treat the person who just saved you from your own stupidity?"

Kathryn's jaw tightened, but she spun around with a smile and stretched up to put her lips against his ear in turn. "Why, Lord Donlon," she murmured. "First you lie to me, then you stand me up, and now you call me stupid. How *ever* do the ladies resist you?" The last few words were more of a snarl than a murmur.

She put both hands on his chest and shoved away from him, then stormed toward the exit, noticing that a pathway had magically opened between her and the front door. Probably more of Lucas's highhandedness. All of his people seemed terrified of him. Maybe he wrapped them in silver chains and made them sleep in their coffins if they were bad boys. She'd read stuff like that in her research, although the sources were all fictional, so she was pretty sure it wasn't real. Especially since vampires weren't actually dead, which eliminated the whole coffin angle. And why the hell was she worrying about bullshit like this right now?

Kathryn finally made it out of the crowded club and stopped for a moment on the sidewalk to enjoy the simple pleasure of breathing fresh air again. It was cold, but the icy air felt terrific on her overheated face. She didn't linger long, knowing Lucas would probably be right behind her. She didn't feel up to trading barbs with him anymore, and she started toward the parking lot. She hadn't been sure when she'd started out tonight if coming to the club was the smart thing to do, but it had turned out well overall. She'd confirmed that Daniel had been here and that Kurt, at least, had expected him back. And while she'd been certain all along that her brother hadn't gotten lost somewhere in the backcountry, it was good to know that Kurt had looked for him and not found him.

But where to go next? The strongest lead she had was still Alex Carmichael, despite what Kurt had said about the vampire's pickup habits. She had no evidence that her brother's disappearance was linked to some obsessed fan, after all. Perhaps Carmichael had financial problems and hoped to extort money in exchange for Dan's release. There'd been no ransom demand, but then one wasn't necessary. The big money was all Dan's. All Carmichael needed was a computer, and Dan could pay his own ransom. She made a mental note to check her brother's bank accounts. She'd done a standard run before leaving Quantico, but she should be monitoring daily for any unusual activity. Things like ATM withdrawals or wire transfers.

So, sticking with Alex Carmichael as her prime suspect for the time being, he definitely wasn't going to be found in this tiny town, especially not if he was holding her brother somewhere. Tomorrow morning, she was going to pack all of Daniel's gear and her few things into her rented SUV and drive to Minneapolis. If there was a lead, it was in the city where Carmichael had a business and friends. She felt certain of that. She was also certain that Lucas knew more than he was saying, but she didn't know the right questions to ask. Until she did, she was wasting her time trying to get anything out of him.

Kathryn pulled the keys out of her pocket as she came around the corner of the building and into the poorly lit parking lot. She lifted the fob and looked up as she aimed it in the direction of her SUV.

Impossible. But there he was, big as life and so gorgeously masculine that even in her anger she had to admit it. Lucas Donlon was leaning against her truck, arms crossed over his chest, legs casually crossed at the ankle, looking as relaxed as if he'd been hanging around all evening, even though she'd just left him behind in the club.

"When have I ever lied to you?" he asked far too reasonably.

Apparently he'd been paying attention to her parting shot in the club. Kathryn sent him a dismissive glance and beeped her locks open, hoping God would intervene and zap his perfectly sculpted ass where it rested against the driver's door of her vehicle.

Lucas laughed. "If you want to spank me, *a cuisle,* I'd rather you use your hand."

"As if," she muttered, and then frowned. Had he read her mind? She dismissed the notion as soon as she thought it. He'd simply reacted to the slight vibration of the electronic locks opening, and then, being who he was, had come up with the most risqué comeback he could think of.

"What do you want?" she demanded. "And how the hell did you get out here before me?" She could have bitten her tongue as soon as she asked the question.

"You first. When have I ever lied to you?" he repeated.

Kathryn eyed him impatiently. "Alex Carmichael?" she said.

"What about him?"

"Oh, please. Don't add insult to . . . insult by pretending you don't know what I'm talking about. Carmichael Galleries. You knew I was looking for an older man named Alex, especially someone who was interested in my brother's work. Put one and one together, Lucas. You're not a stupid man."

"You think Alex—"

"Yes. Alex. Carmichael's first name, which you conveniently didn't mention the other night in your office."

"Actually that's *not* his first name—"

"Blah, blah, blah. That's all I'm hearing from you. I don't care if it's his first name or his tenth. You knew it was significant and didn't say a word to me about it."

Lucas eyed her intently, and Kathryn became aware that they weren't alone in the parking lot. There were at least two other vampires lurking on the edges, and his lieutenant Nicholas suddenly appeared around the back of the SUV.

She frowned. Nicholas looked like someone had sliced off half his face, or at least tried to. What the hell?

"What happened to you?" she asked, walking the short distance between them and reaching out to touch his cheek without thinking.

He flinched back with a quick look in Lucas's direction.

Kathryn spun around. "Did you do that?"

"What?" Lucas demanded. "Hell no!" He straightened abruptly to his full height, taking two hard strides until he was right on top of her, golden eyes glittering with anger as he loomed over her. "Look, Kathryn, there are things going on that you don't know about. Things that are every bit as important as your missing brother. Nicholas was seriously injured last night. He shouldn't even *be* here, but he is because you were too stubborn to wait one fucking day—"

"I might not *have* a fucking day, don't you get that?" she yelled at him. "*Daniel* might not have a day. For all I know your crazy friend is—" Her voice broke off. She couldn't say out loud what she feared might be happening, what she feared had already happened. She shivered, suddenly freezing cold. She hugged herself, even though she knew the sudden cold owed more to her emotional state than the temperature.

"Kathryn," Lucas said softly. "Ah, don't. We'll find your brother." He pulled her into his arms. He was so warm. She hadn't expected that, had somehow thought vampires would be cold even if they *weren't* really dead. It was tempting to stay there, but she didn't.

"You don't know that," she muttered, shrugging away his arms, even as she instantly regretted the loss.

Lucas's lips flattened. "Fine. I don't know it, but I believe it."

"What if—"

"Don't say it, *a cuisle*. Let me tell you something about vampires. Especially vampires who frequent blood houses. When they find someone they like, someone who catches their fancy for whatever reason, they take them home for a while. Don't you know anyone, a friend, a relative, who's met someone in a bar and spent a lost weekend with them?"

"Lost weekend?" she repeated.

"Sex, Kathryn. A weekend in bed, fucking your brains out with someone new, someone you might never see again, or maybe even someone you'll end up marrying and having a passel of brats with. But the point is, vampires make a habit of it. They find someone . . . well, tasty, and take that person home for a while. It's completely consensual. Any vampire caught forcing a human these days is dealt with severely by his rightful lord."

"I don't see what vampire sexual habits have to do with—"

"If Alex Carmichael does have your brother, and I don't think he does—"

"*I* think so, and so does my gut. And I trust my gut a lot more than I trust you."

"Ouch," he said, giving her a wounded look. "Okay. I'll grant that someone has your brother, though it doesn't have to be Carmichael. But whoever it is," he continued, overriding her when she started to speak, "he's taken a fancy to your Daniel and taken him home for a spin. Your brother will turn up, a bit exhausted, no doubt. Maybe short a pint, but otherwise fine. You'll see."

Kathryn took a step back, putting more distance between her and Lucas. He was one of those people who touched easily, but his touches were too distracting. She couldn't afford to let him do that to her.

"Why didn't you tell me Carmichael's first name, then?" she persisted.

Lucas gave her an impatient look. "Because I didn't want you hunting him down if he was innocent. My people have been hunted and killed by humans as long as we've been alive, and for no reason but foolish superstition. If Alex is guilty, I'll let you talk to him. But not until I know for sure."

"How will you know?" she retorted. "I'm the only one looking for him."

"Not true. I set my own people to tracking him down as soon as you left that night."

"Did you find him?" she asked curiously.

"No. Although we know where he is."

"And," she said leadingly.

"He's in Chicago, which means I can't get to him."

"It's a short flight, Lucas, and you have a plane. So why not?"

Lucas's face tightened unhappily. "Chicago is out of my jurisdiction."

"Well, who rules it then? I'll talk to him instead."

"You will not," Lucas said sharply, and his eyes were suddenly sparking gold fire as he stared at her.

Kathryn took another step back, nearly stumbling as the narrow heel of her shoe hit a small rock, and her ankle tried to turn. She caught herself, avoiding Lucas's helping hand, and glanced down, irritated again that she'd bothered to wear this stupid outfit. Lucas hadn't dressed up, or maybe he had, given the nature of the club. He was wearing all black, including leather pants, and okay, she needed to look somewhere else, because . . .

"Is that blood?" she demanded suddenly, her gaze flashing up to meet Lucas's. "What the hell? First you've got Nicholas with half his face torn off, then those wild men invade the club all hyped up with what I'm told was some sort of post-conflict bloodlust—which *thrilled* everyone in there but me, apparently—and now you . . ." She took a longer look. "Your pants and boots are covered in blood."

"It belongs to Nicholas—"

"Oh, no, it doesn't. Not unless the two of you are way more familiar than I think you are."

"For Christ's sake, Kathryn," Lucas snapped, his lovely Irish lilt becoming more pronounced as he grew more irritated with her.

"I want to know what's going on, or I'm calling the authorities," she insisted. "They may not give a damn about my missing brother, but they're sure as hell going to care about what's happening in that club."

Lucas glowered down at her, his jaw flexing visibly. Suddenly he smiled, and Kathryn wanted to back up even farther.

"Very well, Kathryn," he drawled. "I'll tell you what you want to know. But not here in the parking lot."

"My motel room, then," she said, wishing she could yank back the words as soon as she said them. Her motel room? First, it was a dump. But second, she was inviting Lucas back to her motel room? Lucas of the sexy smile and tight leather pants? Was she out of her ever loving mind?

"Tempting, but I think not," he said, and she breathed a sigh of relief.

"Is there a quieter bar somewhere—" she began.

He laughed easily. "It's late, and this is a small town, *a cuisle*. But I've a place in mind. We'll take my truck."

"I can drive—"

He shook his head. "The roads are dark, and you don't know the way. My driver will take us."

"But what about—"

"Do want answers or not?" he demanded with sharp impatience.

Kathryn sighed unhappily. "All right," she agreed. "But how will I get back from wherever you're taking me?"

"Worried I'm going to kidnap you?" he scoffed lightly. "Very well, I'll send someone to bring your truck by later, so you can make your escape . . . should you desire."

Kathryn eyed him distrustfully, but nodded. She didn't know if it was important to her own investigation or not, but she wanted to know whose blood Lucas was wearing and what had happened to Nicholas's face. That sure as hell hadn't happened in a bar fight. She was also really curious about what secret dealings were going on with vampires in general. How many humans had been given a chance to peek behind *that* curtain? It was her curiosity that decided it. She'd go with him tonight and hear what he had to say. But tomorrow morning she was leaving for Minneapolis to continue her own investigation.

LUCAS RESTED A loose hand against Kathryn's lower back, escorting her over to the big Suburban, which was standard transport for dignitaries and vampire lords these days. It was black, naturally, and the windows were so darkly tinted they blended seamlessly with the metal all around them. Even the trim was a matte black, and since his vampires didn't need headlights to see, there was nothing to give them away when they traveled through the night.

Nicholas opened the back door, and Lucas offered Kathryn a hand up, which she refused, of course. He smiled slightly as she grasped the grip bar instead, forced to turn slightly sidewise in order to take the step up in her black cocktail dress. And what an enticing cocktail dress it was, too. He would love to see her in that dress without those ugly leggings. He was only sorry the night had turned out as it had. But there was hope yet.

He followed Kathryn into the SUV, sliding over next to her on the bench seat. She stiffened slightly, then relaxed, as if her initial reaction had been automatic rather than intentional.

Nicholas climbed into the front seat next to Mason and waited for Lucas to tell them where they were going.

Lucas considered going back to the main house. It was comfortable and safe, and Kathryn knew it already, so she wouldn't be suspicious. But there were too many people there. Too many phones, too many decisions needing his attention.

"The homestead," Lucas said and felt Nicholas's surprise ripple down their link. He didn't comment, however. Neither did Mason. But then Mason wouldn't. Only Nick was high enough in their hierarchy to occasionally question something Lucas did.

They cleared the town limits, and Mason switched off the headlights.

As the town faded farther and farther behind them, the night grew darker. Mason turned away from the main highway, and Lucas was aware of Kathryn staring out the window intently, probably trying to keep track of where they were going. She was a control freak, but in this case, it was pointless. Even in daytime, there were few recognizable landmarks out here. And by the time they reached their destination, she would be totally lost.

He stretched an arm along the back of the seat, barely brushing against her long, blond hair. He wanted to bury his face in it and draw in her scent. He loved the smell of a woman's hair, clean and warm and fragrant with whatever shampoo or perfume she used. It was one of his favorite parts of seducing a woman. And Magda had been right. He very much wanted to seduce Kathryn Hunter, though he wasn't exactly sure why. The FBI agent wasn't his usual type. Of course, some people would say he didn't *have* a usual type, that his type was pretty much anyone female.

But that wasn't true. Yes, he loved women, but he didn't want to seduce every woman he met. He liked making them smile and laugh, liked bringing pleasure to a harassed woman's night, if only for a few minutes. But that wasn't seduction.

Seduction was the slow, exquisite game of persuading a beautiful woman to come into his arms. To dance with him, to share long and languorous kisses in front of a fire. He loved to stroke a woman's body until she was trembling with desire, until she opened herself willingly, inviting him between her legs and into her body.

That's what he wanted with Kathryn. But why? As Nick had said from the first, she wasn't some local cop, she was FBI, and that spelled trouble. Vampires had too many secrets to be consorting with federal agents of any kind. Sure, there were vampires toiling in the depths of Quantico, along with just about every other federal agency, but that was different. Those vampires had a clear allegiance to a master, who for most of them was Duncan as Vampire Lord over the Capital territory.

But Kathryn owed no allegiance to anyone but her government. For Lucas to seduce her, to let her see even the tiniest fraction of what made vampire society tick, to risk having that information carried back to her bosses in Quantico? Why would he desire such a thing?

Lucas crooked a finger and captured a lock of Kathryn's hair. The answer was simple. Because he wanted her. Because she was tall and blond, with long legs and a terrific ass. Because she was smart and disciplined and always in control. A pain in the ass who would fight him tooth and nail for every inch of progress he made in this seduction, and he loved a challenge.

But also, because she'd come all this way and had risked the displeasure of her superiors to track down her brother. Because family was important to her, and her brother was the only family she had left. Because family was important to Lucas, too. And he had none.

Because she had a heart deeply buried beneath all that discipline, and before the night was over, he intended to steal it.

Chapter Nine

KATHRYN TRIED TO keep track of the turns they made, of how far they traveled. But even with a waning moon that was still mostly full, there was nothing to see beyond the dark windows of the big SUV. Maybe if she'd been from around here, if she'd hiked or camped in these hills, she'd have been able to conjure a map in her head of their location, but for a city girl from Virginia, the landscape was a monotonous blur of nothing in the middle of nowhere. Some part of her brain was clanging with alarm, telling her she should be worried about being way out here, all alone, with a bunch of vampires. But no matter which way she looked at it, she just didn't believe that Lucas would hurt her. Yeah, he'd been less than honest, and he was definitely dangerous, but the kind of danger he represented to *her* had nothing to do with houses in the middle of nowhere.

She shifted a bit, exquisitely aware of Lucas's arm on the seat behind her. It made her feel awkward and insecure, like being back in high school and not knowing if the boy was just stretching his arm or if he really liked her. Kathryn wasn't that too-tall, gawky girl any longer, but she wasn't exactly a femme fatale, either. She knew men noticed her. After all, she was a nearly six foot tall blonde, in excellent condition, with a reasonably pretty face. But it usually ended with the noticing. She was a little too self-assured, her college friends had told her, a little too cool. She frightened men off. As if she'd want a relationship with a man who was intimidated by any woman with a backbone.

Lucas wasn't intimidated by her. He wasn't intimidated by much of anything as far as she could tell.

Not that it mattered how Lucas felt about her. She wasn't here to be seduced by anyone, much less someone who'd intentionally withheld critical information. That was the same as lying in her book. Even if the liar did come wrapped in a very sexy package. She sighed quietly and focused very hard on the meaningless shapes blurring past outside the car, trying to ignore the slight tug on her hair that told her Lucas was playing with it. Damn vampire.

They turned down a dirt road. It was much rougher and looser beneath the tires, and there were obvious dust clouds billowing past the windows.

The big vehicle didn't slow down at all, though, despite the occasional hard bump and the sound of rocks pinging against the undercarriage. Kathryn leaned toward the center of the SUV, trying to see out the tinted windshield. She thought there was a house up ahead, but couldn't be certain.

"We're almost there," Lucas said, his deep voice melodic and smooth. Kathryn felt a tremor of desire skim along her nerves and moved back to her side of the seat. She couldn't see anything anyway, and getting too close to Lucas undermined her determination to hate him.

Although, that wasn't really true. She didn't want to hate him. Quite the opposite. But she didn't trust him. He lied as easily as he smiled. How could she have any kind of relationship with a man like that? *Vampire*, she reminded herself once more. He wasn't a man at all.

The SUV came to a sudden stop, skidding a little bit on the dirt road. The driver shifted into parking gear and turned off the ignition. Kathryn quickly unbuckled her seatbelt, eager to be away from the enforced intimacy of the darkened back seat. She didn't wait for Lucas, but popped open the door on her side and stepped out, coughing a little at the accumulated dust lingering in the air.

She looked around and saw they'd arrived at a house . . . of sorts. She couldn't see much, but even the moonlight was enough for her to see that the structure was ancient by American standards. Not historic like the castles of Europe, as one of her favorite comedians would have said, but definitely built more than fifty years ago. Way more than fifty years, in this case. Either that or whoever had built it had a really lousy set of construction skills.

It appeared to be made of wood plank. It was small—she would guess no more than 1200 square feet at best—with a covered porch that was sagging both underfoot and overhead. The wood appeared dry and gray by moonlight, and she could only imagine it would be worse in the bright light of day.

Kathryn studied it doubtfully. *This* was where Lucas planned on having their private conversation? Did it even have plumbing? And what about heat? She hoped it didn't use one of those wood-burning stoves, because those things smoked, and the smell was impossible to get out of her hair and clothes.

"It doesn't look like much from out here," Lucas murmured against her ear.

Kathryn managed to stifle most of her jump of surprise, but not all of it. She turned a glare on him, but he only winked playfully. Next time he snuck up on her like that, she was going to shoot him. Let him see how funny he found it then. Sneaky bastard.

Nicholas came around the side of the house. He'd apparently gone around back for something while she'd been, um, admiring the architecture. He hurried over to where she stood with Lucas and handed her the keys to her rental. She gave him a questioning look.

"It's parked on the side of the house," he told her with a quick wink. "The driver took a different route out of the city and beat us here." He turned to Lucas. "My lord?"

"We'll stay here," Lucas responded to the unvoiced question. "You guys know the drill. Kathryn and I will be fine in the main house. Make the usual arrangements for morning."

Main house? Kathryn thought to herself. There was something smaller than this? She turned her head, searching the surrounding area, but couldn't see anything that resembled a living structure. *Wait. Morning?*

"Yes, Sire," Nicholas was saying. "Should one of us perhaps remain with you, and—"

"I'll be fine, Nick. Kathryn won't shoot me, will you, *a cuisle?*"

Kathryn gave him a dirty look. Clearly she was going to need an Irish translator app for her phone. He'd used that particular word several times, and she could tell from the context that it was probably some sort of endearment, like *sweetheart* or *honey*. It had *better* be something like that. If it was *babe* or *baby* or, God forbid, anything like *little one*, she was going to set him straight. Just as soon as she figured out what he was saying.

"Kathryn?"

She smiled to herself. He sounded worried that she hadn't responded right away to his question about shooting him. "No," she said finally, letting regret flavor her reply, "I don't plan to shoot you."

He gave her a narrow look at her regretful tone, but told Nicholas, "Settle in for the night, Nick. You'll know if I need you."

Nicholas was plainly unhappy about the arrangement, and Kathryn wondered if he actually thought *she* was a danger to Lucas. But he followed orders, giving his boss a nod and disappearing around the back of the house.

"Where are they going?" she asked Lucas, as he started for the porch.

"There's a bunk house out back. They'll be quite comfortable."

Kathryn doubted that. Just as much as she doubted she was going to be too comfortable in the *main* house, but what the hell. She'd come this far, and she wasn't staying long anyway. She followed Lucas, stepping gingerly onto the sagging porch, imagining the narrow tip of her high heel going right through the boards if she wasn't careful. But it was surprisingly firm, not even sagging under Lucas's much greater weight as he strode to the front door and inserted a key. The door lock was very sturdy for such an old structure, and a closer look revealed that the doorframe had not only been reinforced, but the door was also more than it appeared. She was no locksmith, but . . . she tapped her knuckles on the door's surface. It was steel.

Lucas glanced at her. "Looks can be deceiving, Kathryn." He pushed on into the house with Kathryn on his heels. She was curious now. How much of what she'd seen was just for show?

Lucas whispered a few words, and Kathryn felt the brush of something along her skin, like static electricity. All at once the room lit with warm light. Candles flamed up on the mantle, but most of the light came from several shaded lamps throughout the room, which was definitely not what she'd expected.

And then it hit her. She'd just witnessed . . . magic? Impossible, but what other word was there to describe it? Lucas had whispered, and suddenly there was light. If it had been only the lamps, she would have assumed some vampire version of clap-on/clap-off, but candles? She strode over to the fireplace and took a good look at the fat columns of lightly scented wax. The flames appeared real, but . . . she licked her fingers and pinched the wick on one of them as a test. It sizzled out between her fingers, and Lucas laughed behind her.

"The candles are quite real, as is the flame. I abhor those fake, electric ones. There's no romance."

Kathryn spun to face him with a narrow look. "Who said anything about romance? We're here to talk."

Lucas tossed his jacket aside and shook his head in mock dismay. "Such a practical woman you are, Kathryn Hunter. It pains my heart. There is romance everywhere. Or there should be. The world would be a better place for it."

"Uh huh," she said skeptically and studied the old house with new eyes. Someone had gone to a lot of trouble to give the appearance of disrepair on the outside. But in here, there was no pretense. Whoever had decorated the main house at the ranch had worked on this one, too. The living room was small—there was no faking that—but it was filled with comfortable-looking furniture. A huge overstuffed couch of reddish brown leather, with two chairs that matched it in both size and color, occupied the space in front of the fireplace—which flared suddenly to life.

Kathryn gave Lucas a sharp look, and he grinned back at her, doing an elegant little gesture with his hand like some sort of stage magician. The only thing missing was a triumphant "ta-da!" And wouldn't she like to know exactly how he did that? Nothing she'd read indicated that vampires had real magic, beyond their extended lifespans, that is.

She turned her back on his far-too-pleased-with-himself expression and continued her perusal of the room. A rectangle of dark wood, pitted and scarred beneath a thick resin finish, sat atop a chunk of natural rock and served as a coffee table. Most of the floor was hardwood, but a large area rug of a deep, rich red sat beneath the table. Looking all the way to the right, Kathryn saw a kitchenette that was little more than a sink and a microwave with a small set of cabinets and a bar refrigerator underneath. A small kitchen table of pale pine stood next to the window with four chairs, one on each side. Vampires didn't require much in the way of kitchens, she supposed. The table was probably more for extra seating than potential dinner guests.

She glanced up and found Lucas watching her size up the place. "This is very nice," she commented, running an appreciative hand over the soft leather back of the couch.

"Not what you expected, though," he teased.

She smiled in spite of herself. "No," she admitted. "But you're a sneaky guy."

Lucas clutched his chest. "And once again, you wound me."

Kathryn rolled her eyes and walked to the other side of the room. There were two open doors; one led to the bedroom. She did no more than glance at that one before quickly moving on to the other, which was a guest bathroom, with only a sink and toilet. She wondered if there was a master bath off the bedroom, but had no intention of finding out. This was clearly Lucas's hideaway place, which meant that was his bedroom. Not going in there. No way. Nuh uh.

"Would you like a drink?" Lucas asked, strolling over to the bar like a big, lazy cat. Did the man never simply walk?

"Water, if you have it," she replied politely. "I have to drive back to the motel later."

Lucas gave her an unreadable look, but pulled a bottle of water from the fridge and handed it to her after twisting the cap off with an audible crack of the plastic seal. She thought it likely that he did that on purpose, to demonstrate that there was nothing in there but water.

For himself, he took a crystal tumbler from the cabinet and poured an amber-colored liquor from the matching decanter on the counter. The smooth scent of fine whiskey filled Kathryn's nose. She wasn't a whiskey drinker, but her father had been, and the scent brought back memories of her childhood. She couldn't say they'd been better times, but maybe they'd been less complicated.

Lucas took his whiskey neat. He indicated the furniture in front of the fireplace, and Kathryn moved around the big couch. She was tempted to sit on one of the chairs instead, but that would have been too cowardly. So she sat on the couch, far enough from the middle that it didn't invite any intimacy. Something poked her side as she settled into the cushions, reminding her she was still wearing her Glock. She unclipped the holster from her belt and laid it on the coffee table.

One side of Lucas's mouth lifted in a smile as he circled the table, then fell gracefully onto the couch and put his back in the corner opposite hers, one knee cocked up on the cushions.

Kathryn took a small sip of the cold water. "So how do you do it? How do you light candles and fireplaces and turn on lights without touching anything?" She flipped her hand in the general direction of the fireplace.

He shrugged dismissively. "I am Vampire. Has no one told you what that means? I would have thought the FBI would know that much at least."

"Maybe they do, but I don't. You said you'd answer my questions if I came with you. So, enlighten me."

Lucas regarded her with a thoughtful expression, then asked, "What *do* you know about vampires? Or rather, think you do."

Kathryn blinked, somewhat surprised that he'd given in so easily. She didn't trust "easy," especially not when it came to Lucas Donlon. But she wanted answers, so she'd play along for now.

"Not much more than what's commonly known," she admitted. "And I assume a good percentage of that is fantasy."

"Most of it, I'd wager," he agreed, and took a slow sip from his glass. He eyed her for a long moment. "Do you believe in magic?"

"No," she said instantly. "But I believe something can *look* like magic, if one doesn't understand how it's done."

"Or if one cannot do it, while another can," Lucas agreed.

"Exactly. So how do you do it?"

"I cannot explain it," he said matter-of-factly. "It would be like Einstein trying to explain how he was able to see the universe the way he did, or a football quarterback trying to explain how he's able to hit the precise spot his receiver will be seconds before the man gets there."

"Einstein?" she repeated archly.

Lucas laughed easily. "I knew you wouldn't like that one. That's why I threw in the quarterback. No pun intended."

Kathryn groaned, but she couldn't help smiling at the same time. He was so damn charming, even when he was being arrogant. Quarterback indeed. She was pretty sure he thought he was Einstein, not some football hero.

"Okay, Einstein," she drawled. "But please try to explain to this mere mortal what you feel when you do it. Do you just think it, and it's true? Can every vampire do that?"

"No, to both questions. Every vampire is changed in some way by the transformation from human to vampire. But very few have the extraordinary levels of power necessary to become a vampire lord."

"And you, of course, are one of the few."

"It's not vanity, Kathryn, but fact. And did you not just tell me that one cannot argue with the facts? I will admit, however, that I can't take any credit for my abilities. It's a twist of fate, and no one, not even the most powerful among us can predict who will be a vampire lord and who will not. On the other hand," he continued deliberately, "I can and do take credit for what I have done with those abilities. Even Einstein had to discipline his genius."

Kathryn couldn't argue with that. "But what about the fire and the lights? Is that unique to you?"

"I would like to claim it, but, no. If a vampire is powerful enough, he—or she, though most vampires are male for reasons I'll not get into at this moment—can manipulate energy. That is probably not a scientifically accurate description, but that's what it feels like when I do it. Even for vampires, however, the laws of physics still hold. I cannot create energy. I can only effect change on what is already there. I simply do with raw energy what you would do with a match. The effect is still the same. I'm just skipping a step or two."

She regarded him silently, careful to keep her thoughts from her face. She'd bet she wasn't the first person to underestimate Lucas Donlon. To assume he was nothing more than a handsome charmer with no meaningful thoughts in his head. The laws of physics! Not her best subject. Not her subject at all, come to think of it. She'd avoided the science and math listings in her college catalog with a diligence that bordered on some sort of phobia.

"As I said earlier, Kathryn," Lucas commented quietly, "things are not always what they seem."

"You're right," she conceded.

"Of course, I am," he replied predictably. "But enough about the secrets of Vampire. Tell me, why do you think Alex Carmichael is involved in the disappearance of your brother?"

"I'm not sure I do. Right now, he's only someone I want to talk to."

"How much did Kurt tell you when you talked to him at the club tonight?"

Her first thought was to wonder how Lucas knew she'd talked to Kurt at all, but then she frowned as she considered the phrasing of Lucas's question. He clearly already knew at least some of what Kurt had told her, and in the next moment, she realized that Kurt had only spoken to her at all because Lucas had okayed it.

"You knew about Kurt and Daniel," she said.

"Not when you came to me. But I told you I started my own investigation that night. I would have told you all of this if you'd given me time, however, events intervened. My presence was demanded elsewhere, and you went to the club without me."

"The blood on your pants."

"One thing at a time. How much did Kurt tell you?"

Kathryn didn't say anything for a long moment. On the one hand, it seemed as if he'd been keeping information from her yet again. On the other, it was entirely possible he was telling the truth. That he would have told her what he'd found out if whatever the emergency was that had pulled him away hadn't happened, and if she'd waited the extra day and gone to the club with him.

"All right," she said. "Kurt told me he's worried. That Daniel came into the club two nights in a row to see *him*, and when he didn't show up the third night, Kurt went looking for him and couldn't find him. He stressed to me that he *really* looked, which, given your demonstration with the candles, I now take to mean that you all have ways of looking that are not available to the rest of us."

Lucas nodded absently. "Some, though it depends—"

"On the vampire," she finished for him. "Yeah, I got that. But what about Kurt?"

"Kurt is my best tracker. He not only knows your brother, he knows that part of the Badlands. If he says Daniel isn't there, he's not there."

"Which brings us back to Alex Carmichael," Kathryn insisted.

"It could be someone trying to set him up."

"I'm aware of that. I know my job, Lucas. But at a minimum, I need to talk to him. His assistant confirms that Daniel is a favorite of his in the gallery, and yet he recently removed a major exhibit of my brother's work. I'm not talking about anything you bought from him. This take-down was so recent that it was still in progress when I was there today, which—"

"You went to Chicago?" Lucas demanded with far greater urgency than she would have thought necessary.

Kathryn frowned. "No, Minneapolis, why?"

"Nothing," Lucas said, shaking his head. "What else did you find there?"

It wasn't *nothing*, Kathryn thought to herself. It probably had something to do with the so-called *events* which had kept Lucas from making their club date tonight. The same *events* that had torn Nicholas's face up and left Lucas covered in blood. She'd get it out of him eventually, but she wanted to know more about Carmichael, so she answered Lucas's question first.

"What I didn't find," she continued, "was Carmichael. He was not only out of town, but supposedly unreachable. And in a time when even children have cell phones, that makes me think he's avoiding me."

"I told you, he's in Chicago. But that doesn't mean anything. He's based there. He has his main gallery there."

"So why won't he call me? I'm sure his assistant had him on the phone two minutes after I walked out the door, letting him know I'm on his trail. And speaking of trails, the local one here has gone cold. I think it probably went cold within hours of Daniel's disappearance, that whoever has him took him away from here long ago. Kurt's information only confirms it. Which is why I'm going back to Minneapolis tomorrow, and from there I'll go to Chicago, if I have to. There has to be a reason why Alex Carmichael is so determined to avoid me, but he can't hide forever."

"You're leaving?"

Kathryn shrugged. "Unless I find a reason to stay. I've already packed most of my brother's gear. It's too valuable to leave in that motel room, so I'll take it with me."

"You can leave it at the ranch. It will be perfectly safe."

Kathryn studied him. Daniel's gear would certainly be safer at Lucas's ranch than in her SUV, but then she'd have to come back here to retrieve it, especially if, when she found him, Daniel wasn't up to coming back for it himself.

"Maybe I'll ship it home," she said instead.

Lucas studied her in turn. "You still think I lied to you."

"You *did* lie to me. A lie of omission to be sure, but still a lie."

"I didn't know if Carmichael was involved. I still don't. And I'm not willing to sic the FBI on him without evidence."

"I'm not the FBI, not in this case."

"Don't split hairs, Kathryn. You know what I mean."

"Not really. I only want to ask him a few questions."

"That's all any of you want, and pretty soon you're compiling databases of who we are and what we can do, and the next thing we know the peasants are after us with pitchforks and torches."

Kathryn scowled. "Pitchforks and torches, Lucas?"

"A movie caricature, to be sure, but the sentiment is valid. We've been hunted before, and we've no intention of being hunted again. We're stronger now, smarter. We've learned to hide in plain sight, and to use your laws and culture against you."

"So you lied about Alex because you were protecting him?"

"Not only him, specifically, but, yes. I told you, I have my people checking him out. If I find anything, I'll tell you. If not, there's no harm to Alex or to you. This is my town, my territory. If a vampire is committing crimes here, it's my business."

"And mine," she reminded him pointedly.

Lucas shrugged.

"You don't think so."

"Alex is Vampire. By our laws, he is responsible to his master and no one else."

"His *master?* Talk about caricatures. Do you make him eat flies if he disappoints you?"

Lucas gave a bark of laughter. "That's a good one. But I'm not Alex's master. His master is in Chicago, as a matter of fact, which is why you don't want to go poking around there."

"Why not? I came poking around *here.*"

"Not nearly enough for my taste," Lucas murmured. "But then, I'm a much nicer guy than the vampire who rules Chicago."

"I'm not looking to make friends, Lucas. You all may think you're not subject to our laws—which are yours, too, since you live here—but believe me, you are. What's this vampire's name, in case I need to question him?"

Lucas stood abruptly. "Drop it, Kathryn."

She watched in surprise as he moved restlessly around the room, finally stopping near the small kitchen. A sofa table matching the distressed wood of the coffee table was pushed up against the wall there, with a big book standing open on one of those old-fashioned book stands, the kind people, or museums, used to put a particular book on display, like a work of art or something. On the wall above the table was a collection of framed prints and photographs, most of which looked fairly old.

Kathryn set her water bottle down and walked over to see what he was looking at. Her eyebrows shot up when she got a closer look at the book. It was a Bible, its pages old and fragile looking, but with the elaborate margin and text embellishments typical of that type of book. The reds and blues were somewhat faded, but the gold appeared to be gilt rather than ink, and it still gleamed.

Kathryn wasn't religious, and so she didn't know if publishers still put out these types of Bibles, or if everything had gone digital by now. But she'd had a friend in childhood whose mother had a Bible like this. The mom had made them wash their hands before touching the delicate pages, but had always been willing to show it to them. She'd especially enjoyed pointing out the front pages, which had listed her family's ancestors going back several generations.

Lucas's book was open to just such a page, but this book was far older than her friend's mom's had been. This Bible had a genealogical listing that started in the 16th century, and that was just the page Kathryn could see. It was obvious that the previous pages went back even further. She looked closer and saw that, although there were several surnames mixed in through the various marriages, only one surname was present throughout, and that was Donlon. This was *Lucas's* family bible. And wasn't that interesting?

She peered closer and saw that the family tree stopped altogether in the late 18th century. The last marriage was Lord Donal Donlon and Moira Keane, which joining produced only a single child, a daughter named Brighid. But after that, nothing. Kathryn scanned the previous generations, but didn't see Lucas's name listed anywhere. She was dying to turn the page back and find out exactly when he'd been born, but didn't quite have the courage to touch the antique Bible with her unwashed fingers—a lesson lingering inconveniently from her friend's mom.

Stymied by good manners, if nothing else, Kathryn straightened and checked out the framed pictures on the wall instead, half-expecting to find more of her brother's work. But most of these were far too old to be Dan's. Several were of the same thing, a gray stone castle, with twin towers and crenelated battlements. She looked more closely. There were two images of the castle at the very top which weren't photographs. One appeared to be an ink sketch, while the other was a watercolor. Lower down there were four separate photographs of the same thing, ranging from sepia to black and white, and then what she assumed to be the most recent one, which was in full color. In it, the sun was shining in a cloud-dotted blue sky, highlighting the emerald green lawn which rolled down the hill in front of the castle.

"Castle Donlon," Lucas said right next to her.

Kathryn's heart caught. She'd been so engrossed in the images, she'd almost forgotten he was standing there. She glanced over and saw him watching her.

"I hope you don't mind," she said, feeling embarrassment heat her face.

"Of course not. They're on the wall to be seen."

Maybe. But Kathryn had a feeling not too many people saw them. This place had the feel of a retreat, not a meeting house.

"The Bible," she said hesitantly, then forged ahead. "Is that your family's?"

Lucas eyed her silently for so long that she thought he wasn't going to answer. She was ready to apologize and withdraw back to her corner of the couch when he said abruptly, "It is. The Bible and the castle, both."

Kathryn swallowed, not daring to ask, but oh she *really* wanted to know where Lucas fit in.

His mouth curved in a lopsided smile. "The castle is mine now. I bought it . . . a long time ago and had it refurbished."

"Do you live there?"

"No, I live here," he said distinctly, as if explaining the obvious.

"Yes, but, do you, I don't know, vacation there or anything?"

"Vacation," he repeated, then seemed to think about it. "No. I visit once a year, if I'm lucky, and only for a few days. Sometimes less, depending."

"On what? If I owned something like that, I'd visit all the time," Kathryn said enthusiastically.

"Would you? Those old castles can be drafty, not to mention the bad plumbing."

Kathryn tilted her head thoughtfully. "No. You said you refurbished. I bet it's been completely modernized. It might look like a castle from the outside, but I bet the inside looks more like this." She waved to indicate the tastefully decorated room around them. "You enjoy your comforts, Lord Donlon."

Lucas dipped his head noncommittally, but Kathryn knew she was right. Feeling bold, she decided to take advantage of his seeming willingness to talk.

"So who owned the castle before you?" she asked, thinking it must have been some distant uncle or cousin, because Lucas had already told her about growing up poor. Whoever owned that castle wasn't poor.

"My grandfather owned it."

Kathryn frowned. "Your grandfather," she repeated, then gave him a dirty look. "I thought your grandfather was a poor dirt farmer with a broken-down plow horse?"

"I may have understated his position somewhat," he said, flashing a playful grin that didn't quite make it to his eyes.

"Somewhat? That's a fucking castle! Did you grow up there?"

"No," he said curtly. The playfulness fled his expression, and she knew she'd touched on a sensitive subject. "I told you the truth of that," he continued. "I visited the old man once, although *visit* might be an exaggeration. My mother took me there when I was no more than six years old. The two of us were living on the streets, starving and cold most of the time, and that bitter old man turned her away. He wouldn't even let his own daughter sleep in the barn. We left and never went back."

"I'm sorry," Kathryn murmured, hearing the pain in his voice.

"It happened a very long time ago."

"How did you come to own it then?"

"I bought it. Land and titles both. I had the greater claim, certainly better than the cousins who ran it into ruin. But they wouldn't have seen it that way, even if they'd known who I was, what with me being a bastard and all. On the rare occasions I sleep there now, I feel the ghost of my grandfather howling in the eaves because the bastard's taken over his precious castle. Gives me sweet dreams every time."

"And your mother?"

Lucas nodded at a small, oval frame to his left, almost eye-level with where Kathryn was standing. "My mother," he said quietly. "She died when I was seven."

Kathryn leaned in close. The frame held a delicate watercolor of a young woman with long, curling black hair that tumbled over her shoulders. The pose was meant to be serious, but the artist had captured the slight up tilt of her full, red lips, the laughter in her eyes that were so much like Lucas's.

"She was beautiful," Kathryn said honestly.

"She was."

"How did she die?"

Lucas turned toward her almost angrily. "How does a young woman die on the streets of Dublin? She was sixteen and pregnant when her father cast her out for the sin of being unwed. Barely twenty-four when she died. Of cold, hunger, disease? Who knows? I was too young to know such details. I only knew she was dead."

"I'm sorry," Kathryn said again. "I don't know why I'm prying into this. It's none of my business."

Lucas reached toward her without warning. Kathryn flinched, but all he did was tuck a wayward strand of hair behind her ear from where it had escaped her ponytail.

"You can ask me anything you'd like," he said, arching an elegant eyebrow. He took a sip of his whiskey, maintaining eye contact over the rim of his crystal tumbler.

Kathryn recognized his attempt to shove back painful memories, to reassert his devil-may-care mask. She remembered what it was like to pretend everything was all right when it never would be again. So, she played along, returning his look with a teasing half-smile. "All right," she began, and then almost chickened out, blurting in a rush the one thing she really wanted to know. "When did you become a vampire?"

Lucas raised both eyebrows in surprise. She supposed it was from her temerity in asking such a personal question. "Well, now, Kathryn," he murmured, moving so close that she could feel the whiskey-scented moisture of his breath along her jaw. "*That* is a *very* personal question. The sort of thing one shares with very good friends . . ." He leaned even closer and put his lips next to her ear. "Or lovers." He lowered his mouth to kiss the soft skin below her ear, and she shivered.

"Which one are you, *a cuisle?*" he whispered.

Kathryn's heart was trying to break out of her chest, it was pounding so hard, making it difficult to draw a full breath. She knew she should say something clever and back away, that it was foolish to get personally involved with Lucas Donlon. But there was a part of her that rebelled against always doing the right thing, always being the dutiful daughter, the responsible sister, the perfect Bureau agent. The part that was buried so deep inside her that she forgot it existed most of the time. The part of her that wanted something more. Maybe it was the vulnerability he'd shown with his pictures on the wall, the anger that still hardened his voice when he spoke of his long-dead grandfather. But she suspected it was more than that. Lucas was like a blazing fire. You knew he was dangerous, that nothing good would come of it, but you couldn't resist the pull, the brilliant heart of a flame you knew would heat you all the way to your marrow, even as it burned you alive.

And there was only tonight. She was leaving town tomorrow.

She reached for his whiskey glass. Locking gazes with him, she brought it to her lips and took a long drink, feeling the whiskey heat all the way down her throat to her stomach. "Which would you like me to be?" she asked quietly. "Friend or lover?"

Lucas's eyes flared a gold that put the fire's heart to shame. He reached for her, wrapping his arm around her waist and pulling her against the hard length of his body. "Be sure, Kathryn."

"I'm sure."

He took the whiskey glass from her unresisting hand and set it on the table so delicately that it made no sound at all. Kathryn watched the amber glow of the liquid, her stomach in knots even though she knew this was what she wanted, what she'd wanted from the moment she'd walked into his office and seen him for the first time. But now that it was here, now that the fantasy had become reality . . .

Lucas gripped her chin with gentle fingers and lifted her face to his. His mouth curved in a warm smile, but his eyes . . . they burned with desire. For her. The knowledge that he wanted her as much as she wanted him calmed her as nothing else could have. She curled her arms around his neck, rising up on to her tiptoes to brush her lips against his. Not a kiss, not yet. Just a feathering of her lips, back and forth, as his eyes grew hotter, his gaze more intense.

Lucas's arm tightened around her waist, holding her in place so that she couldn't have moved away if she'd wanted to. His other hand dropped to the curve of her butt, cupping both cheeks in his long fingers and squeezing, pressing her against the hard ridge of his arousal.

Kathryn's eyes, still captured by his, grew wider, as Lucas thrust his hips forward, making certain she felt every inch of his erection. She did. Oh, God, she did. She fisted one hand in his silky, black hair and licked his closed lips. Once, twice, then bit down gently on his lower lip demandingly.

Lucas growled. As if a switch had been thrown, heat flared between them like a warning that everything they'd done so far was adolescent flirting. And the adults were now in the room.

Lucas crushed his mouth against hers, forcing her lips to open. He stabbed his tongue into her mouth, pumping it like a small cock, conquering with sweeps of his tongue, tasting every inch of her mouth with such shocking speed that Kathryn could only submit. She finally fought back, demanding her share in return, tangling her tongue with his as they battled for dominance.

This was no romantic first kiss in the moonlight. This was the kiss of two people who'd hungered for each other for days, wanted, waited for this moment. Their kiss was hard and full of passion, a clashing of teeth and tongue, biting and licking, mouths mashed together so that Kathryn could barely breathe.

She made a small sound of distress, and Lucas threaded his fingers in her ponytail and tugged her head back. "Breathe," he commanded, his own breath sawing in and out.

Kathryn nodded wordlessly, her eyes never leaving his face.

"Damn it," Lucas swore, then took his arms away long enough to rip his T-shirt over his head, before pulling her against him once more.

Kathryn's gaze shifted to the very image of male beauty that was his body—wide shoulders thickly padded with muscle, tapering to smoothly defined pectorals lightly dusted with black hair which narrowed to a thin line over six pack abs that made her want to weep with their sheer perfection. Her eye was drawn down further to the low waist of his leather pants and the bulge that was stretching the leather so tight that it was gleaming with the strain of it.

She heard someone moaning with need and realized the sound was coming from her own throat. Her eyes shot back to Lucas's face, and then they were kissing again, their mouths crushed together as he tried to get her jacket off and Kathryn tried to help him. With a cry of frustration, she broke their kiss and shrugged the jacket down her arms, letting it drop to the floor.

Lucas growled, fisting handfuls of her tight dress as he dragged it up over her hips until it was bunched around her waist. He yanked her against him, then swore softly.

"What the fuck were you thinking with these stupid leggings?" he muttered, shoving his hands down inside the waistband and pushing the tight pants down until he was cupping her nearly bare ass.

"I was thinking I didn't want to fuck anyone," she snarled right back at him, unbuckling the wide belt and stripping it from her waist.

Lucas laughed breathlessly. "Good thinking since you didn't know I would be there."

Kathryn's response was lost as Lucas pulled the dress off over her head, then stepped back to eye her half-naked body. Kathryn blushed hotly, even though she knew she was in good shape. But the sweep of his gaze was like a caress, a brush of warm velvet over her skin, from the taut muscles of her stomach, to the swell of her breasts above the cups of her plain, white, cotton bra. And, oh God, why hadn't she bought a new bra when she bought the dress?

"I didn't plan on being ravished," she pulled back to explain breathlessly. "It's my work bra."

"Because you didn't know I would be there," he murmured again. "But since you're no longer working—" He pulled her close, grinding his erection against her, while he reached around and unhooked the clasp on her bra with a quick twist of his fingers. "—I think you should get rid of it," he whispered, then laid a sweet trail of gentle kisses down her neck and over the delicate bone of her clavicle.

Kathryn felt the bra give way, felt the delicious release of her heavy breasts from the tight binding of the sturdy bra. She let go of Lucas long enough to slide the straps down her arms. Ever the neat one, she tried to catch it with one hand rather than let it fall to the floor, but Lucas grabbed it and tossed it away, his gaze burning as he eyed her naked breasts for the first time. They seemed to swell under the force of his blatant desire, her nipples tightening as tiny shocks of lust tingled from her breasts to her abdomen and lower, where her pussy was clenching eagerly, demanding that Kathryn give it what it wanted. And it wanted Lucas.

Lucas cupped her breasts reverently in his long fingers, his thumb playing with her sensitive nipples, strumming back and forth until Kathryn thought she'd climax before they ever made it to bed.

"Beautiful," Lucas whispered, bending enough to take one nipple into his mouth and sucking hard.

Kathryn moaned. She didn't want to be admired. She wanted to be fucked. She fisted both hands in his hair and tugged him away from her breasts and back to her mouth. She pressed herself against him, rubbing her breasts against the wonderful hard planes of his chest, feeling the rasp of his chest hair against her nipples.

Lucas dropped both hands to her ass, swearing when he encountered the stupid leggings once more. "Fuck this," he snarled and dropped to his knees, dragging the offending pants down her legs and over her bare feet . . . which put him exactly at eye level with her sex, which was covered in nothing but a black, silk thong.

Lucas leaned forward and kissed her through the thin fabric. "Is this your work thong, too?" he teased.

Kathryn tangled her fingers in his hair, gasping when he slid a single finger under the triangle of silk and into her already wet pussy. Her hips thrust toward him as if they had a will of their own, and Kathryn threw her head back in sheer wanton pleasure. She felt sexual in a way she never had before. Desired and beautiful, as if there were no more rules. Some part of her brain knew this wasn't her. There were always rules. But the sight of the beautiful male on his knees before her overwhelmed everything except the hunger to have Lucas Donlon deep between her thighs as quickly and as often as possible.

She laughed with pure joy at the sensation.

Lucas surged to his feet, his fingers still buried inside her, pumping in and out, her wetness growing hot and slick, drenching his hand. He lowered his mouth to hers, and they kissed again, hungry, full of desire and need. It was an almost frantic kiss, as if they couldn't get enough of each other, couldn't meet fast enough.

"Bed," Lucas gasped against her mouth. He started backing Kathryn toward the bedroom, stopping every other step as their kiss deepened, making them forget everything else. Finally he growled and lifted her against his body until his erection was nestled in the perfect V of her legs. Kathryn responded instinctively, wrapped her legs around his hips for balance and to get closer to the thing she wanted, his cock buried inside her.

Lucas kept walking, carrying her into the bedroom as if she weighed nothing. Kathryn felt delicate and feminine and oh so sensuous.

He dropped one knee onto the bed, laying her down and stripping away the triangle of silken thong. It was soaking wet. Kathryn could feel the moisture as he dragged it down her leg, could smell her own arousal. She stretched on the bed, hands above her head, arching her back and lifting her breasts in offering.

Lucas's eyes were fixed on her like a giant jungle cat's, not moving at all, a predator sizing up his prey. Kathryn's heart began to pound as some primitive part of her brain registered the danger and went into fight or flight mode. She pressed a hand against her chest, telling her stupid heart to calm down, because this was what she wanted, and she wasn't going anywhere. She stroked her hand downward, scraping over a swollen nipple, smoothing over her flat belly and dipping between her legs.

Lucas's predator's gaze watched her hand every inch of the way, flaring with a gold light when she spread her legs and slid her finger between the swollen lips of her pussy.

"Take off your pants," Kathryn ordered. He grinned viciously as his gaze shot up to her face.

Kathryn didn't trust that grin, but she watched eagerly as Lucas stood away from the bed and stripped down to reveal nothing but luscious, naked male. He was commando beneath all that leather, and Kathryn wanted to cheer. His cock sprang forward, hard, long and thick. She couldn't take her eyes off of it as he stalked toward her. She felt even more like a tasty gazelle frozen under the gaze of a big cat, about to be gobbled up.

Yum. She could hardly wait.

Lucas crawled onto the bed, covering her body and pushing her knees up and out, pressing her legs wide with his hips, as he began a teasing sort of thrust with his cock. She could feel the hard length of his shaft sliding in her wetness, pressing her plumped folds open until he was rubbing against the very place she most wanted him.

"I'm going to fuck you first, *a cuisle,*" he said, pressing his erection against her until her pussy began clenching in desperate need.

She almost shrieked in denial when he sat back suddenly, then groaned as he plunged two fingers into her vagina, pumping in and out while rubbing her clit until she was so wet, she could feel the moisture coating the inside of her thighs. Lucas licked his lips hungrily, his eyes half-lidded until they were twin slices of gold fire watching his fingers slide in and out of her dripping folds, his thumb circling her clit. Kathryn moaned, pinching her nipples and squeezing her thighs around his hips in a desperate bid to relieve the ache.

"We'll make love after," Lucas said in a low voice, as he licked his fingers, then stretched out above her. She was swamped with lust and had to concentrate to understand the words. "But first . . ."

He reached down and positioned his cock between her thighs. She could feel the firm tip barely nudging into her eager pussy and immediately lifted her hips, trying to force it deeper. Lucas chuckled, then flexed his perfect ass and slid into her with a slow, irresistible push. His shaft was long and thick, filling her more completely than any lover she'd had before, stretching her inner walls until every nerve was bare, singing with the velvet brush of his cock as he went deeper and deeper, until she felt the slap of his balls against her ass, the tap of his cock against her cervix.

Kathryn closed her eyes against an overwhelming wave of pleasure, the delicious sensation of his erection filling every inch of her. She gripped his ass and opened her eyes to find him watching her. They held each other's gaze for a moment, and then they went wild.

Their mouths met in a clash of teeth and tongues as Lucas began pumping furiously, fucking her fast and hard as Kathryn rose up to meet every stroke. Her breasts were crushed against his chest, her nipples so sensitized that it was almost too much, streaks of desire racing from her breasts, over her belly and down between her legs, where they crashed against the exquisite pulse of her swollen clit, against the slide of Lucas's thrusting cock, then raced back up again to torment her breasts in a never-ending cycle.

Lucas's hands were beneath her hips, lifting her up, opening her even further to his invasion. His cock moved impossibly faster with every stroke, his hips pushing harder, as if he couldn't fuck fast enough, hard enough, deep enough.

He tore his mouth away from hers and buried his face against her neck. His teeth closed gently over the taut tendon there, and Kathryn bit into his shoulder to swallow her scream. Lucas growled against her flushed skin, then stroked his tongue over the skin of her neck, a slow, deliberate gliding of wet heat.

"Tell me it's okay, Kathryn," he panted, his hips never stopping their motion. "Jesus, tell me I can taste you."

Kathryn's heart kicked in doubt, in fear. She could barely think, too overcome with desires she'd never felt before, with a raw lust she'd never known she was capable of. Her brain wanted to think about it, but the rest of her body knew what it ached for, what it wanted *now*. She hesitated for a breath, and then in a flash of insight, she decided. She'd known whom she was going to bed with, known what he was. And she wanted him. All of him.

"Yes," she whispered. "Yes, yes, yes."

Lucas lifted his head and howled, then lowered his mouth once more. He sucked hard on the swell of her jugular vein below her ear, and she felt the rigid edge of his fangs. Her breath froze in her lungs, and then he was biting her, his fangs puncturing her vein with a sharp pinch, and then . . . she screamed as the most intense orgasm she'd ever experienced swept over her without warning. It was like a seizure, her back arching, her skin shivering with need as her womb convulsed, and her pussy clenched like a tight fist around Lucas's cock.

Lucas groaned as her inner walls squeezed his shaft, the sound a deep vibration against her throat that sent fresh waves of sensation trembling along every nerve. He lifted his head, his fangs sliding out of her vein smoothly, like a cool kiss against her hot skin. She felt the quick rasp of his tongue, and then he was fucking her again, pulling his cock out of the embrace of her clutching vagina and slamming it back in, in and out, the friction of his motion heating her inside and out, his hips slamming into hers.

Kathryn dug her blunt nails into his firm ass, spreading her legs wide and thrusting upward, meeting his every stroke until he snarled at her. And then he was coming, his cock bucking inside her, his climax a hot splash against her womb as he lifted his head and shouted her name.

LUCAS COLLAPSED on top of Kathryn, his face buried against her neck where he could still smell the delicious scent of her blood. He was waiting for her to explode, to be furious that he'd taken her vein while she was in the throes of her climax. But even if she did, it was worth it. He'd had hundreds, thousands of lovers over his long life, but he couldn't recall a single one who could match the heat, the urgency of what he and Kathryn had just shared. Even so, he hadn't intended to take her blood like that. He'd thought they would have a fast round of fucking to get the initial hunger out of the way, and then have a slow, romantic bout of lovemaking, during which he would seduce her into accepting the true experience of a vampire lover. Instead, he'd been so desperate in the frantic passion of their coupling that he'd all but begged. He'd seen the indecision in her expression and known how close she'd come to saying *no*, but then everything had shifted as some wild something had lit up her eyes, and, amazingly, she'd said *yes*. More than once, as he recalled.

But now, in the calm aftermath, with her brain returning to its normal sober and rules-following self, she was no doubt cursing herself and him, too. And so he was surprised again when she ran a caressing hand down his back, when she entwined one of her legs with his, her foot massaging his calf absently.

He pressed his lips against her neck and rose up on his elbows so he could see her face. She gave him a lazy half smile, then tugged his head down and kissed him thoroughly.

"Everything you advertised and more, Lord Donlon," she said, her husky voice the stuff of a man's fantasies, especially when the woman it belonged to was naked beneath him.

"Happy to oblige, Special Agent."

Kathryn laughed softly. "Hmmm. Tell me, is it true what they say about vampires?"

"I don't know. What do they say?"

She lifted her hips against his, and his cock, still buried deep inside her, jumped happily. Kathryn made an appreciative noise, and it was Lucas's turn to laugh.

"Oh, that," he murmured, and flexed his hips, causing his rapidly growing erection to glide in and out of her soaking wet pussy. "Yes, *a cuisle*, it's true."

"Excellent," she purred, and wrapped her leg around his hips. She began to move beneath him, her body rippling along his like warm satin.

Desire coursed through Lucas's bloodstream once more. Her core was already heated and wet, her inner walls still trembling and so sensitive that she was already on the verge of an orgasm. He watched her face as he plunged deep inside her once more, her eyes closed, skin flushed and glowing with moisture. He lowered his mouth to hers and licked the seam of her lips. Kathryn tightened her hold on his neck and pulled him closer, her mouth opening as his lips met hers, their tongues curling in a slow, erotic dance. They knew each other better now, knew the rhythm of the other's body, the taste of the other's mouth.

Lucas felt his gums split as his fangs emerged, lusting after another taste of her blood. The sharp points scraped along Kathryn's tongue in the midst of their kiss, and her eyes flashed open, going wide with surprise. He knew what she was seeing, knew his eyes had gone completely gold with desire, with hunger. He nearly lost it when her tongue reached up to explore his now fully distended fangs, twining around the hard enamel, pressing the flat of her tongue against one sharp point until it nicked her flesh. A tiny drop of blood swelled, filling his senses with the honeyed taste of Kathryn. Lucas growled.

Her nipples went rock hard against his chest, and her abdomen flexed beneath his as she moaned softly. "Lucas," she whispered. "I can't . . . oh God, I don't know if I . . ." And then she cried out, thrusting against him frantically as her womb contracted in another climax, her pussy trembling as it squeezed around him.

Lucas smiled against her soft cheek, smugly satisfied with himself as he continued to pump his cock in and out. Her body was so hot, so wet and soft. He wanted to fuck her for hours. He wanted to make her scream in ecstasy until she had no voice left.

He kissed her again, forcing her lips to part beneath his, her breath coming in pants as she groaned over and over, the sounds coming from deep in her chest. Lucas flicked his tongue up and stabbed one of his fangs deep enough into his own flesh that blood welled up instantly. Not the tiny drop that Kathryn had bled, but a steady flow. He coated her mouth and tongue with his blood, giving her no choice but to drink. Not that she fought it. Kathryn got that first tiny taste of his blood and began to swallow greedily, her tongue twisting around his, sucking hard, then sweeping every drop of it from her mouth, and pushing into his to claim the rest.

Her moans became a needy keen as his blood hit her throat and was absorbed into her bloodstream. She began bucking beneath him, murmuring his name over and over again like a mantra . . . or a prayer. Lucas growled and slammed his hips into hers, his cock growing impossibly hard as her body closed around him, as she scraped her dull nails up his back and dug strong fingers into his shoulders.

Lucas licked the side of her neck, wanting another taste of her blood, waiting for . . .

"Do it," she whispered, her voice a rasp of need. "Do it, do it, do it, damn it!"

Lucas sank his fangs into her neck with no further warning. With the first hit of the euphoric in his bite, Kathryn's entire body seized around him, her back arching to press her beautiful breasts against his chest, thighs tightening around his hips as her pussy grabbed hold of his cock and didn't let go.

Lucas snarled against the skin of her neck, his fangs still buried in her vein. His cock bucked, trying to dig deeper into her body. His balls tightened, pressure building as his own climax roared down upon him, irresistible, hot, demanding. He shoved his cock past the trembling grip of her vaginal walls, burying himself inside her until he could go no further, and then he was coming, pumping almost mindlessly as he filled Kathryn's womb with his hot release, searing his claim to her inside and out. And God save anyone who tried to take her from him.

KATHRYN WAS becoming one with the mattress. She couldn't move. Didn't want to. Had she ever in her life felt so satisfied, so utterly sated? Something twitched deep inside her, sending a fresh ripple of pleasure out to tweak her clit one more time. She bit back a groan. Is this what having sex with a vampire did to a woman? Turned her into a sex machine? She almost groaned again, but this time the groan was because she'd even *thought* the words *sex machine*. Next she'd be hearing cheesy background music in her head.

So she'd had sex with a beautiful man, and it had been terrific. Okay, more than terrific. Life altering. She should be thanking her lucky stars instead of bemoaning the fact that she'd climaxed three times in one night, which was probably more times than in all of the last five years combined, not counting her trusty vibrator. And Lucas was far, far better than her vibrator. The man was a god. No, actually, he was a vampire. No wonder all those women at the club were squealing like hungry pigs when those big, bad boys had walked in. Not, she was sure, that any of them could hold a candle to her Lucas.

Her Lucas? When had be become *her* Lucas?

Good thing she was leaving tomorrow, or rather later this morning. She couldn't afford to get tangled up with a man or a vampire, especially not one who lived in South Dakota and currently had an insufferably smug look on his face.

She narrowed her eyes at him, but he just grinned back at her and flexed his perfect ass one more time. She couldn't help it. Her body responded, squeezing his cock and making her nipples harden like puffy, pink pearls.

"Insufferable," she muttered.

"At least," he agreed readily.

Kathryn fought it, but she laughed, then slapped his butt. "Get off of me. You weigh a ton."

Lucas rolled away cheerfully, wrapping his arms around her so she came with him. He patted her ass in turn and kissed her swollen lips.

"You're delicious, Kathryn Hunter."

Kathryn lowered her head so he wouldn't see her blush of pleasure. No one had ever told her she was delicious. For that matter, she'd never even *felt* delicious before. But at this moment, she did. Lucas had done that.

Time to change the subject.

She raised her head from his chest and met his steady gaze. "What is it with your eyes?" she asked. "They go completely gold sometimes, and I think they actually give off light."

"They do," he agreed. "It's a vampire thing. When our power comes up, or when we see something we lust after," he added, lifting his hips so she could feel the still-hard length of his cock against her thigh, "our eyes change. The greater the power, or the desire, the brighter they glow."

"It's pretty."

Lucas smiled.

"Are everyone's eyes the same color? Or does it depend? I mean, your eyes are kind of a goldish hazel all the time anyhow. But what if they were blue instead?"

Lucas shrugged. "It's different for everyone, although most vampires, the rank and file, so to speak, simply gleam red. Those of us with greater power are more unique."

Kathryn rolled her eyes, although she had to agree that Lucas *was* unique. "So pretty eyes go with being a vampire lord, then," she said.

"Among other things, yes."

She studied him for a moment, then said seriously, "Lucas."

"Kathryn," he mimicked, matching her tone.

"Where did all that blood come from on your pants earlier? And what happened to Nicholas?"

Lucas stared back at her for a long moment, his hand growing still against the skin of her back. She thought he wouldn't answer, or that he'd come up with another lie, but then he surprised her by saying, "Vampires are territorial, Kathryn. Viciously, obsessively territorial. Vampire lords even more so than others. And we're violent. It's in our blood. Whatever it is that makes us Vampire amplifies aggression until it's a constant thing, something we have to work hard to discipline, so we can function in our day-to-day lives.

"As a vampire lord, I rule a territory. To every side of me, there is another territory, another vampire lord. These territorial boundaries are old and well-established, but occasionally, someone decides he wants more. When that happens, we go to war."

"War?" she repeated, frowning. "You mean like shooting and killing?"

"Killing, yes. But there's very little shooting involved. Vampires are capable of using weapons of all sorts. I'm sure you noticed the MP5s used by my gate security, along with several other guns or knives you probably didn't see. This is mostly to impress humans who might think to test my security. But the truth is that our best weapon, the one we use against each other, is ourselves. Vampires are strong, fast and deadly. As I said, we're a violent people."

Kathryn mulled over what he was telling her. "So you're saying another vampire lord is trying to take some of your territory."

"Exactly."

"And you had some sort of confrontation with him that got bloody."

"Not exactly, but close enough. You needn't worry about Nicholas, by the way. By tomorrow morning, there will be nothing but a fresh scar, a day later, not even that."

"You can heal that quickly?" she said in disbelief.

"Some of us. And some of us need help. A vampire lord rules his people, but he has an obligation to them as well. What is it your Bible says? 'To whom much has been given, much will be expected?' I'm certain your priests would be appalled to see it used thusly, but it is never more true than among vampires. We live it every day."

"How does it work? The healing, I mean."

"We don't know the science. We don't want to know. And we certainly don't want humans to know. They'd be chasing after us with those pitchforks again, but this time for our blood."

Kathryn stared at him, nearly face to face. They were lying so close. Naked skin to naked skin, their bodies fitted together perfectly, as if they'd been made for this one moment. He gave her a crooked smile, and she felt her heart swell.

Oh, no, she bemoaned silently. Not Lucas Donlon. What the hell was wrong with her?

"Kathryn, *a cuisle*, it is nearly dawn."

She blinked at him blankly before it hit her. Vampire. Oh. My. God.

"What happens?" she asked with some urgency. "Where do you have to go? Do you have a special—"

"Coffin?" he supplied dryly.

"No, of course not," she snapped. "But maybe a basement or something?"

"I'm touched, *a cuisle*, but no. I do like my comforts, and this bed is perfectly fine. However, there *are* security precautions. Steel shutters will cover every window and door moments before sunrise. These walls, as you may already have surmised, look flimsy, but are, in fact, rather severely reinforced."

"What will you—"

"I will sleep. I have little choice in the matter."

"I should go, then," she said hesitantly. She didn't want to offend him, but now more than ever, Kathryn felt the need to get out of town, to flee to the Twin Cities or anywhere else, as long as it took her far away from Lucas Donlon. He was a temptation, a complication, that she couldn't afford. She had a job back in Quantico. A job she had fought and clawed her way into. She tried to imagine what her superiors would say if she became involved with a vampire lord. Most of the people at the FBI viewed vampires as criminals, and *that* was just the regular run-of-the-mill vampires. Vampire lords were viewed with far less favor, if that was possible.

"I *need* to go," she said more urgently.

Lucas gave her a puzzled look, as if aware of the turmoil inside her head and not understanding the cause of it. That look tugged painfully on her heart and made her want to cry. Another thing she hadn't done in years.

"Kathryn?" he said, with obvious concern. "Are you all right?"

"Yes." She shook her head, as if that could brush away her feelings. "Of course. But I really do have to leave. I have things to do tomorrow, or rather later today, and I don't want to compromise your security."

She forced herself to push away from the embrace of his powerful body, from the warmth in his golden eyes. She leaned down for one final kiss, then jumped up and headed for the bathroom before he could see the tears filling her eyes.

Lucas let Kathryn go as she hurried away. He wasn't as sensitive to emotions as his friend Duncan, but even he could tell that there was some sort of battle going on inside Kathryn's excellent brain. Guilt, maybe? She'd probably broken some FBI rule or other about sleeping with witnesses. Although he wasn't technically a witness, since he hadn't seen anything. Or maybe she was feeling guilty about enjoying herself instead of spending every moment searching for her brother. Given what he knew about their relationship, that seemed likely. He could even understand it if she felt that way.

He flexed his abdominal muscles and sat straight up in bed before swinging his legs over the side. He wasn't the kind of man who lay in bed while his lover dragged her clothes on and scurried out the door. Kicking the ruined leather pants to one side, he pulled a pair of fresh sweats out of his closet and slipped them on, along with a matching gray T-shirt. He strolled out to the living room and located Kathryn's clothing for her—her dress, shoes, jacket ... even those ridiculous leggings she'd donned to protect herself against unwanted attention at the blood house. As if a pair of pants would deter any vampire worth his salt.

Walking back into the bedroom, he shook out the articles of clothing and laid them on the bed in a neat pile, then searched around the bed until he found the tiny black thong she'd been wearing. He was tempted to keep that as a memento, but decided not to tease her, and laid it on top of the dress next to her sensible white bra. He took a moment to imagine Kathryn's beautiful breasts encased in silk and lace instead of ordinary cotton, her dusky rose nipples visible as they rose up hard and pressed against the sheer silk.

The bathroom door opened to reveal a naked Kathryn, and his cock sprang instantly to attention. Lucas caught her around the waist as she hurried past, pulling her against his body. He dipped his fingers between her legs and found her still hot and wet from their lovemaking.

"Are you absolutely certain you have to go?" he whispered against her ear.

Kathryn closed her eyes, leaned her head against his shoulder, and expelled a long sighing breath. "I wish I didn't," she murmured, her husky voice breathless with desire. "But I have to get up early in the morning. I have things to do."

Lucas kissed the side of her neck and released her, but not before slipping one finger into her wetness and bringing it to his lips for a taste.

Kathryn's eyes flared she watched him taste the cream coating his fingers. "Delicious, *a cuisle*."

"Not fair," she breathed.

"I don't play fair," he said. "Remember that, Kathryn."

Lucas watched as she dressed, taking pleasure in the heat of embarrassment that colored her cheeks. He helped her on with her jacket, then walked her outside and gave her a lingering kiss good-bye, a promise of things to come. He waited until she was safely in her vehicle and away before entering the security code to initiate the daylight safety measures. The steel shutters he'd mentioned to Kathryn deployed instantly, sliding down in near silence over every door, window, and vent, until the exterior walls were a solid steel surface and nearly impregnable. *Nearly*, because anything was possible. Only death was 100 percent safe.

Lucas felt the hot sun peeking over the horizon as he stripped away his sweats and fell into the bed. He lifted the sheets and smelled Kathryn, not her perfume—she didn't wear any—but her arousal, the scent of their lovemaking. His cock hardened at the reminder, and he stroked it absently, thinking of all the things he had yet to enjoy with his luscious FBI agent.

He was still smiling when sleep took him, and he dreamed.

1791, Kildare County, Ireland

Lucas crouched small and silent in the great hall of his grandfather's castle. Or so his mother told him. He'd never known before today that he *had* a grandfather, much less one with a castle. But it was certainly grand. As big as the cathedral in town where he and his mother lived, bigger even when one added in outbuildings and stables.

He'd wanted to linger in those stables. There'd been horses there, great, beautiful beasts like the ones ridden by the lords and merchants in town. He'd entertained the fancy that he might be permitted to ride one, this being his own grandfather's estate and all. But his mother had snatched him away, and the man she called *Father* had quickly dashed any hope Lucas had of getting near the animals. The giant of an old man had barely acknowledged Lucas's existence, and certainly not as a blood relation. He'd taken one look at Lucas standing there holding his mother's hand, then spit to one side and walked away.

Which was how Lucas came to be hiding behind a chair, spying on his mother and the stern-looking old woman facing her across the hearth. He peered out from behind a fur throw that smelled of dog. Probably the giant wolfhounds he'd seen roaming his grandfather's castle, the ones the old man gave far more affection and attention than his grandson.

Lucas was only six, and he didn't understand much of what old people did, but he knew what it meant to be spat upon. And it wasn't a good thing. Especially not from one's own grandfather.

But the old man wasn't here now. Only the woman his mother had told him was his grandmother—another revelation. Lucas hadn't known he had family other than his mother before today, and suddenly he had grandparents, and probably more. Some of his friends had grandparents, and they had cousins and all sorts of relations to go with them.

"You look a fright, Brighid."

His grandmother's voice drew him back to the drafty room, his narrow chest swelling with outrage at her words. His mother was beautiful! He'd heard some of the men in town, and even the women, comment on her beauty, though he didn't need anyone to tell him what his own eyes could see. On the verge of jumping up to defend his mother's honor, he abruptly sank back down, remembering that he was spying on the women. They would only send him away if he was discovered, and he had a feeling important things were being said, things he needed to hear. There had to be a reason his mother had brought them so far to this grand castle. She'd told him this was home, but it didn't feel like home. The only home he knew was the single room they shared back in the city.

"Forgive me, Mother," Lucas's mother was saying, her usually gentle voice hard with some emotion he didn't understand. "It is difficult to maintain a proper wardrobe when one barely has enough food to eat."

"There is no need to be coarse, Brighid."

"Oh, no. By all means, let us not be coarse."

"Bitterness does not become you, child."

Lucas's mother laughed. "What do I have to be bitter about? That my own father disowned me? That he left me and my child to starve on the streets?"

"It is your own sins that brought you to this. And you are not starving in any case. A bit thin perhaps, but the boy looks healthy enough."

"Lucas is perfect," his mother said fiercely, and Lucas swelled with pride.

The old woman only lifted her lip, as if she'd tasted an ale that had gone sour. "Your father would take you back. Make a good marriage for you, despite your . . . unfortunate situation. There are men who would not mind a young, strong woman. Men who would be willing to overlook your earlier indiscretion."

"Indiscretion? I was raped, Mother."

"Lord Danford staunchly denies your hysterical accusation. Why would he have bothered with a silly girl like you? His lovely lady wife had already given him two strong sons, and she has given him another plus a daughter since then. You do your father little honor with these fantastic tales. Danford is a loyal friend and supporter of your father, one of his most valued associates."

"Obviously an associate of far greater value than his only child . . . or his grandson."

"That bastard child is *not* your father's grandson."

Lucas's mother stood abruptly, her hands clenching in her skirt the way they did when she was upset. "I know not why I came here," she said. "Or why I thought anything would have changed."

The old woman looked up at his mother, unperturbed by her distress. "You should consider your father's offer. Lord Jamie is looking for a new wife now that poor Deirdre passed so suddenly."

"Suddenly?" his mother scoffed. "She was thirty years his junior when they married! The poor woman probably welcomed death after being chained to that vicious old man for so long. How many babes did he force on her? Ten, twelve? Which birth finally killed her, Mother?"

"Really, Brighid. Your time away has made you most uncouth. You must school yourself if you hope to reclaim your father's good will."

His mother made a noise like a laugh, but it wasn't a happy sound. "His good will? Why? So he can bury me along with *poor* Deirdre? And what of Lucas?"

"You would have to get rid of the boy, of course. There are men, I'm told, who will take on unwanted children as laborers. It is a productive life. The best such a child can expect."

"My *son* is not unwanted. Farewell, Mother. Lucas!"

He jumped up, eyes wide as he realized she'd known all along he was there.

"Come, sweetling," she said softly, holding out her hand. "We are leaving."

Chapter Ten

South Dakota, present day

KATHRYN CURSED as she drove away into the pale, predawn light. It had been a huge mistake to sleep with Lucas Donlon. She never dated men she was *seriously* attracted to. Sure, she liked good-looking men, intelligent men, but the ones she dated were looking for the same thing she was—a casual hook-up, scratching an itch, maybe a few pleasant dinners together. After all, men did it all the time, so why couldn't she do the same? Her brother said she was avoiding commitment, that after a lifetime of raising *him,* she had no desire to raise anyone else, including a husband, or even a boyfriend. She'd always denied it, not because it wasn't true, but because she'd never wanted him to think he'd been a burden, that she'd ever regretted even one day of his life.

But in the privacy of her own heart, she knew he was right. She wasn't looking for a relationship, had no desire to find the perfect man to settle down with. So, why in God's name had she weakened enough to spend any time at all with Lucas, much less to have sex with him? Did she love him? Hell, no. It was far too early to think that. But she hungered for him in a way she never had anyone else. She'd just left, and already she could think of nothing but the next time she'd see him. Her body was already so sensitized to his touch that the mere thought of him had her breasts plumping in anticipation, her thighs squeezing together against a need so strong she knew she could climax if she moved . . . precisely . . . the . . . right . . . way. She shuddered as a mini-orgasm trembled through her body.

This was ridiculous. Awful. A complete disaster. She had to get away from Lucas Donlon, as far and as fast as possible. Thank God she was finished with her investigation in this town. She had only to figure out something to do with her brother's equipment, and she could be gone. She certainly wouldn't be leaving Dan's cameras and stuff at Lucas's ranch, though she knew it would be safer there than anywhere else. Unfortunately, the ranch was probably the least safe place in the world for *her* right now. Or ever.

She could ship the stuff home. No, even better, ship it to her office. A quick email to warn them it was coming, and they'd make sure it was held until she got back from vacation. Vacation. What a laugh. More like a nightmare. Her brother was still missing, and she was wasting time screwing a good-looking vampire. She shook her head. Good-looking didn't come close to describing Lucas Donlon.

Focus, Kathryn! Right, the equipment. Okay, so she was shipping it. But that meant boxing it up securely. Dan's cameras weren't the kind of thing you could simply toss into a FedEx box with some Styrofoam peanuts. She frowned. Had she even seen a FedEx place in town? She needed one of those big ones that did packaging as well as shipping, and she couldn't remember seeing one locally. Which meant she'd have to travel to the nearby big city, "big" being a relative term. But that would take time, and she needed to be gone before it got so late that she could, in any way, rationalize waiting for sunset. Because her body was already bombarding her brain with images of a naked Lucas between her thighs . . . on top of her, beneath her, inside her . . . Oh God, she needed to put some miles on the road and fast. No airport. There weren't enough flights, and waiting for a plane meant more delays, more time for her body to win the fight against her brain.

Her GPS dinged, warning her that the main highway was up ahead. At last! She turned off the primitive dirt road and onto the pavement. The rising sun set fire to her rearview mirror, and she squinted, nearly blinded by the reflection before shoving it aside and pressing the gas pedal as far down as it would go. She could probably talk her way out of a speeding ticket. The sheriff knew who she was after all, and . . .

That was it! Her brains must be more scrambled than she'd thought if it had taken her this long to consider the obvious. She could leave Dan's camera equipment with the sheriff. He'd hold it for her as a professional courtesy, if nothing else.

This was why she avoided emotional entanglements. They made her stupid.

Two hours later, the tiny town was behind her as she raced toward Minneapolis. Sheriff Sutcliffe had been more than happy to help her out, had even volunteered to arrange appropriate packing and shipping if she needed it. Kathryn had declined, not sure if she wanted to go that far yet. It would all depend on where her brother was—and what kind of shape he was in when she found him. Because now, more than ever, she was convinced he was alive and that Alex Carmichael had him. What was it Lucas had said? If a vampire met a human he fancied, he took the human home for a while to play with, to taste.

And what could be more intriguing for a vampire like Alex Carmichael, someone who bought and sold beautiful art for a living, than a few weeks with a man whose work he admired? Her brother was alive. She simply had to find him and Carmichael before the novelty wore off.

LUCAS OPENED HIS eyes, feeling troubled and not at all refreshed from his day's sleep. He rarely woke this way, but then he rarely dreamed anymore. And never of the only time he'd visited Castle Donlon as a child. That visit had marked the end of his innocence. Everything fell apart after that, although as an adult he understood that things had been getting worse for some time before then. His mother had lost her seamstress position, which had been the thin thread between them and starvation. Desperation had driven her back to Kildare, to sacrifice her pride in hopes of getting help from her father before it was too late.

If she'd been willing to throw away her son that day, to throw away Lucas, they would have taken her back. He understood *that* now, too. Brighid had been their only child, and old Donal Donlon had been desperate to secure an heir for his estate, someone in a direct line to himself. His wife, Brighid's mother, had been too old to bear another child, and the church wouldn't let him set her aside. So he'd been willing to take Brighid back, to marry her off to someone acceptable to his needs, if not to Brighid's, in hopes of securing a legitimate heir.

But Lucas's mother had loved him, despite the circumstances of his conception. He hadn't understood what rape meant when he was six, but he did later. And he'd marveled that his mother had loved him despite it, loved him so fiercely that he'd never doubted it, not for one moment.

But love didn't put food on the table, didn't pay the rent on their pitiful room. So she sold the only thing she had left. Herself. It shamed him still that she'd been forced to such dire straits because of him. It was why he rarely thought about those times. Why he wasn't going to think about them anymore this evening either.

He sat up and drew a deep breath into his lungs. And he thought of Kathryn. He snagged his cell phone from the side table and punched in her number. It went to voice mail, so he disconnected and dialed the motel instead.

"Motel," a man's voice said, apparently feeling no obligation to announce *which* motel, since there was only the one in town.

"Hunter, room eighteen," Lucas requested.

"Nope. She checked out this morning."

Lucas froze. "She what?" he asked in a voice so cold the poor night manager stuttered his reply.

"Sh—she checked out, sir. First thing this morning."

Lucas disconnected and threw the phone down before he crushed it. She'd run. He'd known there was something off about her emotions when she'd left this morning, and now he understood. It wasn't that she felt nothing for him, because he knew she did. She'd wanted him just as much as he'd wanted her last night, and even this morning she'd clearly wanted to stay. So why leave town so abruptly?

He snapped his fingers as it hit him. Kathryn was a control freak. Why the hell else had she become an FBI agent, one of those uptight clones of rigidity in their identical suits and ties? It had been written all over her that first night she'd met him, in her buttoned up blouse and neat-as-a-pin pants suit. Always in control. But there was no such thing when it came to feelings, especially not when the sparks were flying like they had between them last night. Kathryn hadn't fled because she didn't want him, but because she did. And it terrified her. Finally something she couldn't control, so she'd fled the scene rather than face him. He grabbed the cell phone again, intending to call her on her obvious cowardice, but changed his mind. He didn't need to go begging after a woman's attention. They usually came begging to him. This one hadn't, and it pissed him off. But there were other ways to corner his personal FBI agent, and he intended—

His phone rang. "Yeah, Nick," he answered.

"Sire, we have a target to retaliate against Klemens."

Lucas growled deep in his chest. "Fuckin' A. Where is it?"

"Rockford. A hundred miles from Chicago, give or take."

"We'll have to fly. Have the jet prepped, and give Minneapolis a call. Klemens will know the minute I cross the border, so I want a helicopter waiting for us on the ground in Chicago. We'll chopper from there to Rockford. And tell Thad he's invited to the party. He can bring any of his survivors who can fight. No civilians. Warriors only. This isn't going to be pretty."

"Yes, my lord, when—"

"Have the SUVs out front in ten minutes. Payback's a bitch, my friend."

Chapter Eleven

THAD WAS WAITING for them when they landed at Chicago's Executive Airport, located in a suburb just north of the city. Chicago was Klemens's home city in every sense of the word. He'd been born there as a human and now ruled from there as a vampire. He'd know by now that Lucas had crossed into his territory, though he wouldn't know precisely where just yet. And by the time he figured it out, Lucas would be on the move. Lucas didn't envy the vampires closest to Klemens tonight. They'd be bearing the brunt of the vampire lord's anger, and rumor had it that Klemens didn't spare anyone when he was displeased.

"I brought only two from the enclave, my lord," Thad was saying. "More wanted to come, but you said fighters only, so—"

"Absolutely. This is going to be bloody, Thad. I know you can handle it, but what about the others?"

"Both skilled fighters, my lord, and well-motivated."

"I trust your judgment. Zelma," he said, turning to greet the head of his Minneapolis nest as she joined them. "Everything set?"

Zelma was dressed in the same black combat clothing as the men. At no more than five and half feet tall, she was dwarfed by Lucas and the other warriors, but she was all muscle and skill. Female or not, Lucas had seen her fight and had no qualms about including her in the night's festivities.

"The transport helicopter is waiting, my lord," she replied. "With Thad's three and your ten, we'll be twenty strong once we get there."

They started across the tarmac at a fast walk, heading for the waiting helicopter. "You have recon on the site?" Lucas asked.

"I sent two scouts ahead as soon as Nick called. They drove, taking two separate SUVs, just in case we needed ground transportation once we got there."

"Good thinking. What do you know about the place?"

"It's an older house, two-story brick, on nine acres, which is a point in our favor. It's hell doing battle in a fucking suburb. This place has lots of trees, lots of cover. There's only one way in if you approach by car. It crosses over a small creek with a bridge. One ancient outbuilding, which my guys don't think is being used at all. Last report I had, one of them was trying to get closer to be certain, and maybe get a head count from inside the house."

"I don't want Klemens's people warned, Zelma. If he can't do it quietly, tell him to back off."

"I told him the same, my lord. They both know the ground rules." Her phone rang, and she checked the screen. "The scouts," she told Lucas, then answered the call. "Talk to me."

While Zelma got the scouting report, Lucas and the others were climbing aboard the helicopter, getting situated among the vampires already inside. Lucas and Nick settled into two of the most forward seats. The others shuffled deeper into the passenger bay. It said something, Lucas thought to himself, that he felt it necessary to own three of these heavy transport helicopters. His border squabbles with Klemens had been going on for as long as he could remember, almost from the first day Klemens had seized the Midwestern Territory for himself. Klemens had never been satisfied with the limits of his holdings, even though the boundaries had been drawn and well-established long before he came to power. Lucas had been ruling the Plains Territory for nearly a hundred years before Klemens showed up next door. And the bastard had been a thorn in his side ever since.

He looked over as Zelma stepped up into the helicopter. Nick stood, letting her take the seat between them, so they could both hear her report. Before he sat again, he leaned into the pilot's compartment and gave the order to take off.

The noise from the copter ratcheted up quickly. Lucas grabbed the headset hanging over his seat and put it on, as Zelma and Nick did the same. Zelma glanced at Lucas, and seeing his nod, produced an iPad and pulled up not just a picture of the house but a map of the grounds, as well.

"Klemens only purchased this place ten years ago. The old real estate listing is still there, and my computer guy pulled up the plat from the tax records. The scouts have it, too, and say it's pretty accurate. Doesn't show the surrounding landscape, of course, but I'm more interested in the structures."

Lucas nodded. "What about numbers?"

"The scout who took a look is no master vampire, so it's a best guess. He says more than ten, fewer than twenty. All on the ground floor and, he assumes, the basement."

"The basement is almost certain," Nick commented.

"Agreed," Zelma said. "And we have to assume the number of fighters is on the high end of his estimate. If it's lower, fine. If not, we're prepared."

"I'm not worried about numbers," Lucas reminded them impatiently. "I'll know who's in that house as soon as I'm on-scene."

Zelma dipped her head, clearly embarrassed. "Apologies, my lord."

Lucas nodded his understanding. He could feel battle lust beginning to grow in the vampires filling the big helicopter, the hunger for blood and violence. Zelma was a strong vampire and a good leader, but she wasn't immune to it, either. Even Nick's eyes were beginning to glow around the edges as his power rose in response to the thickening air of violence, and Nick had seen more battles at Lucas's side than anyone else here.

Lucas took the iPad from Zelma and studied the target. There was no cover directly around the house. They'd be approaching in the open and uphill, but if Klemens's people weren't expecting them, that shouldn't be a problem. The question was whether Klemens had sent out an alert to all of his vampires when he realized Lucas had crossed his border.

"Can you call your scouts without giving away their position?" he asked Zelma.

"Yes, my lord."

"Do it. Ask if they've seen any indication that Klemens's people have been warned, any sudden burst of guard activity."

"Klemens knows you're here," she guessed accurately.

"Of course. But did he think to warn this particular barracks?"

Zelma's thumbs flew as she opted to contact her scouts via text. It was growing far too noisy in the helicopter for anything but a shouted conversation. Her grin grew as she read the response and when she looked up, her eyes were glowing red with eagerness.

"Nothing, my lord. They've located a single lookout and will take him out on your command."

Lucas frowned. If this were one of *his* border staging areas, he'd have at least two fighters on patrol at all times. On the other hand, this particular house wasn't that far from Klemens's main headquarters in Chicago, so perhaps they felt secure enough not to bother. They'd learn the error of their ways soon enough.

"Tell them to hang back, wait until I get there. I want to see for myself before we commit to anything." He flicked a switch and spoke to the pilot through his headset, "ETA?"

"Twelve minutes, Sire. We're putting you down in a field a mile distant and downwind. They shouldn't hear a thing."

"Excellent." A mile run was nothing for his vampires, but he'd have to be sure they knew the battle plan going in. Once they were on the ground and running, they'd be on the hunt, their blood flowing hot, adrenaline pumping.

Lucas grinned savagely. This was going to be sweet.

LUCAS STOOD perfectly still and stared up at the old house. As Zelma's real estate photo had shown, it was an older two-story brick with a pitched roof and a small sun porch to one side. He let his power wash lightly over the house, slithering into every crack, cupboard and closet, up every stair and down into the basement. He smiled. Klemens was going to be furious.

"Seventeen vampires, one a master," he murmured. "And no humans." This last was a relief. Humans would have greatly complicated his task tonight. He'd handle the master himself, although Nick or even Zelma could probably do it as well.

"The scouts were right, just the one lookout. Take him out now. Quietly, Zelma. I want no warning bells. We're going in hot. A blitz attack—surround the house, overwhelming force. They're clearly not expecting anyone, and they're sure as hell not expecting *me*."

Zelma said a single word into her throat mike. They were all wearing similar communication gear, except Lucas. He didn't need electronics to communicate with his vampires, not once he unleashed the full measure of his power.

"Ready, my lord," Zelma and Nick both whispered at almost the exact same time.

Lucas climbed the hill slowly, loosening the bindings on his power a little more with every step he took. Living among humans meant wearing a mask. Not just a pleasant face for the locals to see, but lashing his power down tightly so he could walk on the street without buffeting humans and vampires aside, without rattling the walls when he grew angry, or sending entire rooms full of humans into an irrational panic they didn't understand. He was a vampire lord. He was power incarnate, but he rarely bared his true face to the world.

Tonight was one of those times, and he reveled in the beauty of it, as his power streamed out, surrounding him, waiting to be tapped, waiting for the taste of an enemy's blood. The darkness around Lucas lit with golden fire as his eyes reflected the rise of his power. Unnatural winds began to toss the trees overhead, growing stronger until the trees themselves bowed before it, thick trunks groaning as they gave in to the unstoppable force. Lucas swept his arms forward, gathering the wind and tossing it at the house. It hit with a thundering crack of sound, like a sonic boom. Windows spidered, then shattered. Shingles flew from the roof, and the sun room collapsed.

From inside the house, he heard the first cries of shock and fear. No matter how stalwart Klemens's warriors were, they had just become aware of the monster waiting outside in the dark. And they knew death had come to call.

"Go," Lucas whispered onto the wind, and every one of his vampires heard it as if he'd spoken directly into their ear. They responded with a roar, crashing through doors and windows, racing into the house from all sides, howling for blood. Lucas cast his essence deeper into the house, seeding the air with terror, with every nightmare his enemies had ever dreamed. The screaming started as his vampires struck, the disbelieving cries of nearly immortal beings as they died.

Lucas's attention was drawn to a single vampire in a corner of the house, near the fireplace. It was the master vampire, the strongest of Klemens's creatures present. "Mine," he said, and walked through the gaping hole where the front door had once been.

Several of Lucas's vampires surrounded him as he strode forward. The fighting still raged deep in the house, a few diehards holding out against the inevitable. But the master vampire was waiting for Lucas, crouched in an attack position, fingers curled into claws and fangs dripping blood over his lower lip. His eyes were wild with fear as he looked upon Lucas, but they were filled with determination, too. He was too young to know his fate was already cast. Still, Lucas had to admire his courage in holding out as long as he had—and in remaining standing at all in the face of Lucas's power.

Time to end that.

"Kneel," Lucas commanded softly and drove the vampire to his knees with a hammer blow of power.

The young master grunted in pain as his knees cracked against the hardwood floor.

"What are you orders from Klemens?"

The vampire glared at the surrounding vampires, then met Lucas's gaze defiantly. He knew, as Lucas did too, that Klemens would be on his way soon, if he wasn't already. Lucas's invasion of Klemens's territory would have been enough to put the Chicago vampire lord on alert, but the violent death of so many of his vampires at once would be a beacon telling him where Lucas had attacked. And this young master vampire thought he could hold out until his Sire arrived.

Lucas smiled. "He'll never get here in time," he told the vampire almost sadly. "I'll be long gone, and so will you."

The vampire blinked as he took in the meaning of Lucas's words, but remained defiant.

"I can take it from your mind, boy," Lucas growled impatiently. "It will be less painful if you just tell me."

The vampire responded by spitting a glob of blood at Lucas's feet, and Lucas laughed. "I like your spirit. Too bad it's wasted on that bastard Klemens. The hard way it is, then."

Lucas sifted his power into the young master's brain, immobilizing him even as he rooted through the vampire's thoughts. He flashed quickly through recent memory, seeing Klemens's hateful face and then a safe. In the basement. How quaint.

He withdrew from his captive's head and took a step back. The vampire was slumped forward, head hanging, chin nearly resting on his chest. But he was still breathing. Lucas considered his prisoner. He had everything he needed from this one, or at least everything the vampire had to give him. The only thing left was death. He couldn't afford to leave the enemy vampire alive, but he could kill him painlessly.

With what was clearly a supreme effort, the young master vampire raised his head. His eyes were unfocused, and he blinked several times before he was able to glare his hatred at Lucas once more. "My Sire will kill you," he rasped. "I'll see you in hell."

"Probably," Lucas replied cheerfully, then slammed his fist into the vampire's chest and ripped out his heart. "But you'll see your beloved Sire there long before you'll see me."

The vampire crumbled into dust. Lucas's vampires swore and stepped back quickly to avoid getting splashed with any of it. Why they bothered, Lucas didn't know, since they were already liberally painted with the blood of their enemies.

"Nicholas," he said, almost casually.

"Sire?"

"There's a safe in the basement. I want everything that's in it. Everything. Zelma, get that helicopter over here to pick us up, then detail two of your people to drive the SUVs. I want them gone before we leave."

While Nick and Zelma ran to follow his orders, Lucas gazed around the demolished house. His people had taken him literally, coming in from all sides. Every door and window he laid eyes on was destroyed, and someone had actually broken through the wall from the sun porch. The air was thick with the dust of too many dead vampires. It was a musty stench, with an overlay of old blood. He heard the helicopter come in to hover overhead and strode back through the house quickly. He might not mind the smell of his dead enemies, but he didn't want to be covered in their dust from the helicopter's rotor wash, either. He kept going until he was under the dark trees, then took a moment to cast his awareness out, searching for Klemens.

Ah. There he was. And as mad as a wet hen.

Nicholas, he sent to his lieutenant's mind. *Get everyone on the helicopter now.*

He sensed Nicholas's attention and then the urgent emotions of his vampire warriors as they rushed to obey. The SUVs were already gone, their red taillights flickering through the trees as they turned onto the main road, heading away from Chicago to avoid passing Klemens's incoming gang on the road. They'd head for the Iowa border, which was Lucas's territory and less than a hundred miles distant. At vampire speeds, that was little more than an hour's drive. Lucas and his helicopter troops would fly directly to Minneapolis. The jet that had flown them to Chicago had already departed and was waiting for them there. But Lucas would bed down for the day in Minneapolis again. Although this time, he'd be sleeping in his private penthouse condo, not bunking in the basement vault of the Minneapolis house, no matter how comfortable it was.

Between the looming sun and his crashing adrenaline, Lucas was definitely ready to rest. He was pleased with the night's work, however. He'd flipped Klemens the finger by flying into his own capital city for the raid and then destroying seventeen of the vampire lord's warriors and stealing whatever data there had been in the safe. It had been a very satisfying night, definitely one for the good guys—which he had no doubt he and his vampires were. He was looking forward to crashing in the giant bed he'd had custom-made for his Minneapolis penthouse. Only one thing was needed to make it a perfect night. Kathryn Hunter. But somehow he doubted she'd be waiting for him.

Minneapolis, MN

Kathryn woke sluggishly, confused by the complete absence of light. She had a full two seconds of alarm before registering the sounds and smells of a hotel. Right. Minneapolis. Hotel. Blackout curtains. She'd driven all day yesterday, intending to confront Carmichael at his gallery last night. But she'd been so worn-out by the time she arrived in the Twin Cities that she'd wisely put off the confrontation and fallen straight into bed instead. She might be carrying a badge, but Carmichael was a vampire, and she wasn't even the slightest bit suicidal. The last thing she wanted was to challenge him when she was too tired to think straight.

She fumbled for her cell phone to check the time and was surprised to see she'd managed to sleep several hours. Of course, now she was wide awake and faced an entire day with nothing to do but wait for sunset and vampires.

She rolled out of bed and started the coffee maker. With the first lifesaving cup of caffeine burning its way through her stomach, she checked her email, hoping against hope that there'd be something from Daniel or even his agent, Penny. But no luck. Not that she'd really expected it.

Trolling for ways to kill time that didn't involve daytime television, she'd decided to put down on paper everything she knew—a timeline beginning with Dan's last known activities and adding in everything she'd discovered so far. That took all of an hour and got her nowhere. She didn't need a visual aid to know the details of this case. They were imprinted on the back of her brain. She saw them whenever she closed her eyes, like a nonstop video display that just kept repeating over and over again.

Finally, in a bid to retain what little sanity she had left, she pulled on her workout clothes, including the winter weight leggings she'd packed especially for this trip, and took the elevator down to the lobby. The hotel had a gym, but what she really needed was some fresh air and sunlight. There was a group of men in suits hogging the front desk, so she wandered over to the concierge desk, which was unstaffed at this early hour. Buried amidst the many tourist brochures, she found a runner's map which detailed several excellent routes, broken down by stamina and level of training. Since Kathryn ran every day, and that didn't include the extra training she put in on the Bureau's cross country trails, she chose the most challenging route, pulled up the hood on her sweatshirt and headed out into the sunny Minneapolis morning.

Halfway through the route, she found herself near the same huge mall where she'd bought the black dress she'd worn to Lucas's club on Friday, just two days ago. Remembering when she'd worn the dress made her remember when Lucas had helped her take the dress *off*, which then reminded her of the plain white bra she'd been wearing *underneath* the dress. She frowned. Her ordinary work bras were the only ones she'd packed, other than her sports bra, which was even worse. But, getting naked with Lucas had made her choice of bra seem stodgy. They made sense when she was working. She couldn't have some lacey thing outlined beneath her cotton blouses, couldn't have her breasts bouncing around every time she walked. But that didn't mean she had to be sensible all the time. Besides, a girl could never have too much underwear.

That was her story, and she was sticking to it.

Decision made, Kathryn detoured and jogged into the mall itself. She knew there was a Victoria's Secret inside, because she'd passed it by the day she'd bought the dress. If she'd known she was going to be disrobing in front of Lucas Donlon, she might have stopped. But this morning, she found it easily and started inside, suffering a moment's hesitation when she caught a reflection of herself in the plate glass window. In her leggings and hoodie, with no makeup and a ponytail tucked under a sweaty baseball cap, she obviously wasn't dressed for lingerie shopping. She almost didn't go in, but then two women walked out and gave her the kind of look usually reserved for someone trying to bum money for booze on the street corner. That decided it. Kathryn's father had always claimed that the one way to make sure Kathryn did something was to suggest that she couldn't. She thought she'd outgrown that impulse, especially once she'd gotten old enough to figure out her dad was using it against her. But apparently, it still worked.

Casting the two women a dismissive glance, she yanked off her baseball cap, pulled the scrunchy out of her ponytail and fluffed her hair, then strode into the shop.

An hour later, she'd spent nearly two hundred dollars on lingerie that most likely no one would ever see but her. God knew, she wouldn't be wearing that lovely sea foam green lace and silk set to work, and since that was the only place she ever went . . . Ah well. She did date occasionally, and she could always dance around her condo in it.

Leaving the store, she stopped and put the bag on the floor near her feet, tugged her hair back into its ponytail and covered it with her cap. Then she hooked the bag over her arm and geared herself up for the run back to the hotel.

By the time she hurried into the lobby, she was both sweaty and cold. The sky, which had been sunny earlier, had clouded over. It wasn't cold enough to snow, but a light rain had started on her last mile, and her running clothes weren't meant for rain. Not to mention she'd been worried about her new, expensive lingerie being ruined.

She raced up to her fourth floor room, taking the stairs to avoid forcing anyone to share an elevator with her stinky, sweaty self. She stripped off her clothes, took a long, hot shower and settled onto the bed with some reading material she'd brought for the plane. She made it through two pages before drifting off to sleep.

She dreamed of making love to Lucas Donlon and woke feeling guilty about not having told him she was leaving, not saying good-bye, or even leaving a message. She usually wasn't so cowardly. Maybe she'd call tonight. Talk to him from the safety of several hundred miles distance. She could always claim she'd decided at the last minute, and tell him truthfully that she'd been so tired when she arrived last night that she'd fallen straight into bed.

Logging onto her laptop, she checked the website for Alex Carmichael's gallery. A new show had opened yesterday, but tonight was the big gala opening event. She glanced at the clock and knew she wouldn't make it on time. She had serious bedhead and would need to wash and dry her hair before socializing amongst the trendy types. She shrugged. Better to be fashionably late and look good, than the alternative.

Chapter Twelve

LUCAS WOKE THAT night with a feeling he hadn't had in a very long time—the visceral satisfaction that came from having tasted the blood of his enemy, and knowing he'd struck a powerful blow. He stretched, joints popping with the effort, his muscles feeling loose and relaxed. The only thing he needed now was a beautiful woman in his bed, with both her blood and body hot and pumping for him.

Only one woman came to mind, however. Kathryn Hunter. She thought she could hide from him. She clearly didn't understand who and what he was. He rolled over and snagged his cell phone, punching up Nick.

"Sire," Nick answered at once, sounding as if he'd just woken. Which he had.

"Can we track Kathryn's cell phone?"

"Probably, but I'm not sure we want to. The phone she uses is government-issue, and she *is* FBI, my lord."

"Right. What about the rental car then? Don't they all have transponders these days?"

"They do, and we can. I already made note of the rental company she used, so it won't take long. I'll get our people on it."

Lucas disconnected and threw the phone down. He lay back on the pillows and began stroking his cock lazily, pumping his fist up and down as he remembered the taste and feel of Kathryn. She thought to escape him by running, but he was Vampire, the ultimate predator. And for a true predator, there was nothing more exciting than the hunt. Especially one with the promise of blood and sex at the end. He groaned as he climaxed, his seed spilling between his fingers and over his clenched fist. And he knew that before the night was over, the only fist around his cock would be the silken heat of Kathryn Hunter.

KATHRYN STARED at the questionable example of cubism on the wall of Carmichael's gallery and wondered how the same gallery that showcased her brother's photography could also feature this. Even as she thought it, she knew it was stupid. Alex Carmichael would probably sneer at her and tell her that a person of taste recognized it in whatever form it took. She didn't know about taste, but she did know that many of the world's premier museums hung all sorts of work, from Monet to Andy Warhol and everything in between. Still, she stared at the oil painting in front of her with its bold colors and puzzling composition, and couldn't make it work. She snuck a sideways look at the price tag and decided it was just as well, since it was far beyond her decorating budget.

She smiled, thinking that Dan would have chided her, saying that art was not for *decoration.* Her smile disappeared as she glanced around the crowded gallery. She'd come here hoping to find Alex Carmichael. More than ever, she was convinced he was the key to her brother's disappearance. But so far, he was a no-show, and the champagne was beginning to dwindle.

She tapped her foot impatiently, wondering if she should give up and go back to her hotel.

"What do you think?"

Kathryn nearly jumped out of her shoes at the question. Jarred out of her thoughts, she turned to stare at the man who had somehow sidled up to stand right next to her without her even noticing.

Great instincts, Hunter. Good thing he's only interested in art.

She glanced in his direction, and they shared a smile. He was nicely dressed, with short, dark hair, and not at all bad-looking. Two days ago, she probably would have called him handsome. But that was before Lucas Donlon had destroyed her perceptions of male beauty forever. She turned her attention back to the painting so her fellow art lover wouldn't notice the scowl brought on by that last thought.

"It's . . . rather bold, isn't it?" she commented, trying to be sociable. The observation was ambiguous enough that it could be admiration or criticism, whichever he preferred.

"It is," he agreed enthusiastically.

Admiration it is, she thought to herself.

"I love the color in this work," the man continued. "Too many cubists lack the courage of their art. This says boldly, 'This is who I am, take it or leave it.'"

Kathryn stared at the oil painting and nodded, though she personally thought it said something more along the lines of, "I never moved beyond the small box of crayons."

A ripple of movement across the room caught her eye as Francoise, Alex's perky assistant, touched the tiny Bluetooth device in her ear and abruptly took *perky* to a whole new level. The woman had been working the crowds all evening, apparently playing hostess in her boss's absence. Kathryn had noticed her eyeing the door more than once and had optimistically guessed that Alex himself would soon make an appearance.

And now Francoise was *finally* hurrying eagerly toward the entrance.

Kathryn felt her own excitement pitching higher in anticipation as she followed Francoise's eager progress and saw three big, black SUVs pull up out front. Ignoring the valet attendant, they parked at the curb, one in front of the other. Doors popped open and bodyguards spilled onto the sidewalk like a SWAT team, but wearing nicely tailored suits instead. One of them came around from the street side, and Kathryn got her first good look at him.

Her stomach plummeted. It was Nicholas, which could only mean one thing.

Kathryn shifted slightly to the right, so she was no longer in direct sight of the front door. It was easy enough, since most of the gallery goers were shuffling the other direction, going *toward* the doors to get a better look at the new arrival who they clearly understood was someone important, maybe even famous. From the whispered conversations all around her, they didn't know exactly who it was, but speculation ran the gamut from a movie star to the mayor or the president. No one seemed to think it was Alex, but then Kathryn already knew that. It was a vampire all right, but not the one she had come here to find.

Outside, Nicholas took a last look up and down the street, then opened the back door of the middle SUV. And there he was. Lucas Donlon in all his glory, looking devastatingly handsome in a black wool suit, with the thinnest gray pinstripe, and a bronze silk tie with some tiny gold pattern gleaming against his white shirt. His too-long black hair was neatly combed away from his face so that he was the very image of a successful Wall Street titan. He was perfect. Damn him.

Over at the front door, Francoise was beside herself with joy. She waited right in front of the glass door like a child who'd just spotted Santa. Her face was glowing, her hands clasped and tucked under her chin, as if she couldn't contain her excitement.

Two of the bodyguards entered first—Kathryn recognized Mason as one of them—and then Nicholas and Lucas behind him. Obviously well versed in vampire protocol, Francoise waited until Lucas approached her, and then she gushed like a schoolgirl.

"Lord Donlon, this is such an honor!"

Get a grip, woman, Kathryn thought sourly, shifting again to put more people between her and Lucas, concealing her while still letting her see everything.

"Who do you think that is?" her art lover companion asked.

Kathryn glanced at him, irritated at the distraction. She'd forgotten he was there. Fortunately, he'd spoken without looking at her because, like everyone else in the gallery, he couldn't take his eyes off Lucas. "I have no idea," she all but snarled in his direction.

"Francoise," Lucas crooned, drawing Kathryn's attention back to the spectacle. "Don't you look lovely this evening."

Sickening. He probably says that to every woman he meets.

Francoise tittered, her cheeks lighting up like stop signs.

"Is Alex around?" Lucas asked, scanning the gallery.

Sneak. Liar. Sneaky liar. He's probably been communicating with Alex this whole time.

"No, my lord," the assistant was saying. "I expected him, but—"

"Francoise, love, call me Lucas. And I think I'll just look around myself, if that's all right."

"Of course, Lucas. Just . . ." She stretched up closer to his ear and whispered something too softly for Kathryn to make out. Whatever it was made Lucas chuckle. He stroked his hand down the woman's skinny arm, which had her positively beaming with pleasure.

"Let me get the show catalogue for you," she said breathlessly.

It's a wonder she can speak with her tongue hanging out like that, Kathryn thought viciously. She watched Francoise mince her way over to pick up one of the glossy catalogues. *And what's with the 'Francoise, love' crap? Lucas was such a fucking dog. She'd absolutely done the right thing in—*

"The dress looks much better without the leggings," Lucas observed from right next to her.

Kathryn cursed her stupidity. She'd been so focused on Francoise that she'd forgotten the biggest threat in the room. She should have slipped out the back door the moment she recognized Nicholas coming around the SUV. Assuming this stupid gallery had a back door. But it had to have one somewhere. There was a fire code. Not that it mattered, because she'd let herself get so distracted that Lucas had somehow managed to sneak up on her. Fucking vampire.

"Lucas," she managed to say. She turned to face him, meeting his gaze head-on. Which was her second mistake of the evening. His eyes were more gold than hazel tonight, and they were filled with a mixture of hurt and reproach. The reproach she could have dealt with, but the hurt . . . Damn him.

"I didn't expect to see you here," she said.

"Obviously. Who's your friend?"

"Friend?" she repeated, puzzled, then remembered the art lover. "Oh. That guy? I have no idea. Someone who doesn't understand color, that's for sure."

Lucas gave her a smug smile, and she realized belatedly that she should have lied, should have let him know he wasn't the only handsome man in the world who was interested in her. And in the next breath, she cursed herself for the traitorous thought. What did she care if Lucas was jealous or not?

"Kathryn, *a cuisle*, you forgot to mention *when you left my bed* yesterday that you were departing immediately for Minneapolis. Isn't that odd?"

Kathryn narrowed her eyes at him. No, it wasn't fucking odd, and he knew it. "Something came up," she said tightly.

"Really? What?" he replied, his anger rising to match hers.

"Why do you care?" she demanded.

"Why don't you?"

Kathryn caught her breath. The question struck her to the heart, and she could tell by the satisfied expression on his face that he knew it. She looked away from his accusing gaze and focused on the expensive art instead.

"A big fan of cubism, are you?" Lucas murmured in her ear.

He was standing far too close, but Kathryn refused to move and let him know it bothered her. "What do *you* know about it?" she muttered.

He laughed softly. "Probably more than you do. I'd wager your brother's the only artist in *your* family."

"Why do you say that?" she demanded, vaguely insulted, even though he was right.

"Because *you* are far too buttoned up to be an artist."

"I am not buttoned up," she snapped, still staring fixedly at the poor distorted women in the painting.

"Please. You're the very poster girl for buttoned up."

"You have no idea—"

"Oh, I think I do. I also happen to know that you unbutton very nicely when motivated."

She shot a sideways glare in his direction. "It's hardly appropriate to discuss that—"

"Really? But it's okay for you to discard me like a used condom and leave town without even saying good-bye?"

Kathryn's mouth dropped open in a gasp, and she turned to stare at him. "I can't believe you said that!" she hissed furiously, her gaze darting around to see if anyone was listening.

Lucas faced her, his eyes snapping gold sparks. "And I can't believe you left me."

They were standing toe-to-toe, so close that all Kathryn would have to do was raise up on the balls of her feet, and their mouths would meet. She knew what he would taste like, knew the feel of his hard chest against her breasts, the span of his hands as they circled her hips while he drove himself between her thighs.

She drew back, shocked at her own thoughts. Thoughts she could see mirrored in Lucas's fierce gaze.

"Where's your truck?" he growled.

She swallowed on a dry throat. "I took a cab."

"Fine. We'll take mine."

"Lucas—" she started, then stopped when he turned to stare at her as if daring her to protest.

When she didn't say anything, his expression softened. "We'll talk."

Kathryn nodded and didn't object when he took her hand and headed for the front door. Her fingers slipped into his as naturally as if they'd been holding hands for years instead of a single day.

She was doomed.

Chapter Thirteen

THEY BARELY SPOKE on the ride to Lucas's penthouse. Kathryn was painfully aware of Nicholas and Mason sitting in the front seat, and she didn't know what to say anyway. Lucas was still holding her hand, pressing it against his thigh, which struck her as terribly intimate. But then, what was more intimate than what they'd done last night?

They crossed a bridge. She didn't know which one. There were so many in the Twin Cities; it seemed almost every street had a bridge. She saw a sign saying they were crossing the Mississippi River, which meant they were probably now in St. Paul. A few more blocks, and all three SUVs made the turn toward a tall glass and steel building that sat nearly on the riverfront. Parking was underground, with the entrance protected by a human guard, as well as a solid steel barrier. Someone in the front SUV clicked the remote, the barrier rose, and the garage swallowed them whole.

Lucas apparently had some pull with the owners' association, because they pulled into the three parking spaces closest to the elevator. As soon as they stopped, the other two SUVs emptied out, with vampires deploying throughout the garage. One of them punched the call button for the elevator, then stepped inside and checked it out before holding the door open and giving a nodding okay.

Lucas opened his door and stepped out into the garage without ever letting go of Kathryn's hand. She frowned, especially when she had to balance herself to get out of the SUV, but he didn't look at her, just shifted his grip and waited.

Kathryn sighed. He was going to be difficult about this. She just knew it.

He didn't say a word until they were in his penthouse. It was on the top floor, of course, with dynamite views of the river on one side and what she assumed was the Capitol building on the other.

"Beautiful," she commented.

Lucas still didn't say anything, although he did release her hand to head for the wet bar on the far wall. They were completely alone. Some of the vampires in his security contingent had stayed on the ground floor. Others had peeled off on the floor just below this one. Only Nicholas rode all the way to the top with them. He'd checked out the entire condo, then gotten back into the elevator and presumably joined the others somewhere. Kathryn had studied his face covertly, looking for evidence of the ghastly wound he'd been sporting only two days ago. There was nothing. He was completely healed, just as Lucas had told her he would be.

Lucas poured himself a drink at the bar and strolled back to where she was standing in front of the window overlooking the river.

"What happened, Kathryn?" he asked quietly.

She gave him a quick glance. "I don't know what you mean," she lied.

"Let me refresh your memory, then. You fucked my brains out night before last—"

"I told you I had things to do. I drove all day yesterday to get here—"

"—and apparently you couldn't wait to get out of town. I talked to the motel manager. You must have gone directly there from my bed, then packed up and left with the sun barely above the horizon."

"And what do you mean I fucked *your* brains out?" she snapped, seizing on the one thing she could dispute, since everything else he'd said was pretty damn accurate. "I wasn't the only one in that bed, Lucas. Brains were fucked, and fun was had by all."

Unexpectedly, he grinned. "You missed me, didn't you? Oh sure, the first couple of hours you were just focused on getting away, but then you started thinking, doubting . . . and you missed me. Did you dream about me?"

Kathryn's jaw clenched. "Arrogant," she muttered.

He laughed. "Yeah, but I'm right."

She rounded on him. "Why are you here? Why Carmichael's gallery?"

Lucas took a leisurely sip of his whiskey, eyeing her over the top of the crystal tumbler. When he lowered it, he said, "I would think that's obvious."

"You're . . . conspiring with him," she accused. "With Carmichael."

"No, *a cuisle*, I've been hunting." He turned and set down his drink on the marble inlay of a nearby table.

"What does *acushla* mean, damn it! What are you calling me?" She frowned as the rest of his words caught up to her. "Wait, what do you mean hunting. Hunting what?"

Lucas wrapped his long fingers around her hip and tugged her up against his body. "It's not a what, it's a who. A certain FBI agent." He lowered his mouth to hers.

Kathryn intended to resist him. She wasn't going to kiss him, and she certainly wasn't going to grab him like a starving female and rub up against him wantonly. But that's what happened. One second she was determined to walk away, and the next they were inhaling each other's oxygen, kissing hungrily, biting and licking, her arms around his neck, his fingers twisted into her unbound hair, wrapping it around his fist and tilting her head back to plunder her mouth. And his other hand . . . her breath stalled in her lungs as his other hand crushed her hips against his so she could feel every inch of his erection, long and thick and as hard as stone against her belly.

LUCAS FELT A curl of satisfaction as Kathryn moaned a protest against his lips. "I don't want—" she began, even as she sucked his tongue into her mouth.

"I know," he muttered back. "Neither do I." But he couldn't stop. There was something about her, something that drove him mad, like a hot poker stuck straight into his fucking brain. He *had* to have her, desperately needed her beneath him, her hot pussy soaking wet as it sheathed his cock over and over again.

"Damn it," he swore softly and tugged her tight black dress up over her hips.

"Wait!" Kathryn protested weakly. "The window."

"It's one-way," Lucas ground out and stripped the dress off over her head. He hissed when he saw what she was wearing underneath. Gone was the sensible white cotton bra, and in its place, pale silk and lace, barely cupping her full breasts, with a tiny matching lace triangle between her thighs.

"You've been shopping," he said, rubbing one hand over her firm and practically naked ass, while he caressed her breast with the other, thumbing her pink nipple until it poked out against its silky enclosure.

Kathryn was working determinedly on his belt buckle, ripping open the button to his pants and sliding the zipper down. He stiffened, in more ways than one, when she took him in her hand, her graceful and strong fingers gripping him tightly as she began to stroke up and down.

"That's your fault," she complained. "You made me feel ugly with my white bra."

"You could never be ugly, *a cuisle*. I rather liked it, actually, though I do like this better. Now tell me," he tugged her long hair, forcing her to look up at him. "Who did you think was going to see this beautiful and sexy new underwear?"

She smiled innocently, but the gleam in her eyes gave her away. "Jealous?"

Lucas acknowledged the feeling. It wasn't something he felt very often, but she was right. He *was* jealous. He didn't know how long this obsession between them was going to last, but as long as it did, no one was touching her but him.

"Never," he lied. "But I'm a possessive son of a bitch, Kathryn. As long as we're doing whatever this is, no one but me gets to see your underwear." He lowered his mouth to her neck and bit softly.

"Oh, ah," she said, her breath coming in pants. "What if I—"

Whatever she was going to say was lost in her gasp of surprise as he slipped two fingers between the wet folds of her sex. Jesus, she was hot. Slick and silky and so ready for him.

"That's it," he growled. He pushed her against the wall next to the window and ripped away her new lace panties, tossing them aside. Shoving his pants down and freeing his cock, he lifted her up and slid between her legs. She responded just as eagerly, wrapping her legs around his waist, her arms over his shoulders as their mouths met once again, kissing hungrily. Lucas sank his cock into her creamy center, feeling the warmth of her body surround him, her channel so tight, her trembling inner muscles caressing him as he thrust as deeply as he could. He paused for the space of a breath, holding perfectly still, feeling the pulsing of her pussy all around him, her heart pounding against his chest, her breath warm and moist along his cheek. They hung there for a long moment. And then he started moving, slowly at first, easing himself in and out, relishing the satin glide of her juices along his shaft. With a long, slow thrust, he plunged as deeply as he could go, feeling the touch of her cervix against the head of his cock. Kathryn made a noise deep in her throat and did a little ripple of her shoulder muscles from side to side, like a cat that's had a taste of catnip. One side of his mouth lifted in a grin. He liked that—the idea that he was her catnip. Kathryn's eyes flashed open to meet his, and it was kindling to the flame. Suddenly, he had to have her, had to hear her screaming his name. He growled and began slamming in and out of her body, not going for finesse but for completion. He needed to spill inside her, to mark her in a way that no one else could.

Kathryn was making little noises with every thrust of his cock, gripping his shoulders and digging in with her fingers until he knew he'd have bruises by the end of the night. It made him happy. He wanted to carry her mark, too. He lowered his mouth to her jugular, feeling the plump vein beneath his tongue, the rush of her blood, faster now as her heart began to dance in anticipation.

"Lucas, Lucas . . ." she was moaning now, a lover's plea as he fucked her hard and deep.

"Kathryn," he whispered, and sank his fangs into her vein, pushing past the slight resistance of her soft skin, the thin wall of her pliant vein, and then her blood was rushing down his throat like dark honey, heated and smooth.

Kathryn's legs scissored around his hips, her nails scraping his back. Her pussy clenched around him as the orgasm rolled through her body, her blunt teeth sinking into his shoulder as she screamed, her hips bucking against his until he felt his own climax building in his balls, roaring down his shaft and filling her completely.

Lucas retracted his fangs and licked up the last few delicious drops of her blood. He kissed the small puncture wounds, knowing they'd be sealed in seconds and completely healed in hours. Kathryn hung onto him, her arms limp around his neck, her legs trembling in reaction to their explosive lovemaking.

He glanced down at himself and chuckled. He was still more than half dressed. His pants were around his ankles, and at some point his shirt had been ripped open, but he still wore his jacket, and his tie was still in place. Kathryn lifted her head at the sound of his laughter. She followed his gaze and started laughing, too. Until he saw a tear drip from her eye.

"Kathryn?"

"What is it between us, Lucas? It's like . . ."

"Spontaneous combustion," he supplied. "Fire and gun powder. I get near you, and I have to touch you. I touch you, and I have to be inside you. Not later, but right *now.*"

"Exactly," she agreed. "Sort of. I mean, in my head, I'm saying *no thanks* and walking away, and the next thing I know I'm all over you."

"So, it's all your fault, then."

"How do you figure *that?*"

"Vampires are predators, Kathryn. When you run, my instinct is to run after you, and I can run a hell of a lot faster. So if you'd just throw yourself at me first thing—"

"In your dreams, asshole," she snapped, rapping her knuckles on the back of his head.

"Ow," Lucas said, laughing. "You've got some muscles, woman. And speaking of muscles . . ." He palmed her butt with both hands, lifting her higher. Kathryn's eyes widened as if just realizing they were standing the way they'd ended, with him buried between her lovely, long legs which were still wrapped around him.

Her face heated. "Oh, my God. This is what you do. Look at me! I'm up against a *wall!* Naked! And in full view of whoever happens by—"

"I told you. The glass is one-way."

"Whatever. Put me down, you big oaf."

"*Oaf* she says now. That's not what you called me when you were creaming all over me a moment ago."

"Lucas!"

"What?"

"You can't just say things like . . . I thought we agreed this attraction between us was unhealthy. You know, the whole fire and gunpowder thing?"

"I never agreed to any such thing. It is definitely explosive, however. A fast-burning flame. And the best way to deal with that is to let it burn out naturally. We need to spend several days having wild sex in every way imaginable. You know, to get rid of this unhealthy impulse."

"You would think that. Besides, we tried that the other night as I recall. It obviously didn't work."

"Pfft. That was nothing, my sweet. A flame this hot needs more than a single night."

"You're just trying to get me back into your bed."

"I don't need you in my bed; I already have you up against my wall."

She blushed again. He loved making her blush.

"I wish you wouldn't say things like that."

"Like what? Are you not up against my wall?"

"Lucas," she began sternly, then gasped as he began moving inside her, taking advantage of the moisture from her recent orgasm which had left her pussy warm and creamy and perfectly lubricated.

"Shall we set fire to the wall, *a cuisle*, or would you rather use the bed? It's a very nice bed."

Kathryn didn't answer right away. Her eyes were closed, her expression dreamy as he glided slowly in and out of her sexy body. She licked her lips slowly, and it was Lucas's turn to groan.

"You're killing me here, Kathryn. If you want to move to the bed, tell me now, or it's going to be too late."

Her eyes fluttered open. "Bed," she managed.

Cursing the undignified position he found himself in—only Kathryn could have driven him so insanely hungry so quickly that he left his shoes on, his pants around his ankles—he nonetheless cowboyed up and delivered. Unwilling to pull away from Kathryn's welcoming heat, he cupped her ass with his hands, holding her in place as he toed off his shoes, then stepped out of his slacks, leaving them in a pile on the floor. Kathryn's legs tightened around him as he carried her to the bedroom, their mouths feeding on each other as if they hadn't just brought each other to mutually screaming orgasms moments earlier. She was right about one thing. This attraction between them was hotter than any he'd experienced in his long life. And he could see it ending only one of two ways—either they'd stick for a while, maybe a very long while, although he wasn't willing to go too far down that path, even in his thoughts. Or they'd burn out quickly and end up hating each other.

Either way, he thought, as he laid her on the bed and proceeded to strip off his jacket, shirt and tie while still managing to keep his cock buried inside her, he intended to have her in his bed every night as long as it lasted.

KATHRYN SCRAPED her fingers through the fine, black hair on Lucas's chest. Lucas's hard, muscular, gorgeous chest. Why couldn't he have been a troll instead of a god? She'd have been in and out of South Dakota, no looking back, eyes straight ahead and looking for her brother, and then back to Quantico. Instead, she was all twisted up in vampires and secrets and one *gorgeous* lover. And, sure, she was making some headway in finding Daniel, but she was losing her heart in the process. She sighed.

"Whatever you're thinking, stop it," Lucas grumbled, his deep voice sated and sluggish.

"Who says I'm thinking anything?"

"You sighed."

"I breathed."

He laughed. "If I said the sky was blue, you'd say it was green. Though, I haven't seen the daylight sky in so long, it might well *be* green by now."

"The sky is still blue. And I'm not that bad."

"Oh, aye, you are. But I lo . . . can't keep my hands off you anyway."

Kathryn heard the catch in his sentence and wondered what he'd been about to say. She thought about possibilities and found herself smiling goofily. She hit the brakes hard on that thought. Time to change the subject.

"So, how old are you?" she said quickly. "I mean, you told me the other day that only lovers could ask that question, but I'm pretty sure I qualify now."

"No doubt of that."

"So, fess up, old man. How old?"

"I was born in Kildare, Ireland in 1785."

Kathryn blinked. "But that makes you," she did some quick math in her head, but Lucas beat her to it.

"Two hundred and twenty-seven years old, give or take a month. I was born in winter, that's all I know."

Kathryn sat up, staring at him in disbelief.

"You must have had some idea," he said, gazing back at her calmly.

"No. I mean, well, yeah. But . . . I don't think anybody, at least not anybody in authority, knows you're that old. I mean . . look at you! I know twenty-year-olds who don't look this good! Are all of you that old?" She knew she was rambling, but couldn't stop herself.

Lucas only grinned. "You think I look good?"

Trust him to pick out the one flattering thing she'd said. "You have a mirror," she said dismissively. "And I'm sure you spend plenty of time in front of it, too. So don't pretend you don't know what I'm talking about."

"Fine," he replied, sounding completely put upon. "No, not every vampire is the same age as I am."

"Are you never serious?"

"Believe me, Kathryn. I can be deadly serious when the situation calls for it. But lying in bed, naked, with a beautiful woman I've just fucked until she screamed my name—" He laughed when Kathryn gave him a threatening glare. "—is not normally a time that calls for solemnity. However. Just for you, *a cuisle*."

He pushed himself up on the pillows and put his hands behind his head. "There are many vampires younger than I am, and a very few who are much, much older. The important thing to remember when dealing with vampires, Kathryn, is that age and power are not necessarily the same thing. I'm two hundred and twenty-seven, and that seems old. But I have several vampires in my territory who are far older than that, and they are sworn to my service because I protect *them*, not the other way around. If one of them were to challenge me, he'd be dead before he got the words out. That's how it works. Humans speak of leaders holding the lives of their followers in their hands, but with vampires, it is quite literally true. My vampires have blood in their veins and air in their lungs because I make it possible."

Kathryn studied this new, serious Lucas. If all one saw was the public face, the handsome playboy charming his way through a crowd, it would be easy to underestimate Lucas Donlon. Fatally easy.

"How does it happen?" she asked softly.

He gave her a puzzled look.

"How does someone become a vampire? Is it like the books?"

"I suppose that would depend on which book."

"All right. How did *you* become a vampire, then?"

"Ah. Now *that's* a long story." He reached out a well-muscled arm and flicked the tip of one of her nipples. "If you come back here," he added, dropping his arm to her waist and tugging her toward him. "I'll tell you."

Kathryn gave a mock scowl and cupped her breast protectively, mostly for effect since Lucas never did anything that hurt her, not even in the deepest throes of their passion.

Lucas responded by leaning forward and taking the offended nipple in his mouth, kissing it gently and swirling his tongue over and around in a soothing caress.

"Better?" he murmured.

Kathryn could barely breathe. Some emotion she'd never felt before was squeezing her chest like a straitjacket. She stroked her fingers through his unruly hair, then nodded wordlessly, and let him tug her down into his arms. "Tell me the story," she whispered, knowing, even as she asked, that she was playing with fire, that with every word that passed his sensuous lips, she'd be sucked deeper into the flame that was Lucas Donlon.

Chapter Fourteen

1801, London, England

LUCAS DONLON SIDLED through the crowds in the busy square, his practiced eye searching for the next mark, the next fool. That's what they all were. Fools. Clustered mindlessly around the opera house forecourt, without the sense God gave a mongrel dog. At least a dog was smart enough to guard its treasure, even if it was only a tasty bone.

He scrambled up to the roof of a nearby building and crouched low, smiling privately at the image of himself as a mongrel dog among the sheep below. He'd always wanted a dog, but when his mam had been alive, she hadn't wanted the mess, and once she'd died . . . well, he'd had enough trouble keeping himself fed, much less a dog. And there was Dublin's Constabulary to contend with. They'd tried more than once to throw him into one of those priest-run prisons for wayward boys. He'd preferred to take his chances on the streets. At least there he was free—free to keep the few coppers he managed to earn running errands for the whores who'd been his dead mother's companions at the end of her life. Free to steal whatever else he could get his hands on.

Inevitably, he'd run afoul of the Constabulary one too many times and been forced to leave Ireland behind. And not without a few looks back, either. Ireland was his home, but he'd promised himself that he'd return someday when he was a rich man. He'd be wearing fine clothes and riding a beautiful horse like those his grandfather had owned. He only hoped that heartless old man was there to witness it.

Lucas pushed aside thoughts of the grandfather who'd left him and his mother to starve on the streets. The old man was *An Tiarna* of his own lands. His servants lived better than what he'd abandoned his own flesh and blood to endure.

Lucas surveyed the milling crowd. He was still as thin as ever—his meals weren't regular enough for anything else—but at sixteen he was too tall to slip easily through the crowd as he'd once done, plucking purses at will. He had to choose his target more carefully these days, had to move decisively, make the grab and get away with no one the wiser. Because he was too old for a boys' home. If he was caught now, it would be prison for him, and for a very long time, too.

His eye fell on a tall man, black-haired like Lucas himself, but with eyes just as black as his hair. He stood out even in this fancy gathering, supremely arrogant in an arrogant crowd. The man was dressed finely, his breeches clean and tucked into shining, knee-high leather boots. His gleaming white waistcoat was richly embroidered, and his coat was the finest wool, expertly tailored to fit such a big man. The only flaw in this sartorial splendor was the absence of a hat, as though he disdained the need to hide or shelter beneath its brim. All of that said money and position to Lucas's well-trained eye. Unfortunately, his well-trained *brain* was telling him there was something not right about this one. He didn't have the look of the other fools, with their eyes everywhere but where they should be. Lucas's experience was telling him that not much slipped by this dark-eyed stranger.

The man called something over the heads of the crowd, and Lucas turned to look. Another aristocrat, nearly as tall as the dark one, but pale instead, with hair as red as any Lucas had seen on the streets of Dublin. Lucas strained to hear what was said, but they were speaking a strange tongue, and he couldn't understand a single word. The pale man responded in the same language.

Foreigners, then. Lucas grinned. What a feat it would be to steal a purse from this one. None of his thieving friends in the rickety hovel they called their own had ever managed such a grab. It was risky, but he was certain the purse would contain enough coins to make it worthwhile.

Lucas's gaze followed his new target, observing the way the foreigner moved among the crowd, the way his clothes shifted around his purse, and the purse itself. Well-crafted leather, but with a narrow strap that would fall easily to the small, sharp knife Lucas carried up his sleeve. He studied the mark longer than he normally would have. With most of his marks, he could simply slip up behind them, dip a hand into a satchel or slice a strap, and be gone before the fool even knew he'd been there.

But when the purse was rich enough, one had to be extra cautious. Such people frequently had companions or even guards to be wary of. It paid to take a few moments and observe.

With this man, this tall, dark foreigner, he'd take those few moments and more.

Lucas finally made his move when the bells sounded, and the mingling gentry began shuffling toward the front doors of the opera house. He swiftly descended from the roof and hung back in the alley, scanning the crowd one last time, checking the location of the various watchmen who always lingered nearby. Once set upon his course, however, he didn't hesitate. He moved through the crowd with the ease of long experience, dropped the knife into his hand, strolled up to the mark and slid the knife beneath the strap of the foreigner's purse. A flick of his wrist and . . .

Long fingers curled around his wrist with surprising strength. Lucas raised his eyes in shock and met the cold, black gaze of the dark man. The man smiled, and it chilled Lucas to the bone.

"I believe that's mine," the man said, his voice deep, the English words heavily accented.

Lucas clenched his jaw and stood to his full height, straightening his shoulders. If he was going to go down, he'd do it with a man's dignity.

The dark man's expression warmed fractionally. "I've been looking for a boy," he said. "You'll do."

"I'm no boy," Lucas spat back at him.

The man laughed. "No, you're not. But you'll do anyway."

"AND THAT'S HOW I met Raphael," Lucas said, running a hand up and down Kathryn's arm.

She waited for him to continue, frowning when he didn't.

"What's the rest of the story?" she demanded.

He shrugged. "That's it."

"But what about the vampire part?"

"The vampire part?" he repeated, laughing.

"Stop it." She pinched his stomach, or tried to. Lucas's washboard abs didn't leave much to pinch. "I want to know how he turned you into a vampire. And when. Because you don't look sixteen years old, bud. I don't sleep with babies, no matter how old they really are."

"So far you haven't slept with me, either," he murmured, nuzzling her jaw while one hand snuck up to cup her breast.

Kathryn turned into his embrace, unable to help herself. Every time he touched her, her body responded, as if it was programmed into her genes. She curved one leg around his thigh and began stroking herself along his hip.

Lucas made a rumbling sound deep in his chest and bent to suck gently on her neck. Kathryn shivered. She put her lips next to his ear and whispered, "Tell me when you became a vampire."

Lucas slapped her ass playfully and pulled away from her to lie back on the pillows. "Why do you want to know?"

"Because I'm curious. How does it work?"

"I'm not going to tell you that. If you ever become a vampire, you'll find out. If not—" He tugged a length of her hair. "—you won't. Which, as far as I'm concerned, means you'll never know. I like you just the way you are."

"Spoilsport. I hate secrets."

Lucas laughed again. "We all have them, *a cuisle*. Even you."

Kathryn scowled at the Irish endearment. He never *had* told her what it meant, but she didn't want to derail their current conversation to ask, so she let it slide.

"Well, at least tell me what happened after that night," she said instead.

Lucas gave a dismissive shrug. "Raphael needed someone to be his daytime eyes and ears. It wasn't like now, with everything done on the Internet and all sorts of places open twenty-four hours a day. Someone had to deal with the hundred and one things necessary to running a household, things that needed doing during the day. Even vampires need clothing and supplies, and there were social necessities, mail and such. Invitations to events like the opera. Raphael and his people weren't high profile, but they travelled in very ritzy circles."

"So you were his errand boy."

"Something like that."

"For how long?"

"How old do I look to you?"

"Twenty-seven," Kathryn said immediately.

"Close enough. After a few years, Raphael decided to leave Europe. I went with him, of course. There was nothing left for me in England, or Ireland, either. And my life with Raphael had been better than anything I'd known before that. For the first time, I wasn't hungry every night. I had a clean, safe place to sleep and decent clothes to wear. So, I booked ship passage for all of us and dealt with the captain and crew, safeguarding the vampires as they slept, and arranging quiet *encounters* at night so the vampires could feed discreetly. Once we arrived in America, Raphael gave me a choice. I chose to become what I am."

"What if you'd chosen otherwise? What would he have done?"

"He'd have kept me on as his daylight guard, or given me enough money to set myself up doing whatever else I decided. Loyalty is important to him."

Kathryn studied him for a moment, surprised by the honest emotion she heard in his voice when he talked about Raphael.

"You love him."

Lucas nodded. "He's my Sire. That's the most important relationship any vampire has, unless he takes a mate. Even then, the two—Sire and mate—are equally significant to him. But more than that, Raphael was the first person, other than my mother, who ever treated me like I was worth something. I would give my life for his without hesitation."

"Well, please don't."

"Don't what?"

"Don't give your life away." She looked up and held his gaze so he'd know she was serious, but then, feeling the need to take a step back, she added, "I'm using it right now."

Lucas regarded her intently. A slow smile curved his lips, and he said, "No promises. But if you're nice to me, I'll do the best I can."

"I *am* nice to you."

"I meant . . . right *now.*"

Kathryn felt something hard brush against her hip. "Oh, that," she said playfully. "I'm sure I can come up with something nice for *that.*"

DANIEL WOKE TO the sound of voices. He lay still, afraid to move, not wanting whoever it was to hear him and stop talking. There'd never been anyone but his kidnapper before. No one for either of them to talk to but each other. But now . . . yes, that was definitely a woman's voice.

His breath caught as he hoped, briefly, that it was Kathryn, that she'd found him, and the FBI was going to break in with guns blazing. Or at least with badges flashing since it didn't sound like there was much shooting going on out there. But it wasn't Kathryn. Her voice was much huskier than this woman's, sexier, or so his friends told him. She was his sister. He didn't want to think about whether her voice or anything else about her was sexy.

The woman out there, whoever she was, was agitated, her voice rising in volume and emotion.

"I'm telling you, that FBI bitch is cozying up to Lucas, and that's not good."

"Maybe you're just jealous. You've always had a thing for him."

"Fuck you!" the woman snapped. "Besides, they left together. How's that for proof?"

"Whatever," his kidnapper muttered. "What difference does it make?"

"We need to end this. You never told me his sister was a fucking FBI agent."

"How the hell was I supposed to know something like that?"

"If you'd hit up his business agent right away, like we discussed, it wouldn't matter. We'd have the ransom, and this whole thing would be over already."

"There's more to this than money, for God's sake."

"Not for me there's not! Especially now that Lucas is involved. I'm not risking my life so you can get your rocks off with your boyfriend in there."

"He's not my boyfriend. He's an artist."

"Yeah, well, he's a *rich* artist, and I'm sending the ransom demand before it's too late."

"No!" the man said immediately. "I mean, not yet. I need to make a phone call later tonight. Then we'll work something out."

Daniel grinned. So Kathryn *was* looking for him. He'd known she wouldn't give up easily. A door slammed outside the room. It was a little distant, like down a long hallway, and the noise usually meant his captor was leaving for a while. In this case, he thought it was probably the woman leaving, but had the man gone with her? But no, a key turned in the door lock, so someone was still here. He steadied his breathing, feigning sleep. It was a skill he'd perfected over his weeks of captivity, and he was quite good at it. For some reason, the man was always reluctant to wake him. Maybe he thought an artist needed his sleep or some crap. Daniel didn't know and didn't care. If it kept his admirer away from him, it was a good thing.

The door opened slowly. Daniel could feel him standing there, staring at him, but he was used to it and didn't move. A moment later, the door closed, but he remained still. His captor tested him sometimes, popping the door open quickly, trying to catch him. It had worked the first time he'd tried it, but not since then, because Daniel wasn't a fucking idiot. Although he was beginning to think his *kidnapper* might not be playing with a full deck.

The lock clicked solidly into place, and footsteps moved away. The distant door slammed, and Daniel was alone once again.

LUCAS FELT THE bed shift as Kathryn left. He cracked his eyes open and saw her gathering her clothes, sneaking looks over her shoulder. Did she really know so little about vampires? He didn't sleep, not the way humans did. Not at night, anyway. And his daytime sleep was more like unconsciousness, at least physically. His mind could be active, but his body would refuse to cooperate.

Kathryn tiptoed out of the bedroom while Lucas fumed. This was getting to be a habit, and one he didn't appreciate in a lover. He followed silently, stepping into the living room as she pulled the black dress over her head.

"Kathryn."

She jumped at the sound of his voice, spinning around and almost falling as she struggled to get the dress pulled down far enough that she could see him. She would have fallen if he hadn't caught her.

She slapped away his hands, giving him an angry look. "That wasn't funny."

"None of this is funny," he snapped back at her. "I thought we were past the sneaking-out phase of our relationship."

"Relationship? Is that you call this?"

"Well, what the hell do you call it?"

She took a step forward and got up in his face. "We're having sex. And, frankly, I shouldn't even be doing that. I'm supposed to be looking for my brother, not rolling around in bed with you."

"You *are* looking for your brother, but even you can't do it twenty-four hours a damn day."

"I need to find Alex Carmichael, and I'm beginning to think no one wants me to talk to him, including you."

"Is that right?" Lucas snarled. "News flash, Agent Hunter. I've had my people looking for him ever since you told me he left with your brother. I want him found just as much as you do."

Kathryn matched his angry stare at first, then seemed to deflate as she stepped back and sank onto the couch. "I need to find Alex, Lucas."

Lucas crouched in front of her and took her hands. "I know, *a cuisle*. And we will. He can't hide forever."

"What if he's left town? You said he had a different master. Will he go to him?"

"Possibly. Although Alex set himself up in Minneapolis for a reason. I think he prefers living here."

"I don't understand any of this. I don't understand how all of you can live in this country and not be in the system. There are no prints on file for him anywhere. He owns a business, but there are no permits, no ownership documents. The building where his gallery's located is owned by a corporation that's nested so deeply, it would take months for me to track it back to the real owner. If this was an official investigation, I could put some techs on it, but it's just me, and I can't find him."

She looked up, her eyes filled with tears. "I need to find him, Lucas." A tear rolled down her cheek, and she froze, immediately turning her head and hiding behind her hair. No emotion, no feelings. Not for his Kathryn.

Lucas sighed. "I've put feelers out everywhere I can think of. And Alex knows me. He'll call as soon as he gets word that I'm looking for him."

"I thought you all could just—" She sighed impatiently and waved a hand in the air. "You know, telepathy, talk mind to mind."

Lucas fought back a smile, knowing she wouldn't appreciate it. Not in her current state. "If Alex was my child . . . a vampire I had turned myself," he added when she gave him a puzzled look. "If he was one of mine, I could contact him without needing a telephone, so to speak, but he's not."

Kathryn stood abruptly, shoving her hair back. She looked around the room until she spotted her purse, then went over and started pulling things out. Her gun. He hadn't known she'd brought one along, although if he'd given it a thought, he'd have smelled the damn thing. Next came her FBI badge in its small, black portfolio, and finally, a black scrunchy, which was apparently what she was looking for. She finger-combed her hair into a high ponytail and secured it with the scrunchy. Lucas had a few of those himself. He'd been known to go months between haircuts, until his hair irritated him enough that he broke down and got it cut again.

Kathryn turned to face him from across the room, her cheeks scrubbed free of tears. "It must be getting late for you," she said, not looking at him.

Lucas studied her, wondering what event in her life had caused her to withdraw so completely into herself. Wondering if he'd ever find out.

"The sun will rise in . . . forty-five minutes, give or take a minute," he confirmed.

She looked at him then, her eyes wide with surprise. "You can tell that precisely?"

"When your life depends on it, you learn."

He could see she was intrigued. Perhaps that was the way to Kathryn's heart. Give her a mystery to solve. Assuming he wanted to find her heart at all. Maybe he'd be better off taking a page from her playbook. A few nights of wild sex, then good-bye, nice fucking you.

"What will you do today?" he asked her.

She bit her full lower lip, considering. Lucas watched avidly, thinking how much he'd like to be the one doing the biting. He almost missed what she was saying when she finally spoke.

"I don't know that there's anything I *can* do during the day. The only lead I have right now is Alex Carmichael."

Lucas thought about what might happen if Kathryn went looking for a vampire who didn't want to be found. Even one as relatively harmless as Alex.

"Promise you won't go looking for him without me, Kathryn. You don't know what you're dealing with."

She drew a breath, and he could tell she was going to brush him off just like she'd done every other time. But then something changed her mind.

"Okay," she said unexpectedly. "Call me when you're ready to go tonight."

She turned away, but Lucas used his vampire speed to cross the few feet between them, snaking an arm around her waist before she even saw him move. Her eyes widened in shock, but her pupils flared with desire as he tightened his hold.

"I'm ready now, *a cuisle*."

Kathryn's face heated as Lucas flattened his hand over her perfect ass, pressing her against his erection.

"What about—" she began, but her words were cut off as Lucas's house phone rang. He frowned. He wasn't expecting any calls, and certainly not this close to sunrise.

"Saved by the bell," he murmured, then gave her a quick, hard kiss and strode over to the bar to pick up the phone, checking the caller ID as he did so. His eyebrows shot up, and he stilled, listening to Kathryn's footsteps as she walked into the bathroom and closed the door.

He hit the Talk button. "Alex?"

"My lord," Alex Carmichael said breathlessly. "I don't have long. I need to meet with you."

"What's wrong? Do you need help?"

"Not now, my lord," he said, still breathing hard. "There's no time. Can you meet me tomorrow night?"

"Of course. At the gallery?"

"No," Alex said instantly. "Too many ears. I have a property in Saint Louis Park, an old warehouse. It's empty, abandoned. I bought it on spec, but—Forgive me, my lord. You don't care about that. The point is, it's empty. No one will look for us there. I can send you the address."

"Text it," Lucas told him, and gave him Nick's business cell number. "How far is it?"

"Just a few miles, my lord. Fifteen minutes' drive from Minneapolis."

"Two hours after sunset, then. I'll be there."

"Thank you, my lord," Alex said fervently. "Thank you." And then he was gone.

Lucas disconnected with a frown, then immediately called Nick.

"Sire?" Nick answered, sounding just as surprised as Lucas had been when Alex called.

"Alex Carmichael just called."

"That's not possible—Which line?"

"The house phone."

"Where the hell did he get that number?"

"Good question. Better question . . . why does he want to meet me?" He heard the bathroom door open behind him, heard Kathryn's high heels tapping across the hardwood floor.

"I don't like it," Nick said.

"No, neither do I. Something's not right. He sounded . . . frightened, but determined at the same time."

"Klemens is behind this somehow."

"I think you're right, but I have to go anyway."

"Sire!"

"Nick, I need to hear what he has to say."

"My lord. Lucas. Please. You like Kathryn, and you'd like to help her. I get that. But it's not worth risking—"

"This isn't a debate, Nick. You'll be getting a text with the address. An old warehouse in Saint Louis Park."

"That's right outside the city," Nick said unhappily. "He obviously knows you're here."

"I'm sure Francoise was on the phone with him the moment we drove away from the gallery." Lucas felt more than heard Kathryn's attention spike at the mention of Alex's gallery manager. He turned around slowly and found her staring at him, her purse in one hand, weapon and badge once again safely stowed inside.

"Please tell me you're not planning on going alone."

"I'm not an idiot, Nick. You and Mason."

"And a team, my lord. Please."

"You and Mason, Nick," he repeated. "He's already terrified. I don't want to scare him away."

Nick groaned. "You're killing me here, Sire."

"I'll bring Agent Hunter along for good measure, how's that? She's armed and dangerous."

Kathryn narrowed her eyes at him, and he grinned.

"Do I have a choice?"

"No."

"Then tell me what time tomorrow night, and we'll be ready."

"Alex and I agreed on two hours after sunset, but let's get there a half hour earlier than that."

"Yes, my lord."

Lucas smiled at the glum resignation in his lieutenant's voice as he hung up. Kathryn was on him an instant later.

"Whom are we meeting?" she demanded.

Lucas gazed down at her beautiful face, her lips still swollen from his kisses, her blue eyes bright with excitement. And all he wanted to do was drag her back to his bed. She stared back at him and must have read the desire in his gaze, because her cheeks heated, and her heart began to race. She licked her lips, and Lucas followed the quick movement of her pink tongue.

"Who—" she repeated, then had to swallow when her voice came out raspy and dry. "Whom are we meeting, Lucas?" she said, trying again.

"Alex Carmichael," Lucas provided, cupping her jaw in his hand and lowering his mouth to hers for a lingering kiss. It was all he had time for. The sun was very nearly above the horizon. Not that Kathryn would be interested in sex anyway. Not once she'd heard Alex's name.

She grabbed his hand, squeezing his fingers as she pulled away from their kiss. "Carmichael? Does he have Daniel?"

"He didn't mention your brother," Lucas said, sighing in resignation, "and I think he would have if he had him. But we'll have to wait and see."

"Damn it," she swore. "Wait. He gave you the address. Give it to me, and I'll check it out today. If Daniel's there, I can grab him. If not, no harm, right?"

Lucas gave her a patient look. "The location is an abandoned warehouse. It's doubtful Alex is there now. If he is, the building will be secure enough that you won't be able to do anything but stare at it from the outside."

"You can't know that. Give me the address."

"I do know that, and, no, I won't give you the address, because if you storm in there without knowing what you're doing, someone might end up dead."

"You mean your buddy Alex."

"No, actually, I meant you. But, yes, Alex might also be a casualty. A vampire at rest is completely defenseless. I won't help you with that."

She stared at him, her jaw flexing with tension. "You don't think Daniel is there."

"No, I don't."

"All right. We'll play it your way."

"Yes, we will. You can let yourself out." He strode toward the bedroom, miffed at her single-minded obsession with her brother.

"Wait!" she called. "What time—" She yelped in surprise as the automatic steel shutters rolled over the windows and locked with a loud thunking noise.

"Be here at sunset," he said over his shoulder. "You've got three minutes, or you'll be locked in here until then."

Kathryn shot a quick glance at the shuttered windows, then back at him. She grabbed her purse and coat, then surprised him by racing over to give him a quick kiss before running for the door.

"I'll see you at sunset," she called as she hurried out of the penthouse.

Lucas gazed after her in bemusement. Maybe there was hope for her yet. He pressed a button on the security control panel for the penthouse, overriding the lockout on the elevator. A second button push, and a screen deployed, showing him Kathryn in the elevator, then switching to the lobby as she exited the building. She was on her cell phone, presumably calling a cab. She shouldn't have a problem this early in the day.

He leaned heavily against the wall as he entered a code to remove the override. The system reasserted itself immediately, bringing the elevator back to the penthouse level and locking it there, while securing both the elevator door and the front door to the suite with the same steel shutters that covered the windows.

Lucas knew the moment the sun topped the horizon. It was a flame inside his head, a thousand pound weight on his chest as he fell onto the bed. His last thought before the sun stole his awareness was that Klemens was using Carmichael as bait. That this was payback for the death of his vampires in the Rockford house.

Chapter Fifteen

"I DON'T LIKE IT."

Lucas glanced at Nicholas, not at all surprised by his lieutenant's pronouncement. "Of course, you don't," he commented, then turned his attention back to the decrepit warehouse where Alex had set the meet. "I'm not crazy about it myself."

"How do we know who or what's waiting in there?" Nick insisted.

Kathryn made an impatient noise. "We'll never know if we stand out *here* all night."

"Actually," Lucas said, giving her an apologetic look, "I can tell you right now who's in there. And that's Alex Carmichael."

"You can tell," she said faintly, and then her expression fell. "Only Carmichael?" she said, disappointment dragging on every syllable.

"Yes. I'm sorry, Kathryn."

"You warned me," she said resignedly. "I didn't believe you."

Lucas ran a comforting hand down her arm. "Your brother's not there, but that doesn't mean Carmichael doesn't know where he is. He asked to meet us for a reason."

"Sure."

"Nicholas," Lucas said, reaching a decision.

"Sire."

"Kathryn and I will go in alone. You and Mason—"

"My lord! Carmichael belongs to Klemens. What if it's a trap?" Nick demanded, echoing Lucas's own concerns.

"That's why I want you and Mason out *here*. There is no one in that building, human or vampire, except for Alex. And I think I can handle him on my own. But if it's a trap, if Klemens plans to send a force in after us . . . then I need you out here, keeping watch and ready to call in the troops."

"I could call them now, my lord. They're geared up and waiting for the word."

Lucas considered it. This entire setup was damn odd. But Carmichael was a decent sort who had always chafed under Klemens's rule. He'd never had the courage to leave the other vampire lord's territory, but he'd spent much of his time in Minneapolis, nonetheless.

He shook his head. "There's no one in there, Nick. Come on,

Kathryn," he said, holding out a hand, "let's see what Alex has to tell us."

She looked at his hand, then drew her Glock instead. "I'm with Nick on this one," she said grimly. "I don't know who this guy Klemens is, but there's something not right about this meet."

Nicholas gave Lucas a meaningful look, which Lucas ignored. "As you will, *a cuisle,*" he said to Kathryn. "But, let's go see."

The building was old and deeply weathered. The brick was pitted, the mortar missing in chunks big enough that an observer could have peeked inside if one had been so foolish as to put an eye up to the small holes presented. Lucas wasn't that foolish. He strode up to the sheet metal-plated front door and gave the handle a tentative yank. It was unlocked. Clearly Carmichael was expecting them.

The door opened outward. He checked to make sure Kathryn was ready, then pulled open the door and went in ahead of her. He might not think there was a trap waiting for them, but he wasn't going to bet Kathryn's life on it. He was far less destructible than his human lover.

Dirt and grit scraped underfoot as they crossed what had been a small reception area. There was an ancient metal desk in one corner and what he assumed were the remains of a chair in pieces behind it. Wires, both phone and electrical, poked out of the walls, and patches of carpet spotted the concrete floor like a brown fungus.

"Nice," Kathryn commented.

"Alex did say it was abandoned."

A second door stood open to the interior. Lucas crossed over to it and saw that the rest of the building had been a manufacturing facility of some sort. There was a central open area with heavy mountings still bolted to the floor, although the equipment had been removed for the most part. What bits remained were unrecognizable, at least to Lucas. Around all four sides was an open mezzanine with three separate floors, each facing out onto the manufacturing area. Offices lined the mezzanine walls, some with doors still closed, others gaping open. Whatever glass had been in either the doors or the open frames next to them was long gone and littered the floor underfoot. A metal railing that had once provided a barrier between the mezzanine levels and the open factory was rusted away with big gaps where it had fallen, or been ripped, away completely.

Lucas scanned the area, his senses wide open. His gaze fell on the industrial-sized elevator, which appeared to be in relatively good shape. Alex was clearly maintaining it for his own use, despite the ramshackle state of the rest of the building.

The double doors slid open a moment later, and Alex himself stepped out.

"Forgive me, my lord. I meant to be waiting here when you arrived."

Lucas dipped his head briefly in acknowledgement. "Alex, this is Special Agent Kathryn Hunter, FBI. I don't believe you've met."

Alex smiled faintly. "The infamous Agent Hunter. You've got Francoise in quite a tizzy."

"I don't know why. Unless one of you has something to hide," Kathryn responded coolly.

"I admire Daniel's work a great deal, Agent Hunter. But regrettably, he is not with me."

Kathryn remained silent, but Lucas could feel her tension and distrust like a buzz saw along his nerves.

"Why are we here, Alex?" he asked, wanting to get this over with.

"Please, my lord," he said, gesturing at the elevator. "What I have to say is best said in private. I have a very pleasant apartment of sorts downstairs, a place for when I need to get away. No one knows about it, but me. And now you, of course."

Lucas studied the other vampire, looking for deception. If Alex tried to tell an outright lie, Lucas would know, but beyond that, it was difficult to say. Alex didn't belong to him. Still, he was in Lucas's territory, and he had to know that Kathryn, at least, didn't believe a word he was saying. Nonetheless, he seemed perfectly relaxed. Maybe it was only because he was in his private lair, someplace he felt secure. Or maybe he had nothing to hide.

"All right," Lucas agreed. "Is there light enough for Kathryn?"

"Of course, my lord. I frequently work down there."

"Kathryn?" Lucas said, glancing at her in question.

"Sure, why not?" She'd re-holstered her sidearm, but Lucas noticed she hadn't replaced the safety strap, and her hand rested lightly on the butt of the weapon.

"Lead the way, Alex," Lucas said, gesturing toward the open elevator.

The elevator's descent was smooth. Despite the disreputable state of the building, the vamp had clearly maintained the elevator in good condition, which made sense if he came here often to sleep in the basement. The lack of security was surprising, but perhaps there was more to it than what Lucas could see. At a minimum, Alex could probably lock down the elevator and make the lower level inaccessible during the daylight hours.

Lucas glanced up at the floor numbers over the elevator door and frowned abruptly. They had just passed B1 and were descending to B2. "There's a subbasement?" he asked sharply.

Alex nodded. "It's one of the reasons I bought this building. No one seemed to know what the original owners stored down here, but I assume it benefited from the cool conditions. I had the entire site tested for contaminants just to be safe, but there was nothing here."

Lucas accepted the explanation, but couldn't shake a growing bad feeling about this little adventure. Clearly, Kathryn was having the same reservations, because she edged out to one side and a half step behind him as the elevator slowed. Defensive tactics 101. Never give your enemy a concentrated target.

Before the doors to the elevator opened, Lucas sent his power sweeping outward, searching for enemies. Alex surely felt the brush of it, but he didn't offer a protest of any kind, not even an assurance that it wasn't necessary. And it suddenly occurred to Lucas what was bothering him about this setup. It was Alex himself. No vampire liked to have his lair invaded, and especially not by a vampire as powerful as Lucas, who was also the sworn enemy of Alex's master. But it wasn't that Alex was too nervous, it was that he was too *calm.*

Outwardly, Lucas gave away nothing, but privately he cursed his own arrogance and let his emotions leak to Nicholas, who was waiting upstairs with Mason. If the shit was going to hit the fan, he wanted Nick firing on all twelve cylinders from the get-go. The doors opened, and he stepped out into the subbasement, scanning from wall to wall with every sense he possessed. Nothing. So why—

"Forgive me, my lord," Alex said from behind him. "He gave me no choice."

Lucas spun around to find Alex still standing in the open elevator door, his left hand punching a series of buttons on the control panel. Locking it down? Or . . .

In a flash of insight, Lucas understood everything Alex had done. He grabbed Kathryn and threw her toward the back wall of the elevator two seconds before the world exploded, and the entire building collapsed on top of them.

Chapter Sixteen

THE FIRST THING Kathryn registered was dirt. Everywhere. It filled her eyes, her mouth, her nose. It covered every bare inch of skin and crawled down her blouse. She coughed, a horrible hacking sound that she wouldn't have believed could come from her own throat. She went to lift her hand, to brush the filthy hair from her face and bit back a scream of pain. Her arm. Something had happened to . . .

"Lucas!" She'd meant to scream his name, but what came out was little more than a raspy whisper of sound. God, she hurt. With every sense that returned, every nerve ending that came to life, she hurt more.

"Lucas?" She tried again, a raw croak this time. Still no answer.

She struggled to make sense of what had happened, her thoughts thick and slow as tree sap on a cold day. She tried to blink, to open her eyes and realized they were already open. That there was simply no light. Total blackness.

Closing her eyes again, she went back to first principles and took inventory of her body, wiggling toes, flexing muscles, bending knees. So far, so good. She moved her right hand cautiously. Her wrist was sore, strained most likely, her upper arm bruised and aching, but her hand worked, her fingers flexed. That was good news. She was right-handed.

Her left arm hadn't fared so well. The earlier pain had grown to a steady throb that beat in time with her heart. She reached over carefully and felt the warm wetness of fresh blood. That was bad, but probably not fatal.

Kathryn tried to roll over, so she could sit up, but there was a weight on her legs. Reaching down, she felt around with her good right hand and found some sort of metal sheeting. Grabbing an edge, she lifted it enough to bend her knees and shift her legs out from under it before letting it fall back into place with a clang and a fresh cloud of dust. She pulled her knees up to her chest and held on for a moment, shivering. Was she going into shock? She dismissed that possibility. Her arm wasn't bleeding enough for that. Internal bleeding was possible, but her quick inventory didn't seem to indicate any internal injuries.

She needed to remember. She needed to know where Lucas was. She needed *light*.

Her hand slapped down her hip and met the reassuring bulk of her

Glock. Hoping against hope, she felt her way back along her belt and nearly laughed in relief at the touch of her small FBI-issue Maglite. She pulled the metal cylinder out of its holster carefully, not wanting to risk dropping it in the dark. Gripping it firmly, she clicked it on and froze.

Alex Carmichael's subbasement. She *knew* they shouldn't have trusted him. Treacherous, fucking vampire. She shined the flashlight upward and recognized the elevator, or what was left of it. Lucas had grabbed her at the last minute, throwing her back into the elevator with Carmichael who'd been saying something, fiddling with the elevator buttons and then . . . A sudden panicked thought had her flicking her light across the elevator to the corner where Alex had been standing, half expecting to find him staring back at her. But the only things left of Alex Carmichael were the clothes he'd been wearing, and those were literally punctuated by the big honking piece of steel that had ended his life. So the son of a bitch had ended up going suicide bomber on them, blowing up the whole fucking building and himself with it.

And Lucas . . . She struggled to picture those last moments. He'd thrown her into the elevator and then . . .

"Lucas!" She did scream his name this time. Her flashlight showed a tangled mound of wood, metal and concrete where the basement room had been. Could a vampire survive something like that? What if one of those pieces stabbed him in the heart, just like Alex? Was there a pile of dust and clothes under there somewhere that used to be Lucas? No, he was too much alive to die so uselessly. She wouldn't believe it. She *couldn't*. The pain she felt at the possibility of Lucas being dead was startling. When had he come to mean so much to her?

She shook herself mentally and put aside such thoughts for later. Lucas was under there somewhere, still alive but hurt, and she had to find him. She remembered Nicholas and Mason waiting outside. They'd know something had happened—it would be hard to miss an explosion of this size, after all—and they'd be bringing help, but would they be able to dig through the rubble and get down here?

Kathryn shot the Maglite's beam straight up over her head. The elevator wasn't going anywhere, that was for sure. Even if the shaft and its pulley mechanism had survived intact, the elevator itself was bent like an empty juice box. A fresh jolt of fear speared her gut. She was more than a touch claustrophobic. It was a control thing, but knowing that didn't make it any easier to breathe. Not when she thought about the tons of stone over her head, about whether anyone would dig them out before the air ran out—or the wreckage crashed down on her head.

She scanned what was left of the basement one more time. Was it still a basement if there was no longer a building above it? It was more like a tomb. Piles of rock and rubble on top of them with no way out. She banished that thought quickly. There would be plenty of time to give up later. What she had to do now was venture out into that mess and find Lucas. She couldn't wait for Nicholas and the troops to arrive. Lucas couldn't wait. He'd risked his life for hers, and she wasn't going to leave him out there alone.

There was no room to stand, so she duck-walked when she could and crawled when she had to. What was left of the floor was littered with jagged metal and glass, and she had to check every step she took, every place she put her hand down. It was slow and exhausting, but more than anything she was terrified of what she'd find.

"Lucas." Kathryn kept saying his name, sometimes calling it out, sometimes whispering it desperately. She couldn't remember exactly where he'd been when the explosion hit, so she started at the elevator and worked outward as much as possible. There was an awful lot of tangled metal, big heavy bars torn like paper, all twisted up with each other, the spaces filled in with huge chunks of concrete and dirt. She wasn't an engineer, but some of those beams seemed to be holding up the worst of the rubble from above, leaving small pockets at ground level. From far overhead, she thought she could hear shouting, and every once in a while, the air would fill with the sound of groaning metal. She imagined those thick beams straining under the weight of the demolished building. The first time she'd heard the noise, she'd been afraid something had cracked, and everything up there was about to end up down here. But increasingly, the crashing noises began to sound like an organized effort, almost like a construction site, and it gave her hope of a rescue. But that could take hours, and she had to find Lucas.

"Lucas?" she said again, nearly sobbing. Her chest hurt from trying to breathe the dusty air, her back ached from bending over in the cramped spaces. Her fingers were cut and bleeding from shoving aside jagged pieces of metal and concrete, and . . . she'd begun to fear Lucas might actually be dead.

"Kathryn."

She froze, not sure she'd really heard it. "Lucas?"

"More or less," he said weakly, and coughed.

Her flashlight searched the rubble and found nothing. "Where are you?"

"To the left. *The other* left," he clarified when her light went the wrong way.

She forced herself to search slowly, moving the Maglite's narrow beam back and forth until she at last caught a flash of pale skin, nearly invisible in the twisted mass of steel.

"Lucas!" At first, she was unable to reach him. Kathryn was strong for a woman, but even she couldn't move all of that debris aside, even if it had been wise to do so. Frustrated, she duck-walked around to the left, toward where she was certain the outside wall had to be. Alternating her light between where she knew Lucas was and her current path, she found a tunnel of sorts through the wreckage and snaked into him on her belly, her skin crawling with the knowledge of everything that was hanging over them.

"Lucas," she murmured in dismay, running her flashlight over what little she could see of him. He was all but buried beneath a pile of concrete and rebar, only his head, shoulders, and one arm visible. She shimmied as close to him as she could get, ignoring the pain as sharp bits of rubble tore her clothes and dug into the skin of her knees and elbows.

His eyes opened, gleaming with a golden light that put her Maglite to shame.

"Kathryn." The words scraped dryly, and she wished she had some water to offer him. "You're bleeding," he said. "Are you injured?"

She shook her head, not trusting her voice and feeling foolish. Tears overflowed her eyes, mingling relief with despair. Vampire or not, he was seriously injured. Broken bones, those internal injuries she'd been worried about . . . that was just the beginning of what could be happening to Lucas.

"Sssh, don't cry." He reached for her with his one good hand. "I'm hard to kill, *a cuisle*. You're not rid of me just yet." A grimace of pain twisted his handsome face. He closed his eyes against it, but didn't groan, didn't cry out. It was everything Kathryn could do not to cry out *for* him.

She nodded, not really believing him, but understanding the importance of *him* believing what he said.

"Are you injured?" he repeated, squeezing her fingers.

She swallowed past the knot of grief in her throat. He could have saved himself, but he'd saved her instead. And now he was lying there broken and possibly dying, no matter how much he denied it.

She shook her head. "I'm not hurt. A few cuts. It's nothing." She twisted her fingers in his, then leaned forward and touched her lips to his mouth carefully. "What can I do?"

"The kiss was a start."

She laughed. At least she meant to laugh. It was more of a broken sob, but that was okay. If he could tease, maybe there was hope. Maybe vampires really were tougher than she thought.

"Do you need my blood?" she asked urgently.

He grinned, his teeth flashing white despite the desperate circumstances. "I shall remember this moment forever, Katie mine." He coughed harshly, then said, "A bit of blood would be most welcome."

"How do we . . . I mean—"

"Your wrist will do quite well."

"Oh. Right. Of course." Kathryn propped her flashlight in the dirt, angling it to provide light without blinding either one of them. She was wearing both a jacket and long-sleeved blouse. Both were torn and dirty, but remarkably the cuffs were intact. She pushed the left sleeve of her jacket up to her forearm and unbuttoned the cuff of her blouse, folding it up over the jacket to bare her wrist.

"Do I—"

Lucas took her arm with his free hand and brought it to his lips, kissing the soft skin of her wrist gently. "So soft, *a cuisle*. So fragile."

"Fragile," she repeated. "There's a word not too many people would use to describe me."

"That's because they don't know you like I do."

Her words of protest died unsaid as his warm tongue swiped once, twice over the pulse point of her wrist. Her heart started hammering when he kissed her wrist. She knew the pleasure of his bite, and so did her body. Her breasts seemed suddenly too tight in the confining bra she'd put on beneath her sensible cotton blouse this evening.

"This will hurt, Kathryn," he whispered, his breath blowing gently over her damp wrist. "I'd rather be between your legs, my cock buried in your oh so wet pussy—"

"Lucas," she warned him, her face heating. "This isn't—"

He struck without warning, his fangs sinking into the veins buried deep in her forearm. And he was right. It hurt much worse than when he bit her neck, but only for the few seconds it took for the euphoric in his bite to make it up to her brain. After that . . .

She let her head fall forward, fighting the wave of sexual ecstasy careening through her system. If her breasts had seemed sensitive before, they were sheer torment now, her bra scraping her engorged nipples as if it were the roughest lace instead of fine cotton. Heat built between her thighs, waves of sensation storming up into her womb, her abdomen.

A cry escaped her lips, her body shuddering as the climax hit her. Kathryn buried her face against her upper arm, thankful for the darkness. They were trapped in a basement, three stories of dirt, rock and metal on top of them, and she was having a damn orgasm.

Lucas lifted his mouth from her wrist, his fangs sliding painlessly from her vein. He licked the wounds and deposited another kiss on her wrist, but he didn't let go of her hand.

"Thank you, Kathryn," he said solemnly.

She nodded. But couldn't look at him. She was too embarrassed.

"Katie mine."

"What?"

"Look at me."

She lifted just her eyes in a glance, then back down.

"That wasn't a look. Stop it, Kathryn. This is biology. It's how we survived the centuries before humans moved beyond superstition and into discos."

She smiled despite herself. "Discos?"

"A boon for the vampire community, *a ghrá*. But the true revolution was birth control. All of those beautiful women suddenly free and eager to indulge the sexuality men had enjoyed so liberally for centuries."

Kathryn rolled her eyes. "I'm sure you were very popular."

"Were? I'm wounded. I'll have you know I still am."

"Right. I know what you're doing," she added, meeting his steady gaze at last.

"Besides lying here under this pile of rubble, you mean?"

"How badly are you injured, Lucas? The truth."

"Ah, that. I'm afraid I've a few broken bones under all of this. And may I say, never having broken a bone before . . . it hurts like hell. No, no," he added quickly, hearing Kathryn's involuntary gasp of dismay, "I can handle it. Although I will expect some expressions of sympathy and admiration once this is all over with. Maybe you can stroke my forehead and say things like, 'Poor baby. You were so strong.' That sort of thing." The strain in his voice belied his easy words, his voice thin and strangled as if he was struggling to find enough oxygen to speak.

"If we get out of here, I'll stroke more than your forehead," Kathryn promised.

"I find myself motivated, apart from your delicious blood donation, which will speed things up tremendously. Unfortunately, bones take time to heal, even for a vampire." His jaw clenched suddenly, his eyes closing as his face tightened in obvious pain.

"Lucas?" He grunted in response, so she continued. "Why would Alex do that? Try to kill us like that, and kill himself, too."

"Compulsion," Lucas said, his voice low with effort. "His master and I are enemies. He used Alex to go after me. Alex had no choice in what he did. He wasn't a bad guy."

Kathryn wasn't sure she agreed with that, but she wasn't going to argue with him. "I think Nick and the guys are trying to get down here," she said quickly, wanting to distract him. She lifted her chin to indicate the almost constant noise now coming from above.

"Nicholas has begun a rescue effort," he confirmed in a strained whisper. "But that will take time." His voice eased, his expression lightening, as if the pain had ebbed, at least temporarily. "We'll be stuck here for hours yet. So, while the very special thing in my blood which makes me Vampire does its best to mend my broken bones, you can distract me by talking."

"What should I say?"

Lucas didn't open his eyes, but his mouth curled into a lopsided smile. "Tell me you love me," he murmured.

Her heart twisted in her chest, but she couldn't say the words. Not even jokingly. They were too close to a truth she didn't want to acknowledge. "Please don't die," she whispered instead.

"I'm not going to die, *a cuisle*," he said, letting his Irish lilt roll through the words. "I've still got to get you unbuttoned."

"But how can you heal broken bones like this without—"

His golden eyes opened again, and she could read the pain in them, even as he spoke clearly. "You need to understand, Kathryn. The vampire symbiote doesn't care that my legs are trapped under a huge, fucking pile of rocks. It just wants them working again, and it's taking all of the healing power my body and blood possess to focus on that one task."

"What does that mean?"

"Give me enough time, and I'll move this damned pile of trash off my legs. But then the bones will want to start healing all over again, because they're still under pressure right now, and not even the symbiote can make them straight and sound."

"Oh, God. Lucas," she breathed.

"Hold my hand," he said, his eyes closing once more. "Distract me. Tell me what happened after your parents died."

Kathryn stared at him in the dim glow of her small flashlight, searching his face for any sign that he was manipulating her, using their dire predicament to get her to open up to him, to tell him something personal.

But his face was pale, even for him, and there were lines of pain creasing the corners of his closed eyes. His breathing was strained, and she thought about how hard it must be for him to breathe, how painful to lie there, feeling his own bones healing, and all the while knowing he'd have to go through it all over again once he was freed.

"What makes you think my parents are dead?" she asked, to get him thinking about something, *anything* else.

"It's the way you relate to your brother, the way you talk about him. It's more like a parent than a sibling. Plus all this time we've been looking for him, you've never once mentioned a mother or father. I'm guessing you were very young when they died. Maybe someone stepped in, a grandparent, an aunt or uncle, but you were older than your brother, and you felt responsible for him anyway."

He didn't open his eyes, didn't look at her, but she could feel him waiting for her response. Her stomach roiled at the thought of baring her most painful moments, her private history. But he'd told her his story, a life much harder than her own had been, despite her losses.

"My mother died when Daniel was two," she began. "I was six. My father is still alive."

"Ah. But neither of you are close to him."

"He raised us alone. My grandparents—the ones with the ranch—offered to have us live with them, and my father could come out every weekend and be with us. He said no. We were his kids, and he wanted us with him. But he still had to work, of course. We had babysitters, but I'd already been taking care of my brother almost since he was born. My mom was diagnosed with cancer just before she gave birth, and she started treatments right after.

My earliest memory is my father telling me the day my brother was born that I had to help my mom with the new baby because she was sick. They came home with Daniel, and I remember looking at him and thinking he was my responsibility now. When I was four years old, I already knew how to put a bottle together for my brother, how to heat it in the microwave before putting the cap on. I changed his diaper, although probably not well, and I rocked him to sleep. I was the one he wanted when he cried, not one of our parents. When he was a year old, I came home from my first day of kindergarten, and he was so happy to see me he took his very first steps. To me."

"And how did your father take all of this?"

"It was hard on him. My mom was sick for two years before she died, and I think it was actually easier for him after that. He loved us, but his job was an escape from everything. I can't blame him for that. He did the best he could, and I'm grateful. He could have walked away when my grandmother offered, or pawned us off on my mom's sister, but he didn't."

"But he's still alive. So where is he now?"

"He remarried a few years ago. His new wife is younger, and they have a couple of kids."

"More siblings for you. How lovely."

"I guess. I barely know them. They live in Arizona, and the kids are so much younger."

"And you really don't want any more siblings."

"I don't need any. I have Daniel."

"Hmm." He lapsed into silence, long enough that Kathryn felt a spike of fear.

"Lucas?"

Her heart jumped in alarm when he didn't answer, and she scooted closer, pressing her face to his and listening for his breath, waiting for the brush of warm air on her cheek.

"Kathryn," he breathed, soft enough that she wouldn't have heard it if she hadn't been so close. "Have I told you I love you?"

She kissed his closed eyes and then his mouth. "Hush," she whispered. "Save your strength for the important stuff."

"Love *is* important, *a cuisle*. You wouldn't be here otherwise."

He was quiet after that, resting she supposed. But as long as he was still breathing, she figured the symbiote, as he called it, was still working on him, still trying to heal the devastating damage to this body. Kathryn lowered her face into the crook of her arm, still holding on to his hand. She was achingly tired, and she wondered how long they'd have to wait down here.

She didn't realize she'd fallen asleep until a loud banging noise woke her. She startled awake, eyes wide. Her first thought was that something had given way overhead, some crucial piece of metal framework that had been holding everything else at bay, and now they were doomed.

"That's just Nicholas," Lucas said, his voice much stronger than it had been.

She stared at him. He looked tired beneath the dirt and grime, but his eyes were open and gleaming gold with power.

"You ready to get out of here?" he asked.

"Get out?" she repeated, confused.

"Flash your light up there, will you?" He lifted his eyes to indicate the tangle of metal beams and broken building lying on top of him.

Kathryn frowned, but did as he asked, moving the narrow beam of her flashlight back and forth above them until he grunted in satisfaction and said, "That's it. Do me a favor?"

She nodded, a little worried about what he was planning to do.

"I want you to go back over by the elevator where you were before. I'm not sure what will happen when I start shuffling things around, and I don't want you underneath here."

"I thought you said Nicholas was coming with the rest of the guys. I think we should wait—"

"It's not in my nature to wait, *a cuisle*. Besides, I have a reputation to maintain."

"This isn't funny."

"No, it's not. It's deadly serious. Now, please, Kathryn, do as I ask and go back over by the elevator."

She regarded him unhappily for a long minute, then pursed her lips and nodded her agreement. She'd just started to squirm her way back out the way she'd come, when he stopped her with a hand on her arm.

"No kiss for good luck?"

Kathryn narrowed her eyes in irritation, but felt the smile tugging at her lips. "You better know what you're doing, Lucas Donlon, because I'm not saving your ass again if all of this shit tumbles down on you."

"C'mere."

She scooted forward again and put her mouth against his, intending to give him a quick peck on the lips. But Lucas had other plans. His hand tunneled into the loose strands of her hair, holding her still as he gave her a searing kiss. His tongue slipped between her teeth, twining with her tongue, as his lips caressed her mouth. The tension fled Kathryn's body for a few precious moments as she reveled in the seduction of Lucas's touch, his strong fingers kneading the back of her neck, his kiss claiming her for himself, even if it was only for these few minutes in a dark basement.

He broke away slowly, and she liked to think his reluctance mirrored her own.

"When this is over, Katie mine, you and I are going to spend several quality hours in a big bed with a bottle of good whiskey and no phones."

"Big talk, vampire."

"Big *plans*," he corrected. "Now go. I'm tired of having all this crap weighing me down."

Kathryn scowled. She didn't see how he thought he was going to get out of here without help. Vampire or not, there was just too much stuff in the way, and every bit of it weighed a ton. He waggled his fingers, as if pushing her on her way, so she complied. Scooting backwards, wincing when her injured arm brushed against a jagged piece of concrete, and again when something ripped open her pants leg and added to her cuts and bruises.

"You do understand the concept of moving to safety, don't you, *a cuisle?* One should at least *try* to get there in one piece."

"I *am* trying. This isn't easy, you know."

Another banging noise started up above, this one continuing for some time as Kathryn finally extricated herself from the worst of the rubble and half crawled, half duck-walked back to the dubious safety of the elevator shaft. The sound died down just before she got there, the final metallic ring echoing down the empty space of the shaft over her head.

"You think they're coming down this way?" she called over to Lucas.

"Probably. It avoids going through much of the debris. The alternative would be digging in through the side wall."

"I thought you and Nicholas were, you know, in touch."

Lucas laughed, sounding very nearly like his regular self. "There are limitations. Are you in the elevator?"

"Yes," she snapped irritably

"Get as far inside as you can. And you might want to close your eyes."

Kathryn did as he asked, closing her eyes with an impatient sigh loud enough for Lucas to hear. But inside, she was trembling, her heart racing.

She squeezed herself into a tight corner of the elevator, straining to see in the dark, terrified that Lucas's luck was going to run out, that the next collapse would be one he couldn't survive.

LUCAS CROOKED A smile at Kathryn's sigh of exasperation, He couldn't see her from the awkward position he was in, but he could hear her muttering to herself as she moved around. And he could sense her fear for him, the fear she was trying to cover up with her grumblings.

When he was as certain as he could be that she was safe, he stretched out his power and touched Nicholas.

"Sire?" Nicholas's thoughts were tight with worry.

"Any complications from the human authorities so far?"

"A patrol car came out. Someone heard the blast and called it in. We had a nice chat, and they went away happy."

"Excellent. Are you coming down the elevator shaft?"

"Yes. We had to move a few tons of debris first, but we finally cleared the shaft. We can cut through—"

"No. Kathryn's in there. I'll come to you."

"You're coming up?"

"After I move this fucking heavy pile, yeah. It's going to be . . . bad, Nick. You understand?"

"Yes, my lord. I've got the copter on stand-by if we need it. Are we going to the ranch or staying in St. Paul?"

Lucas wanted to go home to his ranch in South Dakota, but it made more sense to remain in the Twin Cities. The sooner he reached safety, the sooner his body could start healing itself all over again, and he needed to get his strength back quickly. Klemens would know Alex Carmichael was dead, and he would also know that Lucas was not. Clearly he had planned on Lucas perishing in Alex's suicidal explosion, but even though he'd survived, Klemens would assume he'd been injured, leaving him weakened and perhaps vulnerable to attack. Lucas couldn't afford to be weak. Not unless he was prepared to surrender his people and territory to Klemens. That would never happen.

The ranch in South Dakota was his true lair, but the penthouse across the river in St. Paul would have to do. More than anything, he needed a safe place to rest while the vampire symbiote *fixed* what was wrong with his body.

"Make it the penthouse, Nick. As fast as possible."

"Understood, my lord."

"See you in a few."

"Good luck, Sire."

Lucas closed his eyes, picturing the crushing mass of I-beams, concrete and rebar that he'd seen in the light from Kathryn's flashlight. And then he added in the distance between his current location and the nearest wall where the destruction was the least pronounced. He steeled himself against the inevitable pain. He'd told Kathryn his broken bones hurt like hell, but running on them the way they'd been healed was going to be so much worse.

"Close your eyes, Kathryn," he called again, giving her a heads-up.

And then he *moved.*

A blast of pure power lifted the mass of wreckage above him with the groan of tortured metal and shattered rock. It was only a foot or two, and for only a few seconds, but it was enough for Lucas to spin face down and scramble on all fours out from under, reaching the relative safety of the wall with no more than a breath to spare as the massive weight came crashing down once again. The walls shook, and the ground shuddered under the tremendous impact. Everything shifted as the pile of debris settled into its new configuration, dirt and bits of concrete raining down on him like lethal snow.

"Kathryn!" he bellowed over the noise.

"I'm okay," she called back. "Where are you?"

"Don't come out!" he yelled quickly. "I'll come to you."

"Are you sure, I can—"

"Damn it, Kathryn. Stay there."

Lucas crouched near the wall, knees tucked up against his chest, face buried in the protection of his arms until everything stopped moving. He lifted his head again. The air with still thick with particles of who knew what sort of garbage, but they had to get out of here. The pile hadn't been all that stable to begin with, and he feared he'd only made it worse.

He forced himself to his feet, closing his eyes against the agony of bones that had healed bent and out of alignment. If he had to guess, he'd say every bone in his right leg had been broken, plus at least the femur in his left. And his pelvis felt like ground glass every time he moved. That was the bad news. The good news was that the damage to vital organs had been minimal and was already healing. His lungs ached, but that was probably due as much to the thick air as anything else. And his heart was sound. Otherwise, he'd be dead alongside old Alex Carmichael. He wondered if Kathryn had realized yet that Alex's remains were part of the dust she was breathing in. He decided not to share that particular fact.

It took him only a few minutes, inching down the wall, finding his way around the few smaller piles of mostly concrete and crushed furniture that barred his way. There were some electrical wires tangled up in all the mess, but they were dead. Nick had probably cut the main line as a precaution. As

Lucas edged into the open front of the elevator, he straightened as much as possible. He didn't want Kathryn thinking too much about his physical condition. Didn't want her paying too much attention to the state of his legs in particular. She didn't need to know how bad it was.

She was sitting against the back wall of the elevator, head buried in her arms, her usually tidy ponytail hanging loose and disheveled. He smelled fresh blood and frowned. The wound on her arm was still leaking blood, and a nasty-looking gash marked her calf. It was the arm that troubled him the most. Even without a bandage, it should have clotted by now.

"Kathryn," he said softly.

Her head came up, and he saw in her eyes what she'd refused to tell him when he was still trapped. A beautiful smile split her face, and she laughed as she jumped up and came into his arms.

"I can't believe it!" she said, hugging him so tightly it hurt, but he held on anyway. "Does anything hurt?" she asked, moving out of his arms too quickly as she stepped back to survey his aching body.

"Nothing I can't handle," he replied truthfully enough. "We need to get out of here, *a cuisle*. I'm worried about this place."

"Right," she said, then looked at the crumpled elevator ceiling. "Um. You have a plan?"

Lucas grinned and grabbed a quick kiss that turned into a long kiss before he tore himself away. That damn chemistry again. Here they were buried in a hole of unstable rubble, and he still wanted her like he wanted his next breath. And judging from the high color on her previously pale face and the racing of her heart, she was feeling it, too.

"Escape first," he said, dropping his hand to the swell of her perfect ass. "Sex later."

Kathryn met his gaze, her chest rising and falling with rapid breaths. She licked her lips. "Right," she said, never breaking eye contact. They leaned toward each other like two magnets, before seeming to recognize at the same time what they were doing and pulling away.

"Nick's waiting," he murmured, twisting a finger in her tangled hair.

"Okay," she agreed, but neither one of them moved.

Lucas smiled slowly, the smile becoming a grin. "There's a helicopter."

"Even better," she breathed.

"I've got to punch a hole in this damn elevator."

"Sounds dangerous."

"It is. A kiss will make it better."

She gave him a lopsided grin of her own. "*You* think a kiss makes everything better."

"Doesn't it?"

Kathryn cupped his cheek and touched her lips to his. She opened her mouth to say something, but she was interrupted when Nicholas chose that moment to yell down the shaft.

"Lucas!"

Lucas rolled his eyes in disgust, but called back. "You ready, Nick?"

"Ready!"

"That's my cue." Lucas looked around for a likely tool and found a five-foot-long piece of heavy steel bracing that was ragged and torn at the ends. "Stand back, and cover your eyes." He studied the enclosed space with a frown. "Better yet, stand just outside so you're not underneath whatever decides to come crashing down when I do this."

"What are you going to do?" Kathryn asked as she moved to comply.

"This," he said, and rammed the piece of metal up through the top of the elevator, cutting through the damaged ceiling, shoving aside electrical wires and opening a hole. More junk immediately tumbled down into the elevator, concrete mostly, along with snaking lengths of thick, twisted cable that he assumed had once guided the elevator up and down.

But in addition to all of that came fresh air and, high above, the welcome sight of the night sky and Nicholas staring down at him with a worried look on his face.

"My lord!" Nicholas called, his voice full of relief.

"Send us a rope, Nick."

"I'll do one better, my lord," Nick said and gestured to the side. Mason appeared overhead wearing a climbing harness with a heavy rope trailing behind him. He tugged the rope once, nodded to whoever was securing the lifeline, then slipped over the edge, falling freely for the first ten feet before the rope went taut, and he began to ease himself down toward the top of the elevator. Lucas appreciated the thought, but he wouldn't be ascending in Mason's strong arms, no matter how much his aching bones wanted to. But Kathryn would.

"Up you go, Katie mine," he said, gesturing to Kathryn. "Your rescuer awaits."

Kathryn eyed the big vampire doubtfully. "Can't I just scale the side? You know, like a wall?"

Lucas shook his head. "Too dangerous. Too many hazards sticking out, live wires and such," he added, lying just a little.

She frowned, but allowed him to boost her up and through the hole in the roof, where Mason waited. He had to grit his teeth as she went into the other vampire's arms. It shouldn't have bothered him that much, but it did. And the fact that it did told him she mattered more to him than he admitted.

Mason didn't waste any time. As soon as Kathryn was secure, he started for the surface. Not being used to vampire enhanced speed and strength, Kathryn gave a little shriek of surprise as Mason zoomed upward, his climbing boosted by vampires pulling from above. Their ascent was probably faster than the elevator itself would have been.

As soon as they reached the top, Kathryn immediately disengaged from Mason's hold and stepped away from the big vampire . . . much to Lucas's satisfaction. But then the next task awaited him. He sighed, thinking not for the first time that vampire pride and competitiveness was a pain in the ass sometimes.

"Just the rope, Nick," he called up.

Nick peered over the edge at him and opened his mouth to protest, but something in Lucas's expression made him stop. Or maybe it was the waves of aggression floating up out of the damn hole in the ground. In any event, the thick rope was soon slithering down toward him. Lucas grabbed it, then gritted his teeth and began climbing, hand over hand, until he reached the top.

Nicholas grabbed his arm as soon as he crested the edge of the hole, bracing him unobtrusively under the cover of pulling him in for a quick man hug before stepping back. Lucas appreciated the gesture and the loyalty of his lieutenant. A vampire lord could never afford to display weakness. Nick understood that.

Lucas scanned his assembled vampires, seeking the smallest indication of disloyalty. But he found nothing but relief, love, and a steely determination for revenge against whoever had tried to assassinate their master. And revenge was definitely in their future. But not tonight. Lucas was in pain and exhausted. He wanted his bed and he wanted Kathryn.

"Let's go, Kathryn," he said, holding out a hand.

She looked at it, then raised her eyes to study his face. For a moment, he thought she was going to reject him, but then something in her gaze surrendered. She laced her fingers with his, and he sighed inwardly. He was going to need all of his strength for what he had to do next.

KATHRYN EYED Lucas as they rode the elevator to the penthouse floor. Something was wrong. Granted he had to be worn out after everything he'd been through. She was certainly exhausted, and his ordeal had been far worse than hers. It was more than just weariness, though.

He'd held onto her hand all the way here. Not unusual in itself; Lucas was a very touchy-touch kind of guy. But every once in a while on the drive home, his grip had tightened almost to the point of pain, and she'd caught a fleeting expression of distress on his handsome face. He'd told her his bones had healed improperly, that the vampire symbiote would want to fix them once he was free, but . . . did that mean it was working on him already?

"Are you all right?" She leaned close enough to whisper in his ear, softly enough that she didn't think even another vampire could hear. But there was only Nicholas in the elevator with them, and Lucas seemed to trust him above all the others.

"Fine," he said in a voice not at all like his usual cheerful lilt.

She frowned, but didn't push him. Maybe it wasn't kosher for a vampire lord to show pain, even among those he trusted.

When the penthouse doors opened, she started to step out, but Lucas stopped her. "Nick will set you up on a lower floor. It doesn't lock down during daytime, so you'll be more comfortable there."

"Why can't I stay with you?" she asked, hating the idea of him suffering alone through whatever was happening.

Lucas looked down at her, his gaze softening as he cupped her cheek and rubbed his thumb over her lips. "You don't want to be here for this, *a cuisle*. I don't *want* you here for this. It won't be pretty, but, trust me, I'll get through it. And tomorrow night you can do that stroking we talked about."

"Lucas, I'm not afraid of a little—"

"Kathryn. Please."

Her lips flattened unhappily, but she nodded. "Fine. I'll just go back to my hotel and—"

"No," he interrupted. "I don't think you were a target tonight, but Klemens knows about you now, and he may try to use you against me. I don't want you hurt. Give Nick your hotel key, and he'll send one of the daytime guards over to get your stuff."

"Lucas, I may spend most of my time at a desk these days, but I'm still a trained FBI agent. I know how to protect myself."

"And Klemens is a vampire lord. You saw what I was able to do tonight, even as injured as I was. Can you defend against that? Please," he added, when she glared at him stubbornly. "One night. What can it hurt?"

"All right," she conceded. "But I'm going to the hotel with your guard. I'd rather pack my own things."

"And you'll come right back," Lucas clarified.

"Yes, Daddy," she drawled, rolling her eyes. "I'll come right back."

Lucas gave her a tired, lopsided grin, then lowered his mouth to hers and kissed her thoroughly. "My feelings for you are definitely not paternal, Katie mine."

Kathryn blushed, knowing Nicholas was watching and listening to everything, but she reached up and gently stroked Lucas's face from forehead to jaw. "Poor baby," she murmured. "You were so strong, so brave."

Lucas laughed and gave her one last, hard kiss. "I seem to recall other promises were made. I'll expect payment in full when I see you tonight." He looked over her head at Nicholas. "Everything's waiting?"

"Yes, my lord. Would you like—"

"Jesus, not you, too, Nick. I'll be fine." Lucas exited the elevator and disappeared into the unlit depths of the penthouse.

Kathryn watched until the doors closed, but he never looked back. She leaned against the elevator wall then, staring down at her filthy clothes, very conscious of Nicholas standing just a few feet away from her in the confined space. Finally, she looked up to find him studying her.

"Will he be all right?" she asked.

Nicholas blinked. "I wouldn't leave him up there if I didn't believe it."

Kathryn nodded unhappily and said, "Okay, I guess. About this hotel trip . . ."

"Lucas Donlon is my master, Agent Hunter. It will be done *exactly* as he ordered."

Kathryn sighed. She seemed to remember being in charge of her *own* life just a few short days ago. She had to wonder when she'd lost it and when Lucas Donlon had taken over instead.

LUCAS CLOSED THE door of the penthouse behind him, more grateful than words could express to be alone with his pain. It had taken every ounce of energy he had left to keep up appearances, not just for Kathryn, but for Nick and the others, too. Maybe it hadn't been necessary, but it was instinct. Besides, if he'd given in to the agony of his body, he'd have been screaming at the top of his lungs and ripping great chunks out of the SUV's upholstery in an attempt to ease the pain.

He went directly to the security console and, not waiting for sunrise, lowered the steel shutters and locked everyone out. Next stop was the refrigerator behind the bar which was stocked with bags of fresh blood. A hundred years ago, Nick would have grabbed someone off the street and had them waiting for Lucas to drain dry. With any luck that person would have been a criminal of some sort, someone the world was better off without. But Lucas didn't delude himself that mistakes had never been made, or that sometimes there just hadn't been enough time before sunrise to be choosy. The one saving grace was that it didn't happen often. The kind of damage Lucas had suffered tonight was a rare thing for someone of his strength.

And human blood banks were open twenty-four hours a day.

Lucas grabbed a glass bowl from under the bar and filled it with water, then set it in the microwave to boil. While he waited, he tore the valve off the first bag of blood and drank it cold. It tasted awful going down his throat, but once it hit his stomach the cold didn't matter. His body began to use it immediately. The microwave dinged. Using a bar towel, he lowered the water-filled bowl to the counter and eased a second bag of blood into the hot water, releasing the valve slowly.

He was reaching for a third bag to drink cold when his phone rang. Not his cell phone, which was buried somewhere beneath Alex Carmichael's building, but his landline. He glanced at the caller ID, but was already reaching for the phone. He knew who it was.

"Sire," he answered.

"Lucas," Raphael's deep, familiar voice greeted him. "Whom have you pissed off now?"

Lucas smiled to himself. "I am well, thank you. Okay, perhaps not well, but only bent, not broken. Not permanently anyway."

"Any more qualifiers you'd like to add?" Raphael asked dryly.

"It's been a rough few hours. I won't deny it."

"Klemens?"

"Yes, though as usual he didn't get his own hands dirty. A human assassin for you, and poor Alex Carmichael for me. Klemens had him under a compulsion. To his credit, Alex fought it, but it was no contest."

"No," Raphael agreed thoughtfully. "Klemens takes the coward's way, but he does have power when he chooses to use it."

"Well, his time has run out. I have people in place keeping an eye on him. If they can pinpoint his location tomorrow night, I'm going after him."

There was a very un-Raphael-like pause, before he said, "Lucas, be very certain you're ready for this."

"I can handle him, Sire. You won't be rid of me that easily."

"What about the FBI agent?"

"She nearly died along with me tonight."

"That was foolish of Klemens. Her death would have brought unwanted attention, even for him."

"I don't think he knew she'd be with me."

Raphael was silent for a moment. "The FBI agent is *with* you," he said.

Lucas laughed. "What can I say, Raphael? Women love me."

"So you keep telling me. I assume she's not there now."

"Not even I could get it up tonight, my lord. She's safely ensconced downstairs."

"And tomorrow night?"

"Not to worry. When I go after Klemens, it will be a vampires-only invitation."

"You have plenty of blood for tonight?"

"Nick took care of it."

"I'll leave you to it, then. Cyn sends her love."

"Somehow I doubt that."

It was Raphael's turn to laugh. "Be well, Lucas."

"And you, Sire."

Lucas disconnected and threw the phone onto the bar, then raised the warmed bag of blood to his lips and drank it down without pause. The third bag he'd been about to drink cold went into the still-hot bowl of water to warm. He took two more cold bags from the fridge and carried them into the bedroom to drink while he got ready. He'd be sleeping in his spare bedroom this morning. The day was likely to get ugly, and he didn't want the mess or the memories in the place he usually slept. He had less than thirty minutes before sunrise. His number one priority had to be drinking as much blood as possible, even if that meant it had to be cold and tasteless. His body would need all the energy it could get to heal itself. But he desperately wanted a shower, too. He was covered in dirt and concrete dust, and who knew what kinds of crud lived in a building that old. The blood could warm in the hot water of his shower, and if he hurried, he could manage two more units after that.

But any way he looked at it, even with every ounce of blood in the fridge, it was going to be a long, fucking day.

DANIEL IGNORED the now familiar sounds from the hallway outside the room. His tormentor—although that was probably too strong a word unless boredom could be considered torture—had returned for their nightly ritual. He assumed it was nightly anyway, because the man had a job to do, and as far as Daniel could tell, he was still doing it. He'd even shown up in his uniform once or twice. Night after night, he brought food and water, then sat and expressed his admiration for Dan's work, even going so far as to bring some of his photographic books to drool over. Creepy didn't begin to describe it. At least the woman he'd heard the other night had a practical reason for kidnapping him. She wanted money. Daniel would be happy to pay them as much as they wanted if they'd just let him out of this disgusting room.

He thought about how Kathryn had despaired of the mess he created in every room he lived or worked. He made a promise to whatever gods of order were listening that if they'd just get him out of this predicament, he'd be neat and tidy for the rest of his life. Or at least he'd try.

The door creaked open, bringing light with it as his captor flipped the switch in the hallway.

"Good evening, Daniel," the freak said cheerfully, just as he did every night. As if he really believed they were somehow friends, and this was simply a pleasant evening's diversion.

Dan didn't respond, didn't sit up, didn't even look at the idiot. He lay on his uncomfortable bunk with one arm over his eyes and ignored him.

"I've brought you a steak sandwich this evening. Your favorite."

"How the hell would you know?" Daniel muttered.

"Joanie at the coffee shop told me," he said, sounding pleased, and Daniel cursed himself for asking the question.

"I brought you something else, too."

The familiar clicking sound of a digital camera in burst mode had Daniel turning to look.

"What the fuck?" he demanded, jumping up and snatching the camera before his captor could grab it back. "That's one of mine!"

"I know," the creep said in a wounded tone. "Your sister left it all at the sheriff's station for safekeeping. I had to sneak it out."

"What do you mean left it? Where'd she go?"

He shrugged. "I don't know. Maybe she went home."

Daniel's heart sank at this bit of news, even though he told himself it couldn't be true. For one thing, Kathryn would never have left his equipment behind if she was leaving for good. For another—and this was the important one—she would never have given up on him. Kathryn was the one constant in his life, the one who'd always been there for him. He had to remember that, to believe it. His captor was just fucking with his head, trying to make him believe he had no one left. This asshole must be the loneliest person in the world if he thought he could kidnap people and make them his friends. Stockholm Syndrome, my ass.

"Can I keep this?" Dan asked, sparing a quick glance at his kidnapper. Enough to see the man's face light up at the question.

"Of course! That's why I brought it to you. I apologize for not thinking of it sooner. It was completely thoughtless on my part."

Jesus, this guy was pathetic. "Yeah, right. Okay. Can I have my dinner now?"

"Oh no, your steak! It must be cold. Should I microwave it or something?"

He wanted to zap steak? What a moron. But all he said was, "No, that's okay. It'll be fine."

"You're sure, because—"

"I said it'll be fine."

"Oh, okay. I'll just get it from the kitchen then. Would you like a glass of wine?"

"Sure," Daniel said, snapping a quick picture as his captor turned away to bring in the food, covering the small sound it made with his words. "That'd be nice."

By the time his captor returned, the camera was lying on the bed. He noticed and frowned. "You want to be careful with that. Make sure you move it before the lights go off. You don't want to sit on it or anything."

"Yeah, about that. How about you leave the lights on so I can take some shots. Artsy stuff, you know," he added with an inflection meant to flatter the freakazoid into thinking he and Dan shared an understanding of true art.

The nut job's face lit up like Christmas. "That would be splendid!" He frowned as if having second thoughts, but said, "I suppose it can't hurt to leave the light on for one day. But no more than that," he scolded, as if addressing a child.

"Great," Dan said, fighting the urge to tell this creep what he really thought.

"You're welcome," the nut job said primly, then settled down to watch Dan eat as he did every night. "Now, what shall we talk about tonight?"

Daniel didn't answer. He found that the freak didn't really want conversation. He mostly wanted someone to listen to his ramblings, and Dan was more interested in eating. His captor only brought food once a day, and Dan had discovered early on that the man's mood was unpredictable. Some nights he lingered for hours, yammering about his life, his job, whatever tedious tidbits he could resurrect from his clearly deranged mind. Other nights, he grew impatient after only a few minutes, leaving Daniel with a half-finished meal and still hungry.

It seemed likely that tonight would be a long one, given the man's excitement over the camera. But Daniel wasn't taking any chances. He ate the cold steak, the tepid baked potato, even the broccoli, which he generally detested, because one of these nights, this asshole was going to slip up, and Dan would be ready.

Chapter Seventeen

Twin Cities, Minnesota

LUCAS WENT DIRECTLY from his bed to another hot shower when he woke after sunset. The day had been rugged, even worse than he'd expected. To call it *sleep* would be a gross misstatement. He'd been in excruciating pain for much of it, pain that had made the agony of being crushed by tons of debris pale in comparison. He'd woken covered in bloody sweat. The sheets had been soaked red, torn to shreds from his daytime thrashing. His body still ached from the memory of it, while at least a part of his mind kept waiting for it to begin again, not quite trusting that it was over. No human could have survived such torture and remained sane. Even Lucas had never experienced anything like it.

He wrapped a towel around his waist and crossed to the steam-fogged mirror, rubbing a spot clear. His beard was a dark shadow along his jaw. He needed to shave. On the other hand, he had a beautiful woman waiting for him. The choice was easy.

He dropped the towel as he headed out of the bathroom, aiming for his bedroom closet. The sound of a sucked in breath had him turning toward the door.

"Kathryn," he said, unsurprised. He'd known she was in the penthouse. She wouldn't have been allowed *into* the elevator, much less out of it, without his permission. The first thing Lucas had done on waking was call Nick, to assure him he had survived the day, and to tell him to admit Kathryn to the penthouse when she showed up. She'd arrived while he was still in the shower—he'd taken enough of her blood to sense her presence—and he'd been glad he'd had the foresight to close the door to the other bedroom where he'd spent the day. He didn't want Kathryn to witness the evidence of his agonizing recovery.

He took in the welcome sight of her curves in a pair of faded jeans that clung and made him wish she'd turn around, so he could see the perfection of her denim-covered ass. Her feet were bare, her toenails polished in bright red. Like the underwear, a sexy side of his Kathryn that she hid from the world. But not from him. And speaking of underwear, or lack thereof, she was braless beneath a dark blue FBI T-shirt, the edge of a white bandage just visible on her upper arm.

His perusal reached her face and found her eyes traveling up his body in turn, lingering, he was pleased to see, on his growing erection.

Lucas grinned. "Up here, *a cuisle*," he drawled, tapping his chin.

Kathryn blushed right on schedule, but she met his gaze defiantly. "You appear remarkably healthy for a man who was crushed under a building less than twenty-four hours ago."

"Ah, Katie mine," he crooned, crossing over to her and tilting her stubborn chin up with a finger. "I keep telling you, I'm not a man. I'm a vampire."

He lowered his mouth to hers. Their lips met with a spark of recognition, an almost electrical shock of instant desire. Kathryn's mouth opened beneath his, and he swept his tongue past her soft lips in a lazy exploration that very quickly turned into something demanding and insistent. Lucas changed the angle of his kiss so he could go deeper, cupping the nape of her neck in a possessive grip, holding her in place as his other hand dropped to her lower back and tucked her up against his naked body. Kathryn moaned into his mouth, her strong hands sliding from his waist to his back, digging into his newly healed muscles as she demanded in turn. This heat between them was never one-way, it was two combustible elements coming together and creating a fire neither one could control.

Lucas stepped back to grab the edges of her T-shirt and pull it over her head, dropping it to the floor as his fingers swept up her bare back and around to frame her beautiful breasts. They were heavy in his hands as he admired them, her dark pink nipples swollen and erect, standing out against large, pale areolas. He rubbed his thumbs over her nipples, smiling in appreciation as they hardened into tight peaks.

Kathryn grabbed his wrists and rubbed her breasts against his hands like a sweet kitten begging to be petted. She rose up on her toes and brought her mouth to his in a hard, hungry kiss, her tongue pushing against his, fighting for control. He bit her tongue teasingly, enough to establish dominance without breaking the skin, opening his bite almost immediately. But there was nothing teasing about her response as her blunt teeth sank hard into his lower lip, drawing blood. Kathryn swept her tongue over the small injury in a sensuous caress, licking away the few drops of blood. Lucas registered absently that the blood would help her arm heal, even as his body hardened, watching her throat move in a swallow, taking him into her in a whole new way.

"Careful," he growled, "I bite back." He lifted her off her feet, his arms around her back, holding her in a tight embrace as he plundered her mouth, crushing her lips beneath his, flattening her naked breasts against his chest, her skin soft as satin, her nipples like twin pearls.

"Lucas," she whispered, the sound full of desire, but touched with fear, as his blood hit her system, and she experienced for the first time what it really meant to have a vampire lover.

"What do you want, *a cuisle?*"

"You," she said breathlessly. "Can you . . . are you well enough . . ."

Lucas laughed and swept his arm under her legs, lifting her off her feet and carrying her over to the bed. He dropped Kathryn onto the mattress, then reached for the zipper to her denims, pulling it down and stripping her naked in a single move. Holding her gaze, he dropped to one knee between her legs and ran his hands up her calves to her knees. He bent her legs and pushed them wide, baring her sex to his hungry stare. He licked his lips slowly, then looked up again and met her eyes.

"Mine, Katie. Don't forget that."

"Lucas, I—"

He never heard whatever protest she'd been about to make, only the sound of her indrawn breath as he dropped to the bed between her thighs and licked, running his tongue along her slit, opening her outer lips to reveal her swollen pussy, wet and flushed with desire. He licked again, tasting her, swirling his tongue over the sensitive nub of her clit. He narrowed his eyes with lust at the sight of that concentrated bundle of nerves standing up proudly from beneath its hood, hard and red as a cherry, almost quivering with excitement. He pressed his tongue over its eager hardness, and Kathryn moaned, lifting herself against his mouth.

Lucas grabbed hold of her hips with a growl, letting her know that he was the one in control. At least for now. Sex with Kathryn was a delicious battle for dominance, and one he didn't mind losing on occasion. But not tonight, and not in this moment.

He began sucking hard on her sensitive nub, drawing it up further from its protective sheathing as Kathryn bucked beneath him. When the hard, little cherry was swollen to twice its size, when Kathryn's fingers were gripping his hair so hard it hurt, he bit down and tasted the sweetest blood of all. Kathryn screamed as the chemicals in his bite hit the very nerve center of her pussy. Her back arched as an orgasm swept over her, her muscles spasming beneath his fingers, her sex clenching against his mouth. She was crying, tears running down her cheeks with an overload of sensation, murmuring his name over and over again, like a plea for something.

No, not *something*, Lucas thought to himself. He knew what she wanted. What she needed. What they *both* needed. He lifted his mouth from the silky place between her thighs and prowled up her body, licking and kissing, lingering to fill his mouth with her swollen nipples, to lick the sweat from between her breasts, gliding higher until the hard length of his cock rested between her legs, against the volcanic heat of her core.

"Kathryn," he growled. He waited until her eyes opened, blurry with desire as she gazed up at him. And then he plunged his cock deep into her body, groaning as her hot, wet channel closed around him, still vibrating from her orgasm as she welcomed him inside. He pushed into her until he was fully sheathed, until his balls slapped against her perfect ass, and her legs came up and curved over his back.

She wrapped her arms around him, her short nails digging into his back, her eyes closed as the walls of her vagina pulsed and shivered. Lucas leaned down and kissed her eyelids one at a time. She opened her eyes and smiled up at him with such naked emotion that his breath caught in his chest. And then, as if realizing what she'd done, or fearing what she'd given away, she closed her eyes again and began lifting her hips in the timeless mating rhythm, undulating beneath him, so her breasts brushed against his chest as her pussy slid up and down his cock.

Lucas let her control the rhythm for a few minutes, enjoying the silk and cream glide of her body, the graze of her hard nipples over his chest. He leaned down, tucking his face against her neck and inhaling deeply, taking in the scent of her skin, her sweat, and the delicious heat of her blood so close to the surface.

Kathryn's heart was a drumbeat against his chest as her movements sped up, as her hips thrust frantically. Lucas laid a lingering kiss on the velvet softness of her neck, smiling as Kathryn shivered in anticipation. She was panting now, her fingers gripping the back of his neck, her head turned to one side as if offering herself to his bite.

He pressed his lips along the plump swell of her jugular until he found the perfect spot, and then he sucked hard, pulling her vein into his mouth and releasing it. Kathryn moaned and dropped one hand to his ass, fucking him frantically to relieve the beginning of a climax he could feel rippling along his cock.

He lifted his mouth and blew softly on her wet skin. She trembled. Without warning, he bit into her vein, closing his eyes in ecstasy as the warm honey of her blood rolled down his throat, causing his heart to hammer against his ribcage, his nerves to thrum with excitement as heat filled every inch of his body.

Kathryn froze beneath him, as if caught in a moment of time, and then she screamed as every muscle in her body seemed to spasm at once, her legs scissoring over his hips, her arms tightening across his back as her nails dug in, scoring his back until he could feel the warm flow of his own blood. His cock grew impossibly hard as her inner muscles convulsed around him, rippling and stroking his shaft.

Lucas groaned, his fangs still buried in Kathryn's neck, her blood still filling his mouth. Lifting his head, he swallowed, reveling in the unique taste of her as his hips resumed pumping, slamming his cock deep between Kathryn's legs as she writhed around him. Her breath was coming in short, puffing gasps, and she was giving little wordless cries of pleasure that made his dick twitch and his balls tighten, made his climax build to an unbearable weight before it finally rushed down his shaft, a fiery flood of release that splashed against Kathryn's womb, branding her with his heat, marking her as his.

Lucas collapsed against Kathryn's overheated body, his face still buried in the crook of her neck. Lifting his head slightly, he licked away the few drops of blood from the neat puncture wounds, sealing them with the chemical in his saliva. In a few hours, there would be no visible trace of his bite, although Kathryn's body would remember far longer than that. He grinned at the thought.

"What are you grinning about?"

He shifted his gaze and found her watching him. "There are so many things that I don't know where to begin."

"You're so full of shit," she responded lazily. "I know what you're thinking."

"Really? I'm all ears."

Kathryn flexed her inner muscles, caressing his cock, which was still semi-hard and buried inside her. "If you were all ears, boyo, we wouldn't be here at all."

Lucas laughed. "Point taken. But you're avoiding the question. What was I thinking?"

"You were being all me Tarzan, her Jane. Guys always get that smug look when they make a woman come, like no one's ever done it before."

She slapped his ass playfully, but Lucas felt a sudden surge of rage that made him want to fuck her so senseless she wouldn't ever even *think* about another man. His eyes must have gone gold, because Kathryn was giving him a wary look.

"Lucas?"

"What?" he growled, knowing he was overreacting and somewhat shocked at his own anger. Of course she'd had other lovers before him. God knew he'd had more than his share. It was probably all the blood he'd consumed the night before. It had given the symbiote enough power to heal him, but it also brought every other vampire characteristic to fore, including a vicious possessiveness about this particular woman.

"Everything okay?" Kathryn questioned.

He brought his power under control with an act of will and focused on the woman beneath him. "Of course," he lied, and lowered his head to kiss her before rolling off to one side. "I was just thinking about Klemens."

"That's the vampire who sent Alex to kill you?" she asked cautiously.

"Yes. Though your presence must have been a nasty surprise. Not even Klemens is foolish enough to try to murder an FBI agent."

Kathryn shrugged and sat up, tossing her long hair behind her. Lucas reached out to tangle his fingers in the silky strands, tempted to use it to pull her back down beside him, or more specifically, beneath him, so he could demonstrate his superiority to any other lover she might have, past or future.

A phone rang in the other room. Lucas frowned at the unfamiliar tone, but Kathryn patted his shoulder and said, "Nick gave me a new cell phone for you. That's probably it."

Lucas got up and stalked from the room, still pissed at both himself and Kathryn. He found the phone on the table near the door. It was just like his old one and no doubt already contained all of the information his old one did, too.

"Nick," he answered. "What's up?"

"Klemens, my lord. We know where he is, and he'll be there all night."

"Excellent. How much time do you need?"

"We're ready, and the plane is waiting."

"Even better. Give me ten minutes."

Lucas disconnected and strode back into the bedroom, going straight for the shower once more.

"Hey!" Kathryn jumped out of bed and hurried after him. "What's going on?"

Lucas closed the shower door and stepped under the hot spray without answering. Kathryn was not so easily deterred, however. The door opened, and she joined him, pumping a handful of his shower gel and washing herself off quickly as she spoke.

"Where are we going?"

"*We* are not going anywhere. I'm going to pay Klemens a visit."

"Fuck that. He has my brother."

"I don't think—"

"Alex had Daniel, and now Alex is dead. And according to you, he was acting under orders from this Klemens asshole, which means Klemens is probably holding Daniel. I'm going with you."

"One . . . no, you're not. This is vampire business, and it's going to be ugly. And two . . . I don't think Alex ever had your brother, hence, Klemens doesn't either."

"Three," she said, snarkily continuing his count . . . I don't care what you think. And four . . . I don't need your permission to do whatever I want, big guy."

"Maybe, but you don't know where I'm going, either."

"Oh, like I can't find out. Even vampires have to file flight plans, and I can certainly get the tail numbers from your planes."

"And I can put you into a sleep so you don't wake up until it's all over," Lucas ground out.

"And I can charge *you* with assault on a federal officer," she snapped, getting up in his face.

"Then I'll fix it so you don't remember that, either," he responded, shoving his face so close to hers that their noses were touching.

"What the hell is your problem?" she demanded.

"I don't know what you're talking about."

"The hell you don't. You've been pissy ever since . . . Oh, please. Just because I said all guys get smug after sex? What? You're too good to be lumped in with other men?"

Lucas snarled and grabbed her around the waist, shoving her against the tiled wall and holding her there with his body. "*I* am not a man at all. You should remember that."

Kathryn grinned, then licked a drop of water from his chin. "You sure act like one sometimes." She rubbed her foot up the back of his calf, and his cock hardened instantly. "Unfortunately, I don't believe we have time to act on *that*," she murmured.

Lucas bared his teeth and tightened his grip around her, lifting her until his cock was nestled in the soft triangle between her thighs. "There's always time," he growled and pushed into her wet heat, thrusting forward until his shaft was fully seated, their bodies skin to skin in the steamy shower.

Kathryn gasped at the unexpected intrusion. Her head fell back, and her eyes closed, the big vein in her neck straining with the sudden rush of blood, almost begging to be tapped. Lucas bent close, licking and tasting her lips, her jawline, dipping his tongue into her ear before running it roughly over her plump jugular. The leg she'd been rubbing along the back of his calf was now clamped around his hips, pumping gently as she encouraged him to get closer . . . and to *move*. Lucas grinned and began fucking her, thrusting steadily in and out as he squeezed the firm globes of her luscious ass.

"You don't play fair," she breathed as she gripped his shoulders, flexing the muscles of her butt as she thrust against him.

"Fuck fair," he whispered against her ear, then dropped his lips to the delicate skin of her neck and sank his fangs into her honey-sweet vein.

Kathryn jolted when the euphoric in his bite hit her bloodstream, her muscles clenched in anticipation of the coming orgasm. A full-body shudder rippled from her head to her toes, her leg tightening around his hips, holding him inside her as the tiny muscles of her sheath trembled along his shaft. Kathryn cried out suddenly, nails digging into his shoulders as her body fisted around him like a warm, wet glove. Her cry became a keening wail as the orgasm swept over her, and she began pumping against him furiously trying to ease the ache. Lucas lifted his mouth from her neck and licked the twin puncture wounds. He would have liked to take her back to bed, to have wrung every last bit of climax from her trembling body before seeking his own. To remind her of the pleasure he could give her over and over again, and let her try to find a human lover who could match it. Or another vampire who would dare touch her. She was his, or she was no one's. But there wasn't enough time.

He growled at the thought, enraged that she could bring him to this, enraged that he had permitted it. He tightened his hold on her and fucked harder, slamming his hips against hers until he felt the overwhelming heat of his own climax building to a roar, tightening his balls and hardening his cock as he thrust into the tight fist of her body before he came with a shout of triumph, filling her once more with his release.

Lucas eased Kathryn's legs back to the shower floor. She held onto him for a moment, her strong fingers gripping his arms almost painfully tight. Her heart was pounding rapidly, her breasts pulsing with the force of it. It was the exertion of their lovemaking, but also the heat of the shower which had been running the entire time, making the shower stall more like a steam room than a shower.

"You okay?" he asked, bracing her gently.

She nodded and licked her lips. "Point made, vampire," she said, her husky voice breathless, her muscles trembling beneath his hands. "You're definitely one of a kind."

Lucas felt a rush of pleasure, but tamped it down, only permitting himself a slight smile before saying, "If you've finished accosting my manly self, I've got to get ready. Nick and the rest will be waiting for me downstairs."

"Right," she agreed, brushing her wet hair out of her face. She frowned at the wet bandage on her arm. "I'll need to fix this, and borrow some clothes from you. I didn't come prepared for skulking around in the dark."

Lucas released her and stepped back. "That's all right, because you won't be doing any skulking."

"Lucas, be reasonable. I can help you."

"I doubt that. The only thing you'll do is get in the way and end up getting hurt."

She punched his arm hard enough to hurt. "Fuck you. I train every fucking day for this."

"Yeah?" he responded. "If you're so tough, take me down. Right here, right now." He strode out of the shower and into the living room where he found the sidearm she always wore. He shook it loose from its holster. "Here's your Glock," he said, holding it out to her. "Shoot me."

"I'm not going to shoot you," she said, clearly appalled at the idea.

"Take the gun, Kathryn." He pushed it into her hand, and she grabbed it from him, racking the slide to verify its readiness as she scooted back to put several feet between them.

"Stop that, Lucas. There's no external safety on a Glock. This weapon's hot."

"Yeah," Lucas replied dismissively. "I'm terrified. So shoot me."

"I told you," she spit angrily, "I'm not going to shoot you. This isn't a fucking game."

"Do it, Kathryn," Lucas demanded, advancing on her menacingly. "Do it, or I'll take it and do it for you."

She stared at him in disbelief for no more than a few seconds before the gun came up between them. "Stop it," she said. "This isn't funny."

Lucas shook his head. "It's not meant to be funny. I'm making a point. Shoot me." He kept advancing, then purposely let his fangs emerge to press against his lower lip. "Do it, do it, do it," he thundered, punctuating each one with a pounding footstep.

"No further, Lucas," she said, deadly serious now, the gun absolutely steady in both hands.

"Make me stop."

"Damn it." She raised the gun a fraction, and he saw the slightest tension in her right hand as she prepared to pull the trigger.

And then he moved. Two seconds later, her gun was his, and he had her wrapped up tight in his other arm, spitting mad.

"You fucking asshole," she snarled. "Let go of me."

Lucas released her without an argument, and she stumbled several feet away from him. But he held onto the gun. He wasn't a total idiot.

"What the hell was that?" she demanded, her blue eyes filled with fire.

"That, *a cuisle*, was a demonstration of why you're not coming tonight. As you so rightly pointed out, this isn't a game. This is war. And when vampires go to war, people die. A human wouldn't stand a chance." He zipped across the room faster than she could follow and hugged her gently. "And I've no desire to watch you die."

She tensed in the circle of his arms. "Let go of me," she said tightly. She was clearly still angry at his demonstration, but that was all right. He'd rather have her angry and alive, than dead the first time she tried to face off with a vampire on the field of battle.

Lucas released her with a shrug. "You wouldn't have believed me any other way, Kathryn."

She rubbed her wrist, although he knew he hadn't hurt her. Even making his point, he'd been exquisitely careful of her human vulnerabilities. Far more careful than his enemies would be.

"Your arm?"

"Fine," she said. "So I can't match you guys for muscle or speed," she admitted sullenly. "But there's more to a takedown like this—"

"This is not a takedown," Lucas interrupted implacably. "This is war, Kathryn. Call it what it is. Vampires fight to the death."

"*Fine*," she repeated irritably. "But there's more to *war* than hand-to-hand fighting. I can't match you there, I admit it, but I sure as hell can shoot. Give me a decent long gun and the high ground, and I'll be your overwatch."

Lucas opened his mouth to reject her offer, but stopped and eyed her curiously instead. "You can do that?"

"Yes, Lucas," she said patronizingly, "I can do that. You're just like all those assholes at the Bureau who think women only know how to type or play hookers."

"No," Lucas said slowly. "I never thought that." He considered his options for a long moment. "Have you ever killed anyone?" he asked bluntly.

Kathryn blinked. "No," she admitted.

"Ever shot a live human being?"

"Once. Not with a rifle. It was up close. Small town. My partner and I were passing through, actually aiming for one town over in an investigation of what looked like a home-bred terror cell, when four assholes robbed a bank across the street from the coffee shop where we'd stopped for lunch. Locals were outgunned and more than happy to accept our assistance."

"You shot a bank robber?"

She nodded. "One of the four tried to make a break for it while his buddies went down, guns blazing. He was wearing a vest. Body armor," she clarified. "I could have gone for a head shot and made it." She shrugged. "But he'd already tossed his weapon, so I shot him in the leg instead."

"That was good of you."

"I'm an FBI agent, Lucas. I try to apprehend suspects, not kill them."

"Another reason you shouldn't come with us tonight. You can't shoot a vampire in the leg, Kathryn. It'll just piss him off."

She regarded him steadily, her jaw tight with anger, but her gaze thoughtful. "What about you guys?" she asked.

"What about us?" Lucas replied, puzzled.

"Are you going to kill everyone you meet tonight?"

"Well, not everyone," he joked, then sobered at her look of irritation. "The simple answer is *yes*. Any vampire who meets us in battle tonight will die. Some might surrender. Klemens is not an easy master, and not too many of his vampires will be sad to see him go. Unfortunately, the Sire/Child bond will drive even most of those who hate him to defend him. They'll die along with the others."

"That's a pretty brutal way of life."

Lucas nodded. "That's what it means to be Vampire."

"Will there be any humans at all?"

"Not on our side, but Klemens is expecting a visitor, a local mob boss who won't want to be seen. Klemens will probably permit the human to bring a few of his own guards with him, and they'll be human, too."

"Will you wait until the humans are gone before attacking?"

"Definitely not. That mob guy is my distraction. But you shouldn't worry too much about him. He and every one of his guards have probably killed, or ordered killed, more people than either one of us. Well, you anyway. I've lived a long, bloody time."

Kathryn stared up into his eyes, clearly trying to decide if he was joking about his own death count. He wasn't.

"All right," she said, in the tone of one who's made a decision. "Find me some high ground. I can at least take down any guards this mob guy brings with him. I won't kill them unless I have to, but there are other ways of making certain a man stays down. Humans don't have your tolerance for pain. I'll also do my best to cover you against your vampire enemies. What's the best way to disable a vampire?"

"You don't *disable* a vampire," Lucas said bluntly. "You kill him. Hit the heart if you can. If not, aim for the head. Depending on the ammo, it might at least take him out of the game long enough for you to get away. Assuming you're as good as you say."

"I am."

"Okay," he agreed, smiling at her look of surprise. "I keep telling you, Kathryn. This is war. I won't turn away a weapon just because it comes wrapped in a very sexy package."

"A package *you* won't be unwrapping again anytime soon," she retorted.

Lucas laughed. "Tell Nick what kind of gear you need, and if we don't have it here, he'll have it waiting for you when we land. But you follow my orders, Kathryn. No questions asked."

"Hey, that's what we do at the FBI. We follow orders." She strode past him, slapping away the hand he reached out to her. "I have to finish my shower. And I'll need those clothes."

KATHRYN LEANED over the private jet's conference table and studied the amazing array of photographs and schematics from Klemens's Chicago compound. They'd taken off from Rapid City in Lucas's elegant private jet—apparently it really *was* good to be the king. She doubted too many invading forces travelled in such luxury. They were no sooner in the air than Nick produced his files on Klemens and started discussing their battle plan for the night. She wouldn't have thought it possible for a private citizen to accumulate this kind of data, but she was probably being naïve. In the era of Google Earth and the million other Internet sites where one could farm data, a first rate hacker could work miracles. And like everything else, when it came to hackers, there was apparently nothing but the best for Lucas.

"Tell me again how you know Klemens will be there tonight?" Kathryn asked Nicholas.

He glanced at Lucas for permission, then said, "That's a bit of good luck on our part. Klemens has some unsavory human allies in Chicago, including Hector McKinney, who's one of the major crime bosses locally. That's who he's meeting tonight. Now, normally, you'd expect that to mean increased security, but the thing is, Klemens is no fool. He doesn't trust his mobbed up ally and limits the number of soldiers he can bring to their meetings. Of course, McKinney doesn't trust Klemens either, so Klemens makes a big show of limiting his guards, too.

"Like I said, it's mostly for show on Klemens's part. His vamps are all there, but they're out of sight, mostly in the basement."

"So they just hang out in the basement for a few hours?"

"A vampire's basement is not what you think, Agent Hunter. Especially not in the headquarters of a vampire lord. It will be fully built out, with every comfort. But it's still a basement, and it puts the majority of his guards in one place when we attack."

"I see. What about this house?" she asked, pointing to Klemens's nearest neighbor, *near* being a relative term in this case, given the size of the lots. Klemens's house was huge, with a lot size to match. His neighbor's house was just as big, but it had one big advantage from Kathryn's point of view—it was three stories, where Klemens's was two and a dormer attic. That put the neighbor's roof at least ten feet above Klemens, and that was ten feet Kathryn could use to her advantage . . . assuming she could get there.

"That's where you'll be," Nick confirmed. "The owners are in Florida. They leave every year after Thanksgiving and don't return until late April."

"Every year?" Kathryn asked. "How long have you had this guy under surveillance?"

Nicholas shot another glance at Lucas, who was sitting next to her.

"Vampires live a long time," Lucas commented cryptically.

"Whatever that means," she muttered. "Okay, so the owners are in Florida, but a place this big, they must have housekeeping staff, gardeners, even guards. What about them?"

"The housekeeper only stops by twice a week. They do have a security system and a drive-by patrol that follows a regular schedule. Their company policy is to vary their patrols for obvious reasons, but they don't. Also, they literally *drive by*, so unless you're planning on standing on the roof and waving, there won't be anything for them to see."

"So, I'll have the place to myself, then."

Nick jerked his head in agreement. "As soon as we hit the ground in Chicago, you'll be going directly to Klemens's estate. One of my guys will drive you and help you get set up inside the house. Lucas and the rest of us will proceed more cautiously, but I need you up and ready to go by the time we get there. Once Lucas arrives at the estate, there won't be any time to climb over walls and sneak into houses. We'll have to attack immediately."

"You do realize, Kathryn," Lucas drawled, "that you'll be breaking and entering the neighbor's house in order to get up on the roof. You being an FBI agent and all . . ."

Kathryn scowled. She hadn't even considered that aspect of the night's activities, but Lucas was right, damn him. She was breaking the law just by walking into that house. She glanced up and saw the laughter in his eyes at her predicament.

"Smart ass," she muttered. "Okay, what am I doing there?"

"Just what you suggested," Nick said simply. "Overwatch. Klemens's estate is too big for us to cover every possible angle. But if you find the right spot, you should be able to see all but the side farthest from your position. If you see anything wonky, you let me know, and I'll direct the response."

Kathryn nodded. This was good, and she could do it with a clear conscience since it wouldn't involve killing anyone. Hopefully.

Nick shifted his attention to Lucas. "How do you want us to proceed with the assault, my lord?"

"How many warriors do we have total?" Lucas asked pensively, studying the satellite image of Klemens's house.

"Minneapolis is fielding almost their full contingent. They're on the ground in Chicago by now. I also brought in fighters from Kansas and Missouri. They both left last night and arrived during daylight earlier today. With your guard, that gives you at least fifty seasoned warriors."

"And Klemens?"

"Because of his visitor, his visible numbers are limited. No more than ten in evidence, including his personal guard and the team on the gate. But he'll have at least another ten close by, most likely out of sight in the basement. It's possible that with the recent hostilities, he'll have upped that number, but I've got eyes on the compound and expect to have a more accurate count by the time we land."

D. B. Reynolds

"What about the human guards?" Kathryn interjected.

Nicholas gave her a blank look, as if he wasn't used to counting the humans as part of the threat. Which he probably wasn't. Lucas's earlier demonstration had stung—in more ways than one—but it had driven home very explicitly just how outclassed humans would be against even a small force of vampires.

"You said the mob guy would have his own guards?"

A look of comprehension crossed Nick's face, and he nodded. "I expect no more than seven humans, including McKinney."

Kathryn nodded. At least some of the human guards would probably remain outside to keep an eye on the gate, because they wouldn't trust the vamps to do it for them. So, they'd be her first targets when Lucas gave the word. She frowned. What was the word anyway? She drew a breath to ask, but listened instead as Lucas began to detail the attack plan for the night.

"There are only two main entries," he began, "so we'll go in front and back. You'll take out the gate guards first, Nick, but I don't want them dead. I don't want Klemens to know exactly what we're doing until we hit the house. Once we're through the gate, we'll have a small roving force around the house, but most of you will concentrate on the two major points of entry. You take one, and let Zelma take the other. As soon as you're set, I'll start projecting, and you hit the doors. I'll handle Klemens and whoever tries to block my path. The rest is up to you."

"Sire," Nicholas acknowledged with a sharp nod. "I'll tell the others."

Lucas nodded his permission, and Nicholas made his way down the aisle and began conferring with the rest of the vampire force.

"What did you mean, when you said you'd 'start projecting'?" Kathryn asked.

Lucas had been studying the house schematic, but now he looked up at her with a smile that melted her heart. She wanted to resist him, but her face seemed to have a will of its own. She smiled back at him.

He took her hand, playing idly with her fingers as he answered her question. "Vampire lords have unusual talents, some of which are unique to the individual. One of *my* most useful talents is the ability to connect with other vampires on what I think of as a visceral level. It's not telepathy—it's both more and less than that. For example, in battle, I can share my far greater strength with my warriors, boosting them both physically and psychologically. But the other side of this particular talent is that I can also drain away the strength and courage of my *enemies,* can make them believe their worst nightmare is upon them."

"Are there limits?" Kathryn asked, somewhat amazed by what she was hearing. "I mean, why do you need any warriors at all? Why not just zap Klemens and his troops from the get-go?"

"Because Klemens is also a vampire lord. And once he realizes what I'm doing, he'll eventually be able to block me from affecting his people. That will take time—not much time, no more than a few minutes—but it will be enough to give us a head start, because Klemens won't be able to block the initial assault, and the shock effect will be considerable. Especially for the newer or weaker among his vampires. They will be hit harder and recover more slowly, leaving them vulnerable when we crash the house.

"But, in the end, it will come down to a brutal, bloody war of vampire on vampire. At least until I destroy Klemens."

Kathryn gave him a worried look. "But you *can* do that, right? I mean, you're stronger than he is."

Lucas shrugged. "Obviously, I believe I can. I'm not suicidal. Why? Are you worried about me?"

She *was* worried about him. But she wasn't going to admit it. Wasn't going to admit that he was important to her, that maybe she cared more about him than was healthy . . . for her anyway. Instead, she changed the subject by asking, "What about my brother?"

Lucas frowned, as if he knew she had feelings for him and was irritated that she wouldn't admit it. But then he couldn't possibly *know* that. So maybe it was just his considerable ego wanting to be stroked.

"I told you, Kathryn. I don't think Klemens has your brother."

"So you've said, but what if he does?"

Lucas sighed. "If he does, he's probably locked up somewhere. Probably the basement, which is the safest place for him."

"Make sure Nicholas tells—"

"Nick has already briefed everyone on the possibility. We're not looking to kill any humans tonight, and certainly not anyone being held prisoner by Klemens."

He stroked an absent hand over Kathryn's tightly bound hair, tugging gently on her braid.

"The rifle meets your standards?" he asked.

Kathryn nodded. Nick had managed to round up the rifle and scope she wanted before they left Minneapolis. While Nick and Lucas had gone straight to the airport to confer with the various groups of vampires heading out for the battle, she'd gone to a gun range with the Minneapolis security chief to calibrate the weapon and adjust it to her specific requirements. But she didn't think Lucas was asking the question because he doubted the weaponry. He was trying to gauge her mood. He was concerned about how she'd react once the killing started. He hadn't come right out and said anything, but he'd hinted around on the subject all the way to the airport. She would have liked to reassure him, but she still wasn't certain how she felt about it herself. Nothing about tonight's engagement was legal, not according to human law. And her job was to represent that law, a job she took very seriously.

"The weapon's fine," she assured him. "Your guy had already calibrated it to a hundred yards. I just did some fine-tuning. When I look through that scope, it'll be like I'm standing right next to you."

"Well, don't shoot me."

Kathryn gave a breathy laugh and nudged his thigh next to hers. "I won't. I'm very clear about my targets before I pull the trigger."

"Your arm?"

"Sore, but better than expected. Your blood?"

He nodded. "You'll be warm enough?"

That made her turn her head and smile at him, erasing the somber note that had flavored their interaction since leaving Minneapolis. "I'm wearing two of your long-sleeved T-shirts over my own sweater, plus this nice, warm jacket Nick found for me. The leggings are mine, and they're winter-weight so perfectly adequate. I'd rather have my tactical boots, but the running shoes and socks are warm enough, and at least they're black. Do I pass inspection?"

Lucas tugged her braid again, harder this time. "Smart ass. I'm sending Mason with you to the neighbor's." She opened her mouth to protest, but he kept talking. "He hooked up with a maid last week, scored an invite. He's not going to stay. He'll just get you through the house and set up on the roof. The house is supposed to be empty, but there's no sense taking chances."

She nodded, businesslike.

"Try not to shoot any of my guys, okay?"

That was greeted with a sideways scowl. "I told you, the scope is good, and I'm very careful. Besides, according to you, my little gun won't do much damage to a vampire anyway."

"Hey, it hurts to get shot, even if it doesn't kill you."

"So I've heard. I'll do my best."

Kathryn started to say more, wanting reassurance in triplicate that her brother wouldn't be hurt accidentally. But Nicholas rejoined them just as the plane angled left and entered a sweeping turn. She looked out the window and saw the lights of Chicago in the distance.

"Buckle up, Kathryn," Lucas advised her. "This war is about to start."

Chapter Eighteen

Chicago, Illinois

WHEN THEY ARRIVED, theirs was the only jet, hell, the only plane, moving at the small airport. Lucas did a quick survey of the area as he followed several of his warriors down the stairs, then waited as Kathryn descended more carefully, the long rifle case visible over her right shoulder. Mason had tried to carry it for her, but she'd declined firmly. Something about no one touching her weapon. So the big vampire had grabbed a couple of huge duffle bags, pointed out their vehicle and headed off to do his own equipment check.

With Lucas on the ground inside Klemens's territory, everything was in play and moving fast. He had grabbed Kathryn for a final hard and fast kiss when she reached the tarmac. "You stay up on that roof, until I tell you it's safe."

"Yeah, yeah," she said, already securing her various pieces of gear on her body. "I know the drill." She stopped suddenly and grabbed the front of his black shirt, which was just like the ones she'd borrowed from him. "Take care, Lucas," she said, meeting his gaze seriously. "I'll see you on the other side."

Lucas frowned. The superstitious Irish street tough he'd once been didn't like the sound of those final words, even though he knew it had a different meaning in the modern context. He watched her run toward the waiting SUV, watched Mason slam the cargo hatch, then climb into the driver's seat. Lucas tracked the taillights until they disappeared around the main terminal, then followed Nick to his own SUV and the many vampires waiting for his command.

The minute Lucas had landed in Chicago, Klemens had known he was here. He wouldn't know Lucas's precise location immediately, only that he'd violated Klemens's territory. They were counting on the Chicago vampire lord's reaction being stalled somewhat by the presence of his human guest. The mob boss was too egotistical and too important to Klemens's operations to dismiss lightly, which meant Klemens would have to disengage diplomatically, and that would take time. Even if he sacrificed the mob boss and broke away quickly, it would still be a few minutes before he realized that Lucas was literally coming through his front gate.

As they raced down the midnight streets of Chicago, Nick kept up a steady murmur of conversation, checking in with the troops already in place around Klemens's compound—close enough to keep watch on who came and went, but not so close that their presence would trigger any of Klemens's own security. War craft was much easier in this technological age than it had been when Lucas first started out with Raphael. Not that they'd had to fight that many wars on this side of the Atlantic, not once the North American vampire community got a taste of what Raphael could do. There hadn't been that many vampires on this continent then, and those were mostly concentrated along the Atlantic corridor. But early on, Raphael had made it clear that his interest lay in the far West. As long as the vampires whose lands they passed through left him alone, he left them alone, too.

Lucas still thought sometimes about how much easier his life back then would have been with a good pair of binoculars, and maybe a motion sensor or two.

He looked up as the SUV slowed, and Klemens's monstrosity of a house came into view. It looked more like an asylum than a home, but the Chicago vampire lord probably liked it that way.

"Sire."

Lucas turned to Nick. "Everything set?"

"The gate guards are down, and the entry teams are in place."

"The human, McKinney?"

"Still inside, my lord. One of his bodyguards was with Klemens's gate guards, and there's an empty SUV with the door open on the street. I'm guessing the human guard was supposed to remain with the vehicle."

"Is the human dead?"

Nick nodded.

Lucas was glad Kathryn wasn't there to debate the issue. He took a moment to search out every one of his vampires, reaffirming their connection to him, offering strength and courage, as well as verifying their positions around the estate.

"Let's do this, Nick."

KATHRYN SETTLED into position, making sure everything she needed was within reach. She and Mason had broken speed limits all the way across town, getting here in what had to be some sort of record. Once on the scene, they'd set another record, making it into and through the house so quickly that it was obvious Mason had scouted it out ahead of time. The door they'd entered through had been unlocked, and once inside, he'd shown no hesitation. He'd known exactly where to go and had literally carried her up the stairs, simply slinging an arm around her waist and *moving.* It had been exhilarating and terrifying all at once. Getting to the roof hadn't proved a problem either, since she'd already decided she wasn't going to work from there. One look at the steeply pitched roof as they'd pulled in behind the house, and she'd known it wouldn't work. The only place she could have set up securely on a pitch like that would have been the peak, and that wouldn't have given her a good line of sight on Klemens's house next door. So, she'd shooed Mason on his way, then set up in one of the third-story bedrooms instead. It was very nearly as high off the ground as the rooftop, and from the window, she had a nearly 180 degree view of Klemens's estate. She could see any movement along the front and most of the back, as well as the side nearest her position.

The window was one of the older double-hung kind that operated on a pulley system to open straight upward. With the window wide open, she had arranged her sandbags on the broad sill, then set up a Sig SSG 3000, which was nearly identical to the one she used back at Quantico. Setting the rifle carefully on a table she'd pulled over near the window, she lifted her binoculars and swept the scene in night vision mode. Lucas hadn't arrived yet, but the advance team vampires were on the move, taking up positions all around the house.

Raising her field, she checked out the building itself with the night vision off. There were a few lights inside, mostly concentrated on the second floor, a corner room on her side of the building. The curtains were drawn, but the occasional shadow of movement could be seen along the edge of one window. And that was it.

She heard the roar of multiple engines and shifted her gaze just in time to see several big, black SUVs tear around the corner and come to a tire squealing stop in front of the wrought iron gate. Kathryn had a bad moment, fearing they'd been discovered, but then the doors popped open, and she recognized several of Lucas's vampires as they poured through the gate and disappeared into the shadows around Klemens's huge compound.

She kept watching, her eye on the one SUV whose doors remained closed. The night grew abruptly silent. No truck engines, no quiet commands, not even the sound of traffic from nearby Lake Shore Drive. Suddenly, the doors opened, and Kathryn sucked in a breath as Lucas emerged to stand silently, his gaze sweeping from side-to-side, seeming to catalogue every detail down to the exact location of vampires Kathryn had long ago lost sight of. His head turned slowly, his gaze settling on the window where she sat watching, as if he could see her despite all the precautions she'd taken to remain invisible. He shot her a quick grin, then sobered and turned back to face his enemy.

Lucas started forward, surrounded by his troops, and it was a terrifying sight. They were the warriors of their race, tall and bulky with muscle, their eyes glowing an eerie red, like the pits of hell. They were dressed completely in black combat gear, with not a telltale gleam of metal among them. Their weapons varied, some carrying long, wicked-looking knives, others a variety of guns, and some several of both. And all of them, Lucas included, were fully fanged, the white gleam of their teeth a stark contrast to their uniformly somber garb.

Of them all, only Lucas wore no weapons, not even a simple blade. But he was armed more lethally than any of them. The power he'd told her about, the power of a vampire lord that she'd only half believed in, was made real as he strode toward the house. A wind picked up out of nowhere, quickly escalating from a breeze that rattled the trees and sent dead leaves scurrying to escape his footsteps, to a raging storm that stalked the ground ahead of him, pounding the shutters and doors of Klemens's mansion, shattering the windows in their frames. The air, which had been so quiet and still only moments before, was now heavy with a sense of doom, as if the night itself understood that a great battle was about to take place.

Lucas strode forward, dressed in the same black combats as his soldiers, his long leather coat blowing behind him like a cape as the storm of his power spun before him. His black hair was slicked back from his handsome face, and his eyes burned the purest gold, casting a brilliant light on the path he cut across the manicured lawn, a beacon guiding his vampires onward. Kathryn shivered, and not from the cold.

Lucas was several yards from the porch when the door opened, only to be quickly torn from the hand of the man who stood there, bracing himself desperately against the storm of Lucas's power. A piercing white light smeared the frosted yard, giving it a dull, silver cast, and silhouetting two humans. Kathryn immediately dropped the binocs onto the pad of blankets she'd scavenged and placed her eye to the rifle scope.

She centered on Lucas, then moved carefully toward the doorway, marking the two men, first one, then the other. The humans had gone old-school, each carrying an Uzi sub-machine gun, held gangster-style at the hip, with an automatic 9mm sidearm in the other hand. She assumed these were the mob boss McKinney's bodyguards, since Lucas had indicated they'd be the only humans in the house.

One of the two took an aggressive step out onto the front porch, his hair and clothes blowing wildly as he shouted something that the wind tore from his mouth and tossed away. Lucas and his vampires kept coming, as if the man didn't exist. Kathryn swore silently and placed her crosshairs on the foolish human. Lucas might be nearly immortal, but only *nearly*. And she didn't care what he'd said about bullets not taking down vampires. *Enough* bullets could do a lot of damage, and if that guard turned his Uzi on Lucas, it would tear him apart. She sank into her sniper space, her mind and sight riveted to the events unfolding far below, every detail as clear as if she stood two feet away. Her entire world became the small circle of space revealed by her scope. She saw the guard's arm tense as he lifted the gun fractionally, saw him snug the weapon closer to his hip to stabilize it, saw his finger twitch.

She blew out a breath, began her slow squeeze of the trigger . . . and froze as her target disappeared. Moving so fast they'd been nothing but a dark blur across the face of her scope, Lucas's vampires had taken the two human guards down. One moment the two men were getting ready to fire, and the next the doorway was empty, and there were two bodies lying in a huddle on the cold ground. She swallowed hard as one of Lucas's vampires dragged a body up off the ground and sank his teeth into the man's throat, drinking deeply before tossing him aside. She brought up the binocs and took a look. The man was on his back, his head at an unnatural angle, his throat torn out. If he hadn't been dead before, he was now, and she wasn't sure how she felt about that. The human was a gangster and probably a killer, but . . .

But nothing, Kathryn, she reminded herself. Lucas had warned her that this was war. And that guard down there would have happily killed every one of the invading vampires, including Lucas, if he'd had the chance. After all, hadn't she been preparing to do exactly the same thing? If Lucas's vampire hadn't done it first, she would have shot him before he could kill Lucas, and she would have shot to kill, too. But seeing the way he died, seeing him lying there with his throat torn out . . . It bothered her. She couldn't deny it.

She jolted as something like static electricity buzzed over her skin, making the fine hairs on her arms stiffen. Far below, Lucas had lifted his arms as if to embrace the mansion and everyone in it. Then the wind died, and the night went dark and silent as every light in the house, every street light, every distant night light in the neighborhood was doused in the space of a heartbeat.

Kathryn grabbed the night vision binoculars, her fingers trembling as she struggled to hold the lenses steadily enough to see. But there was nothing, only blackness where Lucas had been standing.

She had lowered the binocs, when a flash of movement where there hadn't been any before made her pull away from her desperate search near the front door. She lifted the lenses again and scanned the side of the house, certain she'd seen something move. It had been close to the ground, an anomaly caught in her peripheral vision, not an animal, but there . . . something—a window maybe—was being pushed out from the house. It was little more than a slightly less dark patch of wall, but it was definite movement and, oh, yeah, lots of it.

Kathryn touched the small radio bud in her ear. "Nick." It was only a few seconds before he responded, but it seemed like forever as she watched figures begin to emerge from what was clearly a basement exit. It had to be Klemens's vampires, the ones Nick had said would be hiding from the human visitor, McKinney.

"What have you got, Hunter?" Nick's voice was a welcome noise.

"Lots of movement, my side of the house. I think it's a basement exit of some—"

"On it," Nick interrupted, and then he was gone.

Kathryn dropped the binocs and put her eye to her scope instead. These were almost certainly Klemens's vampires. Lucas had insisted she wouldn't be able to kill them with her rifle, but he'd probably never seen what a .50 caliber round could do. A shot to the head would split a person's skull right down the middle like Play-Doh and pulverize the brain. Not even a vampire could survive that. But she hadn't particularly wanted to kill anyone tonight, so she'd gone with Federal Match Grade .308 Remington 168-grain slugs instead. Sighting on the emerging vampires, she didn't bother with detailed target selection. She just moved the crosshairs from one lump of darkness to the next and pulled the trigger. The first couple howled in surprise as the bullets tore into them. As Lucas had said, it obviously hurt like hell, and it definitely slowed them down. They spun in circles, searching for the shooter, but she just kept firing, and they were soon more preoccupied with evading her bullets than figuring out where they were coming from.

"My guys are on scene, Hunter," Nick warned urgently.

Kathryn stopped firing and switched to binocs as the first of Lucas's vampires engaged their enemy. If she'd thought the death of the human guard on the front porch had been violent, this took it to a whole new level. There was no posturing among the vamps, no jockeying for position, they just stepped in and started ripping each other apart. Knives, fangs, hands curved into claws as they slashed and tore at each other. Heads were ripped from bodies, then tossed aside, the bodies poofing to dust before her eyes. Another vampire was run through with a wicked knife. He grabbed his chest and laughed, until Lucas's warrior stabbed him a second time, straight through the heart. Then he, too, became nothing more than a pile of dust.

Kathryn's heart was hammering, adrenaline setting her nerves on a knife's edge as she watched something she knew few humans would ever see. In moments, there was no one left at the basement window but Lucas's vamps. And not a dead body in sight.

"All clear, Hunter," Nick informed her. "Good work."

"Roger," she managed, her hand shaking as it dropped away from her ear. Dust. Vampires were hard to kill, but they really did turn to dust when it happened. Her bosses at the FBI would be thrilled with the intel she could bring them from this night's activities. She might even get a promotion out of it, maybe something that would get her out of the office and back into the field again. She placed a hand over her pounding heart and thought about loyalties. She didn't know exactly where hers lay anymore. It was a troubling thought.

Someone screamed from deep within the house. Then, as if that first scream had freed them all from a spell of silence, the night was filled with the sounds of battle. It was the stuff of nightmares, and all Kathryn could think was that Lucas was in there somewhere, and she had no idea what was happening. Or whether she'd ever see him alive again.

LUCAS STOOD before his enemy's front door, every ounce of power and knowledge he possessed focused on one thing, spreading fear and confusion among Klemens's vampires. Right up until the moment he'd stepped out of the SUV at Klemens's gate, he'd been using his strength to stop his rival vampire lord from pinpointing his presence. But this close, that was futile. His power signature would be far too strong, and Klemens was far too wily. The minute they'd arrived at the estate, even as he was verifying the location of his warriors around it, and Kathryn, too, in her perch high above the battle, he'd been using his unique talent to whisper in the ears of Klemens's warriors, warning them of invaders sneaking around the corner on a breath of wind, of death tapping their shoulders and snatching away their courage. Their terror fed his power, as rich and sweet as blood from the vein. He didn't relish this part of his talent, this ability to draw strength from the fear of others. But this was war, and if it came down to a choice of who would die this night, he'd use every talent he possessed to make certain it was Klemens and his vampires who bit the big one before the next sunrise.

Lucas spared a thread of power to search for his enemy, the delicate probe slipping through the cracks to search every corner of the eyesore of a house before him. Very soon, he'd have to suck his power back into himself and leave the larger battle to his warriors, because somewhere in there,

Klemens was waiting. No matter how many of the Chicago vampires Lucas's fighters destroyed, the real battle, the only one that really counted, was the showdown between the two vampire lords.

The front door opened only to be torn from its hinges by the raging wind of Lucas's power. He squinted against the sudden shaft of white light as two heavily armed humans staggered into the opening. McKinney's guards, he assumed, and they were getting ready to fire. Several of Lucas's vampires were suddenly in front of him, guarding him with their bodies while two of their number made the dash across the frost-covered lawn and took down the humans before they even managed to bring their weapons to a full firing position. The two men screamed, their voices cut off as their necks were snapped. One of Lucas's vampires fed briefly, ripping out the human's throat as his heart beat its final tattoo. But the feeding was more symbolic than anything else—a predator claiming his victory before tossing the limp body aside.

Aggravated by the bright light, which had no place in a vampire's residence, Lucas reached out and fried the local power grid. The entire neighborhood sank into blessed darkness. Next to him, Nick stiffened to attention, then rapidly deployed several warriors to one side of the house. Lucas heard the repeated pop of several gunshots and glanced up at the neighboring house. A muzzle flash confirmed Kathryn's location, and he grinned. So, she got to shoot her rifle after all. And she didn't seem to be having any second thoughts about it, either. Maybe he'd make a warrior of her yet.

His gaze shifted to the black hole of a front entry. He tugged on the thread of his power and found Klemens.

You should have killed me when you had the chance, he thought mockingly, and let the thought carry to the second story where Klemens waited.

Tonight will do just as well, you mick scum. Klemens's mental voice was filled with venom.

Lucas almost laughed at the petty slur and thought the Chicago vampire must really be worried if he was resorting to such superficial insults. Lucas sent one final nightmare speeding through the enormous mansion, his blood pumping with adrenaline as a flood of terror rushed back to him. He soaked it in, then walked through the front door and up the stairs.

The battle raged as he made his way through the house, his warriors moving silently around him, lethal wraiths who brought permanent death wherever they went. The first screams were the final cries of vampires caught by surprise, still muffled by the blanket of darkness he'd dropped over the house. But as he climbed the stairs, gathering his power back into himself for the final battle, the noise level increased. Vampires howled in agony and roared in triumph. Bodies crashed through walls and tumbled over balconies. Klemens's people fought back viciously, knowing what was at stake, recognizing the depth of their danger. Lucas had no doubt they were being goaded to a desperate defense by their master, who remained tucked away in his place of power, waiting for Lucas, like a fat spider in its web.

Lucas moved swiftly down the second floor corridor, all alone now. Even Nicholas had been drawn away into the frenzied battle raging all around him. Lucas moved with purpose, though he'd never been in this house before, Klemens's presence drawing him as surely as a red arrow flashing in the dark.

He found the Chicago vampire lord in an old-fashioned trophy room. Animal heads were mounted on the walls, and a collection of ancient weapons hung over the huge fireplace where glowing embers revealed the dying light of a recent fire. The room reeked of fresh blood, and Lucas knew he wouldn't have to worry about killing Hector McKinney. Klemens had slaughtered the crime boss, draining him dry to fuel the contest to come.

Klemens appeared out of the shadows, standing from behind the desk. Blood, still warm from McKinney's beating heart, clung to Klemens's clothing and dripped from his fangs. He grinned at Lucas, his hands still curved into the claws that had ripped his former ally to shreds.

"Come to die at last, Lucas?"

Lucas smiled easily, flashing his own fangs as he prepared for the fight of his life. Klemens was powerful, but young as vampires go. He was strong, but inexperienced, wielding his power like a cudgel. He was a gorilla with a big club. Lucas, on the other hand, had power *and* experience. His was a more refined fighting style, death by a thousand cuts. He was going to savor every single slice of Klemens's flesh before he killed him.

Lucas lashed out without warning, carving into the big femoral artery of Klemens's left leg, then immediately snatching his power back into a tight shield around himself. Klemens howled at the unexpected attack and fought back exactly as Lucas had expected he would. A thundering stroke of power slammed against Lucas's shields, a tactic that would have driven him to his knees if he hadn't been prepared for it. But Lucas didn't waste time analyzing his enemy's strategy. Instead, he responded immediately, slashing at Klemens left and right, over and over again, his power like a many-tailed whip whose barbed ends cut into his enemy from every direction, from high and low. Klemens roared as he struggled to protect himself from Lucas's unconventional attack. He flung out a hand, and

Lucas staggered. It was like a huge boulder slamming against his shields, but though they bowed under the assault, they never broke. And like his shields, Lucas never faltered. He snarled his hatred as he sliced the flesh from Klemens's bones, severing arteries and veins, driving the Chicago lord to his knees as his legs gave way, unable to support him.

Klemens gave a deep-throated howl of rage and swept his arms outward. Lucas recoiled as every animal head mounted on the walls came flying toward him at once, physically striking his shields from all sides. It was a desperate move on Klemens's part, meant to distract more than injure, and it nearly worked.

Lucas ducked as a fourteen-point stag head flew at his face, and Klemens attacked from where he knelt, wielding his power just like the club Lucas had imagined. It beat against Lucas's shields from all sides, pounding until Lucas could hear the concussion of air against his shields, a deep resonance like the clapper on a huge bell. And Lucas stood in the middle of it all.

He contracted his shields tightly around himself, making them more secure, even as it drew the blows from Klemens's attack closer to his physical body. But that didn't matter. As long as his shields held, even an inch of protection was enough. From within the cocoon of his power, Lucas studied his enemy. Klemens was bleeding from everywhere, blood pooling around him where he knelt, his flesh hanging in gory strips that mingled with the shreds of his clothing. Lucas changed his attack, no longer wielding a many-barbed whip, but a whippet-thin rapier instead. A sharp needle of power aimed directly at Klemens's heart.

He thrust it outward, felt it penetrate Klemens's shields, felt the vampire lord's shock as it pierced his flesh and burrowed into his heart. Lucas's lips curved into a bare smile of victory as he flicked the rapier once, cleaving Klemens's heart in mid-beat, slicing it in two as it staggered within his chest.

Klemens howled and dropped his shields, scrabbling at his bloody chest, desperately trying to gather the dregs of his power, to heal the unhealable. Lucas was all but certain Klemens would not succeed, but he didn't take any chances. He slashed at the unprotected vampire lord, carving into his flesh and bones until his heart finally surrendered the fight. Klemens died, his final scream of denial echoing in the night long after his body had turned to dust.

Lucas had the space of a heartbeat to savor his victory, a mingling of relief and triumph as he reached out to his vampires, touching each one, affirming their link, reassuring them that their master still lived, still held their lives securely in his power. Then the world collapsed, and he fell to his knees, overwhelmed by the weight of Klemens's subjects, the thousands of vampires suddenly cast adrift by their master's death, crying out in fear and desperation, searching for someone to hold them together, to keep their hearts beating, their walls secure against enemies.

Lucas bowed beneath their demands, his back bent nearly to the floor as he struggled to impose order, to hold onto his own people and still protect those who had belonged to Klemens. Raphael had warned him of this when they'd first discussed the need to confront the Chicago vampire lord. When Lucas had insisted he had no desire to rule the Midwestern Territory along with his own.

Lucas was Vampire, and all that it meant. He was aggressive, territorial, possessive and downright feral when forced into it. But as Raphael had observed with some despair on more than one occasion, Lucas was at heart a cheerful soul, a playboy who enjoyed *life* more than conquest.

So, Raphael had schooled Lucas on how to take Klemens's people under his wing, how to shuffle them safely aside, holding their lives secure until a new lord arose in the aftermath. The territory would be thrown open to all comers. Dominance battles would be fought, and some contenders would die, but eventually a new lord would emerge, and Lucas would be rid of this extra burden.

Lucas sucked in a long breath as the voices died down at last, the drain on his strength diminishing until it was no more than an irritating scrape against his nerves.

"Sire?"

Lucas looked up into Nicholas's concerned face. "We did it, Nick. Ding dong, the bastard's dead."

Nick laughed and offered his Sire a hand up. Lucas took it gratefully. He trusted Nick, and he was exhausted. "Any problems I don't know about?"

"None, my lord. Klemens's people were wholly unprepared. Several tried to sneak out through a basement window, though whether their intent was to run away or defend their Sire, I don't know. In any event, Kathryn gave us warning and kept them pinned down until we got there."

"I heard the shots. Is she—"

"Uninjured, my lord. I've asked her to remain up there until we clear the house."

Lucas gave his lieutenant a quizzical look. There was no reason for Kathryn to remain on watch, and no danger for her here in the house. Nicholas knew this as well as he did.

"I have people searching the house for survivors . . . or victims," Nick admitted. "I agree with you that her brother was likely never here, but—"

"*She* won't believe it until she sees for herself," Lucas said, as understanding dawned. "Right. Okay, get some of our daylight guards here as soon as possible. I want this house secured for at least the next few days. After that—" He shrugged. "I've no desire to live here, but I suppose the next lord might."

"Will we have to stay here until the new lord is figured out?"

"Hell, no."

Nicholas grimaced in agreement. "I've already put in the call to Minneapolis HQ. Daylight security will be on station before dawn. Shall I radio Kathryn and tell her—"

"Lucas!" Kathryn's voice wafted up the staircase.

"Too late," Lucas said.

KATHRYN HAD scrambled to put away her gear and get over to Klemens's house next door. Or rather, what used to be Klemens's house. Nick had radioed to let her know they were cleaning up and to assure her that Lucas and everyone else had survived the battle. He'd asked her to remain where she was, in case anyone tried to make a break for it. She'd done as he asked until she'd spotted several of Lucas's vampires hanging around in the yard, slapping each other on the back in victory. She suspected Nick was trying to keep her away from the house for some reason, and that reason could only have one name. Daniel.

Her heart had wanted her to race over there to see what they'd found, but her brain had insisted she make sure there was no trace of her presence left in this house before she left. So she'd sacrificed the few minutes it took to put the furniture back where she'd found it and tossed the two heavy sand bags out the window. She'd watched where they landed so she could pick them up later, rather than lug them down the stairs. She then closed the window and drew the curtains halfway, just as they'd been when she arrived. She took a final look around the small bedroom, grabbed the rifle case and raced downstairs and out the back door, locking it behind her, making a mental note that someone would have to come by later and set the alarm.

Kathryn deposited her rifle case in the cargo compartment of one of the SUVs idling just outside Klemens's house. The trucks had been pulled through the gates and now stood near the front porch. There was no one around, so she walked into the house via the gaping doorway and stood for a moment, listening. The lower level of the house was mostly unlit, but there was enough moonlight that she could see silhouettes of furniture to either side of where she stood. The hallway to the right had a dim light shining out of it, and she could hear a low rumble that made her think there was an emergency generator somewhere, probably the kitchens. In front of her was a wide staircase that went straight up to a second floor mezzanine that fed into closed hallways on either side.

"Lucas!" she called and started up. Lucas appeared on the mezzanine before she'd climbed more than a few stairs.

"Don't come up," he called down. "I'll come to you."

Kathryn studied him as he descended the stairs, moving with his usual lethal grace, and something more. He looked . . . victorious. It was hard to describe. He was as gorgeous as ever, his black hair attractively mussed, his big body encased in black leather, hazel eyes glittering with gold. But, then, it wasn't so much his physical appearance that was different. It was an air about him, as if he were surrounded by an invisible nimbus of power.

He came even with her. "Do I look that bad?" he half-joked, glancing down at himself.

"No," she said quickly. "Just different somehow."

"Somehow," he agreed with irritating vagueness.

"Klemens?" she asked.

"Dusted, along with most of his cohorts."

Kathryn stared up at him. She hadn't counted, but there'd been a lot of vampires coming out of that basement window, and in a house this size, probably more that she hadn't seen. They were people, just like Lucas and Nick and the others. And just like that they were dead and . . . dusted. She'd seen what happened when a vampire died.

"Kathryn?"

"Yeah. Is this . . . usual? I mean, how often do you guys fight each other to the death?"

"Don't worry, Agent Hunter. It doesn't happen that often, and it doesn't concern you anyway. We choose our path within vampire society, and none of those who died here had to be fighters. They could have been shop owners, lawyers, plumbers, whatever they wanted, and been perfectly safe from all of this. It's like your own military. It's all volunteer."

"That doesn't make it any less of a loss when they die," Kathryn snapped back at him.

"No, it doesn't," Lucas countered tightly. "And there are those, myself included, who will mourn the unnecessary death of every one of these vampires. But my responsibility is to the living, to all of those vampires Klemens held in his power, vampires who *would have died in an instant* if I hadn't stepped up to protect them. So I don't need your judgment, thank you."

"Lucas." She grabbed his arm when he would have gone past her down the stairs. "I didn't mean that."

He stopped a step below her and met her gaze, their eyes even. "No, I don't suppose you did. It's late, Kathryn. It's been a long night, and I won't sleep in this house. We're going back to the St. Paul condo. Are you coming?"

"What about Daniel?" she asked urgently.

Lucas sighed, and she heard the exhaustion in that simple breath. "Your brother isn't here," he said patiently. "My vampires have searched every foot of this grotesque house. There is no one alive within these walls, other than my own people. And there are no fresh graves, either," he added, before she could voice that horrible possibility. It was cruel of him to say it, but she couldn't deny she'd had the same thought.

"How can you know that?" she whispered.

"One, Klemens is . . . *was* too smart to bury victims on his home turf, much less in his own lair. Two, vampires have an incredibly keen sense of smell, especially when it comes to blood and death. He's not here, Kathryn."

Kathryn cast a desperate look around the dark mansion. "I need to—"

"To see for yourself," Lucas finished for her. "I understand. I have a contingent of daylight guards coming in to secure the house. They'll help, if you'd like, and they'll know how to get in touch with me."

"Thank you." She held onto his arm, unsure what to do, but not wanting him to leave angry with her. "Lucas . . ."

He smiled and leaned forward to give her a lingering kiss. "I still love you, Katie mine. We'll be flying back to South Dakota after sunset tonight. Let me know what you want to do." He glanced up the stairs. "Let's go, Nick."

Kathryn stood aside as Nicholas clambered past her to follow Lucas. She looked around and spied a light switch near the front door. Walking over to it, she flicked all of the switches, but nothing happened. Whatever Lucas had done in dousing the lights earlier must have damaged the grid. And it would probably be hours before the emergency crews got out here to fix whatever he'd broken. She sighed and schlepped back outside for the big flashlight in her duffle. She believed Lucas when he said her brother wasn't here. Or at least she believed he believed it. But she couldn't leave this place without seeing for herself, without searching for any evidence that Dan had been here in the past.

And after that . . . She didn't know what she'd do. Because if Alex had never had Daniel, if Klemens had never taken him away, then where was he?

Chapter Nineteen

Twin Cities, Minnesota

KATHRYN STUMBLED wearily through the door of the rooms Lucas had set aside for her in his St. Paul headquarters. It was nearly dark, and she knew Lucas would be waking soon, but she couldn't face him. Not yet. She was grateful beyond belief that he'd made this condo available to her, that her luggage was here with her clothes, her toiletries. She needed a shower. She needed her own soap, her shampoo, her own fresh clothes. She needed something normal and good after spending too many hours searching every room, every closet, every cabinet and drawer of Klemens's house of horrors. His filth clung to her skin, coated her hair, and rooted beneath her fingernails. If there was a perversity that the vampire lord *hadn't* been into, she hadn't found it. He had entire libraries filled with books, computer files, and videos of the very worst kind, pedophilia, snuff films, sexual bondage and sado-masochism—and not the consensual kind, either. And then there had been his private dungeon, the place where he'd indulged his hobbies on a more personal level. Lucas might have been right about the absence of bodies—she'd found nothing to contradict him—but men and women had definitely died in that house.

She drew a deep breath of clean air and stripped down to her skin, then searched the cupboards until she found a box of garbage bags beneath the sink. Every piece of clothing she wore went into a bag, from the coated rubber band in her hair on down, including her sweater and the two shirts she'd borrowed from Lucas, even her athletic shoes and socks. She tied off that bag, then shoved it into a second bag and secured that one just as tightly. Her first instinct was to throw it all away, but she might change her mind later, so for now she simply dropped it in a corner near the door and dragged herself into the bathroom.

Reaching into the shower stall, she turned the hot water on full blast, then leaned wearily over the sink, bracing herself on her arms. She avoided looking in the mirror, glad when the room filled with steam, fogging the glass enough that she couldn't see anything. She felt tainted by what she'd found, and she wondered if she'd ever feel clean again. Turning back toward the shower, she opened the door and nearly stepped under the spray without checking first. Something registered on her tired brain at the last minute, and she put out a hand, jerking it back when the dangerously hot water hit her fingers. Heart pounding, she adjusted the water to just under boiling, then closed the door behind her and stood, letting the water wash over her.

She didn't realize she was crying until the shower door opened and Lucas put his arms around her, holding her while she wept silently, her tears hot against his broad chest, her body trembling with emotion while he held her steady.

"Ah, Katie. We'll find your brother. I promise."

Kathryn couldn't answer at first, couldn't find the breath to do anything but cry. But when she was all cried out, her voice scratchy from her tears, she said, "It's not just Daniel. It's that horrible place. Did you know that he—"

"I knew some of it. We vampire lords don't exactly socialize with one another, so I'd never been to his house before. But I knew Klemens's preferences tended toward . . . degradation, and my people briefed me on what they found before we left. I'm sorry you had to see that."

"You know," she said, sniffing loudly, "I've met some of the agents who work on the child pornography task force, and they've hinted at the sorts of things they deal with. But seeing that awful collection of Klemens's today . . . I'm glad he's dead."

"Aye," Lucas agreed. "I'm only sorry he had to take so many with him."

"But they lived there, too. They must have—"

"Some of them probably shared his tastes, but not all. The bond between a vampire and his children is strong, Kathryn. Even many of those who hated him would have been unable to defy him."

"Then I'm sorry for them, but not the rest."

She felt him kiss the top of her head and tried to pull away. "Don't," she protested. "I'm filthy."

"We'll have to do something about that then," he drawled, his Irish lilt making itself heard.

He reached behind her and snapped open a plastic container, sniffing the contents before drizzling it over her head.

"I can do that, you don't—"

"Let me, *a cuisle*. Just relax."

He turned her around until her back was to his chest, his big body protecting her from the pounding water. His strong fingers massaged her scalp, scenting the steamy shower stall with the fresh smell of her shampoo, filling her nostrils with the cleansing scent instead of the greasy miasma of Klemens's lair. She leaned her head back and let him work, relishing the elegant flow of his muscles, the solid strength of his body behind her. A wave of sadness brought fresh tears to her eyes. She knew this couldn't last. Before too long, she'd have to head back to Virginia, to her job and her life there. She'd have to leave all of this—leave Lucas—behind. Theirs was an impossible relationship. Thousands of miles separated their lives, and that was only distance. She worked for the FBI, and he was a damn vampire lord. How could that ever work between them? She couldn't change who she was any more than Lucas could stop being a vampire. She bent her head, so Lucas wouldn't see the tears. She never cried, and now suddenly, she couldn't seem to stop.

Lucas's fingers stilled, and she thought he'd sensed somehow that she was crying, but then he slid his hands to her shoulders and said, "Prepare to rinse." He turned her slowly into the stream of water, tipping her head forward with a gentle pressure. Once the shampoo was gone, he massaged conditioner in—she'd fallen hopelessly in love with a man who appreciated the need for conditioner.

Her thoughts skidded to a halt. Love? She couldn't *love* Lucas Donlon for all the reasons she'd already told herself.

"Relax, *a cuisle*," he repeated, murmuring against her ear. "I'll take care of you."

Take care of her? What did he mean by that? She didn't need anyone to take care of—Oh.

Lucas's clever hands were rubbing shower gel all the way down her back, over her shoulders and along her arms. He lifted each of her hands separately, washing between her fingers, massaging her fingernails and cuticles, scrubbing away every last bit of Klemens's filth. He moved down to her butt and gave a teasing squeeze before sliding his fingers between her cheeks and lower, slipping one finger into her anus before gliding lower to barely crease her pussy.

Kathryn moaned softly and let her head fall back onto his shoulder. She turned her head and met his mouth. His lips and skin were hot from the shower, but his mouth when she swirled her tongue around was cool and delicious. He sucked hard, pulling her tongue deeper into his mouth before releasing her to trail kisses down her neck to her shoulder where he bit gently on the tender bone of her clavicle.

She felt the cold slide of her shower gel as he dribbled it over her chest, and then the warm caress of his hands, cupping her breasts, teasing her nipples into hard pebbles of sensation as his hands moved lower. He washed her ribs, her abdomen and lower still until he dipped his fingers between the folds of her sex, tantalizing her with toying brushes over and around her clit, stroking the edges of her vagina while denying her even the briefest glide of his fingers into her hungry pussy. Kathryn placed her hand over his, pushing his hand lower, deeper, demanding what she wanted.

But Lucas only chuckled and removed his hand from between her thighs and turned her to face him again. Squeezing more gel onto his hands, he knelt to wash her legs, from her hips to her toes, carefully washing and massaging each leg while Kathryn fisted her fingers in his wet hair, achingly aware of his mouth so close to the center of her desire. She nearly screamed when his tongue suddenly scraped a slow path along her slit, sweeping up the moisture of her arousal before stroking against her clit. His lips closed over that sensitive nub, and Kathryn thought she'd faint as he sucked hard, pulling the swollen pearl between his lips, then letting it slide out again, over and over until it was engorged with blood, until every nerve in Kathryn's body was screaming for release. She squeezed her breasts, pinching her nipples ruthlessly, desperate to assuage some of the pressure, some of the *need,* that was overwhelming her senses.

Lucas reached behind her to cup her ass in his powerful hands, holding her in place as he tormented her, making her feel things she'd never felt with anyone, making her *want* things she knew were impossible. She opened her mouth to beg him to stop, or maybe to keep going forever. She didn't know what she would have said, because at that moment, Lucas closed his teeth over her clit and bit down. She did scream then, as an orgasm stormed through her body like lightning, igniting every nerve ending, firing every muscle, and making every hair on her body stiffen as waves of ecstasy cascaded over her body until she could barely stand. Kathryn tugged on Lucas's hair, crying out her pleasure until the orgasm stole even her breath, and all she could do was gasp his name.

Lucas gave her pussy a final stroke of his tongue, his eyes glowing gold as he looked up at her and licked his lips, visibly savoring the blood he'd drawn from her clit. He stood abruptly, his hard-muscled body sliding over hers as he pressed her against the wall of the shower. She could feel the solid length of his arousal as she lifted her arms around his neck. He gripped her thigh and wrapped her leg around his hip, lifting her higher until he could slide his cock into her eager wetness. Kathryn groaned and closed her eyes, overwhelmed with the velvet over marble sensation of his thick penis pushing into her.

"Open your eyes, Kathryn," Lucas demanded, his voice low and rough.

Kathryn lifted passion-heavy lids and met his golden stare. He held her gaze as he began to fuck her, one hand cupped under her ass, the other pressed against the tile wall as he slid in and out with long, slow movements, letting her feel every inch of his cock as he plunged through her still trembling sheath, his pelvis grinding against her exquisitely aroused clit with every stroke. Kathryn licked her lips, sweat dripping down her face as the hot water continued to pound around them. Lucas's gaze dropped briefly to her mouth, then flashed back to her eyes, his expression growing suddenly more intent as his movements became more urgent. His ass flexed harder beneath the leg she had wrapped around his hip, and he began to pound himself into her, shoving deeper with every stroke, his flesh slapping hers wetly.

Lucas growled, and Kathryn's eyes widened as his fangs emerged. His gaze took on a predatory gleam, as he nipped briefly at her lips and jaw, before finally licking the skin of her neck, his tongue a cool rasp against the big vein beneath her ear. Her heart was hammering, her breath coming in short gasps, when the smooth glide of his fangs replaced his tongue. He lifted his head slightly and bit into her vein.

And then she was crying helplessly as a second orgasm claimed her body, fisting her inner muscles around his cock, turning her blood to molten lava as it rolled through her veins, carrying a pleasure that was nearly too much for her to bear all at once. Her leg spasmed around his hips, her heel digging into his muscled ass as her sex clamped tight, refusing to release him, even as some part of Kathryn was begging for it to stop. Her chest tightened with an emotion she didn't want to acknowledge, didn't want to feel, but it was too late. Too late.

"Too late," she whispered, as Lucas sagged against her finally, both of them spent and trembling.

"Too late for what, *a cuisle*?" he whispered breathlessly.

"I don't know," she lied. "I don't know what I was saying."

Lucas reached behind him and unwrapped her leg, lowering her carefully until both of her feet hit the tiled floor.

"Shall I wash you off?"

Kathryn slapped his hands away and forced a laugh. "You've done quite enough washing for one night. Take care of yourself."

"You're no fun at all," he muttered as he soaped and rinsed himself quickly. When he finished, he leaned in for a last soft and hungry kiss, whispering something against her ear before he pulled away and left her in the shower to finish alone. The words were Irish, so she could pretend she didn't hear, didn't know what they meant, but the truth was . . . She didn't need to know the actual meaning of the words, because it was there in the way he said it, in the soft brush of his lips against her ear, the roll of the syllables off his tongue. He loved her, and it was breaking her heart.

Chapter Twenty

LUCAS WAS JUST disconnecting a call with Nick when Kathryn finally emerged from the bedroom, looking all rosy and well-satisfied. He credited himself with both of those things. She'd been far from either when he'd wakened earlier this evening. He'd known she was downstairs even before he woke. The blood he'd taken from her over the past few days had sung to him of her presence, letting him feel her sadness and more.

"Feeling better?" he asked unnecessarily.

She crossed to him and cupped his cheek in one hand as she kissed him. "Thanks to you," she murmured, then stepped back and said, "If I were you, I'd burn that awful mansion to the ground with everything inside it."

"If it were up to me, I would. But it's not my decision."

Kathryn frowned. "I thought since you defeated him—"

"Killed him," Lucas corrected.

Her lips flattened, but she nodded. "Since you killed him, that everything of his would become yours."

"If I wanted it, yes, but I don't. I'll hold his people safely until a permanent lord emerges."

"How does *that* work?"

Lucas lifted a corner of his mouth in a smile. "I'd tell you, Agent Hunter, but then I'd have to kill you." He moved swiftly, snaking an arm around her waist and tugging her against him. "And I *definitely* don't want to kill you, Katie mine. I have much better things to do with that luscious body of yours."

Kathryn flushed with obvious pleasure and tried to push him away. "Keep your vampire secrets. I don't care."

Lucas laughed, giving her firm ass a final caress before letting her go. "We're going back to South Dakota tonight. And I think that's where you need to look for your brother."

She sobered immediately, and he almost regretted reminding her. Almost. Because he knew that more than anything, her brother's absence haunted her. If Lucas could solve that one problem for her, he'd be happy, but he'd long ago given up believing in happy endings.

"You're right," she agreed. "This . . ." She gestured to indicate the

Twin Cities, their lights glittering just beyond the big windows. "This was a bad decision on my part. I need to go back to the beginning, to first principles. I'll start over, reinterview everybody, check every place again. I missed something. I just have to figure out what."

"I'll help you," Lucas assured her. "My people will help you . . ."

"I have to find him, Lucas. One way or the other. If I don't . . ." She looked away, mouth tight, fists clenched as she struggled not to shed the tears shining in her blue eyes. "I have to find him," she whispered, almost to herself.

Lucas put his arms around her and held her gently, like a piece of crystal that would shatter if you held it too tightly. He only hoped Kathryn was tougher than that, because Kurt had searched high and low, in places Kathryn would never have ventured, and he'd found no trace. Daniel Hunter had disappeared into the wind, and Lucas was beginning to think he'd stay that way.

The Badlands, South Dakota

Kurt quickened his pace as he neared the Ben Reifel Visitor Center. He'd parked his truck in the side lot there earlier, before setting off into the backcountry. He was calling it quits earlier than usual tonight. Lucas and most of the warriors had been out of town. They'd fought and defeated Klemens in his Chicago lair last night and would be coming home later tonight. The club wasn't open, but there'd be a party of sorts at the house, and Kurt would be there to help keep things in order. Once upon a time he'd have been right there with them in Chicago, but he was a bartender now, a business manager. He might get bored with that eventually, might miss the blood rush of a well-fought battle, but for now he was content with mashing a few vampire heads now and then.

Tonight, he wasn't mashing anyone's head. He was looking for Dan. Kathryn Hunter had left town, following Alex Carmichael to Minneapolis. Kurt didn't believe Alex had anything to do with Dan's disappearance. The older vamp just didn't have it in him to do something like that, and why would he have to? He and Dan were business associates, friends even.

No, Kurt was convinced his friend Dan was still here someplace. He didn't know why he believed it so strongly. It was just a feeling. Maybe it was the blood they'd shared that once out in the backcountry. It wasn't enough for a real connection. Dan had been more curious than committed to the exchange. But some gut instinct of Kurt's kept insisting that Dan was near, and Kurt had scoured the town looking for him without success. So, he'd returned to the Badlands, thinking maybe he'd missed something. He was a better than fair tracker and had haunted the wilds of the Badlands every night looking for Dan. Sometimes it was only an hour or two after the bar shut down for the night, other times, when the bar was closed, he'd started at sunset and searched all night.

He paused, pulling back into the shadows as a truck turned off the highway and rolled through the parking lot to the small building used as a sort of office and storage by the rangers. He watched as a familiar figure leaned over to collect a Styrofoam container from the passenger seat, then climbed out of his truck and headed inside, using a key to open the locked door.

Kurt caught the scent of cooked food, and his gaze zeroed in on the Styrofoam container. Kind of late for dinner. Plus . . . he sniffed again. Meat, grilled and going cold, but rare enough that Kurt could still smell the fresh blood. And the man carrying it was a full-fledged vegetarian. Kind of a pain in the ass about it, actually.

Thankful that his truck was out of sight in the unlit parking lot near the visitor center, Kurt gathered the shadows to himself, confident that the desert night would hide him until he wanted to be seen. Once the unexpected visitor had entered the smaller building and closed the door, Kurt glided soundlessly across the parking lot. A sliver of light flashed around the side, and he slipped down that way until he was standing right outside a tiny window. He growled his frustration. The damn window was covered in some type of heavy, black cloth, so he couldn't see anything. He could hear the meat-toting vegetarian talking to someone, though. And he could smell that steak. Someone responded to the first man.

Kurt froze in recognition. Then he had to fight every instinct as he backed away and dialed a number.

LUCAS'S CELL PHONE rang as he followed Kathryn into the SUV outside the Rapid City airport. She'd been quiet on the flight home. It worried him on several fronts, not the least of which was that if they failed to find her brother, Kathryn would never recover. But the other thing was the clear sense that she was pulling away from him, or getting ready to pull away, which was the same thing. It was as if she'd decided the end was coming, and she wanted to ease into the separation gently so it wouldn't tear as badly at her heart. Not to mention what it would do to his.

He checked the caller ID on his cell and frowned. Why would Kurt be calling him?

"Kurt?" he said, answering the call.

"Sire. I've found Daniel Hunter."

Lucas glanced at Kathryn, but she was staring out the window, and, being human, couldn't hear what Kurt was saying.

"Where?"

"Here, my lord. In the Badlands, near the visitor center."

Lucas's thoughts raced as he tried to figure out a way to ask if Daniel was alive or dead without giving away anything to Kathryn, who had now turned her attention from the window and was half-listening to his conversation.

"In what condition?" he asked finally.

"Alive, my lord. I couldn't see him, but I heard him speak, and his captor brought him food."

"And who is that?" Lucas growled.

"Cody Pilarski, my lord. The park ranger. It makes no sense, but that's what I saw."

"Where are you now?"

"I'm there, my lord. My first thought was to go in alone, but—"

"No," Lucas said instantly. "We'll be there within the hour. Don't let him leave, but wait for me if you can."

"Yes, Sire."

Lucas disconnected and dropped a casual arm over Kathryn's shoulder, pulling her closer. "Mason," he said to the vampire behind the wheel of the SUV. "We're going to the visitor center in the Badlands National Park. Do you know where it is?"

"Yes, my lord," Mason responded in a slightly puzzled voice.

"Nick, I want four of our fighters with us. The rest can go to the ranch house."

"Yes, my lord, might I ask—"

Kathryn was staring at him now. Lucas turned his head to meet her gaze and said, "Kurt's found Daniel. We're going to go get him."

LUCAS HAD ARGUED for her to stay in the truck. Like that was going to happen. Kathryn pulled her duffle out of the back of Lucas's SUV and retrieved her Glock 23, checking the magazine and working the slide to verify it was hot with one in the pipe. She clipped it to her service belt, along with her mini-Maglite, then grabbed a scrunchy and tied her hair back, twisting it into a low knot to keep it out of her way. The last thing she grabbed was her FBI ID. Whoever was in there was going into custody. There'd be no bodies in the desert this time. This might be Lucas's territory, and she was more than grateful that Kurt had located Daniel when she had failed, but this was not vampire justice time. She was fairly certain a case like this would be bumped to at least the county level, but Sheriff Sutcliffe would be the one making the formal arrest. She'd call him herself once this guy Pilarski was in custody, and she'd kick herself later for not following up and interviewing Pilarski herself. Right now, she was going to get her brother back.

Lucas gave her a disapproving look as she joined the big vampire confab, but she ignored him. They were parked just down the road from the visitor center. The desert was nearly pitch-black, with only a little bit of moonlight to see by. The vamps could probably see just fine, but she couldn't make out anything a few feet away. She didn't switch on her flashlight, though. All she needed was for Pilarski to glance out a window, see her light and panic.

"There's a small room near the back," Kurt was saying, "along the right side of the building. It's mostly scruff back in there, and the window's covered up with a blanket or something, but you can tell when the light goes on."

"Is Pilarski still inside?" Kathryn asked him.

Kurt nodded. "I've been watching ever since I called you. His truck's the one without the logo. They're not allowed to drive park vehicles for personal use, and that building he's in is supposed to be storage. There're a couple meeting rooms inside, but they don't get much use this time of year."

"What about the back room?"

"If it's the one I think, it's not much more than a storage closet."

Kathryn turned to Lucas. "So what's the plan?" she asked. That was her brother in there, but these were Lucas's people.

Lucas gave her a dry look of acknowledgment and addressed his lieutenant. "Nick, you take the others and circle the building. I don't want him escaping out a window. Kurt, you'll knock on the door. He knows you, knows you hang around the park at night, so it won't trigger his suspicion right away. Get him to walk you farther into the building, and Kathryn and I will come in behind you. I want to know how many are in there before we make a move. If it's just Pilarski, you take him out, and we'll get Daniel."

"Take him out nonlethally," Kathryn clarified. "I want him arrested and charged."

As one, the vampires all turned to look at her.

"What?" she demanded. "He's human, and kidnapping isn't a hanging offense. He'll go to jail."

"And do it again when he gets out," Lucas commented.

"You don't know that. We don't even know why he did it this time. Besides, that's up to the courts, and I'm sworn to uphold the law, whether I agree with it or not."

Lucas rolled his eyes in disgust. "As you wish. Nick, go. Kurt, you're with me and Debbie-Do-Right here."

Kathryn punched his arm, but he just laughed. Bastard vampire probably hadn't even felt it.

It took only a few minutes for everyone to get into position. Kathryn marveled again at the vampires' speed and stealth. It was too bad they weren't willing to hire themselves out to law enforcement, because just offhand she could think of a half dozen situations where their talents would come in handy. Did vampire big shots like Lucas forbid vampire involvement in law enforcement? Or was it just a matter of mutual distrust? She made a note to herself to check with Lucas. Later. First, Daniel.

Kurt climbed the concrete steps and knocked on the screen door. The initial response was silence, but after Kurt knocked again, Lucas leaned in to whisper in her ear that someone was approaching the door.

The door barely cracked open at first, then went wider as Pilarski recognized his visitor.

"Kurt," he said in obvious surprise. "What's up, dude? It's late."

"Yeah, it is," Kurt agreed pleasantly, "but I saw your truck and wanted to be sure everything was cool with you. You need a ride somewhere?"

"Oh, no, man. I'm just catching up on some stuff. You know the government, nothing but paperwork."

Kurt laughed. "Someone needs to welcome them to the computer age. Mind if I come in?"

"What? Um. I'm not supposed to really—"

This was a public building, so Kurt didn't an invitation. He pulled the door open and stepped inside, forcing Pilarski to move or be knocked back.

"Well, okay, I guess for a minute, it's okay," Pilarski hedged. "You want some tea or . . . Oh, fuck. Sorry. I wasn't thinking."

"Yo, Cody," Kurt said easily. "Is that meat I smell? You been holding out on us all this time? Sneaking a burger late at night?"

"No!" he protested as they walked deeper into the building, their voices falling away. "I don't—"

Kathryn missed whatever it was Pilarski didn't do, because Lucas was on the move, leaping up onto the step in a single graceful bound and pulling her effortlessly behind him. He went through the door first, completely silent, no more than a shadow among shadows. Kathryn pulled her weapon and followed, keenly aware of the noise she was making in contrast. Her footsteps were like an elephant over gravel, and her careful breathing sounded like puffing bellows. She glanced around and saw that Lucas was already down the hall, gliding toward a lit doorway where Kurt and Pilarski seemed to have turned off. She heard the slide of a tea kettle on the stove and figured it must be a kitchen or break room.

"I didn't know vampires drank tea," Pilarski was saying to Kurt.

Kurt was standing in the doorway, leaning to one side. As they approached, he pointed to a doorway farther down the unlit hallway. "Sure, we do," he said casually, and straightened to stand in the center of the doorway, effectively blocking Pilarski's view as Lucas and Kathryn slipped past.

The door Kurt directed them to was at the very end of the hall. Lucas was already testing the knob when Kathryn came up next to him, but it was locked with a keyed deadbolt, and there was no key in sight. Lucas glanced over her shoulder toward the kitchen, where the tea kettle was now beginning to whistle fitfully, then he shrugged and kicked the door open.

The smell hit her first. She nearly fell to her knees in grief before she recognized it for what it was. Not death, not a decaying body, but human waste, dirt and rotting food. That bastard!

"Daniel!" she called. It was too dark. She holstered the Glock and pulled her flashlight instead, shining it around the room until she found a bundle of clothes on a cot in the corner.

"Lucas, I can't see a damn thing," she called as she rushed forward, her light leading the way. A greasy, yellow fixture came on overhead just as she reached the cot, and she saw her brother pressed against the corner, his face pale beneath the filth, his blue eyes, so much like her own, staring back at her in disbelief.

"Kat?" he half-whispered.

She reached out for him, but he pushed back against the wall, holding out a hand to stop her. "Don't," he said urgently. "I'm disgusting."

"You're not," she said through her tears. She flicked off her light and crouched in front of her brother. "You're the most beautiful thing I've ever seen."

There was a brief flash of his trademark smile as he said, "I'm not. But I will be. Just get me the fuck out of here, Kat."

Lucas was standing in the wrecked doorway, muttering into his cell phone. Probably calling back Nick and the guys, since the enemy in this case consisted of a lone park ranger. An obviously unbalanced park ranger, but no one they couldn't handle. The vampire lord stepped back, and Kurt appeared in the doorway.

"Hey," he said, his eyes meeting Dan's. "You need a shower, man."

Dan laughed, his eyes filling with tears. "That's what I've been saying."

Kurt crossed the room in three long strides and did what her brother hadn't permitted her to do. He wrapped his arms around Daniel, filth and all, and Dan clung to the big vampire, his shoulders shaking as he cried silent tears of relief. Kurt pulled the blanket away with one hand, saw the metal cuff around Dan's ankle and snapped the chain with an angry growl. Then he looked up and met Kathryn's gaze.

"I'd like to get him cleaned up, if that's okay with you."

Kathryn nodded silently, and Kurt started to help her brother to stand, but at the last minute Dan scrabbled for something under the blankets and came up with a camera.

Kathryn stared, recognizing it for one of those she'd left with the sheriff. "How—" she started to ask, suspicion blooming. "I stored your gear at the sheriff's office."

Dan shook his head, as if reading her mind. "The nut brought it to me, bragged how clever he'd been, stealing it from under the sheriff's nose." He tightened his hold on the camera, lifting it to eye level. "This is gonna win me a Pulitzer, Kat."

"Dan," she scolded.

Kurt urged him toward the hallway, but Dan stopped in front of her and took her hand. "I knew you'd come."

Kathryn tightened her hand on his. "It was Kurt who found you," she said, giving the bartending vampire a grateful look. "I was sure Alex Carmichael had you."

"Alex?" Dan repeated in confusion.

"Later," Kurt said. "Shower first."

Dan laughed a little, gave Kathryn's fingers a final squeeze and repeated, "I knew you'd come." Then, as if the exchange had taken what little energy he had left, he leaned heavily against Kurt, who all but carried him out of the filthy room.

When they were gone, she gave Lucas a hard look. "Pilarski," she said tightly.

"All tied up with a pretty bow, just as you ordered, Agent Hunter," he replied mockingly.

"I know you think I'm foolish—"

"Not at all," he said, then grimaced and covered his nose and mouth with one hand. "But could we finish this somewhere else? Even a human nose must be offended by the smell in here."

Kathryn belatedly remembered the stench, and her stomach roiled. She'd been so preoccupied with Dan . . . Fighting a sudden urge to vomit, she hurried from the filthy room, pushing Lucas ahead of her. "Move, vampire, unless you want me to add to the aroma."

Lucas grabbed her and raced them both down the hall and outside into the parking lot, where Kathryn leaned over, hands on her knees as she sucked in deep breaths of the brisk night air.

"God, that was awful," she gasped. "I can't imagine . . . Hell, *I* need a shower."

"Here comes your sheriff," Lucas commented from where he stood several feet away, probably just in case she lost the battle against her stomach.

Kathryn looked up as Sheriff Sutcliffe pulled into the lot, followed by a second patrol unit, both with their light bars flashing.

"But I didn't call him yet."

"I had Nick call before we went in," Lucas said mildly. He shrugged when she gave him a questioning look. "I didn't feel like waiting around for the local *Garda* to get here. It can take a while for someone to show up in these small towns, especially at night."

Kathryn straightened, then patted Lucas's arm in appreciation as she went to meet the sheriff.

"Sheriff Sutcliffe," she greeted him.

"Agent Hunter," he responded. "How's your brother?"

"Exhausted and hungry, but nothing a few days rest won't take care of."

"You didn't call for a rescue unit?"

"A friend took him in," she said, letting him assume she meant *in to the hospital.* "We thought it would be faster."

"So, he's been right here the whole time," Sutcliffe said, shaking his head. "How'd you find him?"

She nodded. "Anonymous tip on my cell phone about ninety minutes ago. The voice was a man's, but muffled. He said my brother was being held here, and since we were already en route from the airport, we came directly to the park to check it out."

"You waited to call me," he said in obvious disapproval.

"That's correct, sir. I saw no reason to make a scene if it turned out to be a prank. After all, you and I both checked things out here at the visitor center, and nothing tweaked our radar." She phrased it deliberately, making herself just as responsible as the sheriff—maybe more—for overlooking anything that might have indicated her brother was being held right under their noses.

"I see." His gaze traveled over the vampires ranged behind her. There were only three—Lucas, Mason and Nicholas—since Lucas had already sent the others away. He would have sent even those two, but he hadn't been willing to leave Kathryn alone with the prisoner, and Nicholas had refused to leave Lucas alone with the human authorities. Trust-Issues-R-Us, apparently.

"Mr. Donlon and his associates were with me when I received the tip," she explained, feeling only a slight twinge at manipulating the truth.

"Do you know where it came from? The tip, I mean."

"I've already had it checked. The call came from a throwaway cell. Impossible to trace."

"Damn things. Well—" He looked beyond her to Cody Pilarski, who was hanging miserably between two husky vampires. "What have you got to say for yourself, Cody?"

Pilarski lifted his head and addressed the sheriff. "I want to deal," he said sullenly. "This was Belinda's idea, not mine. Hunter'd be dead if I hadn't protected him."

Sheriff Sutcliffe shrugged. "Not my call," he said, then turned to Kathryn, who was still absorbing Pilarski's claim. *Belinda* had been the one who instigated the kidnapping? She was the park ranger Kathryn had interviewed on her first day in town. The one who'd gotten all flustered when talking about Dan. Kathryn had assumed she was smitten, but maybe she'd simply been guilty.

"I'll hold Pilarski overnight," the sheriff was saying, "have the County pick him up in the morning. And don't you worry about him getting bail, no matter what deal he gets. We don't take to kidnappers in South Dakota."

"I appreciate that. And now, the scene is yours, Sheriff. I know I should stay, but my brother needs me. So, if it's all right with you—"

"Don't you worry," Sutcliffe assured her. "I understand, and I know where you work," he added, with a wink.

Kathryn laughed, relieved. She'd known she was pushing it by not hanging around. It was bad enough that her brother, the most important witness, was already gone. "Thank you," she said sincerely. "You have my numbers, and I'll make sure we're available to give our statements."

"You'll be in town?" Sutcliffe verified, proving he wasn't totally gullible.

Kathryn nodded. "A while," she said vaguely, very aware of Lucas's keen hearing picking up every word she said. "You can reach me on my cell."

"Good enough, then. I'm glad everything worked out for you and your brother, Agent Hunter. This is a good day."

"Yes, it is, Sheriff."

Lucas came up behind her, not touching, but close enough that she could feel the heat of his presence. They stood silently until the sheriff ambled over to confer with his deputies, and then Lucas dipped his head to her ear and said, "A while, Kathryn?"

She shivered at the low rumble of his voice and the slight menace in the question. She'd known this was coming. She had to go back to Virginia, her job was there. And her home, such as it was. In a perfect world, she might have stayed in this little town, bought a quaint little cottage and settled down to raise goats, or maybe paint masterpieces. It always happened that way in stories. Unfortunately, this was the real world.

"Kathryn?" Lucas demanded.

She turned to face him, her hand automatically lifting to caress his beard-roughened jaw, her eyes meeting his golden gaze. And her heart twisted. She didn't know how it could have happened. Didn't know why it had happened now, and with a vampire of all people. But she loved him. It was going to tear her apart when she had to leave.

"A while," she repeated, stroking her thumb over his soft lips.

Lucas wasn't fooled. He eyed her suspiciously and said, "We'll talk."

Kathryn nodded. Saying good-bye was going to be hard enough, she thought sadly, but Lucas was used to getting his own way. He was going to make it even harder.

"Do you know where Kurt took Dan?" she asked, changing the subject.

"Kurt lives at the ranch."

Kathryn gave him a surprised look.

"Most of my people do," he explained. "Vampires tend to live in nests. It's safer that way."

"Can I see my brother, then?"

He gave her a narrow look. "Aren't you coming back to the ranch tonight?"

Lucas was far too intuitive for Kathryn's comfort. "Of course," she assured him, even though she would rather have gone to the motel. Kathryn didn't believe in dragging out the inevitable. Better to make a clean break of it. But Dan was at the ranch, and in her heart, she wanted these last few hours with Lucas. Tomorrow would be soon enough for heartbreak.

KATHRYN'S BROTHER was waiting when Lucas finally got home to his ranch. Kurt had him sitting at the kitchen table, a cup of hot tea and the remains of a sandwich in front of him. Lucas eyed the food, then lifted his gaze to Kurt, one eyebrow cocked curiously.

"Judy made the sandwich," Kurt explained. "And we had the tea."

"I see," Lucas murmured. He heard Kathryn come in behind him. Dan had been watching the exchange between Lucas and Kurt, more curious than frightened. Not that he had anything to fear from Lucas—Kathryn would stake him in his sleep if he touched one hair on her precious brother's head. But it was surprising, given his recent captivity, that Dan Hunter retained as much of himself as he did. It spoke to strength of character, and courage, too. Kathryn had raised him well, Lucas thought dryly.

"Can I hug you now?" Kathryn demanded, bypassing Lucas to go directly to her brother's side.

He grinned, and Lucas abruptly saw the resemblance between them. The brother's hair was darker, his features obviously heavier, more masculine, but the eyes were the same deep blue, and that grin was what

Kathryn's would have been if her life hadn't wrapped her up so tightly in responsibilities. Most especially a baby brother.

Dan Hunter stood, and brother and sister hugged. He was a good three inches taller than Kathryn, and yet when they hugged it was the hug of a mother and child. Lucas watched and felt an answering tug in his soul, the yearning of a child who'd never had that kind of security. Or who'd lost it so young that it was only a faint memory.

Kathryn ran her fingers through her brother's hair. "Did you call Penny?"

"First thing."

"Are you going back to California right away?"

"I don't know," he said carelessly. "I never finished what I wanted to do here, and there's the new collection to work on. You said my gear's at the sheriff's? All of it?"

"Yeah," she said, not concealing her surprise at his answer. "You sure you don't want to go home? Or you can come to my place, if you want."

"No. I'm gonna hang out here with Kurt awhile."

Kathryn's sharp gaze flashed to Kurt, who gave her a conspiratorial wink.

"Huh," she said, then turned her attention back to Daniel. "Sit, baby," she said, urging him back into his seat.

Lucas almost growled. She never called *him* "baby," he thought, then nearly laughed out loud. What? He was jealous of her damn brother? Maybe he *should* let her leave if this was what she turned him into.

"Kathryn," Lucas said softly, trying not to sound as irritated as he felt.

She turned to him, eyes wide in dismay. Or maybe guilt. "I'm sorry," she said. "Dan, this is Lucas Donlon. He's been helping me look for you. Lucas, my brother, Daniel."

Dan stood again and took a step closer to Lucas to offer his hand. But his expression, when he met Lucas's gaze, was no longer that of a beloved *baby* anything. It was full of warning and protectiveness, a look that said, *hurt my sister and die.*

"Kurt's told me all about you, Lord Donlon."

Lucas gripped the boy's hand, just managing to curb the instinct to crush his too fragile human bones. If not for Kathryn watching every nuance, he might have.

"You're a lucky man," Lucas said instead, "to have someone like your sister care so deeply about you."

"I am," Dan agreed. "And she deserves the best."

Lucas nearly laughed at the obvious but unspoken threat. He bared his teeth. "Don't push it, boy," he growled

"Stop it!" Kathryn hissed. "Both of you. Dan. Sit down and drink your tea, and I'll see you tomorrow." She turned her glare on Lucas. "Can we talk?"

"Of course," Lucas replied smoothly. "Let's take this to my office." He pushed open the kitchen's swinging door and gestured for her to precede him, giving the brother a dark look over his shoulder as he followed.

"What the hell was that?" Kathryn demanded once they were safely behind the closed door of his office.

"Ask your *baby* brother," Lucas responded loftily. "He's the one who tried to break my fingers with his feeble human handshake." He circled his desk and slumped down into his comfortable chair, picking up a sword-shaped letter opener to play with.

"I can't believe this. You're jealous of my *brother?*"

"If you say so."

"There's no reason—" she started furiously.

"Tell me, Kathryn," he interrupted, raising his eyes to meet hers. "What are your plans?"

She froze mid-sentence. "What?"

"Your plans. You've found your brother, and *he's* apparently staying here. Should be interesting, by the way. But what about you?"

Kathryn stared at him as she sank wordlessly into one of the chairs in front of his desk. "I can't stay here, Lucas," she admitted softly. "My job—"

"Your job. That's it, then? You and I mean nothing?"

"We live thousands of miles apart," she pleaded. "And I don't exactly work nine to five. This is the most I've taken off work in . . . ever. Even if we traded off visiting each other—"

"Which I can't do," Lucas said, throwing the letter opener onto his desk. "Virginia belongs to another lord. I can't go there."

"But you expect me to give up *my* life," she said, making it a statement, not a question.

"Your job is your life? I doubt that. So what's the real problem here, Kathryn?"

"Fine. My *problem* is that relationships have a way of taking over. It starts out being fun, and pretty soon you're giving up time with friends, skipping out on work, and then before you know it, your life isn't your own anymore. It's someone else's."

"News flash, love. That's a two-way street. You're not the only one being asked to give up something."

"But I don't want you to give up *anything!* I don't want either one of us to give up anything. I just want my life to be *mine*. I spent twenty years taking care of my brother, and my father, too. I lived for their needs, their wants, their *everything*, and I promised myself that when Dan was grown I'd never do it again."

"Except here you are," he responded bitterly. "Rushing in once more to save your brother. Obviously, you're not as free as you thought," he added, surprisingly hurt by her words, by the idea that she considered what they had to be a burden, rather than a gift.

"But I *love* my brother. I can't just turn off my feelings, you know."

Lucas stared at her, concentrating on sitting perfectly still, on not showing any of the pain her words were causing him. Not that it seemed to matter. She was completely unaware of what she'd said.

Lucas stood from behind his desk, the big leather chair gliding away noiselessly. "At least not the feelings you have for your brother," he commented flatly. "Be safe, Kathryn. Nick will provide any assistance you require in arranging transportation." He strode across the room, heading for his private entrance.

"Lucas," Kathryn pleaded as he pulled the door open. "Don't leave like this."

But Lucas didn't turn around, didn't even look. There was nothing more to say.

Nick was coming down the hall as Lucas closed the door behind him, Kathryn's words still playing in his head.

"My lord," Nick said, hurrying forward. "I was just coming to your office." He paused, catching the expression on Lucas's face, and probably a whiff of his emotions, as well. "My lord? Did something happen?"

"Nothing. Agent Hunter will be leaving. Give her whatever help she needs. Where's Mason?"

"Down at the stables, I believe, with a few of the others."

"Get him up here. I'm going to the homestead. The sooner the better, Nick."

KATHRYN STOOD in Lucas's office, staring at the door he'd shut in her face. She could open it. She could chase him down and force him to talk to her, to let her explain. But what was the point? Everything she'd told him was true. They *did* live thousands of miles apart, and she'd known when she said it that he couldn't visit her in Virginia. Which meant, regardless of Lucas's fine words about compromise, she'd be the one expected to turn her life on its side once more. Lucas would still be here, on his ranch, with all of his people around him. Still the big, fucking lord of the realm. While she'd be giving up the only thing that had ever been truly *hers*. Her job.

So, instead, you're giving up Lucas?

She swatted away the voice in her head. Who said she'd ever had Lucas to give up in the first place? They'd known each other for a few days, a week. Big deal. They hadn't even gotten past the lust phase of a relationship, much less anything else. Okay, so she'd never actually *been* in lust like this before, but her friends had, and they'd told her all about it. In great, fucking detail. With an emphasis on the fucking. So, maybe that's all this was with Lucas—a few days of great sex.

But even if it wasn't, even if they'd managed to stick it out a month, or a year, it would mean compromising on her job. Being with the FBI was the only thing she'd ever wanted to do. And if she wasn't willing to give that up in order to be with Lucas, then maybe it wasn't love, after all.

The pictures on the wall next to Lucas's desk caught her eye, the ones she'd admired at the very beginning, the ones Dan had taken in Ireland. She smiled sadly, thinking about a young Lucas crossing those fields with his mother, only to be turned away by the very people who should have protected them. She went over and touched the image of a running horse, sighing softly. Maybe Lucas was right. There was no sense in raising hope where there *was* none. Maybe a clean break was best.

So why didn't it feel that way?

Chapter Twenty-One

One month later

LUCAS THREW THE phone down, ignoring the cracking sound as it hit his desk. What was that, the eighth one he'd destroyed this month? Who cared? Maybe someone needed to find him a fucking cell phone that didn't shatter at every little bounce.

"Nicholas!" he roared.

The hallway door popped open, and Nick stuck his head in. "Sire?"

Lucas glowered at his lieutenant. Why the fuck was he standing out there in the first place? He'd been doing more and more of that lately, lurking in the hall instead of staying in here where he belonged.

"What the fuck is going on in Topeka? Emmett just called to complain about zoning on the new compound."

"*Emmett* keeps trying to save money by shorting bribes."

"Well, why the hell is he calling me about it?"

"I'll handle it, my lord."

"Someone better," Lucas grumbled.

"Yes, my lord. Is there anything else?"

Lucas gave him a scowling glance. "No."

Nick ducked back into the hallway and closed the door almost before Lucas finished that single syllable. What the fuck was that? He slumped down in his chair and stared moodily at the empty room. Where was everybody? His eye fell on the pictures of Ireland, the ones he used to love before . . .

He stood suddenly, grabbed the already broken cell phone from his desk, and hurled it across the room where it hit the wall with a pleasing smack, leaving a phone-sized divot in the plaster. That wasn't the first one of those either.

Lucas stared at the pockmarked wall. What the hell was he doing?

"Nicholas," he bellowed once more.

Same thing. The door popped opened, and Nick's head appeared. "Sire?"

Lucas studied him through narrowed eyes, then sighed. "Get the jet ready. We're going to Virginia."

Nick blew out a dramatic breath. "About fucking time, my lord."

Lucas would have thrown something at him, but there was nothing left to throw. And Nick was already gone. Smart vampire.

Sitting once again behind his desk, Lucas swiveled his chair to the credenza and reached for the bat phone, since he'd just destroyed his current cell. Punching the desired button, he listened to the call ring twice on the other side of the country before it was answered.

"Lucas."

"Duncan," Lucas said. "I have a favor to ask."

Quantico, Virginia

Kathryn scanned the empty apartment, looking for anything she might have missed. She'd already gone through every drawer and closet at least three times. Had already swept and vacuumed until the place was far cleaner than when she first moved in. Her landlord wouldn't even have to dust before renting it out again. Not that he'd return her cleaning fee anyway, but it went against her nature to leave it dirty.

She picked up the small box of belongings that was the only thing left. It contained her answering machine and a small lamp, plus the few pieces of mail that had somehow slipped past the change of address she'd filed at the post office. It was mostly junk mail, but it had her name and address on it, and she knew too much about identity fraud to leave it behind. Apparently, her OCD tendencies were in full bloom. It was the stress. She hoped getting out of here tonight would help with that.

Holding the box on one hip, she opened the front door, did a final visual check of the place she'd called home for almost three years, then closed and locked the door. She'd mail the keys back to her landlord on her way by the post office tonight. She had a small Priority Mail box all ready to go—addressed, stamped, bubble packed so the keys wouldn't rattle . . . yep, her compulsions were definitely running the show.

Her apartment was on the third floor, so she took the stairs. The only time she'd ever used the elevator was the day she'd first moved in and yesterday to move out. The stairs were good exercise, and besides, anything that tired her out was a good thing lately. She wasn't sleeping well, either.

The fresh air felt good on her face when she opened the outside security door. She waited until she heard the door click shut behind her, then leaned over and checked to be sure her landlord had removed her name from the list of residents. He had. She snugged the box closer and straightened up when a car door slammed on the street behind her. She turned, registered the fact that the engine was still running, and her hand went automatically to the Glock 23 still clipped to her belt. It was late, and she'd come directly from the office, making a final stop before . . .

"Kathryn."

Kathryn's breath caught in her chest, and she hugged the box so closely against her hip that it hurt.

"Lucas?"

"You don't recognize me?" he teased, reaching out to take the box from her.

She relinquished it to him, even though it weighed nothing. She was too stunned at finding him on her doorstep to do anything else.

"What are you doing here?" she asked. "I thought you couldn't . . . I mean . . ."

Lucas lifted one shoulder dismissively. "Duncan's a friend. He made an exception . . . for one night," he added.

"But why—" Kathryn heard herself stumbling over her words, but couldn't seem to stop.

"I missed you," he said, his beautiful golden eyes meeting her gaze evenly. "You said we could visit, so I thought—"

"But I'm moving," she blurted. "I'm leaving tomorrow."

Lucas frowned. "Moving where?" He took an aggressive step forward. "And with whom?" he demanded.

Kathryn nearly laughed at his outraged assumption that she had taken up with someone new. She'd barely slept in a month because she missed him so much, and he thought she was moving in with her new lover.

She *didn't* laugh, though. She couldn't. Not when he was standing in front of her at last, looking so delicious she wanted to weep.

"Turns out I was wrong," she whispered, her eyes greedily drinking in the sight of him standing on her front walk. "I do want my life turned on its side."

Lucas gave her a puzzled look.

His face blurred as tears filled her eyes. "I'm moving to Minneapolis," she explained. "I requested a transfer. Seems there aren't too many agents vying for that posting. Something about the weather."

"Minneapolis?" Lucas repeated. He stared at her blankly, and then that glorious smile lit up his face. And her heart.

He set the box down to one side and pulled her into his arms. "I missed you, *a cuisle*. I should never have let you leave."

Kathryn choked out a laugh. "I'm not sure you could have stopped me," she said against the warm skin of his neck, "but I'm sorry I left the way I did. And I'm sorry for hurting you," she added, the words nearly swallowed by her sob of relief. She wrapped her arms around his back and held on tight, able to breathe freely for the first time since she'd walked out of his office nearly a month ago.

"Don't be sorry," Lucas rumbled. "Just tell me you love me."

"I do. I love you so much it scares me to death. But living without you . . . it's like a hole in my heart I can never fill."

Lucas tightened his arms around her. "Ah, Katie mine, we'll be all right, then. You'll see."

"I know. Now that you're here, I know."

Lucas dipped his head and kissed her. It was hot and tender at the same time and so very familiar. It was like coming home.

"Can I give you a ride somewhere?" he murmured, his mouth trailing warm kisses all along her jawline before coming back to her mouth.

Kathryn smiled against his lips. "How about Minneapolis? I was supposed to catch a flight tonight."

Lucas laughed, then looped an arm around her waist and gestured at the waiting SUV. "Your carriage awaits."

"That's my rental over there," she said, indicating a mid-sized sedan at the curb. "My truck went with the moving van yesterday, and I have to get this one back to the airport."

"No problem. Nick will handle it. He'll be so grateful you're coming back with us, he'll do anything you ask."

She stared at him, confused. "Why would Nick be—"

He actually looked guilty. "It's possible I've been a bit . . . short-tempered lately."

"Guess I'll have to sweeten you up then. For Nick's sake."

Lucas's laugh was low and seductive. "I'm counting on it, *a cuisle*. I am *definitely* counting on it."

Epilogue

Minneapolis, Minnesota

They watched from across the river as Lucas Donlon escorted the woman into a brightly lit gala, two more beautiful people in a hotel that was already full of them. The event of the year, the papers had called it. The rich and powerful of the state all gathered into one big, fat target. Fortunately for all of them, he wasn't hunting tonight. Tonight was just reconnaissance.

He watched as Lucas leaned over to whisper something private to the woman. She laughed at whatever it was, gazing up at him, her face shining with emotion. It was obvious to anyone with eyes to see that she was in love, and it seemed he returned the feeling. Lucas Donlon in love. Six months ago, Aden would have sworn Lucas would be the last one to fall.

"Who's the woman?" he asked.

"His FBI bitch," Magda supplied, all but spitting the words. There was hatred there. And not just for the woman, but Donlon, too. A woman scorned, perhaps? The very worst kind in his experience.

"Don't worry about her," Magda continued. "Worry about Donlon and his plans for the Midwest."

"I thought he'd opened it up to all comers. The first round's in two weeks," one of the other vampires objected. There were two of them, and Aden hadn't figured out yet if they were serious contenders, or simply Magda's pets.

"That's what he *says*," she responded darkly. "But competitions can be fixed. He and Raphael are thick as thieves, and they have big plans that they're not sharing with anyone."

Or perhaps they're simply not sharing them with you, Aden thought to himself, dismissing the female vampire's fears of a grand conspiracy.

"Raphael's involved in this?" the vamp who'd posed the earlier question protested. "No one said anything about taking on Raphael."

"Scared?" Magda mocked. "Fuck Raphael. He can be killed like any other vampire. Klemens almost got him a few months back. If the fool had hired a competent assassin, Lord Fucking Raphael would already be dead."

"I heard there'd been an attempt, but not who did it," Aden commented. "It was Klemens?"

She nodded. "Hired a human sniper who missed. Should have hired a vampire instead."

"And yet, Klemens is dead, while Raphael lives on," Aden said dryly, tired of her hissing commentary. "I doubt *that's* a coincidence."

"Yeah, so Klemens is dead. Doesn't matter why." She gave Aden a dirty look. He'd interrupted her moment in the limelight, and she was a woman who liked the light. "We're here because Klemens is gone, and Lucas is vulnerable," she continued. "Look at him. I could take him out from here if I had a decent rifle."

Aden doubted that, but he kept the thought to himself.

"So what's the plan?" one of Magda's pets asked.

"We take out Donlon and split the Midwest territory," Magda asserted boldly. "Just remember, Donlon's Plains territory is mine."

"If you can hold it," Aden commented softly. He pushed away from the wall and stood to his full height. "I don't know about you lads, but I've no intention of taking on Donlon. I want the Midwest, and I've no need to skulk in the shadows with angry women in order to get it."

Magda spun around to face him, bristling, fangs bared. Aden gave her a dismissive glance. She was full of bitterness, this one, and set on revenge. But she had no power to back it up, and he had no desire to get caught up in her schemes.

"We'll see how tough you are when the shit hits the fan," she sneered.

Aden brushed dirt from his sleeve. "Yes, we will," he said calmly. "See you in Chicago, lads. Should be interesting."

To be continued . . .

Glossary

A cuisle: Pronounced A KUSH-LA. Literally, this means "pulse," shortened from "pulse of my heart," but colloquially it translates as "darling."

A ghrá: Pronounced A GRAW. Translates as "My heart," used as an endearment

An Tiarna: Pronounced On Teer-na. "Lord" (as in an aristocratic lord over certain lands)

Mo Éireann álainn: Pronounced MAW ERIN AWL-IN. "My beautiful Ireland"

Mo Chroí mo go deo: Pronounced MAW KHREE MAW GUH DOE (The 'KH' sound would be like how Scots pronounce 'Loch'). "Forever in my heart"

Tá me chomh mór sin i ngrá leat: Pronounced TAW meh khoh MOWER shin ing RAW l(y)att. "I love you so much"

Tromluí: Pronounced TROM-LWEE. "Nightmare"

Acknowledgments

As always, I want to thank Linda Kichline for all of her hard work and dedication. These books wouldn't be the same without her. And thanks to Patricia Lazarus for helping me find the perfect Lucas, with his golden eyes.

Endless thanks and appreciation to my very talented fellow writers, Steve McHugh and Michelle Muto, who read these manuscripts before anyone else, and whose input makes them eminently better. To John Gorski for answering my sometimes endless questions about guns, ammo, and pretty much every other lethal thing. To my fellow OWG'ers who provide support and distraction as needed for a tired and/or over-caffeinated writer.

For helping Lucas speak his native tongue, I am very grateful to Tracy Nugent and Beryl Nugent for their help with Irish translations, and to John Hart (gaelicclothing.com) for providing both translations and transliterations. All of them gave generously of their time and effort to keep my Irish accurate, and any mistakes are solely my fault not theirs. For advice about horses, and their training and breeding, my sincere thanks to Valerie Strauss, and, once again, any mistakes I made are mine alone.

Thank you to Judy Peterson for her thoughtful donation to the L. A. Banks auction, and for lending me her name and character for LUCAS. Hope you like her, Judy!

And last but never least, love and gratitude to my family for more reasons than I can count, and especially to my wonderful husband who too often loses his wife to a laptop computer.

51924435R00161

Made in the USA
San Bernardino, CA
04 September 2019